THE SECRET CUCKOO CABARET CLUB

EDGAR D JACKSON

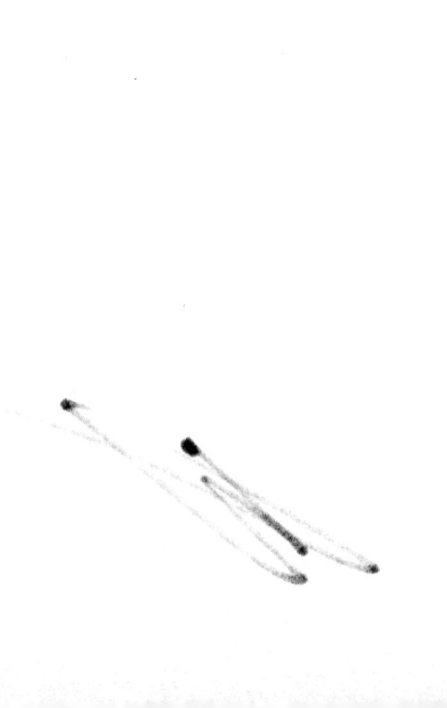

Copyright © Edgar D Jackson 2025

First published in Great Britain in 2025 by IolandaPress
Paperback edition published in 2025
eBook edition published in 2025

The right of Edgar D Jackson to be identified as the author of this work has been asserted in accordance with the Copyright, Designs and Patents Act 1988.

All rights reserved. No part of this publication may be reproduced, stored in a retrieval system or transmitted in any form or by any means, without the prior permission in writing of the publisher, nor to be otherwise circulated in any form of binding or cover other than that in which it is published without a similar condition, including this condition, being imposed on the subsequent purchaser.

No part of this book may be used or reproduced in any manner for the purpose of training artificial intelligence technologies or systems. In accordance with Article 4(3) of the DSM Directive 2019/790, Edgar D Jackson expressly reserves this work from the text and data mining exception.

A CIP catalogue record for this book is available from the British Library.

All characters in this publication are fictitious and any resemblance to real persons, living or dead, is purely coincidental.

ISBN: 978-10683740-0-5

Typeset by Raspberry Creative Type, Edinburgh

CHAPTER ONE

SOMETHING SLEEPS

1

Out here in the quiet, something sleeps. Tweaks, shifts, fidgets. Snores occasionally. Breathes, dreams.

Out here, something sleeps just like things out there sleep. Limbs folded around torso, senses scouring – a jigsaw puzzle of dreams and reality pieced neatly together. It realises its surroundings. It knows itself.

While something sleeps, things continue. The water beneath it foams and tickles against wooden pillars. Beneath the water, life congregates: fish, crabs, mussels, bacteria. A hum of movement and beyond the water, yet more. Houses, vehicles, street lamps, life. The heartbeat is a thick, pounding vibration. Changing in tone, changing in frequency. The souls travel from one place to the next, busy but not busy. Laughs, cries, screams, whispers.

The world out there is vivid, even in the dark. It is alive. But here, something sleeps.

2

Two teenagers enter the water. Splash, crash, holding, pulling. Voices rise higher and higher. And something shifts.

They get closer, heading for the pillars. The pillars are thick and green and slippery with weed, but they want to get there. They want to touch them. One teenager wins the race and pulls the other in. They kiss. They bob. Waves gets louder, and their reality gets heavier. Pushing them, without luck, to a dream.

3

The heartbeat from land grows louder on the wind. Vibrations ripple, teenagers shout, water coughs. And something listens. Its neck twists and its ears open. One second, two seconds, three. Sleep could easily be dipped back into. But not this time. The world is too loud. Even out here, where things are quiet.

Below, two teenagers make a decision. They kiss once more, then return back from where they came. But something is listening now. Something has a heart that beats faster. Something stretches and cracks. Something moves, swallows, blinks, thinks.

Out here in the quiet, something wakes.

CHAPTER TWO

THE BODY

1

Adrian Ramirez began in Metairie, Louisiana, but he ended in Henry Bacon's tap, California.

Henry was a seven year old boy who had trouble brushing his teeth. His mother always said, 'two minutes'. Front and back, side to side, quick lick on the tongue, then done and off to bed. Those were two minutes of Henry's life that he would never get back. Two minutes that he could have spent playing his Gameboy, or reading a comic, or doing something that wasn't as monotonous as standing still and brushing teeth. Sometimes, he would relent. Other times, he would lie. He would turn on the tap and hover the brush underneath, making it wet. He would dab some paste onto his finger and wipe it around his lips. Sometimes he would take two minutes just to think up a plan and put it into action. He even got away with it: toothpaste squeezed under the bath mat, painful ulcer under the tongue. But most of the time, his schemes were a failure. His mother was pretty smart. She would march him back into the bathroom, sit on the toilet, watch him do it for real, then she would bend him over and spank him twice on the butt.

'You wanna have bad breath?' she would say. 'You wanna look like you're British?'

'No, Ma. Sorry, Ma.'

But the next day, Henry would try it all over again. It had almost become a game to him. A challenge between two minds. If he could think of something good, he would do it. Today, however, he didn't have to think of something good. Today, something good thought of him.

It began with a splutter, a cough, a churn. The basin spat water, then stopped. Henry's toothbrush barely received a speck. He tried once more, a small grin cracking between his cheeks. Another cough. Another splutter. The sink grumbled loudly and the tap began choking.

'Ma,' shouted Henry. 'Tap's broken.'

He heard his mother groan in the next room, and Henry stepped down from his stool. She barged into the bathroom.

'How many times, Henry?'

'I'm serious, Ma, the tap's broken.'

'It's not broken, it's working fine.'

'Try it.'

Henry's mother bent over the sink and turned the tap clockwise, watching as it wheezed and gargled, then vomited a few more droplets.

'What the hell have you done?'

'I didn't do nothing, honest.'

'You better be honest.' She rested her head against the bowl and squinted as she attempted to peer up. Then she huffed, left the room, and returned with a long H2 pencil. She turned the tap again and jammed the pencil inside, feeling around roughly before yanking something out and revealing the clog. 'Jesus,' she muttered.

The pencil had caught a thick clump of what looked like human hair. It was jet black, runny, and it clung to the pencil like a squid leaking ink.

Henry watched the tap begin to run normally again. 'Oh. Thanks. Guess this means I should brush my teeth now…' He lifted his toothbrush miserably, but before he could place it into the stream of gushing water, his mother held out her hand and stopped him.

'No. Not tonight, Henry. I don't want you using this tap. I don't want you using any tap in the house, you understand that?'

Henry could hardly believe his luck. 'Yes, Ma!'

He grinned and slid his toothbrush triumphantly into the cup under the mirror. His mother left the bathroom and made a phone call.

2

It was the tenth of October, 2003, and Justin Hadero was expecting a phone call. His wife, Tanita, was two weeks overdue. Since giving birth to George just a few minutes into her morning granola, she was adamant that it was going to happen again.

'He was a morning bird, like me. He had to get up and go, no use hanging around all day. Sarah will be the same.'

Sarah was the name of their unborn second child. The first girl in the family, named after Justin's mother. She had passed away when he was young but had given him a perfect life while she was still around. He had been so excited to name a child after her, he'd considered squeezing the name somewhere amongst the boy's, but his wife had urged him to wait. Kids get picked on for anything these days, and even though it would be a middle name, the bullies would undoubtedly weed it out. Justin was glad he'd listened. George was fourteen years old and he was already being picked on because his voice was taking a little longer to break than others. It was like a game to those bullies: pick the weakest and let it rip. Despite the sentiment, a middle name of Sarah would have given them a whole deck of rigged cards against him.

George Antonio Hadero was the name they had chosen. Sarah Paula Hadero was the name that was coming. Any morning now, Tanita was going to give birth to a beautiful baby girl, and Justin was going to be given a daughter for the first time in his life. He hadn't wanted to wait this long. A boy and a girl was always what he had envisioned, but George's birth had put his wife out of service. She'd suffered badly from post natal depression, and for a while it looked like she would never be pregnant again, but fourteen years appeared to be enough time to put the experience behind her and go for the set.

Now they were just waiting. A few days. One week. Two weeks. The granola servings were getting larger and larger, like Tanita was urging the baby out. She'd even started having two bowls. Nevertheless, the baby hadn't arrived and she was getting impatient. Justin, on the other hand, was content. When Sarah was ready, she would come, and there was no use moping around waiting for her. All he had to do was keep an ear on the phone and a pulse on the pager. When it rang or when it beeped, he would come running, but neither had done so yet. At least, not until now.

Justin had hardly entered his office before the phone rang. He dived over his desk, grabbed it, and yelled, 'Justin Hadero!'

But the voice that came back wasn't his wife's. 'Justin?'

'Who is this?'

'It's me, Gunther. What're you shouting for?'

'Gunther? What the hell are you doing ringing this number? You know the chief's office goes to reception until Tanita gives birth.'

'Yeah, I know. But it was ringing through.'

Justin manoeuvred around his desk and sat down. 'It'll do that. Cherisse gets bagels at this time in the morning.'

'Uh-huh. Most important job of the day.'

'You know it.'

Justin rocked back and picked at his teeth. Gunther was a good cop and friend, but he was a talker. He knew if he got the chance, he'd recite a great American novel, but this was his wife's only way through to him. He had to make it quick.

'Alright Gunther, what do you want?'

'Me and Gate were called before we even got in this morning. Looks like we got a job out here, Chief.'

'I'm sure you can handle it.'

'Naw, this one needs you.'

'Gunther, you know I'm not leaving the office for house calls. Murders and —'

'Murders and homicides only. Yeah, I remember.'

Justin nodded to himself. Since he had become the chief of police in Cuckoo Cove, there hadn't been any major incidents, so the comment was obviously tongue in cheek. But still, Justin was going to stick to it. As long as there was a chance Tanita was still enjoying her morning granola, he was staying in his office and ready for the call.

'Why are you on the phone then?' he asked.

'Why do you think? Murders and homicides only. You said it, Chief. It's time to come out and play.'

A moment passed. Justin heard Cherisse return with the morning bagels, and he took one out of her bag when he left the building.

3

Just on the outskirts of Cuckoo Cove, there was a reservoir. Three hundred feet deep, covering six hundred acres, it had once been the only source of the town's water, but these days it was mostly used as a substitute waterfront for the town's older folk. Cuckoo Cove had a reputation for being a party town. In the summer, old haunts throbbed with loud music, and the beach was littered with drunk and rowdy teenagers. The violence rate was okay for the most part, as they were mainly queer, but the older generation couldn't enjoy the place like they used to. The reservoir gave a far greater feeling of calm. It was a sea away from the sea. Away from the noise and the bustle of it all. Some had even set up tents and cabins, which dotted the verge of the banks like beach huts. It was a place of tranquility, especially when the sun was shining and the day was blue. Only, today wasn't blue. It was grey and overcast, and the sweet retreat of the reservoir felt more like an island of solitude – cut off from Cuckoo Cove, cut off from reality. It felt like a secret, and not a very nice secret at that. It stood quiet and desolate, with nothing but the sound of the breeze and the gentle bobbing of a young man's body to fill the space between silences.

Gaten scratched at his nose as he watched him float. There seemed to be an air of the bizarre about him. The body was stiff, like a mannequin, yet it moved in the water like a plate on a circus pole. The left arm was hooked around his shaved head and the knees were bent under his belly. It looked almost like it had been ejected from an American Airlines lavatory thirty-five thousand feet up and had stayed in that position all the way down. The smell of shit didn't help that thought, but the reservoir always had a slightly froggy smell, so Gaten couldn't put that down to the body alone.

He sniffed again, feeling another barrage of sickness gnaw at his stomach. He turned away from the body and glanced at his watch. As if on cue, a siren sounded behind him, and the squad car of Justin Hadero pulled up. He exited with a half-eaten bagel in one hand and a pair of thick shades atop his nose. He was a handsome man in some lights, but he had an arrogance that squandered his beauty. Like the reservoir, there was a foul stench that hung around the chief wherever he went. It was there as he walked toward Gaten. He was entering a crime scene, but his attention was on his watch, which was already being flung up in front of his face, as if the body was taking time out of his morning. The body itself appeared to moan in apology, and Justin Hadero stopped in his tracks.

'That guy still alive?' he asked unsurely.

Gaten turned back to the body. The skin was a blue-ish grey which had only turned more blue since he'd arrived, a little under fifty minutes ago. 'No,' he replied. 'He's been doing that every now and then. Think it might be air escaping. Like whales, you know.'

Justin came up beside him. 'Is it gonna blow?'

Gaten hesitated, unsure of whether the chief had asked that sincerely. He decided to ignore it. 'Fisherman found him around an hour ago. That's Gunther with him now.'

He pointed over to Gunther and the fisherman, who were standing around a quarter of a mile eastward, just beside one of the cabins. The fisherman had been there since three in the morning. It wasn't until light broke and he'd taken his dog for a walk around the reservoir that he spotted the body. He had called, and then carried on fishing, claiming he was far enough away for it not to be a problem. He was an old man. Probably World War II kind of old, so stumbling across random bodies wasn't too much of a pain for him, apparently. All the same, Gunther told him not to eat any of the fish.

'Jesus...' Justin walked up to the body, the colour draining from his face. 'It is real, right? This ain't a crackpot joke some kids have played on the old-timers?'

'He's real, yeah. That's just rigor mortis setting in.'

'Rigor morwhat?'

'Mortis. It's what happens to the body after death. Gets all stiff.'

'Oh, yeah, that. Yeah, I know that.'

Justin took off his shades and wiped them with his sleeve. He didn't like being told things he should have known as Chief, so Gaten didn't linger on the subject.

'I suppose we should get CSI on this. Get Bert down for photographs and evidence, all that stuff.'

'You think I don't know how this works? This ain't my first rodeo, Gate.'

Gaten nodded, despite the fact he knew the last murder in Cuckoo Cove had taken place around two years ago. Justin had taken the chief's job one year after, and he'd been reaping the rewards of tranquility ever since. He nudged the body with his boot.

'Damned asshole had to pick October, didn't he? With the climate we have, this is the one place in America where beaches actually start to pick up. The mayor's gonna be down my throat.' He shook his head. Then, for the first time since he'd arrived, he took a properly long look at the body. 'What's that on his forehead?'

Gaten looked down and spotted what Justin was looking at. The head of the man was shaved to the skin, and there was a faint black circle around the scalp. Gaten swallowed. He knew exactly what it was.

'Hair dye,' he responded quietly.

Justin stared at him. 'There is no hair.'

'From a wig. The netting. He must have dyed it recently and it stained his head.'

'You think he's queer?'

Gaten fidgeted uncomfortably. 'I don't know, sir.'

'Well, let's hope he is. Lord knows, that'll be a blessing.'

'How's that?'

'Use your head, Gate. If he's queer, the likelihood of this being a suicide triples. Ain't no queer folk get murdered round here. They got themselves for that. Mark my words, if he's queer, this will get forgotten in a day. No panic in the streets. No mayor on my back. Heck, this reservoir could be back open tomorrow. Good job for noticing that, Gate. You've saved me an awkward conversation.' At that moment, the chief's pager gave a funny, small bleep and he grabbed it in a flash. 'Holy shit,' he muttered. 'That's Tanita. She's gone into labour.'

'Congratulations,' said Gaten awkwardly.

Justin jammed the pager back into his belt and began pacing back up the bank. 'Okay, I gotta go. But you know what needs to be done here, right?'

'Sure.'

'Take all the necessary procedures. Call in CSI. No need to block traffic, just cordon off the main entrances into the reservoir. If people ask, don't use the words "crime scene", just tell them we're investigating an incident. Let em' know there's nothing to worry about.' He opened the car door and threw his bagel into the dirt.

'What about you?' asked Gaten.

'I'll phone the mayor from the hospital, let him know what's going on. I want you to stay with CSI when they get here. You and Gunther. Let me know what they say. And goddamn it, make sure that fisherman's gone before they arrive.'

'Will do, Chief.'

Justin Hadero started his engine and the wheels of the squad car churned up clay and dirt. Before he set off, he leant out of his window and called over to Gaten.

'Oh, and find that wig!'

The chief saluted and then, almost as quickly as he'd arrived, he was gone. Gaten watched his car disappear and turned back to the body. It made another squeaking sound. The water around it rippled and bubbled a little. It was so quiet that Gaten heard the weight of the fisherman's line hit the surface of the reservoir. He sighed, pulled out his radio, and began trudging toward him and Gunther.

4

Hunger is a result of ghrelin in the blood and leptin in the stomach sending signals to the brain. This creates what is known as an appetite. A large appetite can lead to obesity, but this is not a choice. It is an addiction. An addiction that riddles the body and forces the hand. Blood, stomach, nerves, the brain, yearning for more. More sustenance. More fulfilment. More.

That is, in many ways, what it is like here. There is a signal. There is an addiction. More is always possible. More is always needed. In time, the hunger can be appeased and the appetite will deflate. But not now. Hunger is the cruellest addiction, because it is necessary to survive. Without hunger, there is no need to sustain the body. It will wither and it will die, and it will never tell itself why. Hunger is a warning shot instilled from birth. It is listened to. It is obeyed. That is what is happening here: more, more, more. Until when?

5

'There was a kid found dead this morning. At least, CSI thought he was a kid. When they got him out the water, he stank. Really. He stank like old shit and seaweed. I vomited three times just being near him. They think he was gay. They think it was a suicide, only they didn't find any cause of death. They've sent him off for the autopsy, so I guess that'll tell us. When they put him on the stretcher, I got a good look at his face. It was bloated, but I could still see the makeup. You know, like blush and mascara. Although that could have been bruises, it was hard to tell. Theo, are you listening?'

'Yeah, yeah, I hear you. Seaweed, vomit, mascara. Sounds like a good night out to me.'

Theodore Dalbret rushed past the television and into the bathroom. He was searching for something and had been since Gaten got home. Gaten's eyes were glued to the television, but he wasn't watching. He was still thinking about the body in the water.

'And the dead kid?'

'Okay, that changes the script a little.'

'I haven't seen something like that before,' said Gaten shakily. 'Not for real. Doesn't it make you scared?'

'Why should it make me scared?' Theo reached behind the toilet bowl and pulled out a thick, curly wig. 'Ah-ha!'

Gaten turned to look at him. His brother was thirty-one, but he looked closer to forty. Being a woman seemed to age him. The lipstick made his skin crack, and the mascara gave him dark bags under the eyes. His face looked leaner too. His cheeks stuck out like jagged stones, and when he placed the wig on his head, it gave him the aura of a dogged rockstar searching for one last lick of fame. Gaten never told him this. It was an uncomfortable subject for him, and he still wasn't sure if he was okay with it, but he made do and kept his words to himself. He turned back to the television as Theo began applying the last of his foundation.

'Like I said,' Gaten clarified, 'the kid could be gay.'

Theo gasped. 'You mean gay guys get murdered too?'

'That's not what I'm saying.'

Gaten looked down at the coffee table, where a stack of Theo's flyers were piled high. They showed his brother in full costume, with a quirky pout and a kiss blown to the camera. Beside him were the words:

SARA DEL BRET
– MON-FRI AT THE PRECIOUS STAR BAR
KARAOKE, DANCE, SING ALONGS,
CABARET AND CALAMITY
PLENTY OF BOOZE BUT STRICTLY NO NUTS!

The flier ended with a line of X's, followed by the bar's telephone number and email.

'It could be dangerous out there,' said Gaten warily.

'Just another night in Cuckoo Cove, honey.' Theo slammed the bathroom cabinet shut, then walked into the lounge and took a swig of some Malibu. His heels made a loud clapping sound on the wooden floorboards.

'I'm just saying, you should be careful. Don't give out too many of those fliers. You don't know who's out there. You're my brother, Theo. I want you safe.'

Theo finished his drink and crossed his arms, tapping his fishnet sleeves. 'Suicide, right?' he asked plainly.

Gaten shrugged. 'That's what they think.'

'So it sounds like some poor kid let this shitty world get the best of him. We've all been there. Good for him for throwing in the towel and knowing when he's beaten. If the rest of us still had nuts, maybe we'd follow.'

'You still have nuts, Theo.'

'I'm just saying, you don't have to worry about me. This town's been gay for years now and no one's had a problem with it. Sure, everyone treats us like aliens. There are threats every day and most of the old folk look like they wanna lynch us by the pier, but I'm as safe as the next person. Besides, we're on the other side of town. It's like a totally different world up there. Maybe they're asking for it more than us. It wouldn't surprise me. I went to a cabaret up there and even I felt like murdering most of the people on that stage.'

'Theo...'

'What? They were murdering *Two Ladies*.'

'You're trying to be funny again. That's your coping mechanism.'

Theo placed his glass on the table and gave a little flick of his heel. 'If it ain't broke, don't fix it.' With a cheeky smile, he walked over to the door and grabbed his keys from the coat rack.

'Just be safe, Theo. I don't want you getting hurt like that kid.'

'Sara, honey. My name is Sara.'

Gaten's brother blew a kiss and waved, and then the door shut and Gaten was left alone. He sat back and turned the volume up on the television, trying desperately to get the picture of the body out of his head. Just like in the reservoir, however, it continued to float there. It rocked up and down, side to side, and nothing he could do seemed to let it sink. After a few minutes, he leapt up from the couch and swallowed some sleeping pills. Then he returned and poured himself a glass of whisky. When he fell asleep, he dreamed of the wig and where it had gone. He was looking for it but he couldn't find it.

CHAPTER THREE

THE PRECIOUS STAR BAR

1

The beach at Cuckoo Cove stretched for nearly three miles. It was bookended by Camp Green Rock and Fort Kraven, named after the explorer, William Kraven, who had discovered the cove back in 1847. He was a renowned captain of the Caledonia, transporting tobacco and rum from the east coast in return for hides and tallow in the west. His company had been wintering near the mouth of Argola River due to an intense storm. On the second day, one of the crew mates spotted a beached whale on the nearby shore. Sensing an opportunity, Kraven set his sights on the cove, only to find the whale had been mostly shed of its carcass. Figuring that there must have been Native Americans nearby, they explored approximately one mile inland and two miles across shore. The cove, however, appeared unclaimed.

After the storm had eased, the Caledonia carried out the rest of its journey and Kraven returned two months later. The whale, by this point, had been entirely dissolved to bone. This time, the captain and his men carried out a more intensive expedition, travelling five miles inland and three miles across shore, expecting to find some form of civilisation. Still there was nothing, although they did note an unusual abundance of cuckoos. Upon returning to the east coast, William Kraven swapped tobacco and rum for human cargo, bringing settlers back to the cove to build a trading post. It was there that they found a further three whales washed up on shore. A crew of men were set the task of retrieving the blubber and oil, and half a carcass was procured the first night. By the next morning, however, the other half had been torn apart.

Afraid that some Native Americans may still be lurking somewhere, Kraven assigned a group of men to work on the second whale during the day, while another group of men maintained a watch overnight. Instead of Native Americans, however, a group of cuckoos scurried out of holes in the sandbanks, spent a few hours pecking at the carcasses, then nestled back inside. Content at the news from his men – although disturbed at the cuckoo's supposed evolution from insect eaters to whale devourers – Kraven blew the sandbanks with gunpowder and set to work on the last of the whales.

Over the next few years, the cuckoos became a nuisance to a growing society, not only due to their unusual meat-eating tendencies, but their incessant *cuckooing* early in the morning and throughout the day. In an effort to get rid of them, Kraven schemed the destruction of all nearby trees and used the timber to construct a pier. He wanted this to be the longest pier ever built and, although their resources didn't allow it to amount to that, the timber they collected was enough to stretch the pier a fair distance into the ocean.

At first, it appeared the scheme worked, but without trees and sandbanks to nest into, most of the beach's cuckoos ended up taking refuge in the framework of the pier itself. Rather than being a societal nuisance, however, the cuckoos became something of an entertainment show, impressing the community with sunset aerobatics as they swarmed above the shallows in search of food. In honour of their newfound role, Kraven changed the name of the land from Kraven Beach to Cuckoo Cove. The skull of the first whale was hung above the entrance gate to the pier. When some cuckoos decided to roost inside it, the skull was admonished with alcohol, chilli peppers and vinegar, and that appeared to do the trick.

2

The sun was wet on Sara's face. Her heels clacked against the sidewalk and normally she liked the sound, but today her head felt precious. It always did after a long night of partying. In a way, it felt like the night before had never really ended; it had just blurred into the morning, and that was always a surefire way to lug baggage. That baggage rested behind Sara's eyes now, and she resisted the urge to rub it away. Her makeup looked good tonight. She had chosen the red and purple eyeshadow and it blended nicely to create a night-sky effect. Her cholesterol spots looked almost like stars, which was a good way to utilise them, she supposed.

The beach was lit in an oily red sheen and the air smelled like salt, smoke and burgers. The sea was calm but frothy, like someone had spilled an oversized tub of bubble bath over the side of the pier. It was eight o'clock on a Friday, so the atmosphere was buzzing. Kids and teenagers bustled across the sidewalks. The ones with hair dye and nose piercings had coffee cups, the ones with tracksuits and buzzed hair had beer cans hidden in brown paper. Some passed her with their eyes on the sidewalk but others stared for a while. *Fabulous*, she told herself. *They think you look fabulous*. When the heckles started, she straightened her back and built up a swagger.

'Hey faggot, can I pop one of your balloons?'

'What does your wife think of those heels?'

'I can see your cock, fairy boy.'

'I'll give you five cents for a blowjob. Or your next best offer!'

Sara went about her daily damage control. She kept her eyes on the road in front of her but she blew a kiss to the most impressive of insults. The blowjob got a wink. She ignored the ones that mentioned anything remotely masculine. She found that those were the most serious, underlined with a kind of anger that only grew sharper if she reacted to it. Cuckoo Cove was a gay town, but there were no gay towns in America. There was only a mirage of acceptance that gay people had to live with. They had always been prisoners in a war camp, but in Cuckoo Cove, their quarters had been made cosy. Their beds were made with linen and their blinds were opened in the daytime, but they still had buckets to piss in. Their clothes still looked the same. That's what the eyes told her whenever Sara walked down the street. She was gay, but that was allowed. She was *allowed*.

When Sara passed the pier, she stopped and removed a pack of Marlboros from her handbag. She lit one and inhaled. She looked at the beach and saw a bunch of kids sitting around a poorly assembled fire. They spoke softly and laughed occasionally. One of them had short curly hair and a nose piercing, and he wore tight fitting jeans that were ripped at the knees. Sara thought she saw him look at the boy in front of him for just a little too long. When the other boy caught his gaze, he looked down and took a swig of beer. She smiled and watched as three of them began to splutter. The cauldron they had created was mostly smoke now and their lungs soaked it in. Their clothes did too. Whatever happened to them that night, whatever route they went down and whatever decision they chose, Sara knew that it would stay with them in those clothes. Those hoodies, those tank-tops, those shorts. Everything that happened would remain pungent inside the fabric. Sara looked at the boy with the nose piercing and hoped that, whatever happened to him, whatever he chose to do, he wouldn't be washing the stench out so soon tomorrow morning.

She sniffed and tapped on her cigarette. A cuckoo fluttered from underneath the pier and landed on the railing in front of her. It tilted its head and stared with white, beady eyes just as Sara took another drag.

'Cuckoo,' she cooed playfully.

The bird didn't blink. It stared at her, she realised, much in the same way that children stared at her. With a wealth of innocence, but a hint of suspicion that had already dawned inside their young and tiny worlds. They knew something was wrong, but they didn't quite know what. It made Sara sad, in a way. That already, before many of them had even uttered their first word, they recognised her as wrong. But then, why wouldn't they? When they were just babies tucked inside pink or blue outfits. They looked at her as if to ask: 'Where's your outfit? How can you get away with it?' The bird tilted its head the other way, clearly attempting to work out the puzzle.

'Man in a dress,' Sara helped it out.

The bird fluttered its wings and chirped, *CUCKOO!* Then it jumped from its perch and flew back underneath the pier.

Sara nodded. 'Cuckoo.'

Then she flicked her cigarette and continued walking.

3

The Precious Star Bar was located on Adamson Avenue, just a five minute walk from the beach. It was lodged between a burrito joint and a small-town bakery. The owner, Carl Vasquez, often referred to it as the meat in Adamson's sandwich. At this time of night, it was usually just the locals running the show, but Sara noticed a group of twenty year old strangers smoking on the doorstep. They wore jackets and chinos. Not the usual type that the Precious Star Bar attracted, but they kept quiet when Sara passed them and one of them even opened the door for her.

'Thanks honey.' Sara flicked her attention to the blonde and gave him a wink.

The inside was illuminated by purple bulbs and Christmas lights that ran the length of the bar. In the corner was a small podium, with a makeshift electric chair in the centre. It was wrapped with tinsel, and a pointed sign above it read, *ELECTRIC SLUT!*. It was used for lap dances during Wednesday's burlesque show, but an elderly gentleman with a denim vest was currently slouched over it, a pint of Budweiser clasped firmly in one hand.

'Hey slut,' Sara called over to him.

The older gentleman caught her eye and whistled. 'Lookin' good tonight, Sara.'

'Always, honey. Always.'

Sara swished her hair over one shoulder and walked over to the bar. Cher was playing loudly over the speaker system, and dry ice was already beginning to churn out of the smoke machine. It filled the air with toxic but strangely comforting fumes. In many ways, the hazy mist had become a part of the Precious Star Bar's personality. It was thick and sickly, but it wrapped around them like some kind of mystical shield. Bloodshot eyes and an unsettled stomach was a small price to pay for the feeling it provided. In many ways, it was the air outside that got Sara queasy.

The woman behind the bar held out a glass of Sara's tipple. Vodka and lemon with lemonade. Sara leant over and gave her a kiss on the cheek.

'How did you know?' she asked playfully.

'I never forget an alcoholics favourite drink,' said Luna. 'It's gonna be a big one tonight.'

Luna was one of Sara's best friends. She was married to the owner, Carl, whose night-time name was Sally. She preferred feminine pronouns but she didn't dress like a girl. She wore a leather jacket lined with black feathers, black leather pants with tassels and she sported an impressive mohawk that came in three, thickly gelled spikes. She would start the evening with her three favourite songs: "Gypsies, Tramps and Thieves" by Cher, "If I Could Turn Back Time" by Cher, and "Dark Lady" by Cher. Then an encore, which was usually a track by Cher.

'What makes you so sure, honey?' asked Sara. 'Are you thinking of changing up your playlist?'

'I think it's time Barbara Streisand made an appearance, don't you?'

'You sure she's ready for that honour?'

Luna stroked her chin with ink-black nails. 'Maybe not. She agitated me with that turtle neck on *Oprah* last night. Maybe "Hell On Wheels"?'

'I haven't heard that one.'

'It's one of Cher's lesser known tracks.'

Sara nodded. 'Sounds appropriate.'

Luna clapped and mixed another two drinks for the both of them. 'I thought you'd be on by now anyway, it's ten minutes past your opener.'

'Sure, that was the plan. I'd just like to play my opener to someone other than Kirk Johnson for a change.' She nodded over toward the electric chair, where Kirk Johnson was giddily tapping along to "Believe"'s outro.

There were only two other people in the bar apart from him. One was a closeted local gay called Tom Butcher – closeted because he had come out of the closet, but had taken all of the coats with him. He frequented the Precious Star Bar every weekend, but he sat like a mute in the corner, sipping his beer through a thin pink straw. Sara had seen him get off his perch just once for karaoke, but he'd fled at the speed of light when a group of teenagers started catcalling him. The other member was Alan Salcedo, warm and friendly, but usually preoccupied with ambushing the first fresh face that walked through the door. He saw the Precious Star Bar as more of a speed dating venue than as the entertainment venue it was supposed to be.

'What about the guys outside?' asked Sara.

'What guys outside?'

'There's about five of them.'

'Are they here to stir the pot?' asked Luna.

Sara shrugged. 'I don't think so. They look like bunnies to me.'

'Oh good. I eat bunnies for breakfast.'

With that, Luna downed her second drink and waltzed to the stage. She was a stout vegetarian, but when it came to eating bunnies, Luna was a certified connoisseur. If they opened that door, Sara knew those boys wouldn't stand a chance.

They did open the door eventually. Granted, the first few times was just to let other people in, but when Luna was done with her set, the five boys had warmed to the light and the Precious Star Bar was speckled with around fifteen people. Sara pursed her lips around the straw in her glass and eyed the blonde. When Luna came to the end of her encore, she swung her hand up toward the mirrorball and let her fingers uncurl. Her nails spun reflections back at the ball, and those reflections warped and exploded again, landing pin-pointedly onto the group of boys. Sara placed her own glass down on the bar and smiled when the blonde looked at her. He was a cute bunny, she thought. His face was lean and tidy. Rosy blotches added some colour into his cheeks, and his hair was parted like two waves hitting together. His jacket looked expensive and so did his pants, which were particularly tight around the thighs. She kept her gaze down there for a while, breaking only when Luna slumped into the stool next to her.

'You keep looking, it'll start smoking soon.'

'It's smoking already.' Sara lifted her glass again. 'Chin chin.'

'Forget it. They only caught the last number. I knew I should have ended with Streisand.'

'I thought you were off Streisand.'

'I'd marry her if it got a few more people in this bar. And I'd do it in a turtle neck.'

Sara chuckled, but her attention was still on the blonde boy. The more she looked, the more she liked him. He was clearly out of his comfort zone, but there was something about him that radiated confidence. He had a good posture, maybe that was it. He had the posture of an Egyptian Pharaoh, standing his ground against an army of anxieties that were clearly telling him to drop tail and run. He didn't run. He listened to his soul, not his head, and the soul was what Sara liked in a man. He looked at her again and Sara fluttered her lashes, determined not to give too much away. She didn't even know if the boy was gay, she was just guessing. But he had willingly entered one of the town's most notorious gay bars, with Luna's unedifying version of Cher's "Dark Lady" demonstrating what he was in for. Sara didn't think much of Luna's voice, but tonight it must have been positively siren-esque. The group of bunnies had heard, and the group of bunnies had taken the carrot, and now they stood in the dizzying light of the mirrorball.

Luna craned her neck. 'What's up, girl? You've gone too quiet.'

'That boy over there, what do you think? Gay or nay?'

Luna squinted through the plumes of fake smoke. 'Hard to tell, he's kinda wibbly.'

'I can see him fine.'

'I thought they were mine to play with.'

'You're married, honey.'

'To a sixty year old man on Prozac. Give me credit, a girl's gotta live.'

'That's what I love about you, Luna. Your never-ending sense of loyalty.'

'Loyalty my ass, those boys are hot. How often do we get men like them coming in here? I'd be stupid not to try one of them.'

Sara finished the rest of her drink. The vodka was strong but the lemon was stronger. It sank into the cracks in her lips, so she clamped her teeth down and chewed the sharpness away.

'Well, leave the blonde one alone. I've got my eye on him.'

'Looks like he's got his eye on me.'

Sara looked back toward the group of boys, noticing that the blonde had indeed diverted his attention to her friend. She felt her heart drop for a moment. 'What's the time?' she asked quickly.

'Nine thirty,' Luna replied. 'Don't worry, you've still got thirty minutes.'

Sara jumped off her stool. 'Can't make them wait that long. I think they deserve a show, don't you?'

She gave Luna a pinch on the cheek, then danced toward the stage.

4

When Sara Del Bret took to the stage, something else took to her – something electric yet soothing, like a toxic shot racing through her veins, making them hum and fizz like the lemon in her drink. She felt alive in ways that she never really felt on the outside. When she had walked along the beach and stopped for her cigarette, she had been happy. But that happiness wasn't real. It was just a numbing gel, something placed on top of something else to make it feel less bad. She experienced a lot of that kind of happiness in her life, but when she was on stage, the feeling was different. This was not a numbing sensation, but a rush of everything that felt good. She feasted on the lights, the smoke, the show, and she became one with it. Sara Del Bret was her true form, but most of the time, she existed in a brief case. When she was on stage, the hinges clipped, the case opened and the real Sara Del Bret was allowed to let rip.

Her show started with a sultry cabaret number, followed by Cab Calloway, Peggy Lee and the fun, bouncing, joy of Harry Ruby. On Wednesdays and Thursdays, she had three backing dancers – Carl's son from a previous marriage and two of the stage hands from Cuckoo Cove's theatre hall. Today, she had no one. But that was okay. The four corners of the stage wouldn't have handled anyone else anyway, because she lived every square inch of it. Her heels kicked into the sky, her dress swished and flew like a bat on a leash, and her voice echoed like she was singing on a lost island in the middle of an ocean. Everything and anything that mattered was her. There was no time, no cause, no reason. It was like she was in space. When the number finished, she stopped and beamed into what felt like starlight. Applause rippled across the bar. The smoke parted just enough to reveal the five boys and she remembered them. She remembered the blonde, who was looking at her now and smiling. She hummed to her audience like she was still singing.

'This next one's dedicated to the boy with the blonde hair.'

She smiled at him and, to her relief, the boy continued to smile back. He said something to his friends. She didn't know if they'd been speaking throughout her set, but she hoped they were quiet for this next one, because it was important to her. She had been singing "Don't Dream It" from the *Rocky Horror Picture Show* since she'd first started performing, and each night it never failed to get the most out of her. She didn't quite know why. Perhaps it came from a place of regret. She'd grown up in the town of Sunnyside, her parents and brother packed like sardines into a tiny apartment. Her dad owned his own shoe company, but he was a slacker, so he struggled to pay rent. He spent most of his afternoons in the local bars. When he came home, he would praise Gaten for the money he made at the local bakery, and scolded Theo for tucking himself in his room and practicing musical routines in front of the mirror. Theo was a volunteer at the local town hall. Every six months they would put on a democratically decided musical, and he would work hard to elevate himself above "Line-less Extra Number Three". His father, however, didn't quite see it as work. For him, standing alone in the bedroom and singing to a reflection was a waste of time and energy, both of which would have been better spent earning something real. One afternoon, Theo asked him how many quarters he'd found at the bottom of his whisky glass, and he clapped him so hard that he left a mark. He tried his best not to listen to him and he tried even harder to get a part, but every six months he never failed to stand three rows from the front of the stage, singing along to a poorly rehearsed chorus number. It took several failed attempts before he realised he had been going for the wrong roles.

It was during the production of *Grease* when Theo ditched the character of Kenickie for Rizzo in the bedroom mirror, and everything seemed to come alive. He remembered his reflection beginning to morph and change. The cluttered bed and drawers dissolved into Rizzo's bedroom, and his voice rebounded off the four walls like he was performing on the biggest stage in Broadway. From that point on, he stopped going to the town hall productions. He knew that the roles he deserved would have to go to someone else, and it pained him that it wasn't his fault. He had been born to play those parts, but like a actor with his suit on backwards, something had gone terribly wrong back in wardrobe. He stopped performing in front of the mirror too, because his reflection judged him. It stared back with its baggy shirt and shorts and seemed to grow a bit paler whenever he performed, as if it knew what it was being made to do was wrong.

One morning, the day after Halloween, Theo's father pushed him into a mountain of shoe boxes. Angry that he wasn't following in his brother's footsteps, he made Theo polish every shoe from every box and, when he was finished, go with him to the store and help to sell as many as he could. Just one percent of income would go into Theo's pocket, and he would do this every day until he could buy the family a steak dinner. The idea was to show him how much hard work went into achieving small rewards, so his pursuit in the theatre industry was really doing no good for anybody.

About a fortnight into his new job, Theo was walking home from the store when he saw a new poster in the window of Sunnyside's picture house. It involved a tall man with dark curly hair, stilettos, fishnet stockings, and a thinly laced, black leather jacket. The man was dressed like a woman, and he stared back at Theo with black shadows under his eyes and a thick clump of lipstick underlining a wickedly confident grin. With the money he had already earned, Theo bought a ticket and sat amongst a group of rowdy young men and women who shouted at the screen and threw their popcorn into the air.

The movie was unlike anything he had seen before. There were men dressed as women, musical numbers about sex and freedom, and a complete refusal to recognise any part of what they were doing as wrong. When he walked out of the theatre, his world felt completely different to when he had walked into it. The next morning, Theo wiped some of the shoe polish around his eyes, then ran up to his mirror to check the results. He saw someone he had never seen before looking back at him. A woman. Without disguise, without a mask. Just a woman. And she was ready for the hard yards. She learned every line of every song in the picture, and when her mother put on a yard sale, she stole one of her dresses and hid it under her bed, putting it on when she sung one song in particular. It was a song that would often make her cry, but she tried not to, because every time she did, her pillowcase became awash with tears and shoe polish stains. The song was called "Don't Dream It", and it taught her that she shouldn't be afraid to be the person she wanted to be. It told her to go out into the world, but not be cynical when the world didn't respond kindly to her coming. It was a song that said, actually, the reflection in the mirror was the only thing that truly mattered. Not the town hall. Not her father's failing shoe shop. Just her reflection. And so long as she was staring at that mirror, and a woman with dark shoe polish under her eyes was staring back, then that really was all that mattered. The rest of them could all get fucked.

Sara never got to play the role of Frank N. Furter. Not properly. But that didn't matter, as she carried that mirror everywhere she went. Here in the Precious Star Bar, she played the role every night. On this stage. To herself, and from herself. It was a gift that said, *I know you're special.* And in many ways, that was the most important thing.

Sara pulled her head back and stared into the lights. The song started and she felt it rise within her breast. She kicked out her knee and began treading playfully toward the corner of the stage. The clouds parted again, and she noticed everyone in the bar was looking at her. She soaked in their admiration, but her eyes remained on the blonde. He was walking now, the fake smoke parting around him like waves. She smiled as he stood in front of her and, when there was a break in the verse, she leant over.

'I'm not stopping the song for you, honey.'

The boy said something back which sounded like, 'They made me do it.'

He handed over what looked like a business card. In the centre was an emblem, two golden antlers, with text just below it.

ASK A DRAG ACT FOR THEIR BRA

Sara turned it over as if she might have read it wrong. Even with two vodka lemonades down her, however, she knew she hadn't. The words remained the same, and the boy that gave her them grinned with two large, twisted front teeth. Her heart sank, but she kept her cool. She stuffed the card into her bra and stood up straight. When she finished the song, the entire bar broke into a round of applause, and Sara bowed like there might be flowers.

5

There was a dull throb in her head when she went outside. Sara stood with her back against the wall, two fingers squeezing a cigarette and another rubbing lightly at her temple. It was nearly midnight, and while that usually meant the night was only getting started, tonight was the first night in a while she was craving her bed. Perhaps it was the incident with the boy with the blonde hair, or perhaps it was Kirk Johnson's terrible rendition of "Don't Stop Believing" – which he had just begun singing for the third time this evening – but Sara could think of nothing better than simply stripping off her clothes and crawling into a nice, warm abyss. She exhaled and felt her cigarette begin to burn her fingertips. She considered lighting another one, but before she could, the door swung open beside her and the bachelor party marched their way out. The boy with the blonde hair spotted her like an eagle spotting a shrew in the long grass.

'Hey beautiful, you got my bra yet?'

The other four boys laughed and Sara put on a forced smile.

'Still warming it up for ya.'

'With what?' The blonde boy giggled like a kid in the schoolyard, and he looked at his friends for reassurance. They gave it to him.

'Give him your bra,' one of them said. 'It's just a dare. He don't wanna fail on the first card.'

'Yeah,' said the blonde boy. 'I mean, it's not like you need it anyway.' He lurched forward, reaching for Sara's chest, and she felt his fingernails dig into her skin.

'Don't fucking touch me,' she yelled, pushing him away and swinging her recently manicured claws into his left cheek.

The blonde boy stumbled backwards and his friends laughed and cheered. Behind Sara, the door to the Precious Star Bar opened again and Luna stepped out into the night.

'What the hell's going on out here?'

The blonde boy wavered, cracking a false, twisted smile. 'Don't fret it. Me and my buddy were just having a friendly conversation.'

'Really? Only, through the window it looked like you were trying to grope her. Listen, I'm not surprised three hours in my husband's bar has turned you gay as a picnic basket, but you can't just start groping the next man you see. There are boundaries.'

'I ain't gay, dude. I'm getting married tomorrow.'

'Really? So I guess you just fancied a try on us before making that kind of commitment, is that it? I'm not sure how your wife would feel about that.'

'We fancied a freak show,' one of the other four boy's raised his beer bottle.

Sara reached into her bra. 'It's alright, Luna. He just wanted his card back, that's all.'

She pulled it out and flicked it over toward the blonde boy. It tapped clumsily against his forehead and fell toward the pavement, but he didn't pay it any mind. He was in a staring contest with Luna, who was eyeing him up with her head dipped, like she might be about to go full rhinoceros and stick one of her mohawk spikes into his chest.

'Come on Daniel,' one of his friend's flung an arm around

the blonde boy's shoulder. 'There's plenty of bras out there. Ones that might actually belong to women.'

The blonde boy was pulled away and the five of them began walking drunkenly down the street. Luna called after them.

'There's a whole collection down in Claire's on fourth street. They might even have some in your size.'

The boys didn't turn back, and Sara was grateful, because she'd had just about enough of this night. She ran a hand through her hair and jolted a bit when Luna took her arm.

'You okay, Sara?'

'Perfect. I think I'm gonna head home.'

'What? Don't tell me those guys got to you —'

'It's not them. It's my head. I'm just not feeling it tonight, honey.'

Sara smiled and her friend smiled back, but it quickly faded when Kirk Johnson broke out into his fourth rendition of "Don't Stop Believing".

'Alright, that's it,' said Luna. 'I'm taking the microphone off him.'

She ran back inside and, despite herself, Sara broke into a quiet laugh. It surprised her, because it wasn't genuine. She did it for herself and for no one. She sighed, then pushed her hair over one shoulder and pulled up her bra. Her heels echoed loudly across the street when she began walking home, making sure to go in the opposite direction of the bachelor party.

6

The route across the beach and back to the apartment was often an empty one, with plenty of room for thought. During

Sara's first two years as a resident in Cuckoo Cove, she believed that the Precious Star Bar was her favourite place on earth. It was funny what the soul could make do with. In a concreted jail house, a shower became a haven, and in Cuckoo Cove, the bar wasn't much different. In the fall of 2000, Jerry Fletcher, the town's most prominent preacher, marched into the place with a phoney court order which told them to close down in two weeks. He was seventy-four years old and senile, but a handful of his congregation still housed demonstrations outside of the doors after they failed to comply. Some had biblical placards that read:

LEVITICUS 20:13

IF A MAN HAS INTERCOURSE WITH A MAN THEY MUST BE PUT TO DEATH

GOD SHOWS HIS ANGER FROM HEAVEN AGAINST ALL SINFUL

1 CORINTHIANS 6:9-11

THOSE WHO INDULGE IN SEXUAL SIN WILL NOT INHERIT THE KINGDOM OF GOD

Other, more simplified placards read:

CUCKOO COVE IS NOT A GAY TOWN

GOD HATES QUEERS

IF GOD LOVES GAYS WHY DID PRECIOUS STAR BAR BURN IN 97?

The latter was a rather obscure reference to the Precious Star Bar's previous identity as a straight nightclub. A small platform had collapsed overnight and ripped through the wiring of a lighting rig. Six months after the incident, the building was sold and re-opened under a different moniker.

Sara remembered Luna putting on a red feathered headdress and tails from the cabaret wardrobe and venturing out to confront them.

'We didn't burn, darling, we rose from the ashes!'

The protestors threw some tangerines that they'd been saving for their lunch break.

They had laughed about it then, but the experience had left an impact on Sara. For starters, it was the first time she realised that there truly were no gay towns in America. Secondly, it showed her that, no matter how much she hoped it would be, the Precious Star Bar was not her favourite place on earth. It was simply a place on earth, more hopeful and less mundane than the rest of them. The blend of ice and heat could form a shield around the noise of the outside world, but it couldn't stop it from forming its attack. The door still swung both ways. Not to mention, the people who walked through it were not really themselves. The righteous, like the boys, walked into the Precious Star Bar with an elevated sense of self-worth. Others, just passing, arrived in good faith but felt like they were owed something just for being there. They walked into the Precious Star Bar like they had crouched into a little girl's Wendy house. The worst, however, were the regulars. They came into the bar like it was a school playground. When Sara was on stage, she sang to paper-men with blank faces. She could stretch out a fingernail and poke a hole in them, and they wouldn't even flinch. They had, in a way, been shaved down to the point of puppets. In the Precious Star Bar, they were allowed to dance and play before the marionette was yanked back and the show was over. It was that feeling again. The same one Sara got every time she walked the streets. None of them could get over the feeling that they were *allowed*, and being *allowed* meant that something, even on a very basic level, was wrong.

Perhaps that was why Sara had felt so put out by the boy with the blonde hair. She had thought that boy was neither here nor there. Not gay, but not altogether like the rest of them. An outsider in the best sense of the word. If he had taken to Sara in the way she had taken to him, then perhaps the world was not so bleak as she had thought. But no such luck. His answer was the one she had known for two years now, and she so wished she would stop trying to rub it out with the wrong end of the pencil.

Sara approached the entrance to the pier and started humming to herself. She found it was her favourite song that passed her lips, the last song she had performed before she got that card. The card. That boy. Why, for heavens sake, did he have to give it to her during that song? A shining light in the middle of nowhere didn't deserve to be tested, so why on earth did he have to shake her? She took out a cigarette and stopped, staring at the whale's skull that dangled ominously above the gate. She didn't know what kind of whale it was, but it was big and brown, with all but two teeth missing. Two cabins on either side of the gate were boarded up with damp planks and nails. They had images beside the doors, both of them faded by salt and water. By the looks of things, they used to sell hotdogs and shakes, with optional extras of sauerkraut and cookie pieces. Out on the beach, the fire pit from earlier was just a pile of red embers. The kids had long since left. They might have been out on the town somewhere, or they might have been tucked up underneath their sheets. The latter was certainly more likely. Cuckoo Cove liked to call itself a party town, but in all truth, most of the parties were put to bed by around twelve. Right now, Sara was completely alone, with nothing but the sound of waves frothing along the pebbles as a signal of life other than hers.

She wiped at her eyes and began moving again, but after a few seconds, something stopped her. The sound of music joined the ocean's pulse, rising cordially in the air. Close but distant. Loud but deafeningly quiet. Sara turned and listened. The pier was pitch dark, abandoned and desolate, but that was exactly where the music was coming from. At times, it was so clear that she could hear brass instruments, following in melody with piano, drums, strings and bass, then cheers, which rose and fell in tandem with what sounded like a cabaret. She took a few steps closer and tried to see if she could spot any lights, but there were none. The pier was dead. It had been for years, and the only souls that occupied it now were the cuckoos. Yet here was a song. Beautiful, gorgeous. And playing out to an invisible crowd like it was fifty years earlier, and the pier was full of life, and buzz, and memories.

Sara frowned and began moving toward the gate, but just as she did so, the music began peeling back and fading, growing quieter and quieter until it dissolved entirely into the crisp, night sky. Then it was just waves again. Quiet, lapping. Sara bit at her bottom lip. She thought for a moment about going to investigate, but a greater pull stopped her. Bed was near, her eyes were tired, it was late, she was alone, and there were no gay towns in America. She turned toward the road and continued the journey back to her apartment.

She thought about that music for twenty minutes until she got to her door. Then she stepped inside, made a cup of tea, climbed into bed, and she didn't think about it at all.

CHAPTER FOUR

THE NIGHTMARE

1

Something here wonders. It does that from time to time. Daydreams. Thinks. It scratches irritably at its ears and occasionally it sighs, phlegm kicking up in the back of its throat. It blinks and the goo between its eyelids makes a squelching sound. It licks when its mouth goes dry. It shivers when it's cold. Something here senses the waves beneath its head and it creates a world on the other side of them. It wonders and then it gets bored of wondering. When the sun comes out, it repositions itself and falls asleep. It dreams about food and its mouth twitches when it's eating.

2

The plant was around two miles from Jason Hancock's front door and it was all uphill. In the morning, he would get out of bed, give his wife a kiss, and jump into the shower without turning the knob. He liked it hot and he liked it cold, so it didn't matter where his wife left it, unless she'd turned it back to the middle. The middle was no good to anyone. When he had washed his hair twice and scrubbed his balls with a bar of soap, he would slip into his jumpsuit and make some eggs in the kitchen. He paired them with apple sauce, buttered potato cakes, and a shot of coffee from his beloved espresso machine. After breakfast, he would place some shop-bought sushi into his rucksack, remove his bicycle from the garage, and set out into the sunrise to make the two mile climb up to the plant. It took him about thirty minutes, depending on how well the espresso hit him, and when he arrived, he would wait for another twenty and have his first smoke. Paolo was usually the next to arrive, and he had the keys to the rolling door. Sometimes he would join Jason for a smoke, but other times he would say he'd quit.

This was the way things usually went, and if it wasn't for the small Ford Taurus that was parked in Jason's smoking spot, today would have been no different. He was just about over the last stretch of hill when he spotted it. The car was at an angle, and he could see that the window on the driver's side was rolled all the way down. Jason used the last of his espresso to pedal faster, hunching over the handlebars until he came up alongside it. The driver was sat with his feet on the dash and a pair of thick, black sunglasses hanging from his collar.

'Ahem,' Jason cleared his throat.

The driver relit a half-smoked cigarette. 'Good morning,' he said, cool as a cucumber.

'Can I help you?'

'Possibly. Do you own this joint?'

Jason had been in water treatment for around two years now, getting his hands dirty in the filter cleaning department. His job sometimes entailed treating microbes and marking water quality levels, but eventually, he wanted to make it at the top. The same top Matthew Torres smiled down at him from. Mr Torres had been in water treatment for thirty-two years, and he'd worked his way up from his jiffies. Now he wore a three-piece Mugler into work, and every day, Jason would feel like marking him: CLEAN / N.A.D.S.O.H. for "Not A Damn Spot on Him".

'Me?' he replied. 'Own this place? Naw.'

The stranger took a quick scan of the stains on Jason's jumpsuit. 'Guess I should have figured that,' he replied. Then he opened the door, stepped outside, and stretched his back. He was shorter than Jason had imagined, with a phoney looking moustache and thin, wiry hair which looked like wilted bristles of a horse brush. 'I'm looking for the manager. Matthew Torres, I think his name is?'

'That's him,' Jason replied. 'But he don't get here till midday. Sometimes not even that.'

The stranger sucked on his bottom lip. 'That's irritating.'

'Can I ask who you are?'

'Officer Wayne Brown. I've been sent to investigate the issues folks have been having with their pipes.' Wayne flashed his badge and Jason stood up a little bit straighter.

'Issues, sir?'

The officer frowned. 'Thought you would've heard…'

Jason shuffled uncomfortably. He nodded, like he might have heard, only he definitely hadn't. Jason didn't hear much about anything at the plant. Not that there was much to talk about. The plant wasn't a hotpot of theatre or scandal. But still, he had spent most of his life feeling out of the loop. He was dyslexic, he was pretty sure, and he never liked feeling that he knew less than other people, even if it was something as dull as a rumour. When he was seven, his mother made him take up the piano, hoping in vain that some creativity might spark up the part of his brain that clearly wasn't working. He never made the first grade. He never even learned to read the music, much to his mother's annoyance. She used to squish the sheet music into his face and scream,

'CAN YOU READ IT NOW, BOY?! IS THAT ANY EASIER?!'

It never became any easier and Jason always hated that. He felt stupid then and he felt stupid now, especially with his jumpsuit on, which seemed to radiate his stupidity like a portrait. Everything about him was there inside brush strokes, so, in a way, he felt relieved that Officer Wayne Brown had seen them and still assumed he'd heard something important. He wasn't about to rob himself of that. If there was something that he should have heard, then he had heard it. He just needed to find out what *it* was.

'Pipes,' he muttered. 'Well, uh, when did you find out?'

'Yesterday afternoon. Got a couple of calls come in, but we left them on hold because a kid had died.'

Jason faltered. Then he nodded again. 'Oh yeah, I heard about that.'

Wayne stared at him. 'You shouldn't have done. It's being kept on the down low.'

'Oh, yeah.' Jason stumbled over his words. 'No, maybe I hadn't heard. Maybe that was something else. Yeah, a dog or something.' He slipped his cigarette packet out of his jacket and lit one up to calm his nerves.

Officer Wayne didn't pay him any mind, however. He sniffed, then blowed, and his moustache bristled slightly in the breeze. He spat onto the tarmac. 'Nothing to worry about. Kid was gay. Cuckoo Cove. Probably suicide, y'know. Still, there's a lot of excitement around the office. Always is when we get close to a murder case, but the calls kind of got overlooked yesterday. When the fourth came in, we figured we should draw straws and I came out short. Now I'm the sucker looking into some sludgy taps when we've got a goddamn real body in our fridge.'

'That's a kick in the teeth.'

'Ain't it?' The officer flicked out his cigarette and crushed it beneath his loafers. He immediately pulled out another one before shrugging toward the building. 'You able to open this joint up?'

'Oh, naw, not me. That's Paolo, the deputy manager. Should be here in around ten.'

'If it's alright, I'll wait with you. Gotta take a look around, at least. Show those folks that we're doing something. Guess we wouldn't like it if we found shit in our water glasses, right?'

Jason suddenly felt himself sweating. Water treatment was a big part of his job and if something had slipped through the cracks, there was a strong likelihood that he would get part of the blame. He shuffled again and asked the officer nervously,

'Did they say what it was?'

Wayne shrugged. 'Black stuff, mostly. Hair, I think one woman said. To think I swapped shifts yesterday. If I hadn't, I would've been the one getting the call on that body.' He grinned and gritted his teeth so hard, it looked like he might chop his cigarette in half. 'With that under my belt, I coulda been a big town cop by Christmas. Ain't that shit luck?'

Jason swallowed and felt his heart begin to beat faster. After a few minutes, he heard the sound of Paolo's Corolla in the quiet, morning breeze. He waited for him to pull into his parking spot, and then he offered Paolo a cigarette and the three of them smoked together. He didn't say another word to Officer Wayne Brown until Paolo clicked a button on the keys and the big door began to roll open.

3

Justin Hadero's office was full of clutter that he had plastered to the walls. From Marfa, Texas:

OFFICER SAVES BOY, 14, AFTER GORGE JUMPING INCIDENT

From Galveston, Texas:

POLICE DEPARTMENT PREPARED FOR HURRICANE DARBY FALLOUT, SAYS CHIEF HADERO

From Cuckoo Cove, California:

VIETNAM VET BECOMES LOCAL POLICE CHIEF

Newspaper clippings were pinned to cork boards like medals, and alongside them, Hadero had mounted photographs of his wife, himself, himself and his wife, and his son. On his desk was a framed picture of an ultrasound. Beside it was a computer, a radio, a coffee mug, a phone, and a cup of pens with the caps missing. The cup was fashioned to look like a gun holster. There was a single, light yellow document just in front of the chair, but Justin Hadero wasn't looking at it. He was fumbling around in his briefcase, a droplet of sweat running into his stubble, and he didn't stop until he retrieved a polaroid. It was a picture of himself, a bundle of blankets in his arms and a baby's face poking out of them.

'Seven pounds, three ounces. Born three o'clock yesterday afternoon. Sarah Paula Hadero. Boy, did I have a long day.' Justin put the picture down on the table and stared at it happily.

'How's your wife, sir?' asked Gaten.

'Tanita?' replied Justin, as if contemplating how she came into the picture. 'Yeah, she's fine. Kind of sick, but I guess that's natural. Take a seat.' He pointed at the chair and Gaten sat down. 'I wanted to say thank you for the work you did yesterday. Something like that is never easy. It's your first body, I'm guessing?'

'Yes, sir.'

'First is always the hardest,' said Justin, as if he was a seasoned city commissioner who'd just wrapped up his fiftieth homicide.

Gaten knew a lot of assholes in Cuckoo Cove's police department, but every day, he found something else to dislike about Justin Hadero. His bleached blonde hair, his arrogant grin, his wall. Everything seemed to mount on top of the other until Gaten felt an almost magnetic draw leading his fist to Justin's face. Today, it was that inflexion on his voice. Gaten knew he hadn't seen death in the way that he projected. He hadn't even been drafted until the last two months of the war.

'What's the prognosis?' he asked, trying to keep his fists relaxed.

'As good as I'd hoped for.' Justin grabbed the document in front of him and handed it to Gaten.

BOARD OF MEDI INVESTIGATIONS:
OFFICE OF THE CHIEF MEDICAL EXAMINER

Gaten scratched at his forehead and frowned. 'That was quick,' he said.

Justin shrugged. 'If the mayor wants something done quick, it's done quick. I wouldn't be surprised if the coroner just scratched the name off his last report.'

He laughed and Gaten kept reading.

DECADENT: FIRST – MIDDLE – LAST NAMES
(please avoid use of initials)
ADRIAN MANE RAMIREZ
AGE: 19
BIRTH DATE: 03/10/1984
RACE: WHITE
SEX: M

Gaten frowned again, peering down toward the bottom of the page.

EXAMINER NOTIFIED BY: NAME – TITLE
(agency, institution or address)
JUSTIN HADERO – POLICE CHIEF
DATE: 10/10/2003
TIME: 14:30
LOCATION OF DEATH: RESERVOIR, CUCKOO COVE
TOWN: CUCKOO COVE
STATE: CALIFORNIA

TYPE OF PREMISES: RESERVOIR
DATE: 10/08/2003
TIME: UNKNOWN

Gaten lingered on the date. He hadn't realised the body had been two days old when he found it, but he guess that went some way to explain the smell. He looked toward the part of the report he really wanted to know.

DESCRIPTION OF BODY: COMPLETE

JAW, TICK. NECK, TICK. ARMS, TICK. LEGS, TICK. COMPLETE, TICK

LIVER COLOUR: PINK-PURPLE, POSTERIOR

BEARD: NONE

EYE COLOUR: BROWN

HAIR: BALD, SHAVED

PUPILS: R 4MM L 4MM

BODY LENGTH: 70 IN

BODY WEIGHT: 190.5 IBS

PROBABLE CAUSE OF DEATH: DROWNING

OTHER SIGNIFICANT CONDITIONS CONTRIBUTING TO DEATH (but not resulting in underlying cause): MARIJUANA, COCAINE/ECSTASY FOUND IN SYSTEM

MANNER OF DEATH: ACCIDENT

CASE DISPOSITION

INQUEST: NO

SIGNED BY MEDICAL EXAMINER'S OFFICE: ANDY STATHUM

While Gaten read, Justin took out a sterling silver zip-light from his chest pocket and removed a pack of brown cigarettes from the drawer in front of his stomach. He sparked one up and reclined back, staring at the polaroid.

'Seven pounds, three ounces. That's normally the average weight of a baby boy, ain't that terrific? I swear most of it's gone into her lungs. You should have heard her. Thought she was gonna bring the ceiling down at one point. I'm gonna be wearing earmuffs this winter, and not because of the cold.'

Gaten remained silent.

'Gaten, you hear me? I said I'm gonna be wearing earmuffs.'

'That sounds like a good idea, sir,' mumbled Gaten.

Justin smiled knowingly. 'You have questions, huh?'

Gaten fidgeted. He knew that he had questions, but he wasn't sure he wanted to ask them. The body of that boy had been floating in his subconsciousness all night, and in his dreams, it had only gotten bigger. It bloated out of the reservoir and into the town, like it was on a night out. Gaten drank in a bar and he saw it in the corner. He went to bed and it hovered over his sheets. It followed him like he had it on a leash, and no matter how hard he tried, he couldn't undo the collar. At one point, he was sure its face morphed and it took on the image of his brother. It found its wig behind the bowl of the toilet and it placed it on its head, still damp. It said, 'found it honey'. And Gaten woke up sweating. Every part of him wanted to forget about that body, but the questions remained like thorns in his side. He shifted in his chair and relented to just asking one:

'Drowning. Does it mean the reservoir?'

Justin smirked. 'That was where the body was found, Gate. Doesn't take a genius to work that out.'

'What was he doing up there?'

'Probably high off all those party drugs. You know what the queer folk are like in this town. Take a hit. Go loopy. Perhaps he thought he was at the beach.'

'But the reservoir is a trek, I doubt he got there by accident, don't you?'

Justin shook his head dismissively. 'You ever been on these kinds of drugs, Gate? He probably thought he was on Rainbow Road, trying to reach the starlight finish line, you can't expect to make any sense out of this kind of thing.'

Gaten swallowed. That was one thorn out. Another, much deeper one remained, and he couldn't quite help it from leaving his lips. 'What about the wig?'

'What about the wig?' Justin repeated.

'It wasn't there.'

'Probably got lost in the current.'

'It's a reservoir, there is no current.'

'Perhaps he left it at home.'

'I don't think so, sir. His head was stained black and bald. These guys care about their appearance. Likelihood was he lived in that wig.'

Justin shrugged. 'How should I know? It's not like it's important. It's a wig.'

'You told me to find it.'

The chief's face flushed a little. He squirmed slightly in his chair. 'I guess I thought it might be important. But it's not. The kid killed himself, Gate. Maybe he threw it away, I don't know. The point is, all the signs say he walked into that reservoir and drowned. There's nothing in the report that tells us any different.'

Gaten sat back and sighed. He glanced at the corner of the room and imagined the body floating there. Still tethered, still watching him. He tried to blink it away.

Justin took back the report and straightened it out on his desk. 'He lived alone. 32 Jefferson Street. No close relatives, only an aunt and uncle who didn't want to identify. I think we can close the book on this one.'

Just then, the phone on Justin's desk rang and he picked it up. It was his wife, Tanita. Gaten sat in silence for a while. He remembered checking in on his brother that morning. He had been nestled like a foetus, lying like he used to do back when they were kids. At least once a week, Theo used to wake up from a bad nightmare, creep into Gaten's room, and lie at the foot of his mattress like a dog seeking comfort. Nearly twenty years later, he still felt that responsibility. No matter how old and no matter how distant, he still felt like he should protect his brother from the nightmares. Only they had become far more real as they had gotten older.

'Any more questions, son?'

Gaten jolted as Justin slammed his finger on hold. He shook his head. 'No, sir.'

'Good. Listen, I admire your tenacity. It's a good thing. But don't give yourself a headache over this one. The kid died. You did good. Let's leave it at that.'

Justin's finger retracted from the hold button and Gaten nodded. He hated it, but for once in his life, he agreed with his boss. Leaving it at that would do well for his mental health. Why pull at the threads of a wig only to weave a nightmare he couldn't fight? His brother would be fine if he kept this one in dreams, and perhaps that was the most admirable thing to do. He stood up from his chair and took a long, deep breath. Yes, he thought. Leave it at that. Leave the kid in the reservoir and his death as the coroner had decided: drowning. Nice and simple. Water was not so great an adversary. And Gaten had already taught his brother how to swim. He asked silently for his leave, and Justin flicked him in the direction of the door.

4

It was midday by the time Sara woke up. She was lying across the bottom of the bed, her left arm splayed above her forehead and her cheek damp with warm saliva. She hadn't taken the time to remove her makeup last night, so half of her face was imprinted upon the mattress. She looked at it and yawned. The ache behind her eyes was gone, and despite not feeling too fresh on the outside, there was a spark inside her that felt light as air. She swung her legs over the bed and walked to the window. She was naked and semi-erect, so she squeezed the blinds to hide her bottom half and stared out onto the town below her. The street was rife with men, women and kids who were making their way down to the beach. Some of them had deck chairs under their arms, others had satchels of food, pizza boxes and bags. On the corner near Mama's Motel, a silver-painted man stood stone-still. When a couple of teenagers passed, he yanked a cord and a plastic cuckoo sprung from the top of his hat. He shouted, 'CUCKOO!', and they screamed and then ran along.

On the other side of the street, some more teenagers sat on Wellington's Well, which was one of the earliest structures of the town still in existence. It once supplied water, but when a third of Cuckoo Cove's population got infected in

1910, it was closed off and abandoned. Now it was used as a popular spot for young folk to smoke out in the open. No one wanted to reach inside it, as it was said that all of the souls that perished from the infection had returned to curse anyone who drank the water. This gave the less superstitious youngsters an easy way to avert justice. If a cop came too close, all they had to do was chuck their spliffs into the bucket and lower it down until it was unreachable. With the superstition ever present in this town, there was no way any law-enforcement officer was going to be dragging that bucket back up, especially if it might drag up an age old curse along with it. Marijuana wasn't worth it, and the kids would only find some other place to smoke besides.

They sat on the well and revelled in their ingenuity, and Sara revelled in it too. Today was a good day to say 'fuck you' to the rules. The sky was blue, the town was buzzing, and Sara felt as refreshed as a slut on heat. The day before had become a blur already, and it didn't hurt her because it didn't matter. That was the good thing about being who she was. The nights could growl and bite, but in the morning, any wound could easily be removed with the swish of a makeup wipe. Sometimes it was as easy as that: washing away the pain and building back even stronger than before. With a little kick of her heel, she walked out of her bedroom, into the shower, then stood in front of the mirror and began making Sara Del Bret as beautiful and strong as ever.

5

She arrived at the Precious Star Bar at two o'clock in the afternoon, which was six hours earlier than her scheduled shift. She felt bad for dipping out early the night before, and had wanted to make it up to Luna by helping with the setup. But when she walked into the bar, she was surprised to find that Luna wasn't even there yet. Instead, she was met by her husband, Carl Vasquez, who was hanging out of the back of the *ELECTRIC SLUT!* chair, fiddling desperately with the wires.

'Goddamn things,' he grumbled.

He was bent so low that his butt was poking triumphantly from his sagging, blue pants. Sara slid her heel into the crack.

'Peekaboo.'

'GODDAMN!' Carl cried and swivelled around, slamming his head agains the arm of the chair in the process. 'Sara, don't scare me like that, you know I'm getting old.'

'I'm sorry, honey, you asked for it. I see an ass, I gotta slip something in.'

Carl rubbed at his head and frowned. 'Slip in a quarter next time, this place is falling apart, and me.'

'I like your wax job, though, was that Luna?'

Carl sat onto his haunches and dragged his hands over his face. 'You know it.'

Sara noticed the liver spots and the arthritis bends in his fingers. He was only sixty, but he managed to look older everyday, especially when he wasn't in drag. He shone and sparkled as Sally Vasquez, but in his grey hoodie and long pants, Carl was just a withered old man grumbling about poor business management.

'I told Luna to sort these wires out weeks ago.'

'What's wrong with them?' asked Sara.

'They're not supposed to blink.'

Sara hummed and trotted over toward the bar. The surface was still lined with liquid circles and sticky blotches of beer. She hovered for a moment, then grabbed one of the glasses and flung the contents into the sink.

'Luna didn't fancy tidying up last night, huh?'

'She's getting lazy,' said Carl, who was back behind the chair.

Sara grabbed a cloth that was hanging from one of the pumps. 'Looks like she started,' she said as she began wiping down the bar.

'Ah, Luna always starts stuff. It's the finishing that she has trouble with.'

Sara grimaced slightly. 'I'm sure she does.'

'What're you doing here so soon anyhow?'

'I ducked out early last night. Bad head. Thought Luna could use some help.'

'I certainly could.'

At that moment, something snapped behind the *ELECTRIC SLUT!* and the lights stayed on a steady red glow.

'Abracadabra,' said Sara.

The hum of the bulbs grew louder and Carl stood up to admire his work. He clapped his hands together. 'That's one down, but we have a lot more to do before tonight. I wanna elevate the stage a little. I don't know about you, but I'm sick to the teeth of being eye level with people when I perform. We should be standing over them like queens playing to a bunch of ants. We should mesmerise them.'

'You mesmerise me, honey.'

'For the wrong reasons.'

Carl walked to the stage and sat down, wiping the sweat from his forehead once again. In the five minutes since Sara had entered the bar, those hands had gotten even older, the face more withered. Carl Vasquez was on a clock that ticked ten times faster than others, and it only paused when he slipped on his wig and strapped lacing around his chest. It was like that for a lot of them, Sara thought. Putting on a true self could stop you in time, like you had become almost ethereal. Sara had that too. Being a woman robbed her of any age. She wasn't young and she wasn't old. She was just herself. Constant and unmoving. Carl Vasquez had never quite allowed himself to take that feeling off stage. He was of the older generation, so he had been taught not to have too much of a good thing. If he was going to die, then he'd better die in the clothes he was born with. Time came full circle in the end. Anything else was a luxury.

Sara began polishing the pumps. 'You feeling okay, Carl?'

'I didn't sleep so good. Sciatica got my hips doing funny dances. I tried to read it off, but my eyes ain't great. Usually Luna reads to me.'

'She didn't read to you last night?'

'No, she didn't come back last night.'

Sara stopped polishing for a second. 'Oh?'

'She thinks I don't know what she's doing, but I know. I don't blame her for it. I'm an old man, I hardly have the stuff I used to. With these hips, I figure sex is like being on a malfunctioning carousel horse.'

Sara grimaced again. She tried to get the image out of her head by focusing her attention on the kegs in the cupboard.

Carl spoke again from behind her, 'You don't know who she went back with, do you?'

'Not sure,' said Sara. 'Like I said, I ducked out early.'

That much was partly true. Sara did know that Luna had been interested in the boys from the bachelor party, but she had assumed that ship had sailed once they had shown their true colours. Perhaps they had come back and apologised. She doubted it. But who else would Luna go home with? Alan Salcedo had made an appearance later in the evening, but she wasn't that desperate. Then again, thinking of that carousel ride, maybe she was. Sara shook one of the kegs and pulled out the coupler.

'We got any more Red Stripe downstairs?' she asked, trying to change the subject.

Carl stood up. 'Sure. You can change it up if you want, I'll get started on the stage.'

'I think I better help you with that. You don't wanna strain yourself.'

Carl gave her a look that could split open the heavens. 'Watch your tongue, girl. I might be sixty, but I'm not entirely incompetent.'

At that exact moment, a plume of smoke flew up from behind the *ELECTRIC SLUT!* and the lights began blinking again. In the darkness of the bar, they looked like red eyes scouring the place. Sara thought about Luna.

6

Out here in the quietness, something thinks to itself. Not in the way most things think. This is something different. Something thinks to itself and its thoughts converge into colours and light. Things that it can sense now flash behind its eyes and it listens to them.

Something has no sight. Nothing to cling onto and form a basis for its reality. Something only knows one thing. Here. Now. How it feels. How it wants to feel. Colours swerve like birds and it grabs one of them. Its belly rumbles. An explosion of emotions. Fading. Space for more. It agrees to itself: more. Then, in its head, it disappears and goes looking for it.

7

When Gaten's watch reached five o'clock, it gave him a little buzz on the wrist. The battery had grown faulty now and the buzz felt like more of a zap which told him: *hey asshole, the day's done, lets get some alcohol into these veins, huh?*

Gaten itched behind his scalp and listened to it. He slid his paperwork for the day – a kid's safeguarding form and a domestic log – into his bag and slurped the rest of his coffee. He had been placed on administration for the day as Julia Wilson was on leave to visit her mother in Florida, but that was okay, because the paperwork took his mind off other things. For now, he was thinking about Jimmy Hartford and his mother, who had become addicted to painkillers. He was thinking about the fight that Gail Santorez had with Liam Jones last night at nine o'clock. The body had more or less disappeared. It floated high above him like a kite hiding in the clouds, and he was looking forward to getting home, pouring a glass of rum, and snipping the string completely.

Gaten swung his bag over his shoulder and said goodbye to his colleagues. Before he could leave, however, the phone on his desk started ringing. When he picked it up, he could tell who it was immediately.

'Hey Gaten,' said the man on the other end.

'Wayne. I'm out of office. What do you want?'

Wayne had only joined the force a year ago, and he had been Gaten's partner ever since. He was a decent guy but a bad cop, so Gaten had promptly asked for someone new. Sadly, the only other option was Gunther, who was only better for the occasional Mad Magazine jokes he would crack on the way to crime scenes. So Gaten had to make do.

'I'm at the water plant,' said Wayne, as if that answered his question.

'Oh yeah, the tap thing. How's that working out for you?'

'Thought about handing my notice in this morning. I figured you all had me down for a meathead. Dodgy plumbing, my ass.'

'Guess you didn't find anything then?'

'Hey, if this meathead is asked to do a job, he does a job.'

'So you did find something,' said Gaten, getting a little impatient.

'Well, not me. I wasn't searching that whole plant by myself, screw that. I gave them my page number and told them to contact me if anything came up. Turns out something did.'

'Fascinating. You're really into the big stuff now, Wayne.'

'Hell yeah, I am. This is something big. It could even help the case.'

'What case?'

'The kid's case. You know, the gay kid.'

Gaten felt his body stiffen a little bit. 'What are you talking about?'

There was silence on the other end, as if Wayne was purposefully drawing this out to make Gaten tense.

'You were looking for a black wig weren't you?' he said after a few seconds. 'Well, we found it. Here in the water plant. That's what's been clogging people's taps.'

Gaten felt his heart sink and the body sink too. Down from the clouds, back into his world. The sagging, blue-grey face and the bald, stained head. It hovered beside him and said,

You didn't think you could get rid of me that easy, did you?

'So what do you think?' asked Wayne after a few seconds. 'You wanna come out here?'

Gaten hesitated. He put down the phone and felt as if his hand had been submerged in the cold reservoir. Like a nightmare following the trail of a dream back into the bedroom, when he reached it back, he was wet and trembling with sweat.

CHAPTER FIVE

LAST NIGHT

1

Are you good enough?

The voice in Luna's head was hers but not hers. It was pale and kind of blue-ish, if thoughts could be colours. It spoke to her behind aching eyes.

Are you good?

At one point, it became so loud that she had to stop walking. She was around half a mile from Adamson Avenue, just alongside Corker's Park. There was a steel fence to her left and an empty road to her right. Luna walked this way every night, and despite the park often housing a drunk or two, she never had any problems. Tonight, however, she didn't feel safe. Not because of the drunks – although there were a few of them – but because of her head.

The question came three times in twenty seconds: *Are you good enough?*

And Luna thought back, *Yes, I am good enough.*

She kept walking, but she felt a little dizzy, so she walked slower than usual. For a minute or two, she thought she might have won, but then, like an eagle swooping down from up high, the voice converged again.

Are you good enough?

It was so real that, for a moment, she swore she could see it in the night sky. The clouds were gone tonight and the stars were potent, but she was sure a few of them were blocked out by its silhouette. Its shadowy silhouette, soaring high above her and circling, talons uncurled and ready to sink.

Are you good enough? Are you? Are you? Are you?

Yes, Luna replied again. *Yes, I am good enough, and I have always been good enough.*

She picked up her pace and felt her breaths echoing inside her chest. For some reason, she remembered her father and her mother, and she remembered sitting on their bed with a tray of tea and cookies. She did this every morning between the age of six and sixteen. She remembered telling them her secret on the ninth of September, 1987, and she remembered her dad getting so mad that the tray fell off the mattress. She remembered how he made her sign up for football practice the next day. She remembered him watching the games and calling her a sissy afterwards. She remembered how he pinched her behind the ear when she quit. She remembered when he gave up hope that this was just a phase. She remembered how he hated her new name. She remembered him saying: '*I appreciate you wanna have a new name but I ain't gonna change the name I gave you.*' She remembered him dying of a heart attack while fixing the gutter above the shed. She remembered not bringing him a cup of tea and cookies ever again because he looked at her hands different.

The memories came all at once, and the voice inside of her lapped them up.

You are good, it said. *You are good, but are you good enough?*

Luna skidded to a halt on the path, and she clung to the fence. She heaved through the gap and vomited into the grass. There was a tent around ten yards ahead of her, and a drunk howled from inside of it.

'Do it in a bowl, pixie boy!'

The voice came back, *I do not think you are good enough and I do not think that you ever will be.*

Luna vomited again, and for a moment, the bars of the fence felt like snakes in her hands. They coiled around her and turned wet and gluey. She wondered whether she had been spiked as she felt her world begin to close in around her. Suddenly, everything was in a bubble. The tent in the park began rustling.

'Didn't you hear me, pixie boy? I said do it in a bowl!'

It rustled and rustled and then the zip opened. The street lamps above her fizzled and glowed, getting brighter and brighter until the entire world was lit up under a big moon. The drunk man stepped out of the tent, and Luna realised he was not a drunk man at all. He was her father. Lean and tall, with wrinkles forming the shape of a 'V' on his forehead, and a patch of grey stubble circling his chin. He pointed at her and screamed,

'ARTHUR JAMES CONRAD, IF I GOTTA TELL YOU ONE MORE TIME, I SWEAR I'LL PICK UP THAT PUKE AND THROW IT IN YOUR FACE! THAT'LL BE A PRETTY PICTURE!'

'No!' Luna cried back. 'No, Daddy! Leave me alone!'
'ARTHUR JAMES —'

She closed her eyes and covered her ears. 'That's not my name! That's not my name! Don't call me that! It's not my name!'

At that moment, Luna could feel the shadow of lights begin to dim again and the rush of blood inside her head started to slow. She waited for a minute or two. When she opened her eyes, the world around her was normal. The fence was cold and still, and the tent was zipped. Her father had disappeared. She wavered, then she lowered her arms, spat out some more vomit and swallowed back the leftovers. She looked around and took a few deep breaths. The sickness peeled away. She attempted to gather herself and reclaim her strength.

Okay, she thought. *I'm okay, I'm good.* She stood up straight and grasped her bearings. Then she looked up into the sky and saw the source of the voice blocking out the stars again.

Yes, it said. *Yes, Luna. You are good. But you're not good enough.*

It swooped down and Luna felt the bubble close tight and something like talons breach the skin of her scalp.

CHAPTER SIX

THE RUNNER

1

The office was tight and dirty. A collection of sandwich packets and empty McDonald's cups cluttered the corner, with stains of strawberry milkshake making the worktops sticky. The computers were grey and dusty and, by the click of the keys, it sounded as if they hadn't been used in a long time. The deputy manager, Paolo Garcia, was sitting on a torn, foamy chair and typing the password into the computer closest to Gaten. He was a sad looking man. The kind of man whose childhood dreams still lingered in his eyes, glowing behind thin spectacles. He coughed into his fist and scratched his butt, which was hanging off the chair on both sides. Gaten leant against a tall, metal cabinet and scrunched his nose at the smell of sweat and chlorine.

'I don't understand how a wig could get through the system,' he said. 'I thought you're supposed to be a filtration plant. Don't you kill bacteria?'

'Filtration and supply,' the scrawny, pimply man spoke up in the corner. His name was Jason Hancock, and he was standing awkwardly with his hands gripped above his crotch, like he was praying. 'Nothing gets through our filtration system, I make sure of that. But things can get into the supply.' He cleared his throat. 'If things try hard enough,' he added.

'How do you mean, try hard enough?'

'I'll show you,' said Paolo.

He clicked a button, and the surveillance footage from two days ago lit up the small, dusty screen. It showed a row of tanks, all of which stood about twenty feet into the air, illuminated dimly by an unseen fog light. The image was dark and grainy, almost like a still picture, except for the rustling trees around fifty yards in the distance. Gaten leaned close to the screen and flicked a glance to Wayne, who was standing in the middle of the carpet, sipping at a steaming coffee cup. Paolo skipped forward on the tape. Ten seconds, fifteen seconds, thirty seconds, sixty. He sniffed and coughed again, then he pulled his pudgy finger from the mouse and pointed toward the figure entering the frame. It was their boy, Adrian Ramirez. He was dressed in dark pants, sneakers, a silky jumper, and he was wearing a long, black wig. He ran jaggedly, like he was teleporting every two steps.

'We couldn't tell who she's running from,' said Paolo. 'But it looks like it's something.'

'He,' Gaten corrected him. 'Who he's running from.'

Paolo frowned at him, then he shuffled on his chair and performed a catholic cross on his chest. Jason swallowed audibly, like the hair of a gay man turning up in people's water made the whole thing even worse. Gaten continued watching the tape. The boy was still running but there was no one behind him. At several points, he turned to look over his shoulder, as if expecting to see something there.

Wayne, who had clearly seen the tape already, sipped at his coffee. 'It's drugs I reckon,' he said confidently.

'That's what the chief said,' replied Gaten.

At that moment, the tape jolted and went dark for a second. When it came back, Adrian had stopped running and was staring straight ahead. He took a few steps back, retreating. Then he moved to the right so fast that Gaten thought the tape had skipped forward a few seconds. The boy clung onto one of the water tanks and started climbing.

'He gonna get in there?' asked Gaten.

Paolo shook his head. 'He doesn't get in. Couldn't. Those hatches are one hundred pounds, ain't no way a skinny boy like that would be able to.'

In the tape, Adrian reached the top of the water tank. Then a few seconds passed and he was making his way down again. The wig was gone.

'Rewind and pull closer on that,' said Gaten.

Paolo obliged. He rewound the tape ten seconds and clicked on the little magnifying glass in the bottom right corner.

'Is there a way you can slow it down?'

'Naw, it just plays straight.'

Gaten pushed a little on Paolo's chair to get a better vantage point. He watched the tape closely. Zooming in had been like pouring ten bags of sand into the screen, but he could still see the boy. For a moment, it looked like he might be hiding. He crouched on top of the water tank, cowering near the edge before pulling on the hatch to try to lift it. It didn't work. He dropped it after a couple of seconds. Then, quickly, he tore off his wig, threw it on the ground, and tried again. He lifted the hatch a few inches and kicked the wig into the gap, letting the hatch drop before returning down the ladder again. The four of them then watched while the boy ran out of the frame. There was silence in the room for a second. Gaten heard the heavy churn of the machines above them. They whirred and bubbled, like they were inside an aquarium.

'Don't people around here keep those doors locked?' asked Wayne.

'Not usually,' said Paolo. 'Like I said, they're heavy.'

'Can anyone get into that part of the plant?'

Paolo shook his head. 'They have to climb over a fence.'

The skinnier man leant forward. 'With signs.'

'The guy's running for his life,' said Gaten. 'I don't think he had time to check the trespassing charge. No, he was hiding the wig.'

'Funny place to hide it,' said Wayne.

Gaten agreed. 'The whole thing is funny.'

'Well, I think it sounds like the chief got it right. This looks like a psychotic episode to me. I should know, my cousin's schizophrenic. She has to take meds. Did they find anything in him?'

'Just party drugs,' replied Gaten.

'Well, there we go.'

Gaten wavered for a moment. He was thinking about the moment halfway through the tape, when things went black, and Adrian stopped running. He had been looking behind his shoulder up until that point. But then he had stopped, looked up, stared directly in front of him, and ran to the right. Something there had made him change direction.

'I don't think that's the whole story,' Gaten said.

'What else could explain it?'

'Perhaps he was running from more than one person. Maybe there was a group of them.'

'Still doesn't explain why he threw his wig in the water tank. Like Paolo said, that takes effort.'

Paolo nodded. 'It does take effort, sir. We ain't ever had a problem with it before.

'Besides,' Wayne continued, 'there's no one else on the tape, you saw it.'

'I don't know what I saw.'

Gaten shot back at him sharper than he had meant to, and Wayne cowered a little. He wavered on his feet, then went back to sipping his coffee. On any other day, Gaten might have felt bad, but as he had already noted, Wayne was a good guy but a bad cop. No good cop could look at that footage and call it an open-and-shut case. He would have to go to Chief Hadero with this. The case would have to be reopened. Or *opened*, as it were.

He presented his hand to Paolo. 'Thanks for your time, sir. Just some advice for the future: lock those hatches.'

Paolo shook his hand, and then Gaten began the normal procedure. Him and Wayne took the two workers information, asked them to print a copy of the tape, and then set their sights on the office and Justin Hadero's desk.

2

'Jesus, how does she normally run this thing?'

It was nine o'clock and Sally Vasquez was showing his crack again. Despite being in drag, his yellow flared pants still sagged halfway down his buttocks.

'It's for effect,' Sara called over from the corner of the bar, where she was sitting with a young man named Tony.

'Is the effect a Nazi gas chamber? Because it's working!'

Sally coughed as the smoke machine blew a few more clouds into his face. He stood on the stage and wiped his eyes, smudging his makeup that had already been lathered on with very little care. He'd spent most of the day fixing up the bar, which meant he'd only had ten minutes to get ready for his set. In many ways, it looked like he'd just been executed by the *ELECTRIC SLUT!* chair.

'Sorry, ladies and gentlemen,' he spluttered. 'Let's try this again.'

Sally broke back into his rendition of Jessica Rabbit's "Why Don't You Do Right?", but not before wiping the sweat from his armpits and choking on some more clouds from the smoke machine. Not quite the sexy, sultry number it was supposed to be, Sara thought.

'Is it always like this?' Tony spoke loudly over the music.

'Normally Luna keeps a tighter leash on things.' Sara turned back to him. 'But yeah, this is basically the gist.'

'Who's Luna?'

Sara sipped some vodka and lemonade from a red and blue straw. 'Married to the owner,' she replied.

'Where's she?'

'Well, if I know Luna – and I think I do – she's probably hanging out of her asshole in some stranger's bed, waiting for him to make her a mac-and-cheese sandwich.'

Tony laughed and Sara laughed too. In all truth, she had been a little concerned about Luna's absence, but her fears were eased when she remembered the summer of 2001, when Luna had got so drunk that she flew all the way to

San Fransisco just to get into a customer's bed. In her drunken haze, she'd assumed his advances were sexual, but actually, he had been a middle-aged Satanist who wanted her to speak at their weekly cult meeting. Despite her appearance, Luna was a devout Buddhist who practiced meditation. She wasn't invited back, and she lost $200 dollars without even so much as a blowjob to her name, but according to her, the whole experience was culturally enriching. Apparently she did the talk. Sara smiled thinking about it.

'She's allowed a day off. She works hard, that girl.'

'And you?'

'The hardest, honey.'

Sara winked, and Tony smiled again. She liked this one. He was dressed well, just a thin moustache out of adolescence, and he was only stopping by on on his way to Oregon for a job interview. He had all the qualities she liked in a man. Young, gay, single, and brief. This would be one night only. No strings attached. She pursed her lips around her straw and tried to lure him in.

'Do you frequent many gay bars, Tony?'

Even in the misty haze of the Precious Star Bar, Tony appeared to blush. 'Not really. My parents are catholics, and so are most of my friends. I haven't told anyone.'

'Oh, so you're closeted?'

He sipped some of his cider. 'Right at the back, along with all the coats and mothballs.'

'Those are my favourite kind of boys, you know. The ones who haven't quite given over yet.'

'Given over to what?'

Sara finished her drink and wiped her mouth. 'Absolute pleasure.'

Tony smiled nervously. 'I wouldn't know what that's like.'

'No, you're used to midnight sleepovers with Salesian priests and intimacy with a wooden cane. You have no idea what it's like to actually feel something. Something different.'

Tony glanced at Sally, who was still sweating from his armpits. 'Looks like he's feeling something,' he said, evidently trying to change the subject.

Sara flicked her hair over one shoulder and looked toward the stage. 'Some people can't stand the heat.'

Tony turned his gaze back to her, and Sara saw the glint of the mirrorball in his eyes. The smoke made him look almost mysterious, but of course, he wasn't mysterious. He was simple, and sometimes that was all that was needed. She grazed her leg against his.

'What about you, Tony? Can you stand the heat? Or do you just sweat?'

Tony swallowed hard. Then, out of nowhere, he took her hand and led her outside.

3

It was raining. The music had stopped, and the night was dying, so it would have been relatively quiet if it weren't for Sally's fury at the smoke machine, and the loud smacking of Sara and Tony's lips pressing together. He was a good kisser, Sara thought. Almost too good for someone who claimed to be closeted. But Sara had gone without action for two weeks, so she let it slide. She pressed Tony up against the wall, and they made out for around thirty seconds before pulling away and simultaneously lighting up a cigarette.

'Cool party,' Tony said awkwardly, like a teenager only allowed out until ten.

'You think so?' Sara replied.

Tony nodded and took a drag. *He's cute*, Sara thought. The kind of person Luna would describe as a virgin bunny who hadn't hopped his first hop yet. In a way, she was glad her friend wasn't here to eat this one up. This one was all hers. She blew out some smoke and kissed him again, this time for around a minute.

'Where's your motel?' she asked after pulling away.

'You wanna call it a night already?'

'Not exactly. We can stay out if you want. I know a few places that are open.'

'What about this one?'

'I don't wanna stay at work,' said Sara. 'Especially tonight, unless choking to death is on your agenda. I don't think Sally's ever gonna get that thing working, and my hands weren't made for fixing machinery.'

'What were they made for?' Tony asked with a devilish grin.

Sara felt herself cringe a little. *Getting cheeky now, are we?*

'Microphones and mickeys, Tony. Microphones and mickeys.'

'What's a mickey?'

'I guess you're not Irish.'

Tony stared at her, confused. 'No, I'm American.'

Sara held back a laugh. *This one's definitely simple*, she thought. Then she took him by the hand and planted a kiss on his cheek.

'From the A to the N, honey. Now let's get out of here.'

With that, the both of them headed down the street to the nearest bar. It was Salvadors, a bar and diner. It wasn't gay, but it was friendly, and the barman knew Sara's brother, so she got a discount.

4

The ambush didn't take much planning. A few minutes in math class, then science, then around ten minutes in the hall between PE and social studies. Steven Harris led the meeting. He was fourteen years old, kind of bulky. A young whippersnapper, according to his gran. A kid who knew what he wanted from the world and paved his own path with a fat mouth and a sharp tongue. He didn't know if that was a good or bad thing, but he liked to think it was. He had razor focus, even as a fourteen year old, and he knew what he wanted. The world had always been very clear to him. He knew what was fair and what was unfair. He knew what was right and what was wrong. And he knew that Theo Dalbret, who was a scrawny kid in the seventh grade, was definitely the latter of both.

Theo had always been a weird kid. He only talked to Mr Gavington, the arts teacher, and it was always about musicals and Broadway. Steven had caught them talking about Elaine Paige on his way to the cafeteria one time, and he had seen Theo recite one of her lines with all the mannerisms of a sissy. He didn't like it, but he let it go, as he had fish to fry that were bigger than Theo Dalbret – less scrawny and with more meat on them. What had happened over the last two weeks, however, Steven had been unable to let slide.

It had begun on the morning of the fourth of September, after the summer vacation. Theo had turned up to math class with what looked like lipstick painted across his mouth. He shrugged it off as vaseline when prodded, but the following day, his skin had become smooth, with hardly any of the usual blemishes that had dotted his forehead and chin the semester before. It was obvious to all of them what was going on. Theo Dalbret, a boy in seventh grade, with an apple in his throat and walnuts down his trunks, was wearing makeup.

Of course, the teachers were having none of it. Most of the day, he got away with what looked like foundation and rouge, but the lipstick had to get scrubbed, and the mascara too, when he came in wearing that. But that didn't stop him from slapping it all back on when the clock hit three thirty. Like a hitter with a coke problem, nothing was going to stop Theo Dalbret from his fix, but Steven Harris knew that the show could not go on.

The meeting of the four boys had gone like this:

'We get him on the way home. St Martin's Street, near the gas station.'

'We get him and we get his brother.'

'Who's his brother?'

'Gaten. Ninth grade. But he's small. We can take him.'

'You sure about that, Derek? Didn't your sister beat you up one time? She gave you a black eye, right?'

'She didn't give me a black eye, she pushed me into a lamp post.'

'Didn't a lamp post beat you up one time? It gave you a black eye, right?'

'Screw you!'

'Guys, let's keep focus. The queer kid. Theo. What are we gonna do to him?'

'CUT HIM!'

'Yeah, cut him up real good. Maybe carve something into him. We'll use Derek's Swiss army knife.'

'Derek has a Swiss army knife?'

'Yeah, I ordered it from Sears. Although, it's not really what it said it would be. It's got, like, forks and spoons and stuff.'

'So you have a spork? Well, great, let's all go to Aunt Lucy's and tuck into a corn-beef casserole.'

'There's still a knife in it, asshole.'

'And it can cut stuff?'

'Hell yeah.'

'No, we shouldn't cut him. We shouldn't do anything that can get us in jail. Besides, he doesn't need it. He's queer. It won't take much to get him in line.'

'So what do we do?'

'We should make his brother lick the makeup off his face!'

'That's gross.'

'You have a sick mind, Lucas.'

'He's got a good point, though. It's the makeup that's the problem. If he wants to be gay, that's fine. Keep it in the bedroom and don't shove it in our face. That's the problem here. He's gay and he's not afraid to show it. We need to make him afraid. Not by cutting him. Just by showing him that we're onto him and we're not gonna allow it.'

'I still think we should do a little cutting.'

'Well, make it discreet. Not anywhere he can show off.'

'So we gonna do this?'

'St Martin's Street. Four o'clock.'

The four boys placed their hands together and did a football chant. Then they walked to American History.

5

Later that day, they congregated in a small alcove near the gas station. St Martin's Street had become pretty desolate since the mall had opened downtown, but that made it the perfect place for an ambush. Each one of the boys was silent. It was raining hard, but the deluge wasn't loud enough that it drowned out the thumping hearts in their chests. They kept close to the wall, huddled together like a pack of predators awaiting a victim. Steven led from the front, keeping a keen eye on the road ahead. The water was beginning to swerve down the sidewalk in a stream, converging near the gas station. He made a mental note to stop Theo there so they could drench him. *The fucker could swim in that*, he thought, and that thought immediately took him back four years. He was at Coral Beach Resort in Florida, and his dad was teaching him to swim in one of the pools. He got so mad at Steven's effort that he ended up throwing him head first into the deep end, and the on-duty lifeguards had to dive in to get him. His dad was given a $1,000 fine for child endangerment, and Steven remembered him saying,

'That's the last time I do something good for you, kid. You wanna be a sissy, that's your call. You wanna drown in this world, I ain't gonna break bones about it.'

His dad was a big-shot lawyer, so the fine wasn't bad, but all the same, Steven had been wanting to make things straight ever since. What was is it his dad had said at the dinner table two nights back?

'A queer coming into our town is like a rock trying to chip its way into a boulder. If we allow this, then a part of our American identity is eventually gonna give. Our great American identity. Someone has to show that boy a lesson.'

Steven was going to show him a lesson alright, and he was going to show his dad something too. That he wasn't a sissy. He wasn't going to drown. He was going to stand up for what he believed in, and he was going to make his dad proud while doing it. He wiped his nose with a sleeve and saw the water rippling by Bateman's Bistro. The brothers came into full view.

'That's them,' Steven hissed at his friends. 'I see them.'

The four other boys bustled excitedly, and Derek flicked a switch on his Swiss army knife to reveal a spoon. He pushed it back in hastily and pulled out the knife himself.

'Everyone ready?' asked Steven.

The other boys nodded in response, and Steven watched as the brothers moved closer. He tried to listen to their conversation over the pouring rain. It became clearer as they came close to the puddle.

'— that's what Felix said, and I think he's right. The grades are more important.'

'I don't care about stupid grades, Gate. I care about me.'

'Yeah, and I do too, which is why I'm trying to tell you to give it a rest for a bit.'

'Is that advice for me or is that advice for you?'

'It's for you, Theo. I'll always look out for you, but this is something I can't help.'

'I think you're embarrassed.'

'Well, so what if I am? It's not like it's normal.'

There was a silence. Lucas whispered something, but Steven hushed him down. Gaten spoke again,

'Maybe if you just wear it at home?'

'How would that make a difference?'

'Well, you won't be showing people. No one will know.'

'Who gives a shit if people know? This is the real me. People should like me this way.'

'But people don't.'

'People? Or you?'

'Stop doing that, Theo. I'm only trying to help.'

'So you keep saying. I don't think you're trying to help, I think you're —'

The brothers had come close to the gas station by this point, so Steven turned around to his crew and gave them the all clear. They stepped out together and blocked the path. Gaten stopped and grabbed Theo's shoulder. From the looks on their faces, they both knew what was about to happen.

'SHIT BRICKS, THEO!' shouted Gaten.

The pair of them went to run, but Billy, who had won first prize in the hundred metre sprint last sports day, was already hightailing it toward them. He tackled Theo down to the ground, and Theo let out a sharp cry. Derek grabbed Gaten, but he was a small boy, so he needed help. He got it from Lucas, who snatched the Swiss army knife from his friend's grasp and pushed it up against Gaten's throat.

'HOLD IT, FUCKER!' he yelled.

Steven stood between the brothers and took control. 'Listen, we don't want any trouble. But this is our town and we don't take kindly to faggots. Especially faggots who don't care that they're faggots.'

'My brother's not a faggot!' shouted Gaten.

'Like shit he ain't,' replied Billy. 'I got his mascara all over me.'

He was still on the ground with Theo, holding the boy in a headlock. Theo clutched desperately at his forearm, and Steven noticed that he had painted his nails scarlet.

'I get he's your brother, Gaten. It ain't your fault that he's queer, but we can't let him carry on like this. Like I said, we don't want any trouble. We just want him to get the message.'

Steven glared down at Theo, watching as he gasped for breath. He felt his heart beat harder and the adrenaline course through his veins. Despite the nerves, Steven found himself enjoying the moment. His gran had always said he would do something one day, and now he was doing it. He was protecting his town and taking matters into his own hands. If that didn't make his father proud, he didn't know what would. He knelt in front of Theo.

'If you're gonna be gay, you gotta do it quietly.'

'I'm not afraid of you,' hissed Theo.

'Not even with a knife at your brother's throat? You think some makeup is more important than your own brother? Jesus, you guys really aren't human.'

'You won't do anything...'

Gaten whimpered as Lucas pressed the knife harder against his skin. 'Don't you think that's kind of my call, Theo?'

'It ain't nobody's call but mine,' said Lucas giddily.

Steven edged closer. 'You're right, we don't wanna do anything. But that don't mean we won't. Thing is, Theo, by looking like that, you're making this town look bad. Do you get that? We're just asking you to take it off. That's all we want. Take it off and never put it on again. Then we'll let your brother go.'

A droplet of blood began trickling from Gaten's neck and he shouted, 'Listen to them, Theo!'

'Yeah,' said Lucas. 'Listen to us, Theo.'

The rain continued to pour, and Steven saw a glint of fear and desperation glistening in Theo's eyes. He nodded down toward the puddle of water that had congregated beside the gas station.

'Look, you've even got a washing bowl to do it in.'

Theo didn't react. Steven didn't like that, so he turned toward Lucas.

'Push it harder,' he said.

And Lucas obliged. Gaten screamed out in pain, and Theo held his hands up into the air.

'Okay! Okay, I'll do it! Just don't hurt my brother! Please! I'll take it off, just don't hurt him!'

Steven smiled, and Billy slowly let Theo go. A few seconds of silence passed. Theo crawled toward the puddle and cupped some of the dark, dusty water into his hands. He stared at it, looking deep into his own reflection. Then he poured it onto his face and started scrubbing. He cried while he did it, like a true gay boy. His red and black makeup filled the water around him, and he bathed in it like a pig wallowing in its own filth. Steven got a sudden urge to grab the knife and stick it in his back, but he didn't. Instead, he just watched as the boy cried and choked in the rain, scrubbing his face so hard that the rouge was starting to return as marks. *Look, Dad,* Steven thought to himself. *Look who's drowning now.* A whole minute passed before all the makeup was gone. Then Theo looked up at the boys.

'Okay,' he said. 'That must be all of it. Can we go now? Can we please go?'

Steven bit at his lip. All he had wanted was for the makeup to go and for them to make a statement, but somehow that didn't feel strong enough now. Every inch of him wanted to go further. *Needed* to go further. He felt his dad breathing over his shoulder, and he felt the harsh whip of his belt on his butt. He did that sometimes, hit him when he had done something wrong. Now Theo was the one who had done something wrong, and Steven held the belt firmly in his own hands. He turned to Lucas.

'What do you think, Lucas? Can they go?'

Lucas pointed the knife toward Theo. 'I say we stick him! Slice his nuts off so he can't hurt anyone!'

'Or we just beat him up,' suggested Derek. 'Show him what real boys do.'

Steven wagged his finger, enjoying his role as leader. 'You're right. You're both right. We can't just give him a bath. That's no punishment.'

'You should let him go,' cried Gaten, his voice high and squeaky.

'Or what?' Steven glared at him, then signalled for Derek and Lucas to let him go.

They did so slowly until Gaten stood free. He stared at Steven, and Steven stared back.

'That's what I thought…' Steven hissed. Then he turned to Lucas. 'Well? What are you waiting for?'

Without further invitation, Lucas leapt forward and gave Theo a kick in the face. Like the first of a long line of dominoes, the rest of the boys soon followed. Derek was second, squeezing his fists into balls and whacking Theo as hard as he could in the abdomen. Billy came up behind him and pulled his hair, and Steven kicked him several times in the gut, so hard that Steven swore he heard one of his ribs crack. All the while, Gaten simply stood there, his face drained of colour, his jaw slack. When Steven remembered him, he swivelled fast and got himself ready for a counter-attack, but none came. Instead, Gaten turned on his heels and ran so fast that he could have given Billy a run for his money next sports day.

The beating lasted for around thirty seconds, until Theo stopped making groaning noises and lay motionless with his head in the puddle. After it was done, the boys bought slurpies, ran to the nearest park, and took it in turns to discuss what had just happened in detail. Although the ambush had only taken a few minutes, each had their own stories and funny moments to recall. When it got to Steven's turn, he focused hard on Gaten.

Billy said, 'Oh yeah! What happened to him?'

And Steven replied, 'He ran away. Didn't you see him? He ran faster than goddamn Road Runner on heroin. MEEP MEEP!'

The boys all rolled over laughing, and Steven thought about that pool in Florida. A new pool had replaced that one now, and he couldn't wait to tell his father. He decided he would do it over supper that night. They were having pork chops.

6

It had been eighteen years since the puddle on St Martin's Street, but Gaten remembered it like it was yesterday. He remembered Theo lying in the rain. He remembered the coldness in his bones, freezing him like a damn statue. He remembered the kid, Steven he thought his name was, standing with his fists raised. That was always the worst part of the memory. The figure of that boy, just a silhouette now, standing there with his fists raised and his knees bent. He had been ready for the fight. He had been ready for at least an attempt of retaliation. But no attempt had come.

Gaten, who had protected his brother from nightmares by just being there, could not even raise a fist when those nightmares had turned into reality.

When Theo got better, Gaten assumed he would never climb into his bed again, but he did so two months later. From that point on, however, Gaten resolved to shoving him out.

'You're too old,' he remembered saying. 'You need to get over this stuff now.'

Theo must have assumed he had taken Steven's side, but that wasn't true. The truth was, he felt guilty. It had been easy enough to protect his brother unconsciously, but when Theo had really needed him, Gaten hadn't stepped up to the task. He was a phoney. A fake. And seeing Theo curled up at the bottom of his bed only reminded him of that.

The voice of Wayne singing ripped Gaten out of his thoughts. They were driving in the patrol car, listening to "Reptilia" by The Strokes. After the chorus, the sound of Wayne's pager buzzed in the glove compartment and he stopped to check it.

'Hadero's not in,' he said, squinting.

'Says who?' asked Gaten, feeling his heart pick up a few paces.

'Says Bert. Apparently he's ducked out early to celebrate his daughter. You want me to drop you home? I'm sure this can wait until morning.'

Gaten saw the body of Adrian Ramirez staring at him in the rear view mirror, and he felt his toes begin to tense in his shoes. *Can it wait until morning?* he thought. He wasn't sure. Something about all of this felt so fast and immediate, and he was sure the response had to be the same. He shook his head and tried to get rid of the feeling.

'No,' he said. 'I'll fill in some paperwork and leave it on his desk.'

'I can do that if you want.'

'No, I want it to come from me. I want it done right.'

Gaten looked out of the window, watching the world move past him like a film reel. He watched their faces. Content and oblivious, just like his brother would be at this moment. No one in the town was aware of the horror that had stung that boy. No one in the town knew of the horror that might sting again, if Gaten's presumptions turned out to be correct.

He nestled his neck into the headrest and tried to tell himself otherwise. He didn't know anything yet. It was still just a hunch. But that didn't stop him remembering that puddle. That didn't stop him seeing his brother, who had cried and screamed in pain, needing help, needing something, and only being able to watch as Gaten ran in the opposite direction. He had been trying to make up for running ever since that day. He had even offered his brother a room in his apartment, for quarter the price of rent no less. But it still wasn't enough. He would be making up for that moment for the rest of his life, and he knew he would never be able to completely close the door on it. Nothing he had done so far had even come close.

Gaten sighed and opened the window a little. The world blustered past him and the rain did too. It felt old, that rain. Eighteen years old. He remembered how it hit his face when he ran. He wasn't running now, at least. Not yet anyhow.

7

On the other side of town, there was a bar named Salvadors. Sara and Tony were sitting in the corner, beside one of the three pool tables. Tony had his hand on her leg, moving it dangerously close to her testicles. He planted a kiss on her neck, and Sara pushed him away with a long fingernail.

'Easy now, tiger.'

Tony slumped back into his velvet seat. 'Sorry,' he said awkwardly. 'This is all new to me.'

'I can see that.'

'Is it too much?'

Sara glanced at the other members of the bar. Men, mostly. Shirts tucked into pants and pants tucked into boots. They looked harmless, but a few of them carried, and there were plenty of prying eyes and grizzling lips. The ones who stared would roll up their sleeves and slurp their beers more strongly, as if they thought being in the presence of Sara might turn them into less of a man – like she was contagious. *America's gay town*, Sara thought amusedly. *But it's spreadin' like wildfire so don't get too close!*

She smiled at Tony. 'Here? Yes. It is too much. A look and a kiss is fine, but anything more and peoples eyeballs start melting.'

Tony cupped his beer. 'I don't care what people think.'

'Of course you don't. You've just come out of the closet, clean off the hanger, with a fresh pair of clothes and underpants. Wait until you get some egg on you.'

'Jesus, is it really that bad?'

'Not the first few times. But, pretty soon, those sparkly new clothes get awful sticky, and you'd do anything to avoid the next pelt. It gets hard to wash out.'

'Maybe I should stay in the closet.'

Sara shrugged. 'Gay life isn't for everyone,' she admitted. 'People these days urge you to come out, but once you do, you spend your life fighting all the people trying to drive you back in. I won't say anything either way. You do you, boo. But the closet is dark, and despite what the stories say, there's no Narnia on the other side.'

'I like it out here.' Tony reached over and placed his hand on Sara's.

Instinctively, she darted her eyes around the bar to check if anyone was looking. It looked clear, but she removed his hand anyway.

'You're cute.'

'So are you. Isn't there anywhere we can have some fun?'

'Like I said, you've booked a motel haven't you?'

'Don't you live here?' asked Tony.

'With my brother,' Sara replied. 'But he doesn't take kindly to me bringing home strays.'

'Who says I'm a stray?'

'I don't know you from Adam.'

'Who's Adam?'

Sara leant back, and one of the guests put on a record on the juke box. "Heart-Shaped Box" by Nirvana. A little different to the playlists they would go for in the Precious Star Bar.

'Summer of 1999. A good screw, but a better screwer.'

'Better than me?'

'I guess we'll find out.'

'When?'

'Do you ever stop asking questions?'

'Do you ever stop demanding answers?'

Sara laughed. 'I'm no mystery, honey. This is routine.'

Tony pouted, his eyes glimmering with a drunken glaze that gave him confidence. He was sitting at the table like one of those American gangsters in the movies.

'I could get used to that,' he said.

Sara nudged his knee. 'Like I said, you're cute. Wait for your first egg.'

Just then, a group of six men clattered into the bar and, like the loud flash of a dying lightbulb, the atmosphere changed. They were rowdy, this lot. A few of them walked straight to the pool table opposite them and began shoving quarters down the coin chutes. The others congregated near the bar and began cat-calling the female bar staff. Sara looked at Tony. The confidence had slipped out of him as easily as piss through a pant leg.

'So, my place, huh?' he said hopefully.

Sara grinned and pecked him on the cheek. 'I'll pay the tab.'

She got up and headed toward the bar, where Diego Martel was wiping glasses and eyeing up the newcomers with his fierce Mexican glare. He hadn't spotted her yet, but someone did. The shorter one of the six men. His hair was bleached blonde and his eyes were blue and icy. He walked up alongside her and stopped when he realised what he was looking at.

'Jesus,' he said.

Not quite, thought Sara. *But not far off.*

She cleared her throat in an effort to attract the attention of Diego, but it didn't work. A few seconds passed, and the short man spoke under his breath.

'Goddamn pansy.'

Sara looked at him. 'It's pronounced pilsner,' she said, flicking one of the taps with her fingernail. 'And I'm next in line.'

'I'm talking about you,' the man growled through gritted teeth.

'You got a problem?' asked Sara.

'You better believe I do. This is my town.' He removed a badge from his jacket pocket and flashed it at her. It read, "JUSTIN HADERO, CHIEF OF POLICE".

Sara shrugged. 'And yet you're still second in line.'

'Another vodka, Sara?' Diego stepped in front of her and placed his hands firmly on the bar.

Justin frowned. 'What did he call you?'

'We're just gonna pay the tab, if that's okay.'

'Sure thing,' said Diego. 'That's nineteen ninety-five.'

Sara handed over the money, and Justin spoke up again, 'What did he call you?'

But Sara was already making her way back to the table. She took hold of Tony's hand and marched over toward the double-doors, praying Justin didn't follow them.

8

He did follow them. Sara and Tony were at the edge of the parking lot when the slurred voice of Justin Hadero called out into the night.

'Hey, I'm talkin' to you!'

Sara hesitated, Tony's hand in hers, but she let it go and stopped. Justin looked even smaller in the light of Salvadors. His clothes strained against a beer gut, temporary but noticeable, and the rain on his face made it look like he was sweating profusely. A repugnant man by all accounts, Sara thought. It was a wonder her brother could work for him.

Justin stopped in front of them, his hand hovering close to his holster. 'What did he call you?' he repeated.

'He called me Sara.'

'How fucking —' Justin stumbled over his words. 'That's not your name though, is it? What gives you the right to dirty that name?'

Mother? Sara wondered briefly. *No, not mother. The anger's fresh. It's bloated and temporary, like that beer gut behind his buttons. This is a daughter.* 'I gave it to myself,' she replied. 'It's my name.'

'I gave that name to my daughter, that's how this works.'

Sara nodded. *Bingo*. Although something told her a prize wasn't on the way. Not a nice prize, anyhow.

'My daughter's name is Sarah,' Justin continued, 'and that's for real. Your kind think you can just waltz around taking names for yourselves. What's your second name? Dorothy? You wanna take my mother's name too? I oughta imprison every last one of you. Hang you up by the city hall like the freak shows you are. Lord knows, I would if I could. You're a disgrace. You're wrong.'

Justin spat and Tony took a step backwards. He was noticed.

'You!' shouted Justin. 'I bet you've stolen a name as well.'

Sara nudged him. 'It's alright, Dorothy. You can speak to the nice man.'

Tony's eyes widened, and he let out a little squeak. Justin pulled out his handcuffs.

'You think this is funny? You realise what I can do to you? Your pupils look awfully dilated, maybe I can book you for those drugs you've taken. Your kind are all on it. You kill yourselves with the stuff. I don't care about that, but I do care about the law. I can arrest you right here and now if I like. Save all of us the trouble of looking at you.' He gestured to the invisible crowd that had apparently gathered around them, and he wobbled a bit while doing so.

Sara felt her nerves beginning to relax. The man was beyond drunk. He was wasted. And that didn't make him much of a threat. He would probably slap a cuff on his own wrist if he tried to do it. Tony, however, was beginning to quake.

'We've not taken any drugs, sir,' he said shakily.

'No,' said Sara. 'I mean, coke doesn't count as a drug does it? Everyone takes that.'

'Sara!' Tony gasped.

'DON'T FUCKING USE THAT NAME!' Justin snapped. 'IT'S NOT HIS NAME! DO YOU HEAR ME?! IT'S NOT HIS NAME!'

'I'm sorry,' Tony pleaded. 'I can't afford to go to jail. I don't know her, not really. I was on my way to a job interview. She took me. Sir, please, if I go to jail, they'll know. I swear I don't know her!'

For a moment, Sara wondered whether Tony *had* taken drugs. It would certainly explain the desperation in his voice. But he was a bunny, and bunnies didn't do things like drugs. *They do hop though*, Sara thought. And Tony seemed close to doing just that.

'Like I believe that shit,' Justin slurred.

He stumbled forward, but at that moment, the door of Salvadors opened and Diego Martel stepped into the night.

'What's going on out here?' he called out.

Tony turned and began sprinting down the street, leaving Sara at the drunken chief's mercy. She watched him go, stony faced. The rain pattered against her wig and trickled down to the ends. For a moment, it reminded her of old rain. Her brother's rain. She felt her world go grey, and her throat tightened around something invisible. She had been here before. She remembered.

'It's alright,' Justin shouted at Diego. 'I'm the police.' He swivelled back to Sara and pointed the handcuffs at her, but she turned in the opposite direction. 'Hey! Don't walk away from me!'

Justin called after her, and Sara half-hoped he might try to follow. It would have been amusing to see him fall and land that pretty blonde head of his into one of the nearest puddles. But he didn't. His job was done. And the puddles were reserved for Sara. The puddles were always reserved for Sara. She dipped her head and the rain began swaying, the wind helping her along the road. Like a pendulum, it carried her into darkness.

9

Context. That was what mattered. In another life, the fleeing of Tony might have meant nothing to her. He was a bunny, after all. Inconsequential. A quick kiss, a quick fuck, and then he would be off to Oregon and Sara would be onto the next one by tomorrow. But context was an ugly thing. It created thorns in roses because it had roots, it had life. There was a world underneath it all, and Sara's world had been plenty watered.

She remembered the day it had happened. It must have been eighteen years ago now. She had been with her brother, and they had been ambushed on St Martin's Street. She remembered the water clinging to her face, making paste of her foundation. She remembered the shoes digging into her ribs and the sound of her nose breaking. She remembered, through the squint of her already swelling eyes, her brother running as fast as he could into the rain. He had not been scared to fight, Sara knew it. He had been scared of what she had become. If she had still been Theo, he would have fought for her. He would have fought, and he would have lost, but at least he would have done the first thing. As Sara, however, Gaten had simply run. It wasn't that she was not worth fighting for. Not at all. It was that, on some level – perhaps small, perhaps just a speck – he agreed with the reason she was being beaten in the first place. Those boys saw Sara as wrong, and Gaten had thought the same thing. Why fight a snake that would not bite you? Why fight a snake in the first place? A snake attacked on instinct, on willpower to survive, and those boys had been fighting for survival too. Perhaps not a snake's survival, but survival all the same. They had been fighting for the survival of the American identity. The same identity that would be lost if people like Sara were ever allowed to be accepted.

Eighteen years later, and that acceptance had still not come. Sara's world had been swept underneath America's carpet. Allowed but never accepted. Acknowledged but never made true. Perhaps that was why Sara felt the way she did. Whenever things got close to being normal, and pleasant, and nice, someone like Justin Hadero would always come along and make her remember: *You are not in a gay town. You are not true. And they are not as they seem.*

Once upon a time, Sara had hoped that her brother would accept her. That he would always be a big brother who protected her from the nightmares. But then he had run. She had hoped tonight that she could find normality again. That she could be happy and carefree, and share a night with a boy who felt the same way. But then he had run. And not only had he run, he had shoved her aside and left her at the mercy of someone who wanted her dead. He had abandoned her in the same way that her brother had abandoned her, and on some level, both meant the same thing.

What was it Tony had said? *She took me.* Tony had agreed with everything Justin was accusing her of. He was a closeted gay who had been trapped in a world he was supposed to hate. He had never really liked Sara, he had just been running on his own instinct – an instinct he had never wanted to act on. Perhaps they were all like that. Tony, Luna, Carl. Perhaps they all despised themselves in their own way, because the world had taught them that was the right thing to do. Perhaps they would all run from that puddle. And if the puddle never came for them, perhaps they would create one for themselves. They would do what they were supposed to do, because they were wrong and that was simply the way of it. Living a happy life was never an option. Breaking free would be a sin. How could the world not be listened to when your ear was pressed right up against the glass?

That was why Sara was upset. That context. Those roots. She had grown another thorn, and she wanted it to make her bleed.

10

When she got to the pier, there were tears in her eyes. The rain was still coming down hard, and she leaned into it. The wind was behind her, and she wished for it to blow her away. To blow her into the ocean and submerge her until she drowned. She closed her eyes and stopped for a while. She thought about Tony, and Justin, and Gaten. She thought about herself, and she tried to remember her song, "Don't Dream It", but it wasn't coming to her. The lyrics were lost in the pitter-patter of the tumbling water, and the melody was a loose chain of ugly notes. She told herself to find it, to find her power and her petals, but she couldn't do it. There was just the rain. Just the thorns. Just quiet.

Until, all of a sudden, something else. Another melody, but not the one she had been looking for. Sara opened her eyes and stared at the pier. Out there in the darkness, there was that song again. The saxophones returned. The drums, the bass, the strings. The cheers too. They were all there once again, playing distantly, but presently, like they were right inside Sara's head and yet far out toward the end of the pier.

She took a step toward it. The song was unlike any Sara had ever heard, and it played out into the cold, night-time air like the calling of a cuckoo in the early hours of the morning. She listened to it for a few more seconds, and then the music changed. Like a wave, it pulled back on itself and regressed into the ocean. It went silent, and then, a few seconds later, it came back. It did this for a minute or two. Regressed and returned, regressed and returned. Sara imagined that it was asking her to follow. Like the pulling of fingers beckoning her to come near, it lured her in, and the wind lured her too. She stared at the pier. Dark, empty, and desolate. Yet the song was unmistakeable in its call.

Sara took a step back. She stopped and she thought. Then, because of all the things that had happened that night, and all the other roots that had led her to this, she muttered,

'Fuck it...'

And then she resolved to follow it.

CHAPTER SEVEN

THE SECRET CUCKOO CABARET CLUB

1

The jaw of the whale hung above Sara, open wide, like it was looking for one last tasty morsel. She avoided it by dipping her head. Her hands were curled around the iron bars, which were wet with seawater. She held them tight and spun herself over the top. It wasn't hard. In her childhood days, she'd climbed plenty of trees to hide from bullies in the playground, and even in heels, she had no trouble scaling the gate and slipping down the other side.

She had never stepped foot on the pier before, but she had heard stories about it. After closing in the early 1980s, it had become a makeshift den for the drug addicts known as the "pier dwellers". According to Luna, plans for refurbishment led to the majority being shipped out on the SS Pinafore, headed for the mines in Mexico. Carl had dismissed this as nonsense, stating instead that the dwellers had left of their own accord, when a communal trip saw the whale's head come alive and try to eat them. Both stories seemed hard to believe, but then again, both Carl and Luna had been around five rums down when they had been told.

The truth was, the addicts of Cuckoo Cove's pier had left the place for one reason or another, as it was now just an empty wooden road, with nothing but dilapidated arcades and run down hot dog stalls to symbolise any sign of a previous life. And the music, of course. Always the music. It was there again now, bristling on the wind. It rose and fell like the swell of a trumpet, and as Sara walked further, it seemed to get louder. In a way, it felt like a dream. A wave of magic. Ghostly and resplendent, or somewhere between the two. It was nothing, but something. There, but not quite there. It pulled Sara in like she was lassoed, and no matter how hard she tried, she couldn't resist its pull.

After a couple of minutes, she found herself approaching the end of the pier, where there was a large ballroom, grey and covered with plasterboard. Unintelligible graffiti lined the splinters:

SMT
GB
TL

Some had more meaning:

GARETH <3 LUCY
I <3 CUCKOO COVE
MOLLY BOY 1999

And one particular message made Sara shiver:

I AM THE WHALE N I HAV DARK THOUGHTS

Sara didn't know why that one got to her. Perhaps it was the way the wind travelled through the whale's empty jaw, causing it to whistle softly into the night. Or perhaps it was the way its teeth had hovered over her head when she climbed. She thought about it, but then the music changed, and she thought about it no longer. Sara could hear a voice over the crowd now. Male, tinny, but clear. So clear that his lips could be heard smacking against the microphone. She took a step toward the doors, which had even more graffiti sprayed over them.

I LOST TWENTY BUCKS ON THIS PIER'S PULL MACHINE AND I WANT IT BACK

On any other day, Sara would have laughed at that. But right now, she was lost in the music. The riotous crowd, the vibrating drum beats, the clinking of glasses. She pressed her ear up against the gap in the middle of the doors and listened. The voice became so clear she could hear the accent, a slight hint of New York, and the lyrics became clearer too.

> *'Why be a bum in the slummest of towns?*
> *Here in the night*
> *It's our duty bounds'*

Sara kept her ear pressed to the crack in the doors. She looked down at one of the handles. It had been copper once, but was now covered in green scale. The metal was peeling with salt water, and beside it, there was a latch with an equally rusted padlock. She fingered at it and saw that it was unlocked.

> *'Our duty to get hooty*
> *Our duty to the fight*
> *The wonders of the cabaret*
> *The cuckoos of the night'*

Sara put her hand on the handle and pulled the door a few inches toward her. What she saw on the other side was unlike anything she had ever seen before. While the outside of the ballroom was cold and dilapidated, the inside was awash with brilliant orange light. The majority of the space was a dance floor, but Sara's eyes were immediately pulled to the stage at the far end, lit with spotlight and housing around sixteen band members: four violinists, one cellist, two oboe players, six trumpeters, one saxophonist, a drummer, and a singer. They were all dressed in black tie except the singer, who was a drag queen lavished in makeup and a bright pink wig. The men behind her had their hair gelled back, but that was the only part of them that was orderly. Their clothes were drenched with what looked like foam, and their cheeks were red and sweating. The crowd was not much different. The room was full of party-goers in suits and dresses. They sat around tables covered in gold liners and adorned with food, champagne and glitter. In the centre of the room, two women were standing in a couple of gigantic champagne flutes. They were dressed in silver lace and dancing to the music. One had her leg over the edge, and an elderly gentlemen was slipping some dollar bills into the straps of her ankle. Amidst the chaos, there were wigs, some bright blonde, others silver, black, purple and pink. Men dressed as women, women dressed as men. Everyone was smiling. Sara's jaw dropped open.

> *'Why be a dull in the dullest of bores?*
> *They be the saints*
> *And we be the whores'*

The drag queen waved an arm to the crowd, and a chorus of laughs erupted from the floor and tables. Someone threw flowers at her.

> *'It's our duty to get hooty*
> *It's our duty to get booty'*

She beckoned to the men behind her.

> *'The trumpers on the ol' grandstand*
> *Oh boy*
> *Well aren't they fruity?'*

The trumpeters behind her raised their instruments in unison and began performing a solo. The drag queen sat on the edge of the stage and feigned tiredness. She picked up a long, rippled fan and began fluttering it in front of her face. A woman raised a glass of something brown, and she took it and winked. She sipped at the glass and feigned disgust. Then she sipped again, and again, and again, and chucked it back to the woman. She blew a kiss and trotted back to the microphone.

> *'I can't remember ever feeling this good*
> *Apart from that boy in my ol' neighbourhood'*

In the champagne flutes, the girls continued dancing. They wore silver tinsel around their necks, and they stroked them like they were pet ferrets.

> *'But that was last December*
> *Think his name was Dustin Ember*
> *Got one up on those bitches*
> *Think his —'*

The drag queen stepped away from the microphone and the saxophonist blew out a quickly escalating note. She returned to the microphone.

'— was seven inches!'

The crowd roared with delight. Then, out of nowhere, two members of the party opened the door and barged into Sara.

'Oh!' one of them gasped. He was a middle-aged man with a lean, wrinkled face and thinning brown hair topped with foam. The other looked pretty much the same. Both had bright pink cigarette holders in their hand, an unlit cigarette shoved into each.

'Don't just stand there, girl.' The second man grinned at her. 'You'll catch a death!' He shoved her aside and the both of them skipped onto the deck of the pier.

Sara nodded, and then she stepped into the ballroom.

2

The warmth hit her immediately. It wasn't cold outside, but Sara found herself folding her arms over her torso and feeling a wash of comfort seep into her bones. The party carried on around her and she found herself seeping into it, like it was a bed made of memory foam. To her left, a champagne bottle popped, and the cork landed skilfully into one of the gigantic flutes. To her right, a man grabbed the arms of a younger woman and carried her over to the dance floor. The pink-haired singer on stage grabbed the microphone again.

'They might call us wrong 'uns, they might call us thieves
We're mowing their lawns
We're blowing their leaves'

Something pushed into Sara from behind, and suddenly she found herself swept into a rabble of five women moving closer to the stage. One of them stopped and twirled around the stem of one of the champagne flutes. People cheered, and the gentleman who had slipped money into the girl's shoe slipped some more into the back of her dress.

'But it's our duty to get hooty
And we will, we'll make 'em right
We'll show them to the cabaret, we'll lead 'em to the light!'

The band grew louder, so loud that Sara was half worried the champagne flutes might shatter.

'The wonders of the caaaabaaareeet…'

Cymbals shook, brass squeezed, stage rattled. Then, like rapids plunging over the top of a steep waterfall, everything descended wild and fast.

'THE CUCKOOS OF THE NIGHT!'

The band stopped with one loud, almighty crash, and cheers erupted around the ballroom. On either side of the stage, a cloud of foam blasted from two canisters, and it snowed down upon all of them.

Sara blinked twice and tried to contemplate the scene around her. She felt numb, like she had stepped into a dream, but she couldn't fly or float. When she blinked, the scene didn't change or falter. It stayed just as it had done before. The same stage. The same lights. The same people. Everything was as real as the wig on her head.

'Thank you, darlings.' The singer on stage held up her arms. 'My lord, what a night we cuckoos are having! Give a warm hand to the fellas staring up the back of my skirt.'

The crowd applauded, and the band members bowed.

'I'm so happy you're all here. It's a cold world out there, and we all know it beats you down. I can see a few heads bowed a little lower this evening, but we can do something about that.' She stared into the crowd and shielded her brow with the edge of her palm. 'A hand for our champagne girls, too. It isn't easy dancing in a champagne flute. Although you should be grateful I'm here, those flutes were full an hour before the show!'

The crowd laughed, and the singer soaked in the reaction. Sara saw her chest glisten and sparkle with sweat.

'Anyway,' she continued. 'We've got another number for you all, and then we're going to bring our lovely ladies out for the Cuckoo Cabaret Club's evening burlesque show. Good grief, that's a mouthful. Yes, thank you for the cheers. Who's that out there? Logan? Oh, yes. We all know you're here for the ladies, darling. Aren't you lucky, you've got me for a while longer.'

She nodded to the band members and they raised their instruments, ready to begin all over again. The singer picked up a glass from the edge of the stage, empty except for a few ice cubes melting in the heat of the spotlight.

'Whisky and soda, darlings. Anyone who wants to pop behind the bar and fill me up, that would be wonderful. A glass of whisky and soda would be nice too.' She winked playfully before setting the glass down and stepping back to the centre of the stage. 'My name is Vierra Vicious, and this is my Cuckoo Cabaret Band. ONE...!'

She counted them in, and the band launched into a full rendition of "Minnie the Moocher" by Cab Calloway. Sara watched as the crowd began to dance again. She took a step backwards and felt herself bump into someone. A splash of champagne landed on her dress, and she turned to spot a woman with beautiful olive skin and dark eyes. She was wearing a copper gown with white gloves, and her wig was pulled up into a beehive, filled with pink and purple highlights that spiralled so perfectly it looked like a cherry could sit right on top.

'Sorry honey,' she said absently. In her hands were two champagne glasses, one of which was now half empty. She shrugged and gave it to Sara. 'Ah well, chin-chin.'

She downed her own glass and went to walk away, but before she could leave, Sara grabbed her by the shoulder.

'Excuse me,' she said, like a child who had gotten lost.
'Yes, darling?'
'Uh, you couldn't tell me where I am, could you? It's just, I'm a little confused. I don't belong here. I just kind of walked in.'

'No kidding,' the woman looked at her bemusedly. 'You're in the Cuckoo Cabaret Club.'

'And what's that?' Sara had to shout as the saxophonist ripped into a solo.

'It's a cabaret club for cuckoos. Our kind. The crazy birds. Now, if you'll excuse me…'

The woman turned, but Sara grabbed her shoulder again.

'No, wait!'

'What is it?'

'I wanna know your name.'

The woman looked at her pitifully. 'Oh, bless you. You're like a baby bird left alone in a strange nest. My name is Ava. But I ain't your mother, darling. I'm just another cuckoo.'

'I'm Sara.'

'Lovely to meet your acquaintance, Sara.'

For a moment, it looked like the woman named Ava might fade back into the bustle of the crowd again. But as they congregated, she remained still, staring at Sara with a funny sort of curiosity.

'Tell me, Sara,' she said softly, 'do you like the little club we've got here?'

Sara looked around. 'It feels like I'm in a dream. Am I?'

'Are you what? In a dream?'

'Yeah, in a dream.'

'Well, that depends. Do you want to be in a dream, Sara?'

'What do you mean?'

The band crashed to a halt, and the crowd around them cheered once again. A few more champagne corks flew above Sara's head.

'I mean,' clarified Ava, 'sometimes good things feel that way. Like a dream. We tell ourselves that, because there's no way something so good can exist in our world. It has to be somewhere else, where we can jump and fly, and do whatever we want. A happy world. It makes it easier to make do if we detach ourselves from what should be reality. So I'm asking you, Sara, do you want this to be a dream?'

Sara thought about it. She looked around at the men and women, drag queens and kings, straight and gay. She took them all in and watched their faces. Then she shook her head.

'No,' she said simply.

'Then it's not. And don't let it be.'

'It just doesn't feel real,' Sara reiterated. 'It feels too good to be true.'

Without warning, Ava took hold of Sara's chin and she flinched. It wasn't violent, however. It was light, warm, and her gloves tickled Sara like she was being brushed by a feather.

'Look up,' she said.

Sara followed her gaze to the ceiling. They were standing beneath a glass dome, smudged with dust. A few balloons were hovering against it, slowly deflating. Outside the dome, she saw a sky full of stars.

'Are those stars not the same stars you saw outside?' asked Ava. 'Try and touch them. Go on, try.'

'How do you mean, touch them?'

Ava let her go again and took another sip of her drink. She smiled sharply. 'I'm as real as a pickle, darling. We all are. Now, do you have a cigarette?'

Sara patted her bra and fished out a crumpled packet of cigarettes. 'Yeah, sure,' she said, slipping one from the inside and holding it up in front of her.

'Put it between my teeth,' said Ava. 'Then follow me.'

3

Outside, the rain had slowed. Hardly any light was coming from the ballroom. The dome was a vague, yellow haze, obscured by the dust, while the plasterboards shrouded the party in shadows. If it wasn't for the music, it would have seemed like there was no life in there at all, not even the faint scuttling of some lost hermit crab. And yet, behind the curtain, behind the façade, it was so much more alive than anything Sara had ever experienced. She lit a cigarette and, after a small prompt, she did the same for Ava, who then walked to the banister and sat down upon an old, splintered bench.

Sara followed and they sat together for a few moments, staring at the ocean. Despite the rain, the water was calm. Waves rippled one after the other quietly and softly, almost black under the darkened sky. Beside her, Ava sighed and a plume of cigarette smoke fell across her face. It kept her in a cool haze for a moment, and Sara felt a flutter arise in her chest.

'So tell me about yourself, Sara.' Ava nudged her with her heel.

'Me?'

'You're the one sitting next to me, aren't you?'

Sara hesitated. 'Well,' she said slowly. 'I'm thirty-one years old. I was born a male, but I transitioned when I was —'

'I don't wanna hear about that.'

'You said you want to know about me.'

'I do,' replied Ava. 'But you believe you're a woman, don't you?'

'Yes, of course.'

'You've always felt that way? Even when you didn't know you did? As soon as you came out of your mother's womb, all pink and sticky, you were a woman.'

'Yes.'

'So why bother with the furniture? That's immaterial. It's boring.'

'But it's a part of me,' argued Sara.

'It shouldn't be. We have a male president, right?'

'Right.'

'Do you think he mentions the fact that he's a male when he talks about himself? Do you think he mentions the time he looked down and realised there was a little worm dangling between his legs? No. Because he is what he is, and has always been. It's immaterial. I wanna know about you.'

There were a few seconds of silence. Sara hadn't been able to hear the waves before, but she heard them now, like they were trying to paper over the awkwardness. She couldn't help feeling caught off guard by what Ava had just said. For so long, her transition had been the one thing in life that defined her. It was a big moment. A wonderful moment. And she had never thought to look at it as anything less.

'Okay,' she muttered, closing herself off a little. 'I work in the Precious Star Bar, on Adamson Avenue. Is that what you're looking for?'

Ava smiled and shook her head. 'Not at all.'

'Well what about you? What about all this?'

'Me or all this?'

'Huh?'

'Which one do you want to know about?'

Sara took a few seconds. She thought she would sooner know about the Cuckoo Cabaret Club, but right now, for some reason, she was more interested in the person sitting beside her. There was something about Ava that she hadn't witnessed in a person before. A confidence, perhaps, but something more than that. She felt almost like an alien. Like she might dissolve if she was to walk across the pier and step into Sara's own world. She was different, and Sara wanted to know why.

'You,' she said bluntly.

Ava nodded. 'Me? I'm happy. I was sad for a while. A few months ago, I was close to throwing myself in this ocean and letting myself sink to the bottom. But now I'm happy. I get bad thoughts sometimes. Something goes click, and things feel a bit fuzzy, and some clingfilm goes over the top of my world. But over the last few months, I've learned to embrace that. I welcome my demons like I'm welcoming my friends to the cabaret club, and after a while, they get swept up in the music and I lose them in the crowd. So, overall, I'm happy and I'm content. Thank you for asking.'

There was more silence for a few moments. Sara took it all in.

'Okay,' she said eventually. 'Next question. What is this place?'

'It's a ballroom on the edge of an abandoned pier. Every night, people from all over town gather here to get drunk and have a good time.'

'How come I've never heard of it?'

'It's sort of a secret. Besides, you must have heard of it. What else made you come here tonight?'

'I only came here because I heard the music.'

Ava shrugged. 'So you were listening.'

Sara stared at her, then she looked back toward Cuckoo Cove. The street lights were flickering in the wind. They weren't red, like the ones in the Precious Star Bar, but they still looked like eyes. Mean eyes that were glaring at her, furious she had found some new friends.

'Alright,' Sara took a deep breath. 'I'll tell you about me. I'm sad. I have been for a long time, ever since I got beaten up and left in a puddle. Everything has been awful since that day. I try to make do, finding happiness in small places. But even those places are just a mirage. People pretend like we're accepted around here, but we're not. We're let out at night, but in the day, it's as if we're circus acts that just keep going. People will hide and spit on us like we're vampires. It's like they're worried we're gonna suck their blood if we get too close.'

'I don't think it's blood they're worried about us sucking,' said Ava.

'Sometimes I feel like I never really left that puddle,' Sara ignored her. 'I was choking on it then and I'm still choking now. Only, this is a different kind of choking. It's like I'm being strangled, and the skin's about to crack. The talons are starting to breach and if I bleed, I'll bleed forever. It won't stop, and I'll end up drowning in it. I just wanna be happy. I wanna be accepted.'

Sara looked at Ava, and Ava looked back at her. She wiped away a tear that Sara didn't even know she had.

'You can't have one without the other.'

'I don't have either,' replied Sara.

Ava nodded. With a small flick of her finger, she sent her cigarette flying over the banister and into the water below. Then she placed her heels back onto the decking.

'It's a small thing, this club. But a small thing can be the only thing. The only thing that matters.' She pointed over toward Cuckoo Cove, and the eyes of the street faded slightly, like they were cowering from her touch. 'See the town out there? That's not everything, you know. That's just a small corner of a small civilisation of a small world. We're selective with what we let in and listen to. So make this your corner. Make this your civilisation. And you can make this your whole world. You can find happiness here.'

Sara felt her heart begin to swell in her chest. She didn't know why, but the thought of coming back to the Cuckoo Cabaret Club gave her a rush of emotion. It was like she had been looking for this place for a long time – or rather, she had been listening – only she didn't know it. Now she had heard, and she didn't want to hear anything else again.

'You mean I can come back?' she asked hopefully.

'You're a certified cuckoo now,' said Ava. 'Now give me another cigarette, my lips are getting cold.'

Sara smiled and fished another cigarette from her bra. As she handed it over, her gaze lingered on Ava's lips, and she wished there was another way she could warm them up.

4

Ten minutes later, Sara was back on the dance floor. Ava danced beside her, sweat trickling down her neck to dampen her copper gown. Hardly anyone was sitting at the tables now. They were all gathered around Sara, so tight that it should have been impossible to dance, only it wasn't. Sara had all the space in the world. And what a world it was.

The music had gotten louder now. It felt more like a vibration, like something spiritual which crept through her bones and needed to be shaken out. She floated around the dance floor like it was hers and only hers. At one point, the foam canisters went off again and Sara looked toward the stage. She saw a mirrorball hanging there. It showed her the Cuckoo Cabaret Club's reflection, full of light, full of sound, colour, and her, in the middle of it, moving in and out of the bodies like they were all part of one organism.

The foam landed on her face and she wiped it away like it was tears. It wasn't tears, though. It was just foam. Sara wondered how she could ever feel tears on her cheeks again, so long as a place like this existed. In a way, it felt like everything that had been missing, not just for her, but for everyone. And yet it was a secret. Hidden away at the end of a dead pier. *The best secret in the world*, Sara thought, and in that moment she knew that it was.

When the foam had settled, Sara turned away from the stage and looked up at the domed ceiling. She saw the sparse, yet all encompassing stars, and she realised Ava was right. It was just them, and the dome, and then the universe. They were cut off from Cuckoo Cove and everything else. They were in a world of their own making and, underneath that dome, with the music and the stars, it felt right.

Sara was happy.

CHAPTER EIGHT

THE SOUND

1

Kenny Townsend was better than Harland Thomas in almost every conceivable way. He wore his clothes straighter than him. He cut his hair shorter than him. He got A's in every class, praise from every teacher. He took piano, he learned guitar, he even underwent climbing lessons in the town's activity centre – he had realised he was good when he'd climbed all the way to the top of the school's Indian post, a feat Harland Thomas had never accomplished.

Even his breath smelt better. Harland's breath smelt like sausages and syrup, cooked by his mother in their luxury condo in Fort Kraven. Kenny didn't have any such breakfasts. His mornings would consist mostly of cereal and orange juice, then a hot rinse with mouthwash. He *made* his breath smell better. As a matter of fact, he did as much as he could to better Harland Thomas in every department – scent and ability combined. Yet he still found himself lugging his kit bag through Corker's Park, feeling far more miserable than Harland was likely feeling at eight in the morning. He was probably wrapped up in a goose-feathered duvet right now, dreaming sweet dreams about Dora Lane. But for Kenny, that wasn't an option. Dora had told him as such two weeks ago:

'I'm sorry, Kenny. You're a nice guy. Sweet. I just think Harley's better suited to me.'

She had been leaning against a wall in the school corridor, her hair in two sumptuous ponytails and her two front teeth accentuated by her overbite, making her look like one of the most beautiful rabbits to have ever walked the earth.

'But why?' Kenny had argued. 'What does Harland have that I don't have?'

'You climbed the Indian post didn't you? All the way to the tippy-top-top.' She'd been touching his arm at this point, stroking it up and down in a way that made Kenny squeeze his legs together and pray that nothing showed.

'Yeah,' he'd replied. 'Everyone's wanted to climb that thing to the top, but I'm the only one who did it.'

'Yes, you are. And I was very impressed. Even more impressed that you did it with these skinny little arms. I tell ya what, when you can play football like Harley can, then maybe I'll give you a shot. See, it's not about how high you climb the post, Kenny. It's about how good you look while you're climbing it. See ya around.'

And with that, Dora had hopped off down the corridor, leaving Kenny to run to the gym and sign up immediately to the local football club.

Every Sunday, nine o'clock. Except Kenny always got there earlier. He didn't much like football. He was a thin kid, wiry, with strawberry blonde hair and freckles that covered his face. He had tried to watch the NFL with his dad, as every good American boy should, but ever since his mother had died from the dreaded Big C, his dad had become a lot more mean. It didn't matter how well his team were playing, every Sunday morning there would always be something to get mad about, and there would always be Kenny to blame.

But despite his aversion to the sport, Kenny put his best foot forward. There were just two months before the annual Christmas dance, and he wanted to make sure that when he danced with Dora – because he *would* dance with Dora – his arms would be strong enough to lift her off the ground. He looked at those arms now as he traipsed over the mound and onto the woodland trail. Still small, still wiry. He stopped and pulled an Apple Jacks bar from his pocket. He was supposed to save this for after his pre-practice practice, but his bones felt brittle, and he was also lacking in any sort of energy. The night before had been full of terrors, which they tended to be when he went to sleep thinking about his mother. When she had died, Kenny had been the first one to find her. He had sat by her bed for a whole hour before he raised the alarm, trying to make sense of it all. This beautiful, caring woman. Alive and moving, and then dead. He had said goodbye to his old mother and hello to his new one. He had grown accustomed to the concept of death in as little as an hour, and in that time, he had somehow managed to feel comfortable with it. Only his dreams told him something different. They rummaged into his soul like a drill, and whenever they did, he awoke feeling sluggish and sloppy. Usually, he didn't mind, but he needed to make every football session worthwhile. There could be no skipped beats in the quest for Dora's heart. Puffing his chest out,

Kenny shoved the bar into his mouth and continued walking.

When he got to the football field, the sun had appeared over the tree-line. Kenny slapped his kit bag down onto the grass, pulled it open, and removed his pads. They were still thick with mud from the last practice session, when Jimmy Oliver had knocked him down into the dirt with his head. He wouldn't be so stupid as to let a running back get the better of him next time, so he wiped off the mud and gave himself the chance of a new beginning. He removed his helmet from the bag and dropped it on the white line of the pitch border. Next came the ball – his dad's ball, from when he had been a kid in the fifth division. Old and haggard, it needed to be pumped with air after every practice session, but Kenny still managed to get a good ten kicks out of it, which was something, at least.

He leant back onto his heels and kicked it now, watching it spiral up toward the clouds before descending toward the centre of the posts. It was a good shot. Pinpoint accurate in fact, if only it wasn't short. It was hard to tell at this angle, but the body hanging below the posts kind of gave it away. The ball bounced neatly off its head, bouncing three times on the grass before coming to rest just beside the right post. The body swung a little and Kenny wavered on the spot. The clothes looked like they belonged to a woman, but Kenny could see that it was a man. The arms were bulky like Harland's, and the rope had tightened around the jaw to reveal a pronounced Adam's apple. The hair was strange and spiky, like the back of a dragon's spine, and the face looked almost confused, like its final thought had been attempting to solve a difficult algebra equation.

For a few more seconds, Kenny simply stared at it. Then he ran forward, grabbed his ball, and made for the nearest pay phone. He called the police, and then returned to the field, hoping to put his adrenaline to good use. He knew that Dora would be impressed that he had found a body, but he knew that she would be more impressed if he had done it with muscles. He practiced for a whole twenty minutes on the other side of the field before the cops showed up and asked him to go home.

2

Abigail turned up the heating in her Honda Civic and leant her head against the window. It was chilly out. The wind twisted the rain this way and that, causing tiny spirals to whistle above the ocean and spray sea froth against the distant pier, like the saliva of a lapping dog. She watched it for a few moments, her fingers fiddling around her pen. Then she looked down at her notepad.

6:00AM – SHOWER AND TEETH

6:30AM – GOLD LANE, APARTMENT 7

9:00AM (MAYBE?) – BACK TO BRECKIES FOR NOTES

12:00PM – WRITE UP PUMPKIN PAGEANT BEFORE TOMORROW (UGH)

2:00PM – MEETING WITH GARETH (HOPEFULLY GOOD NEWS)

> 2:30PM – CALL DAD – MRI SCAN ON MONDAY
>
> 3:00PM – RESEARCH
>
> 5:00PM – DINNER WITH MIKE
>
> 7:00PM – SEX WITH MIKE (BEEN TWO WEEKS)
>
> 9:00PM – MORE RESEARCH

She sighed and tapped her pen against the pad. She'd always made organised notes for her tomorrows, ever since she was a kid, but whenever she was actually *living* those tomorrows, she struggled to actually follow them. Sex with Mike was already an impossibility. She had to feel at least a little frisky to honour that one, and right now, she felt far from frisky, and she was pretty sure that wasn't going to change. Calling Dad was also unlikely to be carried through. She loved her dad, but she hated conversations with him, especially over the phone. Not to mention, her mind was on other things. It had been for a while now, and that always left her pretty despondent.

'*Hmm, yeah...*'
'*Oh, really?*'
'*Dang...*'
'*Huh, that's interesting.*'

She always ended those calls with her dad feeling like they were in a worse place than when they'd started them, so she didn't really see the point. Surely it was better to have a daughter who had forgotten, rather than a daughter who simply wasn't interested? Abigail didn't know. Abigail didn't care. And she didn't really want to spend time thinking about it because, once again, her mind was on other things.

The man she was waiting for was late. She had been staring at the apartment for around twenty minutes now, and still, there was no sign of him. Her flask of coffee was already running low. She took a final sip of it and was pondering grabbing some more when the door to the apartment block opened and her man stepped out into the morning. He looked different from his picture. Taller, with bushy black hair and surprisingly toned biceps straining his shirt. But it was definitely him. Abigail sprung forward, flicking down the sun-block mirror and patting her blonde fringe down upon her forehead. She tucked her hair behind her ears and checked her lipstick with a pout. Once content with her appearance, she opened the door and hurried after him.

'Mr Dalbret?' she called out.

The man stopped and turned, wiping away some gunk from his eyes. He looked ruffled, like she'd just woken him out of a dream. 'Who wants to know?' he asked.

'My name's Abigail Finn,' she held out her hand but the man didn't shake it. 'I work for the Cuckoo Correspondence. You're Gaten Dalbret, correct?'

'I'm a police officer, I don't talk to the CC.'

'But you worked on the case, though. The Ramirez case. Your name was on the statement.'

Gaten hesitated for a moment, glaring at her suspiciously. 'And?'

'I just wanted to ask about it. Details.'

'He killed himself. We don't give details. It's called respect.'

'But I'm not sure that he did.' Abigail spoke quickly, attempting to catch him every time he went to turn around. He was a fish on her line, but she knew how to reel him in.

'What are you talking about?'

'I'm not sure it was suicide. And I'm not sure, if you were at the scene, that you can believe that either. Sorry, sir, but what about some respect for me?'

At that moment, the fish stopped resisting a little. Gaten stood still, looking her up and down. His eyes latched a little too long on her legs. She'd worn the skirt especially for today. If the hook didn't work, she made sure the bait was shiny enough to keep coming back to.

'Did you know him?' asked Gaten.

'I did.'

'Do you have any evidence about the case that we should know about?'

'Not evidence, per se. But I did talk to him around a week ago. I did a column for the CC on the new Revelation bar opening on Renters Street. He was going to have a regular weekend slot there. I don't think Adrian would have killed himself, sir. At least, not the Adrian I knew.'

'How long did you speak to him?'

Abigail hesitated a moment. Even in the wind and rain, her cheeks flushed hot. 'Twenty minutes,' she replied. 'Maybe.'

'Twenty minutes,' responded Gaten. 'I knew Adrian longer than that, and he was dead when I met him.'

'You knew a body, sir. I knew Adrian.'

'So you think in twenty minutes, you got enough intel to dismiss the conclusion of our investigation? Or are you just looking for a story? Something to wind the old folks up before Halloween, is that it?'

Abigail wavered. This wasn't how this was supposed to go. 'I'm just doing my job, sir.'

'Your job is to report the news, not warp it into something that sells copies. The news is: it was a suicide. Now find something else to write about. The pumpkin pageant in Marylestone Ranch is going to be the biggest yet, I hear. I'm sure your readers would love to hear about that.'

'That's my twelve o'clock.'

'Make it your nine.'

Abigail stuttered something back, but nothing intelligible came out. She didn't understand it. She had expected this man to be a cop, like all the other cops. Ill informed, slightly sweaty, and no good at a comeback if it wasn't slapping out a taser and jabbing someone in the belly. She thought she'd walk miles around him, but Gaten had cut off the line before she even got the chance of another tug. He turned and began pacing down the street, leaving Abigail to call after him.

'I'll send you Adrian's column, sir!'

He didn't look back. Abigail watched him disappear into the rain, then got back into her car, pinching herself. It had been a long time since her legs had failed her that badly. They were normally a reliable back up. Abigail looked in the mirror and wondered if she'd applied her makeup right. She made a mental note that sex with Mike was back on the table, then she opened up her notebook and scribbled a few new lines into her agenda.

3

The rain was heavy when Gaten turned the corner onto Sycamore Street. It rushed down the sidewalks and slipped underneath people's boots. As he passed Scrum Bistro, just a few steps from the station, he saw the owner, Mohammed, pour some of his morning coffee onto the sidewalk. It pooled briefly, then split into separate streams. For a moment, Gaten imagined Theo lying in the water and the coffee seeping from his head. He shook the thought away and nodded a good morning to Mohammed. He nodded a good morning back, then went back inside.

Gaten thought about the notes he'd made the night before. He hoped they'd be enough to capture Justin's attention, but something told him they wouldn't be. There were too many coincidences, too many conjectures. The nightmare was still a nightmare, and no matter how hard Gaten tried, the pieces still weren't fitting into a realistic picture. But there *was* a picture. Even the reporter saw a picture, though he knew her reasons were likely different from his. She was just an opportunist. One of those busy cockroaches that scuttled a little faster whenever there was a whiff of sour dirt. The picture in *his* head was the one that counted. He just needed Justin to see it too. As a reality, as a dream, as a nightmare. It didn't matter. He needed to make him see it, and then maybe there would be an end to all this. He climbed the steps toward the station and ruffled his hair when he got out of the downpour.

Once inside, Gaten didn't waste any time before inviting himself into Justin's office. The chief waved him in, hunched awkwardly over his desk.

'This better be quick, Gate. My head's pounding like a stuck pig.' His voice was small and croaked, like someone had cleaned out all the phlegm with dentist utensils.

'Big night?' Gaten asked, closing the door behind him.

'You know it. Big and heavy. It's still weighing down on me now, feels like my ears are leaking mush.'

'I heard you were celebrating your daughter.'

'Uh-huh.'

The chief lifted a mug of coffee and downed it. Gaten glanced at his desk. It was cluttered, as usual. He had left his paperwork on the top of the pile the night before, but now that he looked, he could see that it was gone. Justin continued talking.

'My dad hit the road for five days when I was born. I can hardly handle four hours, and I'm four years younger. What does that say about me?'

'Their whisky was watered down in those days,' suggested Gaten.

'Well, it certainly ain't now. I could drink the ocean.'

'Say, Justin, did you notice my paperwork this morning?'

'Hard to miss,' Justin snickered. 'It was lying front and centre on my desk. I guess Cherisse gave you the keys?'

'She did.'

'God love her. Yes, I did have a look. Splitting headache and seeing colours, but I had a look. Thank you for that.'

'And?' asked Gaten nervously.

'And I'm mighty glad you wrote it out. Was it cathartic?'

'Excuse me?'

'The case obviously bothers you, Gate. Sometimes putting things into words allows you to see sense.'

'It's not the case that bothers me, sir. It's the lack of one.'

'Uh-huh.' Justin nodded dazedly, like he had just finished a big pot of stew and was beginning to doze in front of a roaring fire. 'You think we're barking up the wrong tree?'

'I don't think we're barking to begin with. I think we've been complacent since day one.'

'And you think the tape proves our complacency?'

'I do.'

'Well forgive me to differ with you, Gate, but I think it proves just the opposite.'

The chief put two feet up onto the table and removed an apple from the drawer of his desk. He bit into it and Gaten looked at his boots. The soles were fuzzy, licked with boozy stains and tiny granite pebbles that had wedged into the rubber. He must have been out on the town in the same boots, Gaten thought, because he could smell a hot flush of beer when they arose.

'If anything,' Justin continued, 'the tape leaves us in a good position if any questions come up about the whole thing. Certainly a better one than before.'

'How do you mean?'

'Think about it, Gate. You saw the kid on the tape, didn't you?'

'I did.'

'But no one else. The visual covered the majority of the plant, you wrote here. But it was just the kid on the tape.'

'No one else could be seen in the tape, but —'

'Because there isn't anyone else. They don't exist, Gaten. They were a figment of his imagination. It's all here in black and white. I mean, come on, do you think he climbed all the way up that water tank to look at the view? You think there weren't other places to hide that wig? The kid was deranged, son. He was goo-goo, he was gaga. There's no conclusion to be drawn, because there ain't any sense to be made. You put this forward to open the case, Gaten. But I think it's pretty safe to say it closes it.'

The chief leant forward, lowering his apple for a second. 'Coke. Ecstasy. Marijuana – all of it was found in his system. I've seen this before, Gaten, and I can see it again now. There weren't nothing chasing him but his own demons. And this time, he didn't get away. This time he went too far.'

Gaten felt like he wanted to fight back, but he didn't know how to. Instead, he simply stood there. Cold footed, red with either anger or embarrassment, he didn't quite know which.

'I don't know what to say,' he muttered, quite honestly.

Justin shook his head. 'Me neither. I don't know if you're scared about what happened to this kid. Heck, maybe you *wanted* something to happen to him, but the fact is, the case is shut. I understand you went there for the wig. I get that. And I know I asked you to look for it. But the wig's been got now. And it ain't no piece of evidence, it's just a dank hairball. It's irrelevant. And so is the kid. Do you understand me?'

Gaten swallowed. 'I understand...'

'Good. Now leave me to get over my hangover in peace, unless you wanna start investigating my death too. I can tell ya, that one will be pretty open and shut. You killing me with your rattling on.'

Justin laughed and winked, but Gaten didn't see the funny side. He approached the door and opened it onto the now busying office. The smell of coffee hit him. Bagels, too, wafting from Cherisse's booth.

'You want to do something?' said Justin from behind him. 'Head down to the Pumpkin Pageant tomorrow afternoon. Mrs Taggort got in a fight last year over pesticide. You can be security.'

Gaten turned, unamused. 'I'm not going to the pageant, sir,' he said flatly.

And at the same moment, Justin's telephone started to ring.

4

When Sara awoke, she did so with a smile. Her eyes fluttered open and she lay examining the ceiling for a moment. It was cracked and ruffled. Mould clung to the corners like a rash, and the main light was one flicker short of darkness. She usually awoke scolding that ceiling. Hating it. Sometimes even feeling sick because of it. But this morning, it didn't even feel like her ceiling anymore. Sleepy muck clung to her eyes, and the curl of her lashes blurred her vision, so her examination was inconclusive. The ceiling was a white blur. Neither pretty, nor ugly. So Sara smiled and decided on the former.

This morning was a good one. Sara felt better than she had ever felt in her life, and it was all to do with the secret Cuckoo Cabaret Club. Visions of it still flashed in her subconscious. Every thought she had was accompanied by fireworks, and confetti, and singing, and dancing, and gay guys dressed like peacocks, and women with fake breasts, and stars, so many stars, gliding into the distance and away into the ocean of the sky. And, of course, there was Ava. Her face, her legs, her eyes, her lips. Those sumptuous lips, pursing like a clam. And Sara wanting more than anything to open her up and steal whatever was inside.

All of this was buzzing inside Sara's head, filling her with electricity. She wiped at her eyes and jumped up from bed. She hadn't changed last night. Her dress remained clamped to her body by night sweats, and the spatter of alcohol gave her linings a healthy shine. Her wig sat atop her head lopsided, and it tickled her right armpit, so she pulled it off and let out a long, croaky sigh. She smacked her lips. She pursed and tickled the roof of her mouth. She pulled herself onto her feet, and looked out of the window onto the streets of Cuckoo Cove. It was grey, and specks of rain trickled against the panes. But that didn't matter, because Sara could squint her eyes. She did so until the world became a blur, just like it had in bed, and she decided that what was there in front of her was the most goddamn beautiful thing.

5

She had pop-tarts for breakfast. Cherry pop-tarts with some milk. Her knees were shaking and she couldn't stop it, because the electricity wouldn't go away. It sat with her like a warm, fizzy kiss, and when she tried to calm her heart, it only beat faster, hitting against her ribcage like the steady beat of those wonderful drums. The music of the club continued to swirl through her head, making her giddy. She watched the clock like a kid on Christmas morning. It ticked slower than Sara had ever seen it tick in her life. She wasn't waiting for the hour hand to hit twelve, which was when she'd usually head to the Precious Star Bar on a Sunday. She was waiting for the night, for the music on the pier, and to dance on that dance floor again. The Precious Star Bar was just an inconvenience that filled the space in between. She couldn't even imagine getting up on that stage now, performing her song, trying her best to block out the audience. In fact, she was almost sure she couldn't do it.

Why should she do it? After years of service, all that time and struggle, there was nothing stopping her from picking up the phone right now and calling it in. She wouldn't do that to the people she loved, of course. But all the same, she knew she couldn't get up there today. Not after everything that had happened. She needed time. She just needed time to sit and be happy. And wait. All she wanted to do was wait.

Making her decision, she swallowed the last mouthful of her pop-tart and finished her milk. Then she walked over to the telephone and began dialling. Her eyes were still on the clock. She watched it tick, tick, tick – slower, and slower, and slower. Until she was sure it wasn't ticking at all. Sara huffed and waited for Luna to pick up.

6

When Gaten approached the body, he felt a strange sense of calm. This was different from the last time. Although the body of Adrian Ramirez had been small, it had managed to change the world around it, casting its own shadows. Gaten remembered feeling weightless, caught in a breath of wind. He had been slipping down the slope toward Adrian, but actually, he had been walking, one foot after the other, allowing Adrian to pull him in. The body had been a black hole of hideous colour. It had festered in the centre of a garden, and all the trees were stripped, and anything alive was gone, and Gaten was the last thing left to be sucked into its orbit. He had wanted to stop walking, but he couldn't stop walking, because he was a police officer, and police officers didn't stop walking. He had made himself keep going, and when he was within a few inches of the body, he had felt himself being swallowed to the other side, and he had arrived blinking like a newborn baby into a world that looked exactly the same, except it was made from death.

This world now seemed to be the new normal, because nothing changed this time. When Gaten approached the second body, he didn't feel any different. His breathing was normal, his boots were heavy, and his gaze was set. That wasn't the same for everyone else. Officers behind him were holding back, and when he had looked at them, they had stared back like he was a stranger. They seemed totally detached from their reality, and so Gaten had pressed forward, keeping himself set in his own. And now he was as close to the body as he was going to get, and the body was looking down at him, and there was a strand of grass protruding from its lips, and Gaten thought he should say 'hello' like he was greeting an old friend. But he didn't. He simply stared and said,

'Okay.'

And then he retrieved his notebook and wrote: *Death Number Two*.

7

Something here knows everything. The water, the weeds, the wood. It knows the termites that crawl into crevices. It knows the fish that gulp at the sides. It knows us, too. It knows us very well. Something has made a home in our home and something whispers to us when we sleep.

Something here thinks. It thinks about the shore and it realises: no. It might know everything, but it doesn't know every story. The stories are still ripe. Still untasted. It delights in their intricacies, and it wants to feed them until they pop. Something here feels a thrill. A rush of excitement that waters the tongue. Something here feels thankful. Content. It thinks and it realises that there are not enough stories to go around, there are plenty.

8

When Mrs Taggort tended to her pumpkin patch, the day was gloomy and humid. Sweat clamped her white hair to her head, and it felt itchy under her woollen scalp cap. She scratched at it, threw down her knee mat, and began picking worms from the bed. She slipped around ten of them into her pocket, withdrew her snippers, and began punching at the pumpkin vines.

When she was done, five pumpkins were squeezed into her wheelbarrow. The largest was around an inch bigger than last year, but it was no huge improvement. Nothing to write home about or mention to Bob over supper. The rest of the pumpkins lined the corner of the bed, caked in soil and wet fingerprints from when she had measured them. None of them were good enough for the table, but she wouldn't waste them. They were to go into the week's dinners: pumpkin and bacon soup, pumpkin pie, spiced pumpkin soup, pumpkin curry with chickpeas, and perhaps even pumpkin-spiced scones, if she could find it in herself to tackle them. With a heave, she lifted the wheelbarrow and pushed it to the log shed. Bunting was lining the gutter of her house. She had put it all up the day before, which was the latest she had ever left it. She didn't like to get in the pumpkin pageant mood before her pumpkins were on the table. She never won. She was a judge, and self-congratulations were frowned upon in her profession. But still, she liked the compliments when people passed her, and she liked the fact that people *thought* she should win, even though she couldn't.

Wiping her brow, Mrs Taggort raised her head and looked at the sky. It seemed for a moment like a dark cloud had blocked the sun, but when she blinked, the sun was still shining, and the cloud was gone. The only ones that remained were sparse and mildly grey. The rain had been and gone, and now was the time for limbo – that period after rain where the sky took a breath, and looked upon what it had done, and considered whether to feel guilt or keep going. It rarely decided on the latter, and Mrs Taggort was thankful for that, because *something* controlled the rain, and although it got testy, it didn't ever choose destruction.

She had been a deeply religious woman until the age of nineteen, but after an unfortunate incident in 1959, she had changed. She didn't say "God" anymore, she said "something". She didn't call God "he", she called him "it". That was her way of coping with what happened, and she had seen it in plenty of other people too. It wasn't that she had stopped believing, it was just that she'd learned to use her eyes more. Things that deserved loyalty and love were things that she could see. That's why she didn't care about what was happening in Iraq or Afghanistan, or how hungry they were in Kenya. That's why she cared about her Bob, and her cat, and her pumpkins. If anything wanted a deeper connection, then she had to be able to feel them, touch them, know them. The moment God looked into her eyes was the moment she would call him God. Until that day, she would be content with what was in front of her. But no more rain, for now.

A rustle came from behind her, and Mrs Taggort saw Mr Taggort stuffing his face in the sprout bowl. She hissed at him and he looked at her. His face was covered in grey fur and his whiskers were bent on the left side. He was an ugly cat, by all accounts, but she still loved him. She had taken him in after a storm eighteen years ago, and she'd named him Mr Taggort when she thought there'd never actually be one. When Bob came along around a year later, she had explained the situation and he'd been okay with it. The cat had got there first, after all, and you couldn't change a cat's name once it responded to it. Sure, it made the shop-owners confused when Mrs Taggort asked for Mr Taggort's worm medicine, but they were willing to live with that.

'Psst! Hey! Get out of there!' Mrs Taggort pointed firmly at Mr Taggort, and he meowed angrily. 'I've got your din-dins here…'

Mrs Taggort removed the worms from her pocket and flung one of them on the grass. Mr Taggort clawed at it, ate it, and Mrs Taggort walked over to the ledge of the window. She picked up a tub of old seeds and soil, shaking it onto the ground before replacing it with the rest of them.

'More later, if you behave.'

Mr Taggort meowed, and Mrs Taggort stroked his head. For a moment, all she could hear was the two of them. Her breathing, him purring. But then there was another sound. A bird, maybe. Or not quite a bird. More of a baby. She looked toward the road, which lay twenty or so yards from the pumpkin patch. For a moment, she wondered if a car had broken down, because the road was so quiet. But then the sound stopped, and it was just her and Mr Taggort again. She figured it must have been a bird, and went about the rest of her business. Mr Taggort ran indoors.

9

That night, they had leftover lasagne with cherry tomatoes, mixed salad, ginger sticks, cress, and a jug of strawberry water. Mr Taggort had two more worms and some cat food.

Mrs Taggort had lived in the ranch house for twenty years now, and it suited her. The rooms were small and tight, but that made them warm, with smaller shadows, which was good because Mrs Taggort had always been frightened of shadows. Herself and Bob were sitting at the table, and Bob was teasing her through a mouthful of lasagne.

'Where's my pumpkins, pumpkin?'

'Out in the yard,' Mrs Taggort replied. 'You know I don't cut them up until after the pageant is over. If one of my showpieces doesn't make it, I need backup.'

'Backup pumpkins,' Bob repeated, like the concept was funny.

'Crows got one last year, remember?'

'Oh yeah, I remember.'

'Granted I had six clean and good, but you never know how hungry the crows are.'

'Maybe leave them the worms.' Bob glanced down toward Mr Taggort, who had left half a worm bleeding by his dinner bowl.

'But Mr Taggort loves the worms,' said Mrs Taggort.

Bob shook his head. 'Shouldn't feed cats worms. Gives them worms.'

'Mr Taggort has had his medicine.'

'That don't do nothing. They're all still inside him. Waiting.'

'Waiting for what?'

'You seen that movie *Alien*?'

'If Mr Taggort stopped getting worms, he'd wonder why, and perhaps he'd just wonder that I don't like him no more. Like he don't deserve worms.'

'If worms are a sign of your love, perhaps I should be worried about what I eat.'

'Quiet, you. And eat your lasagne.'

Bob eyed his plate suspiciously, then swallowed another hearty mouthful. This was the way most of their evenings went nowadays. Bob teasing, Mrs Taggort fending him off happily. Although most people would see it as pointless busy talk, Mrs Taggort wouldn't have it any other way. Their love for each other was simple, and their talks were simple too. That was the way she liked it. She didn't see the need to complicate things, or talk about anything more than cats or pumpkins. Love was always the simplest and happiest language. She felt sorry for people with long, deep conversations.

'More strawberry water?' she asked Bob.

He nodded and Mrs Taggort filled him up. Some mince had got stuck in his beard, so she leant over and picked it off, flicking it away absentmindedly. Mr Taggort rushed to it and ate it with such delight that Bob frowned and glared at his plate again. Mrs Taggort pulled him out of it.

'You know, I thought I heard a bird just now.'

'Huh?'

'A bird. We were talking about crows, Bob.'

'Oh, were we?'

'Yes, and I thought I heard another bird just now, out in the yard. Didn't sound like one I'd heard before. You like your bird watching, what'll it be?'

'What did it sound like?'

'Like a baby.'

Bob laughed. 'Get serious.'

'I am serious.'

'What bird you ever heard in your life sounded like a baby?'

'I don't know, that's why I'm asking you.'

'That weren't no bird. A baby, maybe.'

Mrs Taggort placed a forkful of salad into her mouth. 'Funny, I don't remember putting baby feeders out.'

Bob shrugged and reclined in his chair. His buttoned belly bloated against the tabletop.

'Listen,' continued Mrs Taggort. 'I heard them birds on the Discovery channel once. All bright coloured ones, made a real funny noise. Perhaps it was that.'

'You thinking of a kookaburra?'

'Maybe.'

'Well, hold on, I'll get on the phone to Australia. Tell them they're missing one.'

'Very funny. Well, what else could it have been?'

Bob shrugged again. The food had clearly made him too tired to tease anymore. 'I don't know. Hey, what's for dessert?'

Mrs Taggort huffed and decided to leave it, but for some reason, the conversation shook her. There was a seed of something strange resting in the pit of her stomach, and she couldn't quite figure out why. She tried to ignore it, but when she did the washing up, she was looking through the window and staring at the place the noise had come from, She wondered why she cared, because she normally didn't care about things she couldn't see. And yet, when she got to watching television with Bob and he fell asleep in his Lazy Boy, she decided that she really did care. She cared a lot. The cry kept playing in her mind, and the seed in her stomach kept growing into something twisted, and knotted, and squeezed with worms.

Mrs Taggort didn't drink often, but that night, she retrieved some of Bob's gin from the top shelf in the kitchen and poured herself a three-quarter glass. She drank it straight, then had another before she went to bed. She dozed off easily, but when she was fully asleep, the sound started again. This time, in dreams.

CHAPTER NINE

THE PUMPKIN PAGEANT

1

Doctor Stathum was exactly as Gaten had expected. Dressed in white, his skin was pale and blotchy, almost green in places, and his eyes were a strange shade of brown. Not hazelnut. That was too pretty. This was a dull brown, like stripped bark that had been left out in a downpour. He stared at Gaten behind thick, rimmed glasses, and his face was twisted with a hidden smile.

'You folks are testing me, huh?'

'Testing how?' asked Gaten.

'Two bodies just two days apart. That can't be a coincidence. This has to be an audit.'

'Do morgues have audits?'

'Only if the auditors are brave enough.'

The doctor's hidden smile revealed itself, and for a moment, Gaten was concerned that he had awarded him that. He hadn't asked the question in jest. It had come automatically, almost distantly. He snapped himself back into the room and cleared his throat.

'Do you have any initial impressions?'

The doctor turned toward the body of Arthur Conrad. He lay flat on a metal table, a sheet draped over his lower half. Slight beads of water flecked his forehead, as if the body was perspiring, but the room was colder than winter. Below his jaw, a thick red mark travelled from the front of the neck to the back, where a tangled knot of gelled hair cushioned him like a headrest. The rest of the hair was still in position, spiked several inches into the air. Not even death had shrivelled the punch of this hair gel, and Gaten rather thought the company should attest to that in their next marketing campaign. He shook out the slightly morbid joke and listened to the doctor.

'Seems pretty open and shut,' he said. 'Ligature marks around the neck, with trauma to the C2 and C3 vertebrae.' The doctor pointed with a pen toward two zones of the middle-upper neck. 'Suggests death by asphyxiation.'

'Anything else on him?'

'Two abrasions to the metacarpus. Contusion to the carpus, possibly a carpal bone fracture. Abrasions on either kneecap, and one on the buttocks. Scarred tissue on the left forearm. Piercing on the genital area, probably recent, given the granulation tissue.'

'Any of those suggest wrongful death?'

'The piercing, maybe. I'd be driven to suicide too if a dick piercing gave me rats.'

Gaten looked at him darkly and the doctor's smile faded.

'I mean, no. All other afflictions are minor. Could have happened falling down.'

'The wrist? You don't think he was grabbed?'

'No, I don't think so.'

'How come?'

The doctor pointed with his pen again. 'The abrasions,' he explained. 'They're to the heel of each hand. That's what would happen if you fall down and try to stop yourself.'

He lifted his own hands and tilted them toward his body in demonstration. Gaten understood.

'Say, officer,' the doctor continued. 'Did they say he was hanging from a football post?'

'Yes,' said Gaten.

'Interesting...'

Gaten waited for more, but it seemed that was all the doctor had to say on the matter. He turned and placed his pen neatly on one of the counters, beside a tray of scissors, shears, and forceps. Gaten felt a little sick looking at them, so he turned to look at the clock instead. It was a cuckoo clock, West Virginian, according to the inscription. Two weights hung below the lever, fashioned white marble, and the woodwork was made to look like maple leaves. Gaten frowned at the thing, then looked back toward the doctor. He was sitting down in his chair now, flicking erratically through some files, a glass of water half-drunk beside him. It was then that Gaten realised the doctor had made this, the mortuary room, nothing less than a makeshift office. The doctor noticed his look.

'Don't worry,' he said, understanding exactly what Gaten was thinking. 'I have osteoarthritis. Makes the stairs harder and harder each time I have to go up them. I spend more time in here. It makes sense.'

Gaten nodded. 'Sure. Sure, it makes sense.'

'You're thinking I've made a home with the dead.'

'No,' Gaten responded, taken aback. 'Not at all.'

'It's alright. My wife thinks the same thing. She works just up the road from me, in the laundromat on Crescent Street. She used to bring me sandwiches on her lunch hour. She doesn't anymore.'

Gaten grunted awkwardly. 'Right, yeah.'

The doctor looked at the clock. 'Huh. One o'clock. The cuckoo's a little slow.'

At that moment, Gaten heard movement above them, and he went to make for the stairs. The doctor raised a hand to stop him.

'It's alright, he'll be brought down by my diener.' The twisted smile had returned on his face, and he didn't try to hide it this time. 'You know what a diener is? That's what they used to call mortuary assistants in the nineteenth century. The people responsible for handling and cleaning the bodies.'

'I should speak to Mr Vasquez before he comes in,' said Gaten. 'Can you not ask your diener to hold him?'

The doctor shook his head, suppressing a laugh. 'Diener is derived from the German word "Leichendiener". It means "the corpse's servant".'

Before Gaten could respond, the door at the top of the stairs had opened and two pairs of footsteps began echoing between the walls.

'Mr Vasquez,' said Gaten as the first man approached. 'I was going to find you before you came down.'

The man in front of him was called Carl Vasquez, but Gaten knew his drag name was Sally. He worked at the Precious Star Bar with Gaten's brother, and while Theo had always described him as "pouty but playful", right now, he was neither. This was an old man with an emptiness in his eyes, standing there as still and cold as the body on the table.

'Why?' he asked distantly.

'To go through procedure,' Gaten replied. 'And to prepare you.'

'Prepare me for what? Yeah, it's her.'

Gaten looked at the diener behind Carl's shoulder, a weedy man with ginger hair. Then he turned back to the doctor.

'I think it's wise that you leave us for a moment.'

'Are you kicking me out of my office?'

The doctor spoke bluntly, but he had clearly meant it in jest, as he had reached the stairs before Gaten could answer. The both of them exited the room and left Gaten and Carl alone. Gaten shuffled awkwardly.

'A closer look, if you would.'

Carl's breathing got deeper, and for the first time, he glanced at the body. Once they were there, they didn't leave. He took a few steps toward it.

'No touching, sir,' Gaten said, but he rather thought that Carl knew that already.

The old man's toes reached the table and he looked down. Gaten could see that his hands were trembling, like he wanted more than anything to touch the body on the slate and pull it into his arms. Hold it tight. Squeeze it to eternity. But they remained by his hips, just inches from the table. He bowed his head.

'Who did this to her?' he whispered.

'Can you positively identify?' said Gaten.

'You know I can.'

Gaten shuffled awkwardly. 'We don't know. Possible no one. The deceased was found hanged in Corker's Park.'

Carl didn't respond. His head bowed lower.

'Do you have any idea why the deceased would do this?' asked Gaten.

'Call her what you want, Officer Dalbret. She can't hear you anymore.'

Gaten stuttered a little, checking himself. 'I'm – I'm sorry.'

'She was happy last time I spoke to her. She gave me my pills. Said she needed to bleed another few years out of me before I kick the bucket, otherwise it might look suspicious.' He laughed silently, his back to Gaten.

'You have a lot of money, Mr Vasquez?'

'No, I was poor before Luna came.' On that last word, Carl's voice choked and sliced in half, like a shard of glass had torn through his voice box. His whole body seemed to sag, and he bowed in front of Arthur Conrad like he was bowing to a queen. When he spoke again, tears were in his voice, like blood from the glass. 'What am I gonna do now, huh? You sly bitch, you left me with them. How could you leave me with them?'

'Leave you with who?' asked Gaten.

'The monsters. I was still hiding under the bed before Luna came. She picked me up, dusted me off, and gave me a spear like one of the characters from her stories. She protected me from the monsters. But the monsters got her.'

'You think he was mentally unstable?'

Carl's laugh wasn't silent this time, it was loud and harsh. 'The monsters aren't in our head, sir. They're in yours.'

Gaten faltered but kept quiet. He watched Carl bow closer to the body.

'Won't you tell me another story?' he whispered. 'A good one. Where we win in the end.'

'I'm sorry,' said Gaten. He was suddenly moved to comfort him. This man was the only family that Arthur had known. The third choice after a deceased mother and father, yet surely the only choice, judging by the way he looked into his eyes. 'You'll see him again. I hope you can take comfort in that.'

'I won't see her,' sobbed Carl. 'If she doesn't tell me another story now, I'll never hear one again.'

Gaten could feel him staring at Arthur's lips, willing them to move, to whisper back and tell him it would all be alright. But they remained still. Blue.

'I'll try to remember them,' Carl whispered. 'I'll take them under the bed with me.'

'He'd want you to stay strong.'

'Yes. She would. Because she was strong. She was the strongest I've ever known. If the monsters can get her, they can get anyone.'

A collection of seconds filled the silence then. Perhaps minutes, Gaten wasn't sure. He watched the clock on the wall while Carl wept, his body still bowed but not touching his lover. The cuckoo still hadn't shown itself. It stayed hidden in its home, the door clamped firmly shut. The minute hand juddered forward one pace, and that was when Carl spoke again.

'What do you think happened to her?' he repeated.

'Like I said,' replied Gaten. 'The evidence points to suicide.'

'And if I told you there were monsters after her?'

'Sir, if you're talking about the public perception of queers in this town, that's all the more reason to follow the evidence.'

'Then you won't mind if I touch her then?' Without waiting for an invitation, Carl planted his lips against the body's. He stayed there for a while, trying to sap warmth where there was none. When he let go, he wavered his hand above the body's forehead. 'Goodnight, my little loon. Sleep better.'

This time, it was Gaten's turn to bow. He waited as Carl hobbled past him, watching as the old man stopped at the stairs.

'There's a tale, you know. A fox chasing a rabbit through the forest. The rabbit jumps into the river to escape and it drowns. What killed the rabbit? Was it the fox, or did the rabbit kill itself?'

He didn't ask the question directly. Gaten wasn't even sure he was talking to him. Carl appeared to be in a sort of trance, staring at the stairs, but not really seeing them.

'You think the fox is responsible because it drove the rabbit into the river?' asked Gaten.

Carl snapped out of it. 'No,' he replied absently. 'I think, in this case, the fox caught the rabbit. I think it tore it to pieces. And the crime scene is being investigated by wolves.'

Just then, the cuckoo clock burst into life. Gaten jumped as the door opened and the wooden bird flung itself from its perch, wings creaking, head tilting, and calling loudly. It remained displayed for a few seconds, then it locked itself inside its house again. By the time it was gone, Carl was gone too. He had climbed the stairs and been replaced by the unsightly visage of the mortuary doctor climbing down.

'Saved by the bell, hm?' the doctor said with that horrible twisted smile.

Gaten didn't answer him. He had a sudden urge to catch up with Carl, only he didn't know why. There was nothing more to say, and he knew he would only pain him further. Only the urge was there, clinging to him like a child, pushing him in the back. The doctor walked around the body and flung the sheet back over the head. He sat in his chair and took a sip of water.

'Verified, I presume?' he asked.

Gaten nodded. He placed one foot on the stairs, hoping to leave this place and never come back, but then there was another urge, an even stronger one that kept him rooted to the spot.

'Doctor, can I ask you a question?'

'Yes.'

'Why did you say the posts were interesting? The football posts, I mean.'

'Ah, well, you asked me if I could see anything on the body that suggests wrongful death. Actually, I can. Just one thing. His size.'

'His size?'

'This man is five foot ten. The crossbar of a football post is, what, ten feet? It must have been a tall effort to shimmy his way up there. Were there trees nearby?'

'Yes,' said Gaten. 'A whole forest.'

Doctor Stathum shrugged. 'That's why it's interesting.'

On the wall of the mortuary, the cuckoo clock ticked and its cogs clunked. It seemed as if the cuckoo hidden inside was still moving, making itself comfortable again. Gaten swallowed. Then he turned, left the building, and didn't look back.

2

The woman was small and toad-faced. Her hair was puffed up in a bush, held in place by a bright pink clip. She wore a fuzzy coat, zipped only halfway due to the size of her breasts, which hovered like two great orbs under a crimson shirt.

'I'm just saying,' she said hoarsely. 'Her pumpkins were laced with flies. I didn't want to have any unfair advantage, so I sprayed them with pesticide. I thought I was doing her a favour. I didn't think it would kick up such a fuss.'

Abigail stood with a cup of coffee in one hand and her notebook squeezed under her armpit. She'd been at the pumpkin pageant for over an hour and hadn't opened it once.

'Then,' the toad-faced woman continued, 'Mrs Taggort confronts me in front of the whole pageant. According to Jermaine, Sue had been walking her dog at the time and had taken photographs. Can you believe that? She papped me. I don't know what she expected. For the Cuckoo Correspondence to pay for the story? What would the headline be? *Local Woman Sprays Pumpkins*? That's hardly going to get papers flying off the shelves. So, anyway, she took her complaint to Mrs Taggort, and I was disqualified as soon as I showed up. Imagine that. I was disqualified for saving a neighbour from embarrassment. I complained, of course, but there isn't really an authority for that sort of thing. It's just Mrs Taggort.'

Abigail nodded tiredly. 'Did she win?'

'Hmm?'

'Sue, the neighbour whose pumpkins you sprayed. Did she win the pageant?'

'Oh, no, of course not. Her pumpkins were completely ruined. No fault of mine, of course. There were just so many flies.'

The toad-faced woman looked down at her shoes, and Abigail huffed, looking around the lawn for a friendly face. She couldn't find one. The pageant was full of forty to seventy year olds who lived on the outskirts of town, away from the youth and the drama and that little thing called real life. In a way, Abigail was disappointed that the pesticide incident hadn't happened a year later. At least then it would have given her something to write about. As it was, the most exciting thing that had happened so far was a little old lady tumbling over and knocking her head against a wheelbarrow. She hadn't had the courtesy to fall *into* the wheelbarrow, of course. No, that would have been too amusing. Or at least fairly amusing. She had tumbled onto her arse and then marvelled at how very big the pumpkin was, and how she couldn't quite believe she had missed it. Then that had just sparked up more conversation about pumpkins, and accolades to the gardener who was responsible for the one that tripped her.

If only she could have fallen into the wheelbarrow. Right in it. Headfirst. And then maybe the wheelbarrow could have taken off down the hill and toward the road. And a truck could have been tearing down the road at full throttle. And the little old lady could have been hit by the truck, and the truck could have tried to stop by sliding into a skid, but the road had dipped, and it had rolled, and it had been carrying oil so it exploded, and everybody was just so shocked. Then maybe Abigail could have had something to write in her notebook. Instead, she had nothing. Not a darn thing.

She was just thinking this when her phone started to ring.

3

When Gaten entered the station, Justin Hadero was sleeping in his office. He thought briefly about waking him, but he knew that his hangover from yesterday was still lingering. When the call about the autopsy had come in, he had said, 'Lord, save me', and flicked Gaten away accusingly. But in all truth, Gaten hadn't been planning on giving him more ear ache. Unlike Adrian Ramirez, the body of Arthur Conrad had been found hanging, so the case appeared to be far more open and shut. It wasn't until the doctor mentioned the forest that Gaten started seeing things differently.

The forest. There had been a whole forest, and yet Arthur had been found hanging from some football posts. Why? What would be the point in shimmying up the football posts when there was a whole forest to make things easier? Was it because he wanted to make a statement? But then, what suicidal person cared about making a statement? Gaten didn't know, but he couldn't get the thought out of his head. Questions lingered there like the body of Adrian Ramirez, tied by a tight string, and no matter how hard he tried to shake them off, they were only getting louder. They would fill Justin's ears soon enough, but for now, he let him sleep. God only knew how much he was going to need it.

While he waited, Gaten approached his desk and, for the first time that day, he sat down. With his right hand, he scratched at his scalp, and with his left, he caught the dandruff that floated through the air. He hadn't had a shower in days. Was it Wednesday? Or was it on the Thursday, before the first body was found? He tried to fill his mind wondering about *that* rather than thinking about the other thing. But to no avail. The bubbles dissipated in the swamp and he was swallowed back into the filthy water. Arthur's eyes were staring at him down there. And Adrian's too, peering at him over his left shoulder. Gaten shook his head and looked down at his table. There was a file waiting for him there with a sticky note that read 'FOR GATEN' placed on top. He picked it up and looked over at Gunther, who was standing by the coffee machine, waiting for it to brew.

'This new in this morning?' Gaten called over.

'How do I know?' Gunther shrugged. 'I'm not Cherisse.'

With a frown, Gaten looked back at the file and read the first few lines.

10/05

SUBJECT: Revolution Bar opening Oct.

INTERVIEWEE: Adrian Ramirez AKA Aurora Amaris, Age 19.

TIME: 12:00:PM

Gaten remembered the woman on Gold Lane, the pretty blonde-haired woman with the chip on her shoulder. This must have been the column she was talking about, still in its handwritten form. He turned it over in his hands, and spotted a note on the back.

Useless to me now but not useless to you

Please read

My number is 555 - 659 - 7079

He flipped the file back over and continued reading.

NOTE PERSON: Aurora wears a light pink dress. Tight. Two feathers on a pink hat. Black wig. Brown eyes. Olive tanned skin. Heels. Long sharp nails, speckled with little plastic diamonds. Skin is shaved. Eye shadow is dark, deep red. Choker. One eye a little lazy. Lipstick red. Fun. Bubbly. Drinks plume. (for type: personality is as bubbly as the plume in her left hand).

NOTE PLACE: Dark. Lighting being fixed. Pink. Bar is long and already drinks in place. Funny names for taps. Jazzy's J*zz. Gorgeous Girlz Cider. Frothy Frocks. Revelations Own. Last one not so funny. Owner looks anything but gay. Blue jeans. Grey short-sleeve top. Overweight. Bald with a stubbly head. Hairy arms. Looks like a construction worker. Entrance has balloons. Pink, grey, and blue.

TRANSCRIPT

AU: I have two minutes darling.

ME: That should be enough

(fluffle)

AU: I can't imagine working in daylight. In fact I can't imagine working.

ME: This isn't work for you?

AU: Look at me. Does it look like this is work? All the stuff outside of here, when I'm not paid by the hour, that's the real work.

ME: What do you mean?

AU: Oh I'm sure you don't want to get too deep too early darling. Let's keep this light.

ME: Do you mean the treatment of gay people in this town?

AU: Where are my manners? I've just realised you haven't got a drink. What's your tonic darling?

ME: Oh that's okay. I'm working.

> (Au leans closer)
>
> AU: So? I'm offered twenty drinks when I'm working and I take every one of them. They're my tips.
>
> ME: I just prefer to keep a clear head at work.
>
> AU: So do I. I really like to see my audience. They're always so beautiful. And looking at me like I'm a phoenix. And they applaud and throw flowers and everything is wonderful. Without those drinks I wouldn't see any of that. It would just be a few gay fatties with tank tops and their hands down their pants. Isn't that right Stanley?
>
> (calling over to the owner. He's knelt working on wiring. Butt-crack showing. He grunts.)
>
> (Au smirks. She sips the straw of her plume.)
>
> AU: Such a hottie.
>
> (fluffle)

Gaten ran a hand through his hair, wondering whether he should bother turning over the next page. Nothing about any of this was game-changing. And it was hard to read. What was "fluffle"? Was it the parts so un-interesting that Abigail couldn't be bothered to write them? If so, why wasn't this whole section marked out as fluffle? Gaten huffed and ventured a brief, un-enthusiastic look at page number two. He scanned it quickly, and then he saw something that made him stop and reconsider. One word. Reservoir. He kept reading.

> ME: So what do you think this new venue will bring to the community?
>
> AU: A safe space that isn't so fucking quiet. Sorry am I allowed to say fucking?

ME: It's okay I can edit it out later.

AU: I'll save you the trouble darling. I think it will bring a safe space that isn't so bleeping quiet. Seriously. Every safe space for our people in this town is bleeping quiet. And bleeping dull. And you need to walk a really long bleeping way to get there.

ME: How do you mean quiet?

AU: It sounds funny right? This being a gay party town. But the truth is the people in this town still can't get their head around us. We scare them. And because we scare them they scare us. You don't see me wearing this getup out and about town. The only ones that do are the ones who have shit for brains. Because that shit is dangerous. Sorry that bleep is dangerous. Oh and sorry I mean bleep for brains. But yes. Most of us get changed in the back rooms of these bars and there's a reason for that. It's not really a gay town. Not until I see a dozen peacocks and pantie bulges on the seafront in broad daylight will I ever think that it is. This is just a town and our safe spaces have to be off limits. Places no one will see us. Mine is the reservoir.

ME: The reservoir?

AU: Yeah, the one near Rambert's Creek. It's where all the old people go to avoid the parties. I find myself going there sometimes when the sun hasn't come up yet. I bring my stereo, light a doobie, and watch the sunrise.

ME: Sounds nice.

AU: Oh I'm sorry you disapprove?

ME: Disapprove of what?

AU: Me lighting a fat one.

ME: Not at all.

AU: You won't put it in though, even though half the people in this town are into that stuff. And ecstasy. And coke. And god knows what else. They all do it. Even the older folk. That's why their eyes burst out of their sockets when they see us. We're like a bad trip. Can't say I blame them though. Heck, I'm on all three.

(REDACT that obviously).

AU: Anyway. That reservoir. It's bleeping bliss. The perfect hiding place. But quiet. That's no good for people like me who have a thousand voices (natting?) away in their head. That's why I was so excited about this bar. It's not in the centre of town. It's on the outskirts. That might just sound like geography but really it's so important. You have to go looking for this place. You have to seek it out. And who are the ones that will seek it out?

(AU gives an over the top bow)

AU: Us darling. Us.

ME: This is the fifth gay bar to open in Cuckoo Cove. Why will this be more attractive in your eyes?

AU: Because of everything I just said. This town doesn't like us. They hate us. All the other gay bars. Adamson Avenue, Main Mall, Bazaar. They're all slap bang in the middle of it. For the "normal" people, they're like zits. Easy to pop. And they do it all the time. I've heard countless stories. None of those places are really safe from them. But us here we're like a boil on Cuckoo Cove's buttocks. There ain't no popping us.

(she lifts her glass and cheers)

ME: I didn't want to move onto this so quickly but it seems you've forced my hand. Do you think this town has a bad attitude toward its gay community?

AU: Oh don't be silly darling. Of course you did. Are you telling me you're following up this interview with Mr Stevens who opened a new delicatessen down on Forest Way? No. Because no one cares. If a bird makes a nest on your front porch, you walk by it no problem. If a bat makes a nest, you have something to say about it.

(fluffle)

AU: I'm not singling you out my darling. You're just doing your job. And I like you. You have pretty eyes. Excellent legs. But no one straight will ever walk in here without wanting to pick a fight. If only a tiny little kitten fight.

ME: I didn't mean to offend.

AU: No offence taken dear. We're strange and we know it. In fact I like it that way.

(fluffle)

ME: What can people expect from your show?

AU: Oh I don't know. Everything and nothing. I'll try to tingle your tickers and tickle your tits. I'll put my all into it every night because that's what us showgirls do.

ME: You're part of a line up of course. Could you ever imagine running a place like this yourself one day?

AU: Playing around with the lights with my ass hanging out like our dear Stanley? No thank you. Darling if this goes well I'm going to be performing on that stage forever. Why would I leave? All any of us want is somewhere to call home. Somewhere not so damn quiet. And I think this will be it. I don't need the reservoir anymore and I like that.

ME: When can we expect your first set?

AU: 14th October. 9PM to 12AM. I'm gonna stir up a storm alright. So if you're queer and feeling lonesome you can come dance as it breaks.

ME: For the record, seeing as this is a gay town I actually think Cuckoo Cove needs more places like this.

AU: Like I said my darling. This is no gay town. There are no gay towns in America.

Gaten stopped reading and picked up the phone.

4

Abigail answered and received a gruff voice on the other end.

'This is Gaten. Can I ask who I'm speaking to?'

'You called me, chick. I knew you wouldn't be able to resist.'

She walked over to a vacant seat beside a lemonade stand, trying hard to keep her balance as her heels sank into the mud. She had slipped on her brown heeled mules this morning because she thought the ground might be dirty, but she hadn't taken into account yesterday's downpour. When she had arrived and wobbled to the first pumpkin table, Mrs Harris had joked,

'Wearable dibbers! That's ingenious, lady. Can I buy a pair?'

The women around her had laughed, and Abigail had laughed too, even though she had no idea what it meant. Garden humour, she supposed.

'Yes,' she said when Gaten didn't reply. 'It's Abigail.'

'Okay,' Gaten muttered. 'Okay.'

There was silence for a few seconds. It seemed like Gaten was trying to work out why he had called in the first place, so Abigail helped him out.

'You read Adrian's column?'

'Yes, I did.'

'And do you still think he drowned accidentally?'

'I'm not sure.'

Abigail shook her head. From across the lawn, she could see the toad-faced woman speaking to Mrs Taggort. She had just placed an award ribbon on one of her pumpkins, but the conversation appeared to be heated. The toad-faced woman was flailing her arms around, and her face was as red as radishes.

'How can you not be sure after reading that?' asked Abigail.

'There are factors that you don't know. He was high at the time.'

'High on what?'

'Ecstasy, coke, marijuana.'

'He said he was on that when he met me, and he didn't seem close to drowning himself then.'

'Like I told you,' said Gaten, 'these people can put on a good show. Heck, that was his job.'

'So why are you calling me?'

Another pause on the line. Abigail heard the toad-faced woman shout,

'I try to help a neighbour and what do I get? Disqualification and then second place! It's a crime, I tell you! It's a conspiracy! You're in this together, you and that dog-loving bitch!'

Instinctively, Abigail reached for her notebook, but then she remembered that if this conversation went the right way, she wouldn't have to be writing anything pumpkin-related ever again.

'The reservoir,' she heard Gaten say.

'Yeah?'

'That's where he was found.'

'I know. I heard you boys closed the road up there. The seniors were furious.'

'If he never wanted to see it again, why would he go back?'

'You tell me, Mr Detective.'

Abigail kept the phone pressed firmly against her ear. She was trying to sound blasé, but in all truth, she was hanging on Gaten's every word. A vision of her handing in the story flashed before her eyes. This one story could be the one to send her on to bigger and better things, a city like New York or Chicago, where murders happened a dime a dozen.

'He knew it. He knew the reservoir.'

Abigail began patting her knee restlessly. 'Okay...'

'Outside of town. Cut off. Isolated. He never wanted to go there, but he did.'

'All on the money, so far. Do they give you awards in detective school?'

'He called it a hiding place. Maybe he really meant it. Maybe on the night he died, he was hiding from something.'

Abigail smirked. 'Something? Alright, Officer Dalbret, don't get creepy on me.'

'Someone. Same difference.'

The toad-faced woman pushed over her table and the people watching gasped. The ribboned pumpkin rolled to a stop in one of the beds, a great crack sliced up the middle. The two women stormed off in opposite directions.

'Abigail,' said Gaten. 'I want to ask you a question, and I want you to give me an honest answer. No stories. Forget about your job for a minute, I'm just talking to you human to human. Do you think he could do it? Do you think there's any possibility the man could lose it and kill himself?'

Abigail thought for a moment. She thought back to her interview with Adrian, his face. She hadn't liked that face. He had been scanning her, assimilating her, eating her up like a foul-tasting cookie. He wanted to know what she really thought of him. He may have been high, but he had also been grounded, more grounded than most people Abigail had met. His liquor went down the right hole, and that was the truth.

Abigail spoke firmly, 'He could have been wearing a noose and I'd say he had a future.'

There was a crackle on the line, like Gaten had just taken a deep breath, and Abigail's eyes narrowed at nothing.

'So is there a case, Officer Dalbret?'

'There's been a case ever since I found that body,' Gaten replied.

Then he hung up, the dead tone lingering. Abigail slipped her phone into her pocket, gave herself a self-congratulatory fist pump, then stood up and strutted back to her car. Her heels didn't dig into the dirt this time. This time it felt like she was walking on air.

5

Mrs Taggort thought: *ungrateful, pumpkin-killing bitch.*

When she had stuck the ribbon on Nancy Gartner's

pumpkin, she had expected a muted 'thank you', a disappointed tut, or maybe even the finger when she had walked the other way. What she hadn't expected was the barrage of abuse that was currently being thrown at her. Nancy was a passionate woman, the whole village knew that. But when it came to vegetables, that passion reached a completely different level. She stood hurling insults in Mrs Taggort's direction, her anger so fierce that some of it was coming out as saliva. Mrs Taggort had tried to calm the situation down, to tell Nancy that really her pumpkin was very good, but all attempts had been obliterated in a whirlwind of foul-mouthed, venomous, and wildly inaccurate accusations. According to Nancy, this whole thing was a conspiracy that had begun over a year ago, when Mrs Taggort and Sue Verity had concocted a plan to eliminate her from the pageant. It wasn't remotely true, of course, but because the fury had sapped Nancy of all logical reason, there was nothing for Mrs Taggort to do except stand still, keep straight, and take all the hits that came her way.

Only that was becoming increasingly difficult, because the sound had come back again. It had started in the morning, just as Mrs Taggort was putting her finishing touches on the pumpkin tables. The sound was everywhere and nowhere – over the hill, yet right up close to her, crying into her face and yet muffled by the clouds. After a few seconds, she had run inside to fetch her husband. After pulling him out onto the lawn, she had told him to stand in the same spot and stay quiet for a moment. Bob had stood for several minutes, his eyebrows raised in curiosity. The noise, however, had disappeared. Rather than humour her further, Bob had given up and patted her on the head. He had said something about 'stress', and left Mrs Taggort to continue with the preparations. But now, in the middle of Nancy's tirade, the sound had resurfaced once again.

Not a bird, but a baby. Surely a baby. It sounded like crying. Like a baby in need of milk, or whose diaper had filled to dripping point. It swirled about the air and filled Mrs Taggort's head, making her heart race and the hairs on her neck stand on end. She glanced left, then right, and then she pressed her temple and felt herself shakily say,

'The baby. There's a baby.'

She looked around at the crowd – who had gathered to watch Nancy's tirade – and found herself searching for a push chair. She looked at Jasmine, a young woman, pregnant, whose thin cotton shirt was swelled into an egg after eight months of growth. Mrs Taggort looked at that bump and found herself thinking, *could it be?* But she shook away the notion almost as soon as it had come and continued her search to the right. It was there that she saw a woman beside the lemonade stand, a phone to her ear, staring intently forward. Could she hear it too? Mrs Taggort wondered whether she could, but then the woman's mouth started moving, and she stared down at her heels, so again, the notion had to be dismissed. Hopelessly, Mrs Taggort turned back to Nancy and said again,

'Someone has a baby. I'm sorry. There's a baby crying and someone needs to know about it.'

'Oh, so you're calling me a baby now?' Nancy laughed bitterly. 'Well, that's rich. I'm putting forward genuine complaints about how things are being handled, and you're calling me a cry-baby?'

The next few words that came out of Nancy's mouth, Mrs Taggort didn't hear, but she saw her tip over the pumpkin table and storm off toward the road. The next thing Mrs Taggort knew, there were hands on her shoulders and comforting whispers in her ear. It seemed like people were trying to console her, but all she could think about was that sound. The crying. That's what it was. Definitely now. A real baby was somewhere in her garden. In front of her, Mrs Taggort saw Bob rushing toward her. He brought her inside the house and draped a blanket around her shoulders. Then he made her coffee and looked concerned as Mrs Taggort said over and over,

'Baby. Baby. There's a baby.'

6

Later that night, Bob tried to convince her that the pageant had been a wonderful success. Jermaine had continued the awards giving, and Julio had earned first prize, just as she had intended. Mrs Taggort heard what he was saying, but she didn't listen. When Bob saw how pale she was, he walked her up to bed and took a second blanket from the shelf to lay on top of her. He tucked her in and then walked downstairs, and Mrs Taggort heard noises in the kitchen, like banging and the microwave going. She lay staring at the ceiling until Bob came back and closed the door. He had Mr Taggort under one arm and a hot water bottle in the other. He placed them on either side of her and then kissed her forehead. He said something about going back downstairs to watch the news, and that he would be back as soon as the credits rolled. Once again, however, Mrs Taggort didn't really listen. She simply stared vacantly, and the concern on Bob's face seemed to grow even deeper, until even his wrinkles became wrinkled. He turned the light off when he left the room and said something about loving her, and Mrs Taggort wondered briefly whether she would still be awake when he got back. But then her eyes closed and a darkness took her.

7

The darkness here is preferred. It wraps around the body like a blanket and keeps things warm. Something here uses the darkness like a lantern. It scours the plains in a great search. When it finds what it is looking for, it thanks the darkness cordially, and prays that its light and warmth never goes out. Something here is old and crinkled. But the darkness keeps it alive, and gives it stories, and it finds them. It finds them, and it tastes them, and it licks them, and it sucks them, and either it swallows or it spits. Like now. Right now. The story. The great story. It tastes and fondles with its tongue and it wonders: is it good enough?

8

Are you good enough?

Mrs Taggort awoke in the bathroom, the dazzling light momentarily blinding her. She was standing barefoot on the bath mat and it was wet. Water was speckling her shins because the bath was going. The tub was around three-quarters full and it was steaming. The misty, wet smoke trailed into Mrs Taggort's nostrils and she breathed it in, cleansing her system. The whole place was like her very own steam room, but it hadn't clouded everything just yet. On the walls, there were still paintings. A lake with two ducks wallowing on the water's surface. A ceramic of a neat, black cat, sitting straight. A photograph of a dolphin.

Mrs Taggort stood in the centre of the room and listened as the taps roared. She sighed and rubbed at her temples.

Are you good enough?

The voice came again, and Mrs Taggort looked toward the doorway. It was firmly shut. She realised at that moment that her head was still pounding. Something was pulling at the strings of her scalp, threatening to cave it all in. She grabbed her hair and squeezed. Then she turned to the basin and poured some cold water onto her face. She looked into the mirror, and what she saw made her gasp. In the mirror, Mrs Taggort was staring back at her, but she was far younger. Forty-four years younger, if she had to place it. Mrs Taggort was a bright, young, nineteen year old girl. Her skin was smooth and her hair was thick. Her eyes blazed with light, and her breasts were sitting as pert and proper as the cat in the ceramic. She touched delicately at her face, and then her neck, trailing down toward her breast, and she loved the feeling of the journey. It was without crease, without crinkle, and without any sort of bump in the road. Her flesh sparkled in the bathroom light and shone in the dizzying steam, and she spent several seconds just staring at it. After a while, she was interrupted by the voice again. It asked,

Are you good enough?

And Mrs Taggort replied, *Yes, by Lord, I do believe I am.*

The water from the bathtub started splashing her, and she turned to find the bath completely full. A strong impulse caught her then. An urge to go and bathe in it. She realised that she would like nothing more than to wash this body in the hottest water imaginable, spread it over her waist, her breasts, her buttocks, like a cream, and cleanse any trace of that sixty-three year old woman who was still living in her head, tarnishing it with age and wisdom. She bent over to turn off the tap, but as she did so, her belly caught on the sharp rim of the tub and she yelped. Her gorgeous, silvery-smooth hand shot out to steady herself, and it was then that she realised something was wrong. Her body in the mirror had been glowing, but her lower half, which the mirror could not see, was hideously swollen. Her belly button protruded like a clump of cotton, and each side of her tummy was scarred with white-pink lines.

Are you good enough?

Mrs Taggort started to sweat. She touched at her stomach and hated it. She turned to the sink and saw a cloud of steam disperse to reveal a bottle of clear gin. She stared at the bottle and noticed it was half full. Then the voice came again.

Are you good enough?

And Mrs Taggort looked down at her belly and thought, *No, I'm not good enough. I have this thing inside of me that ruins my features, ruins my innocence, and will ruin my life. What would Donovan Lane say?*

She wavered and felt the name rest between her eyes. Donovan Lane. She hadn't thought of that name for many years now. It was a spectre of her past in the shape of a boy, young and good looking, with greased black hair and a careful, cute birth mark that roared invitingly atop his Adam's apple. He was her lover and her friend. A social boy with contacts across the town, and a boy who was evidently going to do very well for himself, because he studied law and Latin, and played football on weekends when the wind wasn't too cold. What would he think? That boy was going to soar so far, and he was meant to do it with Mrs Taggort in his arms, joining him for the flight. What would everyone else think? Those thousands of eyes that were scattered across town would see this young girl, so beautiful and young and optimistic, laden with child. Un-good and unclean. Another whore from the backstreets who had dragged poor Donovan Lane down along with her. What would they think, and what would they say, and would she ever come good in those eyes again?

Are you good enough?

No, Mrs Taggort thought. *Not right now. But I can be. If you just give me a few seconds.*

With a surge of adrenaline, she lunged for the basin and seized the liquor bottle. Then she climbed into the bath and winced. The water was hot and stinging. Not quite the nice, nourishing soak that she had envisioned, more a fiery pool of black froth that engulfed and dissolved her like sugar in a straight coffee. Despite the pain, she stayed put and unscrewed the gin's cap. She lifted the bottle to her lips and began drinking, and with every gulp came the words that had been her only company in this god forsaken room:

Are you good enough?
Closer.
Are you good enough?
Closer.
Are you good enough?
Now.

9

Mrs Taggort opened her eyes and found herself in bed. Mr Taggort was curled up beside her, and Bob was curled up beside him. The room was dark, but there was a fraction of light in the corner, and she used that light to locate the wetness that was irritating her belly. She lifted the sheets and saw her hot water bottle lying atop her crotch, the cap loose and the bottle half empty. She cussed at Bob's laziness. The water had soaked her shirt and when she lifted it, she saw that the water had left hot, red stains around her belly button. She climbed out of bed and walked sleepily toward the bathroom. The light was on and, again, she cussed at Bob. She approached the sink and began pouring cold water into the bowl. When she looked into the mirror, she saw Mrs Taggort looking back at her. She wondered for a moment why she thought that was strange. She touched briefly at her face, like she had been expecting someone else to be standing there.

After a few seconds, the water had reached the rim of the bowl, and so she turned the tap and put a towel in it. She soaked up as much of the water as she could, and then she rung it out and applied it to her stomach. She stood there for several minutes, repeating the motion until the pain had subsided. Then she pulled out the plug, hung the towel on the bathtub, and began making her way back to the bedroom.

Kerflunk.

The sound occurred when Mrs Taggort put her hand on the doorknob. She froze for a few seconds, then turned slowly. The room was empty. The towel dripped and the water was still falling down the drain of the basin, but other than that, there was nothing that could have made that noise. And yet she had heard it. A strange twisting sound, like metal or plastic, being rung in just the same way she had rung that towel. She stood still for a few moments, feeling the thick pulse of blood cascading quickly around her skull. She put her fingertips on the doorknob, and again, the sound came back.

Kerflunkshh.

This time it was accompanied by water. A twisting, and then a sloshing, unlike any noise Mrs Taggort had heard before. She breathed quietly, then tread carefully toward the bath. She looked inside and saw nothing but gleaming white enamel and a few pubic hairs near the drain. With a pale, bony hand, she turned the drain stopper and pulled at it. A clump of thin grey hair came up along with it, covered in a thick, gooey slime and some congealed fluff. She creased her nose at the smell of rotten eggs and salty water, and she placed it back down and screwed the stopper tight. She made a mental note that Bob would have to clean the entire bathroom the next morning, and then she stepped back over to the door.

Kerflunkssshhhh.

The noise came again, thick and fast. Twist, gulp, slosh, twist. But Mrs Taggort didn't turn this time. She decided that the drains must have been clogged, and that was all the more reason for Bob to get to work. She opened the door, turned off the light, and climbed back into bed alongside Mr Taggort.

In the darkness, she lay there and thought back on the day that had just passed. The pumpkin pageant, the screaming Nancy, the crying baby, and then a voice. A dark voice. It climbed into the back of her head as if through a secret passageway.

Are you good enough?

And Mrs Taggort sat up. In an instant, she remembered everything. Her dream, the way she had looked in the mirror, the gin, the bath tub, the steam, curling its way into her nostrils and into her mouth. She remembered her belly and the way it had curved and bloated, and stung when she had slipped herself down into hot water. Then, as she was remembering, there was another noise. The one that she recognised all too well now. A baby crying. But closer. It swirled around the room, and this time, Mrs Taggort could clearly make out the source. It was coming from her bathroom.

Are you good enough?

The voice entwined itself with the baby's cries, and Mrs Taggort looked fretfully at the closed bathroom door. She clasped at her stomach.

Are you good enough?

And Mrs Taggort thought, *Please, no, I'm not good. I'm sorry. I sinned and I'm not proud of it.*

The voice didn't seem to like this answer, so it said again, *Are you good enough?*

And Mrs Taggort thought back, *I was good. I was young, and I was beautiful, and I had the whole world to play inside of. It was my world, and I was good, and I'm so sorry for what happened.*

The baby's cries grew stronger, and Mrs Taggort squeezed her eyes shut.

'I'm sorry!' she moaned helplessly.

The baby roared in reply, screaming at the top of its lungs. Not in the way a baby usually screamed, but like an adult, bellowing at the world and unleashing a wealth of anger that had rested inside it for years. Mrs Taggort leapt out of bed.

Are you good enough?

She walked toward the bathroom.

Are you good enough?

She opened the door and switched on the light.

Are you good enough?

The twisting, slushing, gulping sound was coming from the toilet, and she walked fearfully toward it.

'I'm sorry,' she whispered through her tears. 'I'm sorry. I'm sorry.'

She reached out a hand and opened the lid, and inside the toilet was her worst nightmare. A bloodied baby, squeezed inside the bowl, sucked halfway down the chute, with only its face, a leg, and an arm left to go. It glared at her fiercely and kept crying, and crying, and crying, until Mrs Taggort screamed and slammed the lid shut.

Then the voice said, *You are not good enough.*

And Mrs Taggort felt her head spin in a cyclone and something even hotter than the hottest water gush behind her eyes.

10

Bob awoke at exactly seven o'clock in the morning. The light of the sun was beginning to leak from behind the blinds, and the bedroom was covered in a comforting, orange glaze. He yawned, stretched, then turned to pull Mrs Taggort into a warm embrace. He reached for an empty space, and then he blinked confusedly. On the bed was the hot water bottle, the cap unscrewed, with a dark, damp patch soaked into the space where Mrs Taggort was supposed to be lying. He sat up and looked over toward the bathroom door, which was open.

'Honey?' he called out, but there was no response.

Bob turned and placed his feet on the floor. A soft, strange, squelch greeted him. He glanced down and saw that he had stepped on a worm. He looked around and spotted three others, two of them sliding awkwardly across the carpet, and the third wriggling on the precipice of the bathroom. Bob stood and walked toward the open door

'Pumpkin?' he called out again.

But again, he got no response. He peered around the door. What he saw aged him and put him two weeks away from a fatal heart attack. Mrs Taggort was knelt by the toilet, her body slumped, her arms dangling, and her head plunged inside the bowl. Mr Taggort was sitting beside her, nibbling the worms that were escaping from her dressing gown pocket.

He was purring happily.

CHAPTER TEN

PAIN

1

Kenny Townsend wasn't in the mood for duck.

At eight years old, he'd had the biggest disappointment of his life when his father had taken him on a shooting trip to Lake Tahoot, just east of Corebank, near Cuckoo Cove. They had spent the day in the rain, searching for ducks that had been released into the park by a local hunting reserve that spring. When the dark day moulded into a darker afternoon and the sun began to set behind the clouds, they still hadn't shot anything, and Kenny's father had gotten mad. After a furious rant to the reserve managers, he ordered them to trawl in a dozen ducks from the nearby farm, and Kenny had the pick of the bunch. He chose the plumpest one, much to the farmers annoyance, and they took it home to smoke on the barbecue – which again, they did in the rain. Ever since Kenny had become obsessed with fantasy board games that were threatening his masculinity, his father had been adamant that they should spend more time together. He'd even bought him his own rifle, which Kenny could hardly lift. But by the end of the day, Kenny had not only failed to shoot his first duck, he had been rushed to the hospital due to a fragment of bone getting wedged in his gums. All that waiting, all that anticipation, all that suffering in the bitter rain, only for a duck to posthumously retaliate with a bone to the mouth. Kenny's manhood had certainly been questioned after that. Especially since he had to take five days off school for recovery, which he'd spent in his room playing board games.

He was just finishing another game when he was called down for dinner. His hero, Salvar the Great, was about to enter the Kingdom of Bats, ruled by the nefarious Bat Queen, Transylvicor. She had put the town at peril by morphing them into Night Animals, which were basically vampires, only Kenny didn't like to use that name. He'd heard about the concept of copyright, and if his story ever made it into the comic books, he didn't want to have a costly lawsuit on his hands.

'That's twice I've had to call you, Kenny!' he heard Mandy shout from downstairs.

Mandy was Kenny's dad's girlfriend, and despite movies portraying stepmothers as vicious witches, she was actually pretty nice. While he had his back up initially, nowadays, he wouldn't even be mad if she *did* become his stepmother. He couldn't remember his real one much, and she did put a little light on whenever she was around. A light that his dad never failed to switch off when she left.

'Stop ignoring me, Ken. If you don't hurry up, your duck will get cold!'

'It's a duck,' Kenny grumbled under his breath. 'It's used to being cold.'

He bent the page of his character journal and threw it on his desk. It landed next to two more, both finished, and filled with incredible stories and adventures that spanned the length of Gonagreen, which was the world Kenny had created three years ago. He had first come into contact with D&D in an afterschool activity class, which was run by Mr Gleek – otherwise known as Mr Geek. While he enjoyed the hour and thirty minutes coming up with stories and creating campaigns, it soon became clear that D&D was for the kids at the bottom of the school's social pile. Kenny hadn't been too concerned about that – he was hardly that popular to begin with – but he *was* concerned about what Dora thought of him. Instead of risking it all in a socially-shunned D&D group, he had to buy a set from the local Try N Buy, and he came up with all of his adventures by himself as a solo player. He didn't mind that too much, though. He had always been told that his imagination was too big. Alone, his imagination could soar.

'Cold, Kenny!' Mandy shouted again.

Treading past his makeshift world, Kenny opened the door and saw her staring at him on the other side. She was quite a pretty woman. Her hair and skin were dark, her stomach was slim, and her eyes had a sleek, leafy shine. Kenny could have fit her right inside Gonagreen. As a damsel he would eventually save, of course.

'Couldn't you hear me?' she asked, frowning. 'I said your duck is getting cold.'

'I don't even like duck.'

'You'll like this one. It's a three pound mallard your father shot with his new Beretta.'

'Oh, wow. Now I'm really excited.'

Downstairs, Kenny saw that his dad had placed his football helmet ceremoniously between his knife and his fork. He was already sitting at the end of the table, his sleeves rolled up to the elbows and his chin twitching hungrily over his plate. Behind him, a load of hunting paraphernalia and fishing photographs were hanging on the wall, demonstrating to anyone who took dinner with them just how much of a man he'd been to procure it.

'Kenny, how many times do I have to ask you not to leave your football gear laying around?'

Kenny sat at the table miserably. His dad looked mad, but that wasn't a scary thing, because Kenny's dad always looked mad. He was the exact opposite of Mandy, who always looked like she had just cleaned her teeth with popping candy. Her smile was wide and taut, like Kenny's dad had hooked her from both sides and had reeled her into his life with a couple of four-inch long shanks, and her eyes were always bubbling with enthusiasm. They didn't really seem to belong together, and Kenny sometimes got the feeling that Mandy was just an asset. Like his prized hunting plaques, or the big mouth billy bass that was hung rigidly above the mantlepiece, she was something to look at, and play with, and show off to friends whenever they came around. Only, unlike the big mouth billy bass, Mandy didn't recite any limericks.

She marched into the kitchen now and radiated the same contradictory energy. 'C'mon, Rupe, let him be. You're happy he's playing football, remember?'

'If that is what he's doing.'

'No,' said Kenny, 'you're right. I just enjoy the smell of the helmet.'

Mandy speckled some salt over her dish. 'Probably smells better than your room. What is it with boys and bad smelling rooms? Seriously, it's like farts and crab sticks.'

His dad glared at Kenny mid-chew. 'Well, that's gonna happen if you spend all your waking and sleeping hours shacked up in there.'

'Football practice is two hours,' replied Kenny bitterly. He flicked at the potatoes on his plate and began turning them into mush with his fork.

To tell the truth, that was a lie. Football practice was exactly one hour, but he tended to spend an extra one getting his kicks in and working his quad muscles. He needed to if he was going to rule the dance floor in just two months time, with Dora Lane spinning gracefully at his side. He thought about her again now. That face. Those teeth. That smile. He remembered that time she had sat beside him to copy his homework, and that time he had to hold her hand for a few seconds in the school play. He remembered how she had brushed up and down against his bony left arm when she had told him about the Indian post, and the feeling that had given him in his groin. Dora had been impressed when he'd told her about the body. Her sumptuous brown eyes had grown wide, and her palm had rested breathlessly on her chest.

'A body? You?'

'Yes,' Kenny had replied. 'Me. I found it. And I was brave too. It didn't bug me one bit.'

But after a few minutes, everything had gone back to normal. Things moved fast in the school corridors, and any news, even big news, swept through the halls as easily as a paper aeroplane flew across a classroom. Dora's eyes had watched him fly, and soar, and then crumple back into ordinary paper. And then her eyes had latched straight back onto the eyes of Harland Thomas.

Kenny mashed the potatoes harder with his fork, rueing the very name of him. Harland Thomas. The enemy. The obstacle he would have to face if he wanted to ride with the pretty girl into the sunset. He would do it, alright. He would mash him into the ground as easily as he could mash these potatoes. All he needed to do was work, and build, and maybe find another few hundred bodies before that dance floor was hit by the spotlight.

'You okay, Ken?' Mandy snapped him out of his thoughts.

'Huh? Oh, yeah. I'm fine.'

'You look tired. I hope you're not up all night playing that game. Or is it the body? If you still wanna talk about it —'

'There's nothing to talk about. I wasn't scared.'

'It's okay to be scared —'

'But I wasn't.'

Kenny hated anyone talking to him about the body who wasn't Dora. It was like they expected him to burst into tears any minute, like he hadn't gone to ask for some milkshake at the age of six only to find his mother lying dead in her bed. Granted, she hadn't been hanging from her neck below some football posts, but that was beside the point. He was a grown up kid, and he knew how the world worked. There was the living part, and there was the dead part. He'd pulled that curtain back a good five years ago, and once it was pulled back, there was no forgetting how things looked backstage. And yet everyone was so damn worried about him. At least, everyone but his father.

'Eat your game,' he mumbled plainly.

Kenny stabbed his fork into the duck and began scouring for bones.

2

Once the duck was eaten and a selection of bones rested threateningly on the side of his plate, Kenny was told to get down and help Mandy dry the dishes. He did so with the sound of Madness blaring out of the kitchen radio. Mandy always liked Suggs' voice as the soundtrack for washing up. When it came to hoovering, it was Freddie Mercury, the mopping up was Michael Jackson, and the ironing was half the time Cher, half the time Nickelback. She moved her buttocks playfully to "The Return of the Los Palmas 7", and when the song and dishes were finished, Kenny took his cue to return to his bedroom. His dad, however, had different ideas.

'Returning to bizarro world, are we?' He stood behind Kenny, two trash bags sagging from clenched fists. 'Take these. And don't leave the cans open this time. If you do, you can clean up what the racoons leave behind.'

Kenny took the bags and scowled his way over to the front porch. It was bright out. The moth lamp that was hanging from the roof was working its magic, with around seven moths clinging to the bulb. Legs burning, but clinging. Kenny half-thought that could be a clever analogy for something. Perhaps the way he was doomed by nature to cling onto this misshapen house until it burned him up. Or perhaps the way he clung to the light of Dora's eyes until he started to sting and her heart undoubtedly tore his into flames. Something like that. But Kenny was tired, and his imagination had to be saved for Gonagreen, so instead he simply gawped at the light for a few seconds and then headed across the yard.

The trash can was a difficult thing. Opening it was easy, but closing it required crawling into a nook to push the lid's hinge down. Standing on tiptoes, Kenny clasped the edge of the lid and pushed. It fell open and slammed against the fence behind, and Kenny felt a shot of pain rush through his fingers.

'Shit!'

He checked for blood, but there was none. His fingers were clean and white, with only a smudge of guacamole that had spilled over the bags from the night before. He hummed bemusedly, then he prepared to heave the first of the bags into the can. Before he could, however, another rush of pain shot through his fingers. This time it went all the way up, travelling through his arm before culminating in a weird bulge in his shoulder. Kenny jumped away from the can and dropped the bags onto the grass.

'Ow!'

Again, there was no blood. Nothing to show for what felt like a hot knife that had plunged into his skin. He rubbed himself shakily. Then the pain came again. This time it started in his shoulder, then waltzed like a floating orb over his chest and in around his armpit. For a moment, Kenny wondered whether he was having a heart attack. He'd paid attention in Biology class and he knew that one of the symptoms was a shooting pain in either the left or right arm. This felt different, though. This felt like the pain wasn't sure where it wanted to go, like a mouse desperately trying to navigate through some dark passageway. It scurried from one end of his body to the other, then it went down to his groin, stayed there for a bit, sniffed, listened, waited, and then travelled all the way back up to the ridge of his nose. After a while, the pain stopped feeling like a knife and instead grew a little softer, until it didn't really feel like pain at all, but more a vague and distant thought:

Pain.

The world around Kenny grew quiet. The soft glimmer of the sunset gave its last dance, and the echo of dying light turned into a silent, blue dark. Kenny scratched at his temple. He stood and listened as crickets chirped and tree animals began climbing into the branches. He breathed. Then he scratched again, and in those few seconds, he lingered on the precipice of two lives. One, where he would forget what had just happened and go back to his familiar daily routine. Or two, where the thought would come again, and what followed would be a dizzying haze of something horribly and terrifyingly new.

Pain.

The thought came again, but it wasn't Kenny thinking it. The voice was unlike any he had heard (or thought) before, and it arrived in a part of his brain that felt empty and full of cobwebs. Like the very back, near where the spine turned into scalp.

Pain, pain, pain.

The thought came in threes. There was no pain that accompanied it anymore. No hot knife sticking into his body. Just the thought, and the fear beginning to creep into Kenny's soul.

Pain, pain, pain.

The world around Kenny grew darker, and all of a sudden he felt very alone, even though he knew he wasn't. Because the thought was not just a thought, it was a calling.

A thread between Kenny and something else. Something that he knew was resting somewhere in the nook beside the trash can.

Pain, pain, pain.

Before he could help himself, Kenny took a step forward and crouched down. His shadow spread over the alley, so he shifted to let just a slither of the moth light through.

Pain, pain, pain.

Kenny blinked and spotted something move in the corner. It was small. Just a lump. Budging only slightly every few seconds.

Pain, pain, pain.

It danced with the thought. A shadow morphing into different shapes every time the word clanged in Kenny's head. He squinted. Then, with his heart beating hard, Kenny leant into the nook and reached for it.

Pain, pain, pain.

When Kenny's hand curled over the shape, he knew what it formed almost immediately. He had never touched a wild bird before, but when he was taken to the zoo at five years old, he'd been asked by his mother to stroke an owl that had been clamped to a tall man's glove. He had done so begrudgingly, and the feeling of those feathers felt identical to the feeling in his hand right now. He pulled the bird out of the gap and into the fuller light, and he saw that it was a cuckoo. Its left wing was bent beneath its stomach, and its little face was staring at Kenny with its mouth open, as if it was feigning shock. Kenny stared at it for a few seconds and there was silence in his head. He wavered, feeling a little sick.

Then he realised he was on that precipice again, where his life could go one of two ways. One, back to normal.

This was strange, but not unsolvable. Perhaps he was tired. Perhaps he spent too much time in Gonagreen like his dad said, and perhaps tomorrow all would be normal again. Or two, into the unknown. Where the cuckoo in his hand would confirm what he thought, and everything in Kenny's life would change far more than he ever could have imagined.

With a slight, shallow breath, Kenny pressed his thumb onto the bird's wing and watched as it squirmed in his grasp.

Pain, pain, pain.

The thought came again, and Kenny said goodbye to his old life and hello to his new one.

3

The tears rested on Sara's lashes, twinkling gently in the afternoon sun. The beach was beautiful and quiet, and Sara was sitting alone, crying softly. Her skirt was wet, and she could already feel a rash beginning to form on her butt cheeks, but she didn't care. She didn't care about anything anymore. The sun was shining, but the lights had gone out. Now the only ones that remained were the ones at the end of that pier, and even they weren't glowing yet.

Sara felt more alone now than she had ever felt in her life. Luna had been her best friend in Cuckoo Cove for as long as she could remember, and the fact that she was gone felt impossible to contemplate. Sara had thought that coming to the beach and giving herself a horizon to stare into could make it all fit into place. Like she could mourn and cry, but understand what had happened and make a little sense out of it. But there was no sense to be found, because Luna could not be dead. Not that woman. Full of life, and soul, and vigour, and hot, splendid jazz. How could that person be cold now? How could the music have disappeared from behind her eyes and faded to dust and salt like the wind between these pebbles? Sara couldn't fathom it, and the more she tried to, the more she realised what a mistake it was to come to the beach. To surround herself with a world as beautiful as Luna herself confirmed the very thing she was crying about. How could that setting sun come back the next day when her friend couldn't do the same thing? Where was the fairness? Where was the sense? Where was the natural order of things that all of them had grown so accustomed to? Clearly it was all just another joke. Another lie. Beauty wasn't something any human could understand or appreciate. Beauty came in foreverness. Dependability. The sun would always come back. That's what made it so beautiful. But people like Luna would burn and extinguish, and so what was the point of her? What was the point of anything she had done, or said, or thought? For Sara, Luna had been everything. But really, she had been nothing. Like comparing a firework to the brightest of stars, she had always been doomed to sparkle, then fade, and become instead just a spiralling fallout, destined to get wet in the grass.

And so Sara sat there, and she felt the rash grow on her buttocks, and she cried. One hour. Two hours. Three. Sara stayed in the same spot, thinking the same thing over and over again, until the stones began to shift behind her, and she was joined by her brother who nestled awkwardly at her side.

Gaten was dressed in a black zipper jacket, half undone, and his tie was lying loose and limp on a crinkled shirt.

He sat silently for a few seconds, and Sara wiped her eyes with her sleeve. She removed a cigarette from her bra and dropped one onto her tongue, then she offered the box to Gaten. He declined.

'Sorry I'm late,' he said after a few seconds.

Sara shook her head. 'Don't mention it. You're busy.'

'Yeah but still, I didn't want to —'

'Is it really her?' Sara interrupted him.

Gaten hesitated for a second. Sara knew that he was considering whether to go along with Sara's pronouns or stick to his own rigid religion.

'Yes,' he said finally. 'It is her. Sorry, I should have called you first. It's been very busy at the station.'

'What are you lot going to do about it?'

Gaten shuffled. He took a few stones from the ground and dropped them into his lap. 'Chief Hadero is sure it's suicide.'

Sara laughed bitterly. 'Oh, sure. If the straight, white male who never even knew Luna thinks it's a suicide, then I guess we can all sleep easy.'

'Him being straight and white has nothing to do with it. You gotta admit —'

'What? What do I have to admit? That Luna was trans and so she must have been depressed enough to tie a noose around her neck?'

'There's no evidence that suggests foul play. In fact, we just had a call come in from a witness who reported seeing her acting funny outside Corker's Park shortly before her death.'

'Who was the witness?'

Gaten repositioned himself. 'He's a rough sleeper. Been living in the park for a year or so.'

Sara threw up her hands. 'A straight white male and a whacked out hobo. Oh, well, case closed then.'

'Now who's judging?'

'What do *you* think?' Sara asked Gaten the question directly, looking at him for the first time since he had sat down.

He swallowed. 'I'll always look out for you, Theo. You know that.'

Sara kept staring at him. His face. Downcast and guilt-ridden. *Yeah*, she thought. *Look out for me like you looked out for me in that puddle.* She wondered if Gaten was thinking the same thing at that moment. She wondered whether he even remembered that puddle, or whether that was just a memory he had glossed over in the pursuit of his own, comfortable and ordinary life.

'That's not what I asked,' said Sara.

Gaten began chucking the stones from his lap and onto his boot. 'You didn't give me time to finish,' he replied. 'You gotta admit that you thought it was suicide. When I first told you about the case of Adrian Ramirez, the first thing you said was that he killed himself. If you remember, this conversation was flipped the other way around.'

'I didn't know Adrian.'

'No, you didn't. And we don't know Luna, either.'

'But I do. I know Luna. I *knew* Luna. She wouldn't have done this to herself. She just wouldn't have done.'

Gaten sighed, throwing the last of his stones onto his boot before gathering up some more and placing them onto his lap. He was like a child. If there was sand, he would have brought a bucket and spade.

'Then I'm in trouble,' he said quietly.

'What are you talking about?' asked Sara.

'If you really wanna know, I don't think Adrian killed himself. A woman interviewed him not a few days before his death. By all accounts, he seemed fine. That wouldn't be enough to go on, of course, but then there's the question of his wig.'

'Wig?'

'It turned up at Gordon Hill, in one of the water tanks. He threw it in there himself. Running from something.'

'Something?'

'Someone. You know what I mean. The point is, I expect your friend Luna was the same case. You spoke to her before she died, I guess?'

'Not a few hours before. Yeah, she was totally normal. Better than me, in fact.'

Not too far from them, a couple of teenagers ran from the road and onto the shore. They were trim young men, muscular, wearing bright salmon swim shorts with long, shoulder length hair. They ran barefoot into the ocean, screaming happily as they emerged.

'The other thing you said to me,' Sara continued, 'was that I needed to watch out.'

'Yes,' said Gaten solemnly. 'I remember.'

'So do I? Is there someone killing gay people in Cuckoo Cove?'

Gaten threw another pebble. 'Yes. Yes, I think so.'

Sara took that in for a minute, then she turned back to the boys. They were fast swimmers, and had already reached the halfway point along the seaside pier.

'I'd like to meet him,' said Sara. 'Whoever did this to Luna, I'd like to deal with him myself.'

'I wouldn't recommend that. Besides, right now there is no him. Not until I can convince the chief.'

'Why'd you need to convince him?'

'Because he's the chief of police, Theo. He gives the orders.'

'I've met that man. I met him two nights back. You'll never convince him. He hates us. I don't think he'd care if a thousand of us dropped dead.'

'He's a member of the police department. He does his job, no matter who it is.'

'Do you really believe that?'

Gaten swallowed and remained silent. Out near the horizon, the boys had reached the end of the pier. They bobbed alongside it, just tiny orbs peeking out from the swirling ocean waves.

'Okay,' said Sara. 'Okay, Gaten. I trust you.'

Gaten threw the rest of the pebbles back onto the beach and stood up. 'There's nothing to trust. I'm just doing my job too. But I'll do it the best I can. Are you gonna be okay?'

Sara watched as the boys finally made their way back to shore. The current was working against them. They travelled slowly and their efforts were laboured, like they were swimming on a treadmill. She looked at the pier and then up toward the ballroom, and she thought about beauty again. The real beauty of everlasting things. She didn't know when this pier was built, nor who built it. She didn't know how long the secret Cuckoo Cabaret Club had been going, nor when it would end. Perhaps it would always be a refuge under the stars. Or perhaps it would be gone tomorrow, in some great storm that swept its foundations into wasted bark and mortar. But perhaps that actually didn't matter. Perhaps it was the moments that could be everlasting. She thought about Luna and how beautiful her moment had been, and then she felt the tears coming again. She looked at her brother.

'I'll be fine,' she said, noticing the yellow glare of the sun turn orange on his forehead – the telltale sign of night, and blackness, and the nothing hours that were now so much more than they had been in the dark.

She managed a tearful smile and her brother patted her three times on the shoulder. Then he began walking back up the beach.

4

The glass dome was painted by starlight. The stars were far above Sara's head, swirling in a cyclone with the moon in the centre, like the pupil of a giant eye. Sara stared at it as she twirled around the dance floor. The beat of the music skipped inside her heart and she was covered in sweat. The room was dark, no one was talking, and Sara liked it that way. She was looking up at the dome and thinking about Luna. Tears streaked down her cheeks, and her breaths were shallow and distant. She felt rooted to the spot, spinning around and around, until it felt like she might take off like a samara, all the way up beyond the dome to join her friend in the clouds.

The music wrapped itself around Sara, sinking into her pores. It was different to the night before. Two heavy speakers were propped in each corner, playing songs that were designed for midnights. Beats and drums and heavenly female voices cascaded around the hall, and everyone felt it. There wasn't a single person standing still. Every heart was filled with song, and every body was caught in a state of trance. Everyone was together until it felt like no one was.

Sara felt like she was the only person there, only there were dozens of her, all with the same thoughts and memories. All with the same reason to cry, and to smile, and to dance. There was a synergy that felt as strong as the water and the shore, and while they may have been dramatically different, they were really the same. One soul in one place. Dreaming of Luna.

Sara closed her eyes to the rhythm and stroked her chest. Through the crowd, the bodies dissipated and made way for another. Ava. The woman in the silver dress, with hazel hair and lips like a goddess. She moved slowly toward her, and when she was within a breath, she bowed forward and kissed her on the lips. The kiss was everything Sara thought it would be. Ava's lips were soft and warm, her tongue gentle and sympathetic. Her body was wrapped in salty sweat, and her hips were swaying like leaves. It was the sort of kiss that wasn't rooted in sexual desire, but was something deeper and more important. The sort of kiss you wanted to cry into, like a pillow that rested the head and helped dreams. It felt right, and Sara embraced it. Then, when it was done, Ava took her hand and they started spinning together.

5

Outside, the world was quiet. Ava leant against the rails on the edge of the pier and looked into the waves. Sara stood alongside her, a Bacardi in one hand and a cigarette in the other. A red pulse illuminated the town in the distance. It came from a nightclub on Wilson Street, a place that Sara had been to once before. She had been kicked out by a security guard that night, bloodied and bruised from a fight with some rednecks. She didn't remember much of it, although she did remember giving the security guard a handjob behind the trashcans an hour later. The girls at the Precious Star Bar never believed her. Sara had to go back the next day to ask him for CCTV footage, and for that, she got another black eye. And then a handjob.

That life felt more than a few waves away now. It felt like a lie, and not a white one. A story's web that just kept spinning and spinning, until it finally ended, and Sara was stood on the last page. Luna had been part of that story. She had been one of the comforting chapters between monsters and bad things. Now it was the Cuckoo Cabaret Club and Ava. Sara took a sip of her drink and looked at her. From this angle, she stood taller than the town, but just smaller than the moon, which rested above her head like a bobble hat. Celestial was a good way to describe her, Sara thought. Celestial and sexy, and with a hint of that *other* kind of humanity that fascinated her. She was part of this world, and yet not part of it. She was five foot ten, and yet scratching the moon. She was different in every sense of the word, and yet familiar enough to be comforting. She was a drug, alright. And Sara couldn't help but breathe her in.

'Waves are getting choppy,' Ava said after a few minutes of silence.

She was shivering, and so Sara approached and wrapped her in a warm embrace. She nuzzled her chin into her collar and felt her pulse.

'Where are you from?' she whispered.

'Now she wants to know me.'

'What's wrong with that?'

Ava turned toward her. 'You already know me. Didn't I kiss you?'

'Yeah, so?'

'So what else is there to know but that?'

The waves began smacking against the wooden posts below them, hissing at the foundations of the pier like a cobra with venom. The music from the Cuckoo Cabaret Club was being drowned out, becoming vague vibrations on an electric wind. Sara felt them sizzle.

'You like being a mystery, huh?'

'Didn't I tell you?' said Ava. 'I'm no mystery, honey.'

Sara thought back to their first conversation. She didn't remember her saying that, but then again, she didn't remember a lot of that conversation. Just feelings. Just light and lust and happiness. A lot of happiness. The kind Sara had not experienced before. She remembered those feelings and nestled into them.

'How do you like it?' Ava cut her out of the memory.

'How do I like what?'

'My little club.'

Sara thought. 'I'm in love with it,' she said.

'Oh, wow. You're in love. Those are strong words.'

'Mysterious words,' Sara agreed. 'I imagine you like them.'

'I do. Are you in love with me?'

The words were delicate on Ava's tongue, and they weren't thrown away. They stayed there willingly, purposefully, like they wanted an answer. So again, Sara thought about an answer. Only one came to her.

'Yes. Yes, I think so.'

'Ah,' said Ava. 'You can't think. You're either in love with me, or you just love me.'

'Is there a difference?'

'You tell me.'

Sara laughed without sound. She turned away and pulled another cigarette out of her bra. She was down to her last two now. Although she had started the day with a full pack, each stick had been burnt away to embers and ash. They had joined the wind and rested inside her soul, where they stayed plaguing her, turning things from red to black. She would not be without them, so she sniffed and lit, and again, she thought about Luna.

'Yes,' said Ava, answering her own question. 'Of course there's a difference. Love is outward. Being in love is —'

'Inward.'

'You got it, sister.'

Sara turned back to her and took her in. She started at her shoes, those heels, carrying what must have been such a weight. She looked at Ava's face, waving silver lines in the moonlight, catching and glinting every few seconds when the clouds let it breathe. The waves beneath them grew louder.

'You know,' said Sara contemplatively, 'I've never met anyone like you. You're so...'

'If you say mysterious, I'm gonna throw you off this pier.'

'No, you're so normal. You're everything I want in a person. But being like that makes you abnormal.'

Ava smirked. The sweat on her chest shined too. Tiny beads of crystals layered upon perfectly waxed skin. 'You know why they call people abnormal, and not just different? Because they *are* normal. Or rather, they're everything people want normality to be.'

'Yeah,' said Sara. 'Yeah, that's you. That's this place.'

'Ab,' said Ava.

'Ab.'

'Fab.'

Sara laughed. She took another drag and felt the smoke rest in her soul again. 'I don't know what I'd do if I hadn't found you. Tonight, I mean. I think I might have stayed on that beach. Or I would have just walked right into the ocean. I'd have joined the crabs and weed at the bottom. I would have been happy to. But here you are. Dancing with me, kissing me. Showing me that life isn't as dark as it seems out there.'

The waves began peeling back below them. The cobra was rearing its head, preparing for another strike.

'I didn't think you could do it,' Sara continued. 'Especially today, after what happened. But...' She paused, taking her time. 'You know when you wake up from a nightmare, and it's three in the morning, and you know you have to go back to sleep, but you don't want to in case you slip back into it? This place is the dream when you finally close your eyes. The nice dream that's exactly what you hoped for.'

Ava smiled at her. 'Keep hoping, honey. We'll be here. A nightmare doesn't happen twice. Not if you don't want it to.'

Sara looked back toward the town. 'Nobody asks for nightmares,' she said slowly.

'Oh, but they do.' Ava pushed herself from the rails and walked over toward Sara. With angel grace, she placed one arm on her left shoulder and the other arm on her right. She stared at Sara directly in the eyes. 'You know what I've found to be the perfect cure for nightmares? Never closing your eyes. So stay up with me. All night. Don't leave until the sun starts peeking over that horizon.'

'Don't you think I need sleep after what happened?'

Ava gestured toward the town. 'Out there is the nightmare, isn't that what you said? Cuckoo Cove's where you can close your eyes, but the Cuckoo Cabaret Club? We're no dream, honey. We're real as pickles. So keep them open.'

Sara smiled back at her. 'You really are a mystery. Can't you see that?'

Ava leant forward and kissed her again, quick this time. So quick that Sara could hardly place a toe into the water. The kiss came and went, and then Ava was hanging out of the doorway to the old ballroom, holding out her hand. The song inside was fading to the end, signalled by cheers and chatter, and champagne corks flying high toward the glass dome.

'I see that your glass is half empty,' she said. 'And you're gonna need some more Bacardi for this next track.'

As if on cue, the song inside the ballroom finished and the next one started to play. "Murder on the Dancefloor" by Sophie Ellis-Bextor. More whoops and cheers welcomed it into the world.

'You like Sophie?' asked Ava.

Sara smiled. 'I'm in love with her.'

Ava smiled back. 'That's the spirit.'

Underneath the pier, the cobra struck again. The ocean waves whipped against the wood and into its old and jagged skin, and Sara followed their call back into the ballroom and onto the dance floor.

6

Something here listens to love and whispers. It hangs from metal poles and concentrates, twitching, repositioning, and scratching its teeth against large gums. Beneath its head, the water spirals and hisses furiously. Above it, the hard vibrations of the everlasting house turn soft. Thousands of feet stamp and shake, but something here only thinks about one pair. In the centre, spinning. Spinning and spinning and spinning. And something here waits for the person called *Sara*.

CHAPTER ELEVEN

THE SHADOW

1

'Mrs Taggort? Nice woman. Good teeth. That's unusual at our age. Ya see these?' The old man opened his mouth to reveal seventeen fillings and five crowns. He pointed to the gap where his two front teeth should have been. 'That's from chewing sugar wheat. That's a recipe my ma made. She used to stick it in a pot and drain it in cloth. Could chew on that for a day in the ranch. She called it "sweet". Get it? Sweet. Sugar wheat.'

Gaten closed his notebook and bound it with the strap.

2

'Saw you talking to Arnie, so I thought I'd stick some lemonade on. He does like to chew the fat. Not that he chews much of anything these days, mind. Have you seen his teeth?'

3

'I was there in the morning. Morning of, I guess. She put on that pumpkin pageant, you heard about it? Sends everyone in a two mile radius wild. It's old timers around here, you see. We ain't got much better to do.'

The second old man was a black man, dark warts on his temples, stubbly, greying hair. Gaten noticed thick, coarse hands and scabby nails on his finger tips.

'You notice anything unusual while you were there?'

The old man scratched the back of his neck. 'Not as such, no. I mean, Nancy was playing up. But that's not unusual, she always does. Mrs Taggort seemed to handle herself fine, but I didn't see her much after their argument. I don't know if she came back.'

'Back?'

'Yeah, she got shook up. Course she did. Nancy pushed a table over. Had pumpkins on it and everything. She took it too far. Mrs Taggort went inside. I think her fella made her tea. You heard about him? I know he went to hospital, I hope he's alright.'

'I'm sure he'll be okay.'

'He owes me fifty cents.'

4

'I never hurt her, okay? I hurt a few pumpkins, sure. That's what I am, apparently. Nancy Gartner the Pumpkin Killer. But it was all lies. They wanted to eradicate me from the pageant. Couldn't stand the thought of me winning for whatever reason. Have you come to arrest me?'

Gaten touched briefly at his forehead, wiping tired

sweat from above his brow. 'No,' he replied simply.

'Then what's with the gun?'

He looked down at his firearm, which was dangling just as idly in the holster. 'We always carry, ma'am, nothing to worry about.'

Nancy seemed to relax. 'So how did she die?

'Not concluded yet.'

'That's a shame.' A pause, and a flicker of a smile on Nancy's lips. 'Guess that means no pageant next year, huh?'

5

Gaten walked back to the squad car. Wayne was waiting for him there. On his face were a pair of thick shades, despite the fact the sun had disappeared over an hour ago. He stood chewing gum and watching the dirt spray from Gaten's boots. In front of him was the first of six households that Gaten had interviewed. Arnie, the old man with ruined teeth, was still sitting on his porch, tilting in a rocking chair. His body was thin but his legs were puffy. A thin slice of wheat was hanging from his mouth, and he had the radio on beside him. When Gaten reached the car, Wayne offered him a cigarette.

'You're gonna give in to it any day now,' he said after Gaten declined. 'Bigger the death count, bigger the urge.'

'People have been dying since I quit three years ago. Hasn't cracked me so far.'

The old man giggled on the porch. 'Don't feel like yesterday since I was carryin' on like that.'

Gaten frowned at him. He turned to Wayne. 'Any more out of this one?'

'Nope, but I'm seeing my dentist next week.'

'Probably a good call.'

'Any luck with the others?'

Gaten shook his head. 'Nope. Unless this was all over a dispute with pumpkins, I can't see that anyone had a reason to hurt that woman.'

'Guess this makes you look kind of a fool, huh? How do you explain this one, then? Mrs Taggort was a closeted gay?'

Gaten knew that little chestnut would crop up sooner or later. In fact, he thought it was a little overdue.

'What is it?' Wayne poked him. 'You think she was sucking fish on her off nights at the laundromat? You think she was coming back from the bingo with sticky fingers?'

Arnie giggled into his armpit again. Wayne glanced at him, then opened the car door.

'Alright, you sleep good, Mr Kurdale. Watch that gout now.'

'You ain't askin' me more questions?'

'Not today,' said Gaten. He stamped some of the dirt from his feet and walked around the hood.

'Alright,' the old man mumbled to himself. 'Arnie Kurdale sees some stuff. No one asks him about it.'

'I tell you who you ain't seeing,' Wayne called over. 'His name's Dr Griffiths, his business is on Main Mall and his time's nine to four. You even get a lollipop. Although I'd pass on it if I were you.'

'Arnie Kurdale sees summat strange, and no one asks him why or what. They only ask him about his teeth.'

'Hey now, we didn't wanna know about your —'

'Hold on,' interrupted Gaten. 'What did Arnie – I mean, what did you see?'

Arnie's eyes lit up, and he chewed on the sugar wheat triumphantly. 'Arnie's become important, huh?'

Gaten scowled irritably. 'What did you see, Mr Kurdale?'

'A cloud. On a cloudless day.'

Wayne huffed. 'That's great, Mr Kurdale. You get that down, Gate?'

'Never seen a cloud move that fast,' Arnie continued. 'Two seconds, then BAM!' He clapped his hands and the sound of a whip cascaded across the fields. 'Sunny skies.'

Gaten's frown deepened. 'How do you mean a cloud?'

'I mean just that. Arnie's sitting here on his rockin' chair, chewin' some sweet, enjoyin' the view. Then the view turns dark. Real dark. Just for a moment. I had the fear. You probably don't know the fear. It's a farmer's fear. Black skies, black money. That's what my daddy told me. It all came back to me in a single second, that's how dark it went. All those thoughts and memories and carryin' on. Then poof, sun's shinin'. Arnie looks up, and there ain't nothin' there. Spooky clouds. Can you believe that?'

'You sure it was cloudless?'

'One or two maybe. Miles from the sun, though. Well, they're all miles from the sun, ain't they? But these were real far. Couldn't hit them with a slingshot.'

'And this was what time yesterday?' Gaten asked.

Arnie sucked hard on the sugar wheat. 'Weren't yesterday,' he said. 'This was day before yesterday. Ah, no, yesterday was completely normal. Borin' even.'

Wayne climbed into the driver's seat of the squad car. 'Okay, well, like I said. Watch that gout, Mr Kurdale.'

Gaten remained still for a while longer, staring up at the old man. Arnie leant forward with that mischievous twinkle still in his eyes. Then he began munching on the sugar wheat, folding it down with his gums before swallowing. He lifted his saggy arm and saluted mockingly. Gaten dropped his gaze and climbed into the car alongside Wayne.

6

Gaten watched as the world whirled past him. Green and grey blurs created a world of chaos, without meaning or order, yet Gaten's thoughts were straight and still. He thought about the old man and the way he had smiled at him. He thought about his saggy arms and his mocking salute, about the cloud and how fast it must have travelled through the sky. At any other time in his life, Gaten would have passed Arnie off as a trouble maker. A bored old wrinkled man who had nothing better to do than invent stories. Only this Gaten was different. This Gaten was three deaths deep and bracing for a fourth. He would have believed anything if it gave him something to grab onto. And this story did give him something to grab onto. This cloud had feathers, and it was flying tantalisingly close to Gaten's grasp, only he didn't quite know why. With his left hand, he turned the radio down and thought. He rummaged through his brain like he was searching for a key in a packed suitcase. He thought about his brother, the beach, the football posts, the third body, the second body, the first body, the water tank, the wig. And then he pulled himself into the now and found himself tangled in that mess of whirring colours. He turned to Wayne and said,

'Take me to the water plant.'

And Wayne knew better than to argue.

7

Abigail entered the building through the small door and imagined bustling cubicles, flying coffees, and scraps of white paper being thrown from desk to desk. The reality was far from that. The Cuckoo Correspondence was a small place on Crimson Avenue, sitting discreetly opposite one of the few straight nightclubs. It was in the basement of a rented property, tiny, with a handful of offices that were more like closets – scrunched-up pieces of paper, like mothballs. She made the short journey from one end of the room to the other, and she imagined doing the same walk around five hundred miles south. She imagined the chaos and ferocity of The Weekender or The LA Print. She imagined the excitement and the confusion and the chatter. Murders, rapes, and court cases – the golden stories that frayed tempers and caused coffees to be downed like tequila shots. She felt warm and happy, and she kept the dream with her as she knocked on the tatty door of Sammy Lavender's office.

'Come in,' came a hoarse voice on the other side.

Abigail opened the door and the image disappeared as quickly as it had arrived. Sammy Lavender was sitting at his tiny desk, a tray of cigarettes askew in front of him, and a single, lonely fan doing its best to wipe the gathering sweat from his face. The room itself was rotten. Speckled mould ate into the window sills and the carpet was torn and dusty. His gym clothes were tossed on the couch, with a stack of crinkled magazines beside them, two of them X-rated. Abigail stood in the doorway and took in the sight.

'Sir, can I have two minutes?'

'I know you were at the pageant yesterday, Ab. But the woman was like ninety years old. If we wrote a news story on things like that, our papers would be nothing but death.'

Sammy's eyes bulged in his skull. His belly overhung the desk a little, only that was more a consequence of the tiny desk and room than his calorie intake. He was a man on a mission. After two heart attacks last September, he had managed to lose three stone in just over a year, and he was looking all the better for it. His fingers were still tubby, though, and Abigail found that slightly strange.

'It's not about Mrs Taggort,' she said hesitantly. 'It's about Adrian.'

'Who?'

'Adrian Ramirez. The dead guy they found in the reservoir.'

'The gay guy? Same story.'

'No, but I spoke to the cop. The one in charge of his case, and the new case, Arthur Conrad. He told me something different. He told me he doesn't think it was suicide.'

'Murder then?'

'No flies on you.'

Mr Lavender looked at her plainly. 'Is that supposed to be funny? You wanna be bunked back down to coffees and biscuits? Actually, my throat's getting pretty parched.'

Abigail took that moment to pull up a chair and sit down. She knew she had to play this smart if she was going to reel Sammy in. He wasn't a man who could easily be manipulated, or persuaded even. She remembered how he used to sit in this office munching on sandwich deals and chugging cold sodas. If he could spend a whole year avoiding burgers and french fries, he could easily avoid a few minutes of Abigail's seduction tactics. She straightened her dress and broke out a bright smile.

'Lay off, Sammy. You didn't even drink my coffees.'

'That's not something to be proud of.'

'Got me here, didn't it?'

Sammy shrugged nonchalantly. 'Yeah, and where's here? Where are you going with this?'

'The cops have given us information on the deaths, but they haven't held a press conference.'

'Why would they?'

'Have you asked for one?'

'Listen, Ab, if you held a press conference every time a gay guy knocked himself over the head —'

'Our papers *and* our screens would be nothing but death, yeah, I know. But don't you think Cuckoo Cove deserves to know if people are getting murdered? Don't you think that's on the police?'

'Who said anything about murder?' asked Sammy.

'Officer Dalbret. He's the guy looking into these cases, and he's the guy who thinks there's foul play. If there's been no press release, it's because someone at the top doesn't want us to know about it.'

There was a pause. Sammy reclined on his chair and his head bumped against the window behind him. *That's it*, Abigail thought. *That bait looks shinier than the rest. Come on, boss. Why don't you come nibble on it?* A sigh escaped from Sammy's lips and he tapped absently upon last week's copy of the CC.

'What do you want me to do?' he asked after a few seconds. 'Run a story contradicting the cops?'

'No, not at all. People would accuse us of fear mongering.'

'Then what?'

Abigail leant back herself, crossing her legs so that her skin showed. 'You've long since wanted a story that goes statewide. And you're right, two dead gay guys isn't gonna do it. Nor is Officer Dalbret's comment. On it's own. But it doesn't have to be on it's own. Not with a press conference on the table.'

Sammy took that in, his puffy eyes narrowing. He looked at Abigail like a journalist would look at her, right past the skin and into her soul. He saw her, then. And she could tell a good part of him liked it.

'Huh...'

'That's the great thing about "off the record", sir,' said Abigail. 'Once it's *on* the record, we can control how it spins.'

Sammy tapped again on the copy of the CC. Then he slowly shook his head. 'You're a rotten journalist, Ab.'

'And I'm a rotten coffee maker. Which one would you prefer?'

The fan in the corner clicked, and another bead of sweat trickled from Sammy's temple. Abigail stared back at him. *Take it. Take it, take it, take it.* She imagined the offices five hundred miles away. Their walls, their carpets, their windowsills, all as clean as a baby's buttocks. She imagined papers flying in the fan and fluttering around the room like golden rain.

'What do you want me to do?' asked Sammy finally.

Abigail rejoiced in her soul. 'Bug them. Bug the hell out of them. Don't stop flooding their phones until the dam breaks.'

8

'Shit, shit, shit. Double shit. Triple shit. Shit on a house. Shit on Gonagreen. Shit on me.'

Pain.

Kenny paced around his bedroom, his hands held firmly behind his back. His heart was beating three times the *okay, everything's fine* amount and his armpits were getting sweaty. Sweatier than normal. And normal was pretty darn sweaty.

'Shit,' he said again. 'Fuck, even. Yeah, fuck. Fucking shit.'

Pain.

'Okay, pain, I get it. I heard you the first few hundred times.'

He turned to the cuckoo in the corner. It was splayed out in the box of his game, propped up in a mound of toilet paper. True to its purpose, the bird had pooped three times already.

'I heard you,' Kenny repeated to himself. 'I heard you in my head. I heard you.'

Pain.

'That's it. That's what I heard. Anything else you wanna say?'

The cuckoo's mouth remained open as if a worm was lodged inside its throat, and its eyes glared widely into Kenny's soul. A few seconds of silence passed.

Pain.

Kenny began pacing again. 'This isn't happening. This can't be happening. Why can I hear you?'

Pain.

'I mean, I thought it was me at first. I could feel pain, like a weird sort of pain. I've felt lots of pain before. Urinary infection. Eczema. Jonnie Carson's fist. But this was different. I felt your —'

Pain.

'Yeah. Your pain. I felt it. But then I heard it. It's like it came out of me, only it was never really there. My brain was confused. It didn't know what was happening, so I felt it, and then I heard it. And that's what was happening —'

Pain.

'I was hearing you —'

Pain.

'I *am* hearing you —'

Pain.

'And you better stop saying "pain" otherwise I'll mash that other wing of yours to mush, I swear to god.'

There was another silence. The cuckoo shuffled and tried flapping a little. All to no avail, unless its mission was to string a slice of toilet paper over its head.

'I'm talking to a bird,' said Kenny dazedly.

With a cold sting of dread, he walked back over to the cardboard box and pulled the paper away from the bird's face. Its dark eyes were still staring at him, its breaths fast and shallow. Kenny glanced at its beating chest and realised that the rhythm of its heart was reflecting his own. For a moment, he felt pity for the cuckoo. But then his pity morphed back into an all-consuming terror.

'I don't understand...'

Downstairs, he heard his dad laughing at the television. The sound of chinking glasses were coming from the kitchen, and that must have meant Mandy was preparing their evening mojito. It was strange, but Kenny half expected his dad to rush upstairs at any moment, like parents could sense when their children were experiencing fear. Only that was stupid. No one could sense anything from another person. Certainly not his dad, who couldn't even tell that Kenny hated him most of the time.

Pain.

And yet, Kenny could sense the bird's thoughts. That was the only way he could describe it. There was a psychic link between himself and the cuckoo that was as real as a conversation. The only question was, did the conversation go both ways? Kenny stared rigidly into the cuckoo's eyes.

'Can you hear me too?' he asked.

The cuckoo blinked. Kenny didn't even know that birds could blink, but the cuckoo definitely blinked.

Pain, the bird shuffled again.

'Yes. Pain. I know you're in pain. And maybe I could help you. But you need to tell me if you can hear me first. So can you?'

The bird's mouth quivered and Kenny swore it tilted its head.

'Say this word if you can hear me... Gonagreen.'

The birds good wing fluttered and its tiny legs twisted to the side. It turned itself over onto its belly and resumed the staring contest.

Gone green.

'No, Gona —'

Kenny gasped. The bird had heard him. It had actually heard him. And that meant they could talk. A million and one questions rushed through Kenny's head. After absorbing them all, he settled on just one.

'Do you need a bird sling?'

The cuckoo dropped its head miserably.

Pain.

9

The grass cracked and crunched beneath Gaten's feet. Warm air lingered in his nostrils, and when he breathed, it felt like the hairs inside singed. While his heart was pounding, his blood felt loose and heavy. His head was hanging, and to Wayne it must have looked like he was examining something, but really, he felt like he was two blinks away from falling into a soft and dreamless sleep. He hadn't had one of those in a long time. Not since the body of Adrian Ramirez had appeared in that reservoir, and then again over his left shoulder, his dried and bloated body tied by the invisible string wrapped around his pinky. Gaten sighed and blinked once, then he lifted his head.

'Something's wrong,' he said, trying to get as much of his beating heart into his voice as possible.

'Well, jeez, three poor fuckers are dead, Gate. Something ain't right.'

Gaten shook his head. 'No, I mean with this place. It's that tape. Something's wrong.'

Gaten scratched the back of his head, staring up at the floodlights, which stood around forty feet tall at the end of the field. Dotted about the place were water tankers, thick with rust. A single camera was attached to the building to the left of them, with a sign next to it that read:

THIS VICINITY HAS 24-HOUR SURVEILLANCE

TRESPASSERS BEWARE HEAVY CHARGE

Gaten remembered the boy running through the VHS blur. He had chosen to cut through the water plant, perhaps believing it to be the fastest route to the reservoir. Something had made him stop. Turn, climb, and throw a part of himself into one of the tankers – the most important part, if Theo was anything to go by. A lot was wrong with that, but there was something more. Something lingering under the surface of that tape, reaching out to Gaten, if only the waters weren't too murky to see it. He remembered the man with the ruined teeth, rocking back on his chair and grinning. A cloud, he had said. Something that had stripped away the sunlight, if only for a small second. *Something*. That was it. The word Gaten had been using for a while now. But why had he been using it? What made that word appear in that clog of whirring colours, and why couldn't Gaten shake it away?

'You okay, Gate?'

Wayne spoke up beside him, but Gaten didn't really listen. He was looking at the floodlights again. The bulbs were staring down at him like large, hovering eyes. His pinky twitched as the string pulled.

10

The office hadn't changed. McDonalds cups still littered the surfaces, sticky and wrinkled, and the computers had gained an extra inch of dust. Except for one, which was playing the night Adrian Ramirez died again. Adrian was running into centre frame, and Gaten felt his sweat begin to go cold as he watched him. Wayne was sitting on one of the chairs, spinning and playing with his watch. Justin stood in the doorway.

'I haven't changed nothing,' he said, as if the investigation had suddenly taken a turn on him.

Gaten ignored his plea of innocence, keeping his attention on the tape as his pinky continued to twitch. *Please*, he thought, but he didn't know why he thought it. Just like he didn't know why he thought: *something*. Although, perhaps he did. Perhaps he had always known. He just didn't want to face it. Couldn't afford to face it. Not after what had happened all those years ago, when he had left his brother lying face first in the puddle. *I couldn't fight Steven Harris. I couldn't fight Lucas, Billy, Derek. If I couldn't fight them, how in the hell can I fight <u>something</u>?*

Ten seconds of the tape played through and Gaten zoomed in. Thanks to the floodlights, the CCTV footage was bright, but he knew it wouldn't stay that way. He remembered the last time he was sitting in this chair, and that split second the tape went black. It would happen again now. Things would go black, and either this case would carry on as normal, or every fear spiralling inside Gaten's gut would be realised. He zoomed in further and watched as Adrian Ramirez turned, the fear on his face as clear as the wig on his head. Behind him, Wayne's watch started beeping, and Justin cleared his throat impatiently. Then the darkness. Gaten hit pause and leaned in close.

How far can you see in the dark?

The floating body of Adrian Ramirez teased him, pulling itself so close to Gaten's shoulder that his pinky ached. He squinted and cupped his face against the computer screen. He saw the outline of the water tank, he saw the quiet sparkle of Adrian's glitter, and he saw the glint of grey grass. He saw and he swallowed, because the tape hadn't faltered. It wasn't a blip, a flash, or one wire not quite reaching the other. It was Adrian's world that had blacked out. A cloud on a cloudless day. Except it was night, and whatever had blacked out Adrian's world must have been big enough to cast a shadow in the floodlights. *Something.*

Wayne finished playing with his watch. 'See anything new, boss?' he asked.

Outside the room, Gaten heard the machines of the water plant churning, bubbling, frothing – a low, watery growl. He unpaused the tape and watched Adrian climb the water tank.

'Yes,' he said to Wayne. 'I see a monster.'

And then Gaten Dalbret thought about his brother.

11

Something here casts shadows. Wings shift and talons curl around rusted iron. Without sight, it cocks its head to the waves and sniffs. Its snout rolls back and black gums seethe with saliva. Crooked fangs. Dark throat leading to a spiral of desires, stronger now than they've ever been. It listens to them. Depends on them. But it has found its food, it knows that now. Something here thinks about its feast, wonders about the soul, its taste, the fulfilment. Something here waits for the filling of a mighty hole in the holy dark.

12

The wind rises. Goosebumps swell. Something here feels the salty air against its fur coat. It feels the metal groan as it moves. It climbs through gaps and scuttles slowly, steadily, clinging with talons and splintering wood. Beneath its head, the waves part and foam. Above its head, the music starts. The secret Cuckoo Cabaret Club awakens, members already in place, songs already sung. Bright lights and hellos and goodbyes and everything in between. Everything is here and nothing changes. Nothing but the person called Sara.

Something here thinks about her, turns her over with its tongue, tastes, shivers, wonders. Things out there have not been enough. Nothing will be enough until the doors of the Cuckoo Cabaret Club close and the feast is complete. But not yet. Not yet. Something climbs a little further, then it lets go and soars into the sky, its silhouette briefly shadowing the moon, making the town of Cuckoo Cove a dark place.

CHAPTER TWELVE

THE CUCKOO'S DREAM

1

The ship lingered on the horizon, listing slightly to the left to counter the storm, and though the rain was hard and hail clouded the view, Kenny could see it. He sat in the bushes, his stomach aching. Sea-berry skins littered his feet, pounded into the sand by heavy water, and their juice was twisting his insides. He raised his head and allowed the hail to fall down his throat. Then he looked at the ocean again and noticed a small boat riding atop a twenty-foot wave, its bow tilted at a forty-degree angle. Four figures were sitting inside, hunched together. When the wave collapsed, the boat shot forward. On either side, oars were cutting into the water, the rowers trying desperately to fall into a rhythm, but they needn't have bothered. The raging wind was taking care of their journey, and within just forty seconds, the boat was already crunching a triangular dent into the sand.

Kenny retreated slightly into the seabuckthorn. More berries fell at his feet, and he glanced at them ruefully. One of the figures roared over the wind.

'Pull her at least ten feet, we don't want her being caught by the tide!'

Through the haze, Kenny could just about make out the face of the figure. It was a bearded man, old looking. Jet black hair tumbled from a furry nest on his head, and a portion of it lay tangled in the straps of his hood. All four men wore dark fur coats, but the attire below their waist was thin and light – knee-length breeches that had turned jet-black in the storm. Three of them finished dragging the boat and turned. One of them spoke, but his accent was so strong that Kenny couldn't understand him. He remained silent and hidden.

'Is it old?' another one said more clearly.

They walked somewhere to the left and Kenny lost them in the clog of bushes.

'Can't be. You see the bone here? Traces of tendon. And here, some skin and tissue still left in the sockets.'

'Lord almighty...'

'Could be scavengers?'

'The job looks too clean for that. We could be dealing with native folk.'

'Damn them.'

Despite the pain in his belly, Kenny managed a brief smile. He remembered the taste of the blubber, the soft drip of salty blood falling down his throat, as cold as rain water. He was disappointed that perfectly good food had evidently been missed in the eye sockets, but the fact that these men – these hard, rough, tall men – had braved fierce waters to discover nothing but a skeleton did amuse him enough to forget it.

'Stewart, Arnold – take the boat back to the Caledonia and load it with axes and pistols. Cover them in cloth for the journey. Alfred and I will stay here and scout one mile. When you return, we'll conduct a full search.'

This time, Kenny couldn't help but laugh. When he did, however, the world around him seemed to shake. The sound that came out of his mouth was unlike anything he'd ever heard before. His throat vibrated and strained, forming a loud, rough call that just kept on going. He started to panic. Over the roaring of the waves, Kenny heard the jangle of footsteps and metal clinking. He let out another laugh, and then another, and then another, and in his frenzy, he tasted a sour clump of bile pull itself up into his throat. Above his head, the thicket was pulled back, and the pale, stony face of who Kenny assumed was the commander glared down at him.

The man said, 'It's just a bird.'

But in Kenny's head, he heard: *I'm hungry.*

2

When Kenny awoke, his head was pounding. The room around him was dark and quiet, with just a slight breeze breathing through the open window. He lifted himself from his pillow and grimaced at the sticky sweat beneath his pyjamas. In the pit of his stomach, he felt ill, so he swung his legs around the bed and paced quickly into the bathroom. Even though he didn't vomit, Kenny knelt in front of the bowl for twenty minutes, twice pulling the chain to feel the cold toilet water rush over his head. When he felt like he was ready to stand, he did so and replaced the bog-water with tap. He showered himself in the sink until his head felt slightly better. Then, quite gingerly, he turned off the light and walked back to his bedroom.

The cuckoo was waiting for him inside. All attempts to form a sling for the bird had failed, and so instead, it rested in a mound of toilet paper and was wrapped tightly in a scarf Kenny hadn't worn since he was five. Its eyes were still wide open, and as soon as Kenny closed the door, he could hear it talking again.

Gone green. Gone green. Gone green.

Another bubble of sick arose in Kenny's stomach, and for a moment, he considered running back to the bathroom. But he didn't. Instead, he pulled up a stool and stared as hard as he could into the box.

'I dreamt about you,' he whispered.

The bird stared at him with its mouth open. *Gone green. Gone green. Gone green.*

'Well, not you. I dreamt about me. But it was like I *was* you.'

Gone green. Gone green. Gone green.

Kenny huffed and leant back on the stool. 'I suppose I should be happy you're not saying "pain" anymore.'

The bird blinked at him and shuffled in the tissue. *Pain.*

'Don't you fucking start...'

Pain. Pain. Pain.

'Yeah, I get it. You're in pain. I gave you a scarf, didn't I? What are you moaning about?'

The bird seemed to think about that. Its good wing shifted a bit, and Kenny sighed, leaning closer to the box again and resting his arms on the desk.

'How is this happening?' he asked, blinking slowly. His eyes were growing heavy. The shock of waking back into this reality had surged the blood, but now it had been a few minutes, the same reality was starting to weary him.

'If I go back to sleep, will I dream about you again?'

The cuckoo remained motionless. Kenny frowned at it, then rubbed his temples.

'I don't want to, you know. If that's you talking to me in my sleep, I don't want to hear it. I'd rather dream about other things.'

Gone green.

'Yeah, Gonagreen.'

The cuckoo twisted. Then, like a faulty clock, it began calling again, and Kenny felt the cold water wash off his skull and the dull, throbbing ache return with a vengeance.

3

Gaten winced as boiling hot coffee soaked his sleeve and streamed down his wrist. He placed the coffee cup on the desk and rubbed his eyes. Gunther and Wayne were sitting on his left, Justin on the right. They were all staring at the collection of faces in front of them. Reporters lined the town hall in four rows, their eyes hungry and their lips baying for a morsel, at least just a *morsel* of a story for their fading newspapers. The ink was nearly out of the pot, Gaten knew. And all of them had come to him for a refill. He saw Abigail in the crowd, a curious smile resting upon one side of her face. He thought for a moment how pretty she looked. That blonde hair, that suit, the way her eyes balanced between a state of seriousness and seduction. Both were one and the same, Gaten knew. She was serious about seduction, and she seduced to get serious. But those eyes would soon be disappointed, because none of them would be getting a story today. Even though there was one to tell.

Gaten leant back in his seat and tried to stop his hands from shaking. A day had passed since he'd stood in that water plant and realised the truth, and a part of him still didn't want to believe it. A shadow could be anything, after all. A trick of the light, a projection, a dream. But Gaten had been living in a nightmare for a week now, and he knew by now there was always a monster lurking somewhere in the darkness.

'Good morning everyone,' Justin Hadero straightened his shirt as he spoke, his gaze glancing toward the three news cameras, which were propped in the corner of the room. 'Thank you all for coming out here today. Lord knows, this town hall needed feet to kick up the dust a bit.'

There were a few bemused huffs at his choice to open with a joke, but the group of reporters let it slide. Their pens had not yet hit pad.

'I wanted to start by acknowledging the tragic deaths of Adrian Ramirez, Arthur Conrad, and Bethany Taggort. Our hearts are with their families, and we pray their souls rest in the holy arms of God. As chief of police, I've never been in charge during a time where there's been such tragedy in such close proximity.

'I understand that the deaths of both Ramirez and Conrad have received extra attention due to their similar choice of livelihood. But I want to reassure the community that we believe these deaths are not connected, and no evidence has been found to indicate foul play. On the contrary, our evidence points to these being isolated events. Both men were known to have sufficient issues with their mental health. Both were on medication, and indeed, both men had been open about their struggles. It is our belief that on the eighth of October and the eleventh of October respectively, Adrian Ramirez and Arthur Conrad lost their battles, and once again, we'd like to offer our sincerest condolences to those closest to them.

'As is evidenced by the case of Bethany Taggort, there is no distinct pattern that would suggest anyone was coerced into taking their lives, or worse, had their lives taken from them. Unfortunately, events like this happen from time to time, and in a small town like ours, when they happen so close together, it hits all the harder. All three souls will be greatly missed by our community, and I want to reassure you that, as officers of the law, we did everything in our power to investigate them fully. I'll now open the floor to questions.'

Gaten took another sip of his coffee, turning his wrist so as not to display the brown stain on his white cuff. He tuned out as the press began firing their questions, focusing instead on the red light of a camera at the back of the room. It was blinking steadily. A single red eye peering over the heads of reporters. He swallowed and placed the cup down again.

'— location of both deaths were unusual? Neither are known suicide spots.'

A young reporter with a brown moustache finished speaking, and Justin Hadero raised his hand.

'I understand the locations were unusual,' he replied. 'This is why we got our best men onto the scene as fast as we could. Both assured me that the evidence points to suicide, and both post-mortems supported this point of view. I should also mention, in the case of Adrian Ramirez, a substantial dose of Class A drugs were found in his system. This could help explain how he ended up where he did.'

'And in the case of Bethany Taggort?'

'Mrs Taggort was found by her husband in her bathroom early yesterday morning. Her death has been confirmed as natural causes.'

'Sources have said she was found with her head down a toilet bowl.'

'As a man called Elvis would surely tell you, we don't choose where we die.'

This joke *was* met with disdain. Some journalists grumbled and crossed their legs, others started writing furiously in their pads, evidently realising that badly timed jokes might be the only thing of note that came out of the day's conference. Gaten looked at Abigail, expecting to see a similar sense of resentment. But resentment was not what he saw. It might have been the lights. It might have been the lack of sleep. But from where he was sitting, he could swear that Abigail was still smiling at him, her pad resting gently on her lap, her legs crossed, and her eyes still sizzling with that delightful balance. She looked totally unfazed by what Justin was saying. If anything, she looked happier now than she did when she sat down. Gaten held his cup but didn't take a sip.

'What I meant to say,' said Justin, attempting to pull the press back on side, 'is that the manner of these deaths are not an indication of homicide. Of course, we took these things into account. But our findings speak for themselves —'

'Should homosexuals in Cuckoo Cove be afraid?'

The woman who asked this question was sat at the back of the hall, her glasses thick and pink and her eyes small and beady. Gaten noticed the chief's jaw tighten.

'There's no reason to be afraid,' he said through gritted teeth. 'This town has long been a safe haven for folk of all identities. Doesn't matter whether you're straight, gay, black, or white.' The chief's voice cracked and he straightened his shirt again. 'My family is Hispanic,' he finished, as if to labour the point.

Just then, Gaten saw Abigail raise her hand and he felt his stomach perform a small backflip. His mind emptied of all thoughts of the monster and instead found a new one to be afraid of. He wished with all his might that Justin would ignore her, and to his relief, he pointed to an elderly gentleman three rows from the front. This question was on the police process and the specific details of Mrs Taggort's autopsy, but Gaten wasn't really listening. His attention remained on Abigail, whose hand remained high in the air, circling slightly like a snake rearing its head. She was still smiling at him.

Justin's answer was short and per-functionary, and when he was done, the elderly gentleman leant back and his gaze flickered across the room again. He gestured toward Abigail, and her hand dropped onto her notepad with a thud. It was a small thud, almost inaudible, but to Gaten, it sounded like an atomic bomb. She began talking.

'Mr Hadero, my name is Abigail Finn, reporter for the CC. Do you know how much taxpayers money goes into this police force?'

Justin swallowed, and it seemed as though everyone else at the table did the same. None of them had been suspecting that, least of all Gaten, whose fear of the new monster had suddenly tripled.

'That would be a question for the mayor, Miss Finn. My concerns are —'

'This *was* a question for the mayor, but I've noted that the mayor is not here.'

Abigail's voice was curt, sharp, seductive, serious. All the things that made her the perfect journalist, and the worst one Gaten could possibly imagine. His hand remained wrapped around his coffee cup, still trembling.

'The mayor isn't here,' Justin confirmed. 'You'll have to forgive that. This conference was rather rushed, as you'll be more than aware. He knows about the situation, and I've assured him that the people of this town are not in any danger.'

'That's excellent. But since the mayor is not here, you're the only person who can answer my question.'

Justin fidgeted with the microphone in front of him. 'I do not know. I'd have to come back to you on that. I'll get my best men on it —'

'It's $3 million,' Abigail answered for him.

Justin raised his hands. 'Looks like I won't need to waste valuable police time.'

'Actually, Mr Hadero, I wasn't asking about the number. I was asking if you knew it. Now you've confirmed that you don't, I can confidently ask my second question. If the police don't know how much the people of this town are paying them, does that explain why you would lie to those people during this press conference?'

The red eye of the middle camera blinked, and Gaten released his coffee cup. He heard murmurs in the room, the faces growing hungry again. Ravenous, in fact.

'Miss Finn, no one is being lied to —'

'Mr Hadero, I received a statement from one of your police officers that the police have been actively looking into Adrian Ramirez's murder from day one. And following information provided by the CC, the case *is* being treated as suspicious.'

Gaten felt the eyes of Justin Hadero flicker in his direction, and a momentary burning sensation lashed the side of his face.

'Miss Finn, I don't know where you're getting your information from, but I can assure you —'

'Mr Hadero, the source of this information is sitting to your left.'

Everyone in the room glared at Gaten. He felt a thousand lasers lash his skin, draining him of blood, until he was nothing but a pale skeleton, staring with dead eyes into the smile of Abigail Finn. Her lips moved, and Gaten read them.

'On the thirteenth of October, Officer Dalbret was given evidence regarding Adrian Ramirez direct from the CC. This was received voluntarily in order to help with the inquiry of Ramirez's death. Later that day, Officer Dalbret confirmed that the evidence had been examined, and that he was treating Adrian Ramirez's death as suspicious. This is recorded and on file. Why is it that a key member of the Cuckoo Cove police force would tell the CC something different to what is being said in this press conference? Do we take it, for instance, that this police force does not trust the people of Cuckoo Cove with the truth? To the point where they would actively choose to endanger their lives?'

The sound of pen and paper echoed across the town hall, every journalist scribbling furiously. To Gaten's left, he felt the gaze of Gunther and Wayne piercing into him, and to his right, he saw the body of Justin Hadero lean right up close to his microphone. He spoke with a gruff, shaking voice, churned up from the depths of inner, inexplicable fury.

'Well, Miss Finn. That sounds like a question for a certain Officer Dalbret. And unlike your last question, he is here to answer it.'

4

The press conference only lasted another five minutes before Justin pulled the plug. In all that time, Gaten remained silent, staring at nothing but the red light at the end of the room. When the conference was adjourned, the journalists charged out of the door like school kids rushing to the cafeteria. Justin Hadero dismissed everyone but Gaten, giving Gunther specific orders to get the mayor to call him immediately.

Once this was done, Justin stood in front of Gaten and smoked, the gel dripping from his hair in a barrage of sweat. He said something about reducing the scraps – tactical stuff to save skins. He said something about betrayal, disloyalty, nerve. He said something about heads being on the block. After a cigarette of his own, Gaten phased back into the world around him. He told Justin about his brother, and when he mentioned Theo's new name, Justin slammed his fists on the table and grabbed Gaten by the chin. Gaten then phased back out and stared at where the red light had been, now an empty space, a corner with cobwebs and dead blue flies hanging there. Keeping his eyes on this corner, he spoke again, interrupting Justin with the most earnest of intentions.

'Sir, what would you say if I told you I believed in monsters?'

Gaten Dalbret did not follow the rest of his colleagues back to the police station. Instead, he was sent home.

5

The wind was gentle. From the sandbanks, Kenny watched the movement of the ocean, pink dust on the waves, reflected against the sky. The scene might have been quaint and beautiful were it not for the racket about half a mile to the right. The crewmen had arrived on their row boats around three hours ago, dragging a collection of picks, shovels and drills toward the sandbanks. After digging trenches for an hour, they returned to the ship, brought back crates of black powder and packed the charges tightly before lighting the fuses and watching them blow. They were making their way down the beach, drawing closer to Kenny, but he wasn't afraid. The first few cuckoos hadn't been so lucky as to get a three hour warning, but Kenny had. So he sat and watched the sunset for a while, waiting for his turn to leave and find some other place to rest for the night. The crewmen couldn't possibly find him. And even if they did, what were they going to do next? Blow the entire coastline?

Chop, chop, chop.

Another explosion. Kenny listened as wet sand hit the water. He wondered exactly what the crewmen were trying to achieve. The cuckoos had taken their half of the latest whale to wash up on their shores, and the crewmen had taken the other. Technically, they had a split of one and a half whales each, and even that was being generous. The crewmen were outsiders, after all. They had no right to ask for any kind of share. But then, Kenny was aware of his limitations, and he knew it wouldn't be long before the crewmen were aware of theirs.

Chop, chop, chop.

Another bang. Louder this time. And Kenny could have sworn he heard the mushy sound of wet flesh landing in the ocean.

Chop, chop, chop.

Perhaps it was time to go.

Chop, chop, chop.

But not before —

Chop, chop, chop.

Kenny shook his head and cursed. 'Who's making that sound?'

Me. You asked what they were going to do next, and I'm telling you. Chop, chop, chop.

The next explosion rattled Kenny's ribcage, so he spread his wings, left the sandbank, and went in search of a well-covered branch somewhere in the undergrowth. Preferably one with fruit on it.

6

In the garden, Kenny found three worms, seven woodlice, and a slug. He dropped them inside a tub with some grass, and then filled a water bottle with the hose. Once inside, he fetched a teaspoon and some sugar and then headed for his bedroom, where the cuckoo was still lying in the corner of the box. It had done several shits in the last half hour.

'Jesus Christ,' said Kenny as he closed the door. 'Do you wanna add diarrhoea to the growing list of afflictions you're struggling with?'

With a heavy sigh, he placed the tub onto his desk, and the cuckoo glanced at it curiously. It hadn't so much as uttered "gone green" or "pain" since Kenny had awoken, and its silence was unnerving. It seemed almost tired, like it was close to giving up. Kenny had never seen a bird sleep, but he was pretty sure they needed it. And yet every time he had stirred last night, the cuckoo had been staring at him, its beady, black eyes reflected in the nightlight. Kenny had never much liked the cuckoos of Cuckoo Cove, but since this cuckoo had gone to the effort of talking to him, he felt at least partly responsible for it.

'I got you something,' he said, opening the water bottle. 'I saw on the Discovery Channel that you can help tired bees by putting some sugar in a teaspoon and filling it up with water. I didn't know if that translated to birds, but I thought we'd try it.'

With his right hand, Kenny grabbed the packet of sugar and flicked some into the teaspoon, dripping some water over it before placing it by the cuckoo's beak. It stared at him blankly.

'I guess that's a no,' Kenny muttered. 'Okay, if you don't like sugar and water, surely you like grass. Every animal likes grass.'

Once again, the cuckoo simply stared at him.

'How about a worm?' asked Kenny finally.

He removed one from the tub, dangling it over the cuckoo's head, and it sucked it up like a string of spaghetti.

'Great. You like the worms. The hardest thing to procure.'

The cuckoo blinked at him twice, then turned its gaze toward the tub on the desk. Kenny gave it another one.

'Go easy on them. We've got some woodlice and a slug in here too, and they're the main course, so you can't fill up.'

The bird finished off the second worm, and Kenny found himself smirking. He'd made dinner for his dad and Mandy once before. The pasta was so undercooked and hard, it sent Mandy to the dentist with a chipped tooth. He was glad to know worms, woodlice, and slugs were a dinner he *could* get right, and he made a mental note to remember that the next time he was asked to cook for them.

When the bird was done with its food, Kenny poured a small pool of un-sugarfied water into the other corner of the lid and watched as it crawled over to take a few sips.

'I've got a friend, you know. Well, not a friend. It's someone I like. Her name's Dora. Dora Lane. She's beautiful, honestly. Her eyes, her smile. She's got these lovely teeth that shine in the school corridor, the one with all the lockers. I don't know, I guess they reflect the light or something.'

The bird kept drinking, but Kenny was almost positive it was listening.

'I've been trying to do stuff to impress her. I climbed the Indian post. It's like this big post in the schoolyard, covered with these Native Indian markings, although I'm not sure they're real. But I climbed right to the top of it. Probably not much of an achievement for a bird like you. It wasn't for her, either. You see, there's another boy in school she wishes I looked like. She likes looking at pretty things, and I don't mind that, because I guess I'm the same. So I'm trying to play football.'

Kenny lay his head on the desk and watched as the bird finished its last few mouthfuls. When it was done, it crawled back into its corner and started pecking at its good wing.

'I could walk you right up to her and say: Dora, I can talk to this bird, and this bird can talk to me. And you know what she'd say back? That's great and all, but have you tried doing it with muscles?'

The bird stopped pecking and renewed the staring contest, glaring into Kenny's eyes like they held the secret of the universe.

'I'm happy you're not saying "pain" anymore. I guess that means my scarf worked. I'm not a doctor, but whenever I hurt a part of myself, I always hold it real tight. And when we – humans, I mean – break our leg, we put it in something called a cast. I say I'm not a doctor, but maybe I am. Doctor Dolittle. You know who that is?'

The cuckoo kept its eyes drawn to Kenny, waiting expectantly.

'You don't watch many movies, huh?'

Downstairs, Kenny heard Mandy arrive back from her afternoon workout. Bags of groceries smacked against the kitchen work surfaces, and a loud rendition of "Our House" by Madness travelled up through the floorboards. In a few moments, she would knock on Kenny's door and ask whether he wanted a milkshake, and Kenny would decline, as he always did, because milkshakes made you pudgy and Kenny didn't have any muscle to waste. He walked over to the door to lock it, then turned back to the cuckoo.

'My dad's girlfriend listens to a band called Madness. I've never been so much as a tiny bit offended by their name, because madness is a thing that will never affect me. But now I'm not so sure.'

The words tumbled from Kenny's mouth without much rhyme or reason, but once they were out, they hung in the room with a strange sort of tension, like they really mattered. The cuckoo seemed to soak them in. Then it began pecking itself again, and Kenny lost it. With an angry yell, he raced across the room, picked up the cuckoo, and held it five inches from his face.

'If you can talk to me, you better well talk to me properly. None of this "pain" shit. No "gone green". And don't go quiet on me either. That's just… that's just rude. I feel like I'm going crazy here, and everything in my life is so different in the smallest but biggest of ways, and if I'm being honest, it really fucking scares me. So if you can talk and you can listen to me, you better say something right now before I lose my mind, shove you in this water bottle and shake you up like a mineral.'

Downstairs, Kenny heard Mandy slam a cupboard door and call up to his bedroom.

'Kenny? Can you help me prepare dinner for your dad? Every time I chop onions, I feel like I've watched *Titanic* three times over.'

There was a silence. The bird stared at him. Then, in Kenny's head, he heard a voice reverberate from ear to ear. It almost had a tinge of humour to it, like it was mocking him.

Chop, chop, chop.

7

Sara watched Gaten approach the ground floor apartments, his face half covered by shadows. A soft speckle of rain had begun pattering against the window ledge, and in the muggy evening air, it oozed an almost sickening smell of salt and seaweed. Sara exhaled a puff of smoke from her cigarette and watched it float up into the sky.

When the door opened and Gaten finally entered, she didn't turn around. She stayed sitting on the sill, her eyes on the streets of Cuckoo Cove. A quiet rumble of thunder echoed through the clouds, and Sara flicked some ash into the mix. She spoke quietly.

'Yesterday I asked if there was someone killing gay people in Cuckoo Cove. You said there was.'

'Theo...'

Sara swivelled and saw her brother standing in the doorway, his body hunched and his skin pale.

'You told that reporter you knew there was a case,' she continued. 'You knew that, and yet you still sat there and let the chief lie. And not just lie, but put everyone in this town in danger. Everyone like me.'

With a strange, airy sigh, Gaten glided slowly across the room and grabbed a bottle of whisky that had been left on the coffee table. He took a glass from one of the cupboards and poured it around a three-quarters full.

'Do you want me to die?' asked Sara.

Her brother took a long gulp of the whisky and sat down onto the couch. His eyes were wide open, but Sara could see an emptiness in them, like they weren't really eyes at all. More like holes, burrowed all the way to the back of his skull.

'I'm not going to answer that question,' he muttered.

Sara stood up. 'Answer it.'

'No, Theo. I don't want you to die. I don't want anyone to hurt you. I don't want anyone to hurt anyone.'

'So why did you do it?'

'I've been telling Justin there's something wrong for days now. He wouldn't listen.'

'Your job is to serve the people in this town, not Justin Hadero. What are you? Spineless?'

Gaten took another gulp of whisky, then tapped the glass twice with his finger. 'I guess so.'

'You remember when we were kids? I used to climb into your bed after a bad dream, and you kicked me out. You were happy for me to fall back into my nightmare so long as you stayed comfortable. Not much has changed, has it?'

'Everything's changed.'

'Tell me how.'

'What?'

'Tell me how things have changed. Tell me what's different.'

'Well, you don't climb into my bed anymore, for a start.'

'You think I don't want to? I didn't stop getting nightmares, Gate. I got tired of getting kicked onto the carpet.'

Outside, another rumble of thunder vibrated from the clouds, but there was no lightning. The night was completely dark. The black ink had stained the page and no colours could break through. Except perhaps one. The secret Cuckoo Cabaret Club was going to get started in just a few hours now, and sometimes there were fireworks. Brighter fireworks than Sara had ever seen before, striking the night sky until it bled with light.

'Nothing has changed,' said Sara confidently. 'I'm still that kid who needs their brother. Yesterday on the beach, I said I trusted you. But you went ahead and lied anyway. Do you even know where I was last night?'

'What do you mean?'

'You believe there's someone killing gay people in Cuckoo Cove, so do you know where I was last night? What about the night before? Or the night before that?'

Gaten put his glass back on the table and refilled it. His hands were shaking, Sara noticed. The bones of his knuckles were squeezing against the skin, turning it white.

'I warned you what was going on the night we found the first body,' he replied. 'I can't control you, Theo. If you want to go gallivanting across the town doing what you do, I won't stop you.'

'You could have tried. You could have held me back. You could have begged me not to leave this apartment.'

'That would've made me the perfect brother, wouldn't it?'

'I'm not asking for the perfect brother, I'm asking for a brother who protects me.'

Gaten shook his head. 'You have no idea what I've gone through the last few days to do just that. I've been putting my neck on the line, fighting god knows how many people. Heck, I've just lost my job trying to protect you.'

'And yet all you had to do was take my hand and hold me back. But you wouldn't do that, would you? When was the last time you took my hand or gave me a hug? When was the last time you touched me?'

'I'm tired of this conversation, Theo.'

'You're not tired of the conversation, you're tired of trying to find answers that don't exist.'

'If they don't exist, why are you asking me?'

Sara thought about it. She mulled over what she was attempting to say, trying to find an open door. 'I guess I'm not asking you anything,' she said after a few seconds. 'I'm telling you, because perhaps you need to know. You don't love me. You haven't loved me since the day I put on this makeup. The brother you loved died that day, and you've simply been putting up with the imposter.'

Gaten stared at her. 'If you only knew how wrong you were.'

'Yes. If I only knew. So tell me.'

'You think I wanted any of this to happen? Everything I've done, every moment I've breathed has been spent in the shadow of the day I ran away from you. Ever since then, I've been ashamed. Ashamed of myself as a human being, as a brother. How could I let you sleep in my bed after that? You think I don't love you. The truth is, I love you so damn much that...'

'That what?'

Gaten swallowed up the last of his second glass. 'Forget it.'

Outside, the rain started getting louder, forming a small puddle on the wood of the windowsill. Sara stared at it for a few seconds before walking across the room to pull the window shut. She heard Gaten pouring another drink, and that familiar spike of anger rested inside her gut. As if she was on autopilot, she then walked into the kitchen and picked up a bottle for herself, but she didn't pour it. Instead, she headed back into the lounge and threw it directly at the wall by her brother's face. The whisky bottle exploded, shards of glass scattering across the floor and a flurry of amber liquid streaming down the paint.

'ARE YOU FUCKING INSANE?!' Gaten yelled.

'Oh, what? This conversation has woken you up now? All it took was a crash and a bang to make things interesting.'

'Jesus, Theo! What more do you want me to say?'

'You can start by saying my name.'

'What?'

'The puddle. You wanted to talk about the puddle, so let's talk about it. They pushed me into that puddle and beat me within an inch of my life because of who I was. Who I had chosen to be. You say you're ashamed of how you reacted, but you're on entirely the same page as them. If you feel ashamed, if you wanna protect me, then call me by my name.'

There was a beat. Gaten sat on the couch like a mannequin, his body tense and rigid.

'Call me by my name, Gaten. I call you by yours.' Sara felt tears start to stream down her cheeks, as ugly and unforgiving as the whisky on the wall. She wiped them away. 'That's it, isn't it? That's just it. You know, I always thought I didn't care. It's just a simple thing and you're my brother. Why would I care? But the thing is, it *is* simple. It's so simple. And that's why I care.'

Another beat. Another cold, lingering silence. Sara almost stamped her foot.

'Goddamn it, why is it so hard?'

'I don't know,' replied Gaten finally. 'You want me to give you a reason? I don't have a reason. You're my brother and I love you. I always did. But when you changed the way you are, the brother I knew wasn't the same person anymore. And I found out very soon that this was a brother I couldn't protect. I resented myself and, yeah, maybe in a certain way I resented you. I resented the person you made me become. Weak and afraid, and so scared I couldn't even stand up for my brother when you needed me most.'

The whisky on the wall began dripping onto the carpet, joining the sound of the rain which continued to patter against the window. The room vibrated with thunder, and Sara let out a long, shaky breath.

'That sure sounds like a reason to me. And a pretty selfish one at that.'

She didn't want to hear anymore. Before any more tears could ruin her makeup, Sara paced across the room and grabbed her fur coat from the peg by the door.

Gaten leapt up from the couch. 'Where are you going?'

'I'm moving out. I'll make sure all my stuff is packed by the end of tomorrow.'

'You have nowhere to go.'

'No, actually, I do. I've met someone. Not that you would care, you don't give two shits about my life.'

'Who have you met?'

'I'll see you in the morning.'

Gaten raced over to her, his arm outstretched, but he didn't touch her. He didn't hold. He stopped himself like there was some kind of invisible forcefield between them. All that connected them were their eyes, their old eyes that knew each other so well, and yet so distantly. A pair of strangers that had crossed paths for years and years, but had never spoken a word to each other.

'You can't go out at night,' said Gaten desperately. 'Not now.'

Sara slipped the coat onto her shoulders. 'Like you said, you can't control me.'

'Theo, the thing that's been doing this... the thing that's out there... it's not a person, it's...'

'It's what?' asked Sara.

Despite the whisky having poured a little blood into Gaten's face, it began draining again. He stood there as white as paper, so pale you could see the veins in his cheeks.

'A monster,' he answered shakily.

Sara laughed. 'There's plenty of monsters in this town, big brother. But I saw the news conference. There's nothing to worry about. Thank you for your service.'

And with that, Sara turned, closed the door, and made her way through the apartment block and onto the street outside. The night-time rain was heavy and the thunder was loud. It took only a few seconds for her wig to get wet. So wet, she may as well have dunked it into the ocean.

CHAPTER THIRTEEN

THE PIER

1

The hot water bottle rested on Kenny's lap, stinging his thighs. The rain outside was pounding the window. There was no lightning, but the nightlight was flickering in the corner of his room, casting bright green beams every half second.

After ten minutes of trying to get to sleep, Kenny gave up with the hot water bottle and flung it down onto the carpet. The cuckoo jumped and Kenny stared at it. In a way, it looked like the bird was waiting. Waiting for his eyes to drop and for sleep to take him. Kenny tried to calm himself down. When he was a kid, his mother used to tell him to count sheep, but Kenny had always struggled with counting, so he didn't find that advice helpful. Instead, he tried to disappear into a world of his own making. A world with devils and demons and monsters, which soon became a world he recognised as Gonagreen.

He entered it again now. He was a warrior with a shining sword, riding upon his noble steed, charging along a narrow road to a castle with tall twisted spires. He didn't know what was waiting for him inside. A dragon, an ogre, a thunder troll, a basilisk. All he knew was that he was ready for it. His hand hovered around the hilt, and his steed galloped at what felt like a hundred miles per hour.

Kenny felt his eyes begin to droop, the green flashes of the nightlight start to dim. But his heart stayed strong, his will unwavering, until he reached the bridge of the castle and the great wooden doors opened in front of him.

2

On the other side of those doors was a beach. Bright and shining. Tiny crabs were scuttling over the grains, their legs clicking against flakes of shell. Kenny was sitting in a mound of leaves and flowers, the sun piercing the skin beneath his feathers. The trees had long gone and their timber was piled about a mile outward, getting wet from the waves. The crewmen were there too, but there were more of them now – hundreds, in fact. Spindly structures were built around them, covered in salty canvases and ropes, some of which dangled from platforms and swung hypnotically in the sea breeze. Kenny was just about to fly in for a closer look when a voice circled around his head.

You see, I told you. Chop, chop, chop.

Kenny felt his body go numb and a sense of hyper-awareness strike him. In that instant, he realised he was dreaming. The world around him wasn't real – the ocean, the beach, the tiny crabs with their spindly, scurrying legs. None of it was real. Even *he* wasn't real. Couldn't be real. And yet...

Very much real.

The voice in his head was very much real, that much he could tell. It echoed through him like a cold wave. He could hear it and he could feel it, and if he tried to shake it off, he knew it wouldn't work. It was like the voice was outside of his dream, calling into it.

Very much correct.

Kenny started remembering elements of his life outside of this beach. The sun in the sky started flashing green, the waves turned into rolling thunder, and the water speckling the stones became rain pattering against the window pane. He remembered lying in bed and staring at the cuckoo in the box.

It's you, he realised.

The voice returned. *Who?*

You. My cuckoo. The one in my bedroom. It's you. You can talk.

No, I can't talk. None of us can talk. But we can think. We were taught to do that a while ago.

Beneath Kenny's feet – or what felt like feet – the sand of the beach began to move, but the wind hadn't changed. His stomach started doing somersaults, but he held firm and kept himself rooted to the spot.

I don't understand. If you're the cuckoo in my bedroom, that means you can talk to me. Why are you doing it when I'm asleep and not when I'm awake?

Your mind is more open when you're asleep. And mine too.

Okay, but why are you talking to me at all?

You're not so special. You're just a child. Children dream when they're awake. You more than most. That's why you heard me.

The sand continued to move, getting faster and faster. Out in the distance, Kenny saw the crewmen disappear, then reappear, then disappear again, and every time they did, the pile of timber on the beach got lighter, forming into multiple platforms that stretched out into the ocean.

What's happening? he asked shakily.

I'll show you, his cuckoo replied.

And then Kenny was up in the air, the wind whistling past his face. He felt cold but hot at the same time, and that sick feeling in his stomach was growing more intense, climbing into his throat until he felt like regurgitating into the ocean. After a few seconds, he was hovering above the crewmen, each of whom seemed to be moving on fast-forward.

Now that he was closer, Kenny could see what was going on in far greater detail. It wasn't just men, but women too. The mountain of timber was now surrounded by iron piles, stone and metal straps, some of which were tied to horses, ridden by people in official looking uniforms. The coastline itself was filled with short stumps where the trees used to be, and beyond the beach and the grass, Kenny could see small buildings, smoke rising from the chimneys and melting into the blue, shiny sky. A lot had changed since he had last dreamed about this place. A lot had changed since just a few seconds ago. The platforms in the ocean were combining together now, stretching into the ocean, and around two dozen row boats and barges were bobbing underneath them. Large, strange looking contraptions were tied down upon rafts, hanging over the water and driving long, iron poles down into the depths.

Years and years and years, said his cuckoo.

Kenny started circling, spinning around and around the buzz of activity as the decking started travelling further into the sea.

It's the pier, he realised. *The Cuckoo Cove pier, that's what they're building. That's where we are.*

At the same moment this thought struck him, something else replaced the anxiety inside his stomach. It was the feeling of dread. All of a sudden, the sun flashed green again above him, and his world was plunged into a strange sort of darkness.

Hungry.

This time, it wasn't his cuckoo talking. It's wasn't anything. It was a memory. Small and distant, but somehow still loud and clear. Kenny remembered his last two dreams. He hadn't realised he was dreaming then. And he hadn't been Kenny in a cuckoo's body, he had *been* the cuckoo. He remembered eating the beached whale, ripping the flubber from its bones, digging with his beak into the soft flesh beneath its fins. He remembered the taste, he remembered the satisfaction, he remembered the anger he felt when the crewmen took the next whales for themselves. He remembered the word "hungry" echoing around his head. But not just his head. Every head. Every cuckoo. Because they were all connected. They were connected through thoughts and dreams, in a maze of colours, with one very dark one in the centre. The one that had started it all.

Years and years and years, his cuckoo said again.

Kenny looked down. The pier looked more like a pier now, though it was still just a skeleton of the pier he knew. He stared for a few more seconds before asking his next question.

But this can't be a memory. How can we be here if this happened hundreds of years ago?

A group of around ten cuckoos hurtled past him then, swooping down toward the waves before shooting up into the clouds.

We share the same thoughts, his cuckoo replied. *The same memories. Over and over again. You felt it too. We're connected.*

But why?

Something has been here for a long time. Waiting. We came to it and it talked to us. For years and years and years. All it had was us. It listened to our thoughts and nestled into our minds. It was so hungry, so we got hungry too.

The pier was nearly finished now. The timber and iron from the beach was just about gone, but the boats and barges remained.

When the people came, his cuckoo continued, *it left us. But over thousands of years, we had learned. Our connections remained.*

I don't understand what you're saying, said Kenny.

But something here is still so hungry. Not for flesh. Something doesn't eat flesh. It needs something else. A single feast that can keep it filled for centuries.

Kenny felt himself flying lower, heading back toward the beach. He spiralled about the sand for a minute or two, watching as the boats and barges travelled east toward the sun, which was setting, then rising, then setting, then rising. And flashing green.

Something here has been given a home. Given a bed. And it's been waiting again. Listening. And getting more and more hungry for the big feast.

Like a rollercoaster, Kenny swerved to the left and began weaving through the framework of the pier, darting between metal poles and timber. He was flying out into the ocean again. The waves beneath him roared, foam dripping from the woodwork like saliva. Kenny noticed groups of cuckoos nesting in the crevices, huddled together and staring at him as he flew past.

I wanted to show you, said his cuckoo. *To say thank you. I thought you'd like to know.*

Kenny continued to fly, coming up to the end of the pier now. He could see a great, black mass waiting for him there.

Something here is awake now. And it's time for you to wake up too.

In the light of the rising sun, the black mass formed itself into something real. What looked like a gigantic bat was hanging upside down from the pier, its wings folded around its torso, its curled talons long and shining. It opened its eyes as Kenny approached and Kenny saw that they were the colour of blood.

He awoke in his bed screaming.

CHAPTER FOURTEEN

AVA

1

Sara knew there would be colours. Above the secret Cuckoo Cabaret Club, a myriad of lights swelled in the dark sky, fluttering like ribbons in the wind. While they could have been fireworks, there was no sound. No whoops, no cheers, no soft hisses as the display fizzled into nothing. The lights hung there with a strange sort of permanence, reflecting on the surface of the ocean to create a sphere of brilliance. What was more strange was that the storm continued. Thunder growled behind the clouds and rain seeped into the wood beneath Sara's feet, making it slippery.

When she approached the club, she saw Ava waiting for her in the doorway. She was wearing black today. A tight leather jacket was hugging her torso, tied across the breasts. Around her shoulders, she wore a dark, flowing cape. On her arms, she had fingerless leather gloves that travelled up to her elbows. Fishnet stockings were suspended just a few inches from her mini skirt, and the makeup on her face was dark and boisterous, with jet-black lipstick, eyeliner, and mascara. Her hair was short and curled this evening, tickling both shoulders and fluttering in the wind as gracefully as the ribbons in the sky. Sara came up alongside her, watching as the lights morphed from green to blue, to purple, to red.

'Hi,' she said quietly.

Ava nudged her. 'What do you think of our little firework display?'

Sara pulled out a cigarette and lit it under the eaves of the club. 'They're not fireworks. They can't be.'

'Double points for my clever cuckoo. You know what this is? It's called the aurora borealis, and it's created just for us.'

Sara squinted at the sky. 'I didn't think you could see the aurora borealis from here.'

'I'm not a scientist,' laughed Ava. 'But do you think the world revolves around you and your preconceptions? It's a loose cannon, honey. It does what it wants. As do we.'

'Even in a storm?'

'Especially in a storm.'

Ava gave her a little peck on the neck, but Sara pulled away. When she did so, it looked like Ava's eyes flashed green for a moment, her irises reflected in the lights dancing above their heads.

'What's wrong?' she asked.

'Nothing, it's just...'

'Just?'

Sara swallowed. She thought about her brother. His empty, pale face. His eyes, like holes, and his tense, shaking hands. She thought about his silence when she asked him to say her name. That simple, beautiful name. *Why couldn't he just say it?* she thought. *Just move his mouth and say it...*

'Sara...' Ava nudged her again, and Sara stared at her.

Even with the new look, there was still something so stunning and wonderful about Ava's presence. Her face was shining, and up close it had a sweet scent of coconut and pomegranate. Her hair looked soft and sculpted. Every strand, every droplet of water resting at the ends, created by an artist. And her eyes, those big eyes, full of mystery. On closer inspection, it didn't look like they were reflecting the colours of the sky. It was like they *were* the colours. All of the colours, all at once.

'Would you come away with me?' she asked her then.

'Come away with you...' Ava repeated.

'Yes. Come away with me. Away from this place. Away from Cuckoo Cove. This isn't a gay town, Ava. People don't want us here.'

Ava smiled playfully. 'There are no gay towns in America.'

Sara wavered. She remembered thinking the same thing a few nights ago. Those exact words. Ava seemed to read her expression.

'We all know it, pickle. We think it everyday. That's why we created this place. Our own little world. That's why we dance and dance and dance.'

'But don't you want more?'

Ava's eyes flashed again, yellow this time. 'What do you mean, more?'

'Don't get me wrong, this club is the best thing that has ever happened to me. The best. But I want every second of every day to be like this. I don't want to be afraid anymore.'

'It's like I told you, Sara. The world we've created for ourselves here, that's the only real thing. Everything out there is just a shadow.'

Sara sighed. She stared at the town of Cuckoo Cove at the other end of the pier, untouched by the display of lights above their heads. It was black and lifeless, its low-glowing lamps shivering in the wind and rain.

'So you won't come away with me,' she said simply.

Ava smiled again. She leaned in close and whispered into her ear, that irresistible scent of coconuts and pomegranates doubling as she did so. 'I'll come away with you whenever and wherever you like. I'll spend every waking moment with you if that's what you want. Haven't you realised by now? I am yours, and you are mine.'

Sara pulled away. 'You'll leave?'

'Who says we have to leave? All we want is each other, Sara. The rest is immaterial.'

The rain continued to pour. It fell as hard and soft as Ava fell into her. The kiss was just as Sara had remembered. A warm bowl of happiness poured into her mouth, making her tremble, shake, shiver, and yet stand more firm and tall than she had ever stood in her life. After what felt like a whole minute, Ava finally pulled back, and Sara saw those eyes echoing the lights of the sky again. Deep red and glowing.

'Shall we go inside?' she asked softly. 'Aurora borealis is beautiful, but this puddle we're standing in is getting deeper. And I don't wanna sink to the bottom.'

Sara nodded and flicked away her cigarette. Then she took Ava's hand and was waltzed into the club.

2

Midnight on the other side of town, and Gaten Dalbret was approaching the police station. The storm was getting heavier. What felt like a barrage of water stuck his hair to his face, making him shiver and quake – or so he told himself. The real cause was probably the whisky. That thick, sickly amber that had circled down his throat like water down a sink, kicking up the fury and creating the fever. He had entered his apartment feeling numb, but now he seemed to feel everything. Anger, guilt, fear, and the fire. All the emotions were swirling through his blood and tensing his muscles, urging him to let it all out, to find the nearest excuse of an instigator and knock them into the dirt. And that was exactly what he was intent on doing.

He made his way up the steps and into the main reception of the police station. Two officers passed him on the stairs, but neither of them batted an eye. Both of them were half asleep, a steaming coffee in each hand and a newspaper folded into their armpits, entirely oblivious to the danger facing them all. They looked like they would hardly blink twice at the videotape, and Gaten knew exactly why. The reason was waiting in his office. He'd known Justin Hadero would be there, seeing as it was his neck on the line this time, but he had no idea how many others he would rope in along with him. Gaten was glad to see it was just two. Wayne Brown and Gunther Price, both of whom sat beside Justin with their shoes up on his desk, a yogurt and a spoon in each hand. Their shoes swiftly left his desk when they saw Gaten marching up to them.

'Gate!' gasped Wayne. 'What are you doing here?'

Gaten ignored him, staring straight into the eyes of Justin Hadero. 'Who gave you the order?' he asked quietly.

Justin remained in the same position behind his desk, glaring back at Gaten with an air of both hatred and disinterest. 'I said you were on administrative leave, Gaten. That means you don't come into work.'

'Administrative leave my ass. I'm fired and we all know it.'

'Then you're trespassing.'

'Breaking and entering, actually.'

Before either Wayne or Gunther could stop him, Gaten picked up the computer from Justin's desk and slammed it onto the floor. Black glass and chunks of plastic scattered about their feet.

'JESUS CHRIST!' Gunther yelped.

'Who gave you the order?' Gaten repeated. 'Don't tell me you believed they were suicides. Who told you to wipe it under the carpet?'

Wayne grabbed Gaten's shoulder. 'What the hell's gotten into you, Gate? You can't be doing this.'

'Call the police, then. Oh, wait, we are the police.' Gaten pointed at Justin. 'Who gave you the order?'

Justin stayed rock-steady, his legs crossed and his expression completely unchanged. 'I give my own orders, son.'

'Bullshit.'

'Gaten!' Wayne pulled him by the shoulder but Gaten shrugged him off.

'When you came to the reservoir on the day of the first body, you said the mayor would want this to be kept quiet. How long has he been whispering in your ear to save his image? How long have you been listening to save yours?'

'You think a few dead gay guys would tarnish the mayor's image?'

'This is a gay town, Justin. It wouldn't help it.'

'You really have no clue, do you? Cuckoo Cove is not a gay town. It's an American town. We didn't choose to have queers frolicking around our doorstep, they chose to be here, and we're abiding because we need to be. The greater good. People can do what they want, when they want, but not to its detriment.'

In the corner of the room, a coffee machine began whirring and breathing steam. The smell of nut, caramel, and soil oozed into the air-con.

Gaten shook his head. 'What are you talking about, the greater good?'

'Jesus, Gaten, quit burying your head in your mommies blouse. Do you think this town would be half as prosperous if it weren't for them? Small American towns are dying, right across the country, but not this one. Why do you think that is? Investment. Nightlife. Tourism. They bring in money, it's as simple as that. Our leniency is keeping this town alive, but there are consequences. Keeping order in a town full of queers is never going to work. These people don't understand order. They'll drink and drown their twisted minds in all the chemicals you can imagine, and it's us that's gotta clean up the pieces.'

Gaten took a step back, gawping at Justin in disbelief. 'You're saying we'll take from them, but we won't protect them?'

'Our job is to keep order. You can't do that for people who don't know the meaning of the word. Listen, Gaten, I don't know what party pills you've been taking. But there is no killer. These people brought it on themselves, plain and simple. That's what I believe. That's what the mayor believes. And that's what we'll make this town believe.'

Wayne picked up his yogurt and let out a smile. 'Perhaps he's borrowed some pills out of the drawer of his brother.'

At that moment, the coffee machine stopped churning. The sound of boiling water died away and was replaced by the sound of ringing. A strange, high-pitched ringing that seemed to dig its way into Gaten's head like a burrowing mole. The world around him flashed white and things went a little dizzy for a moment, like he'd just finished a loop in the world's shortest rollercoaster.

'What did you say?' he muttered.

Wayne shrugged, licking the back of his spoon. 'You said to me yesterday that you saw a monster, right? I mean, come on, Gate —'

But before he could finish, Gaten grabbed him by his shirt and slammed him into one of the office cabinets. For a second, he thought he might punch him, but as soon as Wayne hit the metal, the ringing in Gaten's ears went away. The white flashes fizzled out and he found himself in the room again, like the blood had boiled as fast as the coffee in the corner, and was now bubbling into nothing but hot air. After a few moments, Gaten felt Gunther's arms wrap around him, and he let himself be pulled away.

'Jesus Christ, Dalbret' said Wayne shakily, patting down his uniform. 'I always thought you were a good guy. After what you said to me yesterday, I thought I'd give you the benefit of the doubt. But now I know you're just a psycho. Looking for monsters where they don't exist.'

'He's just tired, Wayne,' said Justin, who now wore a strange, bright smile. 'That's all this is. He just can't cut it.'

The chief tapped his knuckle twice on the desk, and Gaten peered down, finally taking in the notes in front of him. He saw his training reports, case reports, fitness assessments, psychological evaluations. All of them were accompanied by scribbles in the margins:

PSYCHOTIC EPISODES

CONFUSED

QUEER BROTHER

Justin noticed his gaze, picking up a pen with a smug flourish before clicking it into action. 'Now we have another to add to the list,' he said. Then he leant down and wrote the word,

VIOLENT

For a split second, Gaten thought about breaking free and leaping over the table, grabbing Justin by his collar and slamming him into one of his cherished accomplishments on the wall behind him. That's what he had come here to do, after all. To unleash his fury upon a man who deserved it. To hit and hit again until he drew blood. But now he was stood staring into the cold, brown eyes of Justin Hadero, all he felt was a sense of despair. Uselessness. The blood had boiled, and all that had resulted was a split second of hot steam. He dipped his head and felt Gunther's grasp loosen.

'You're going to sweep me under the carpet too?' he murmured.

Justin put down his pen. 'There are no monsters, Gaten. Only the ones we create ourselves.'

Gunther stepped away and Gaten was left unmanned. He felt naked in a way, like he had been stripped of his emotions almost as soon as they had returned to him. Now that numb feeling was swirling through his system again. He was nothing but a cardboard cutout, like they could tap him and he would fall over. With a shaky breath, he turned and walked out of the office.

'Actually, that's not true,' said Wayne from behind him. He walked over to his desk and grabbed a small, pink sticky note. 'Kid called a couple of hours ago. Had a nightmare. Says there's a monster hiding underneath the pier. How about you go investigate that, Officer Dalbret?'

He slapped the note onto Gaten's chest, and although he was now covering the door to the chief's office, Gaten could hear Justin laughing. He imagined him sitting there like a cartoon character, smacking his knee in amusement with tears streaming down his cheeks, unaware of a great black shadow that was rearing its head behind him.

Gaten took the note and left without saying another word.

3

Kenny's rifle was propped inside his dad's cabinet. It wasn't hard to get in there. His dad's hiding place for the key was around the antler of a stuffed elk head, which he'd shot on a trip to Montana and positioned on the wall of the living room. Kenny had seen it hanging there since he was about five. He was twelve now, and the last time he'd touched this gun was a year ago. Thankfully he'd grown at least a couple of inches since then, and while his muscles didn't seem to have grown along with him, it was still less of a huge, threatening thing to carry. He took it in both hands and locked the cabinet, returning the key to the elk on the wall before creeping back to his bedroom. The cuckoo's eyes appeared to widen when he entered, and the word "pain" swirled around Kenny's head.

'Don't shit your pants again,' he said under his breath.

Dropping the gun onto his bed, Kenny paced across the room and opened his cupboard. A large white suitcase was waiting for him inside, half zipped and full of coat hangers. He pulled them out and threw them onto the carpet. The cuckoo jumped and flapped its wings frantically.

Pain, pain, pain.

'I said don't shit your pants.' Kenny broke open his rifle and put it inside the suitcase. Then he clambered down onto his stomach and began rummaging underneath his bed, pulling out a clutter of old board games, dirty socks and underwear.

Pain, pain, pain.

'Would you shut up? I know what you're trying to do.'

Pain, pain, pain.

'Your wing is getting better. I can tell. You're moving it more. If you wanna act like you're in pain, you gotta be consistent. It's called pretending.'

Pain, pain, pain.

Kenny felt his hand close around a large, plastic tub, and he pulled it out. Inside was a variety of objects: action figures, dragon figures, spaceships, comics, and a range of small, skull-shaped candles. He'd bought the latter around a year ago when he had been trying to add a little more atmosphere to his Gonagreen adventures, but it wasn't the candles he was looking for. He began pulling out the contents of the tub one by one.

The bird fluttered its wings again and toilet paper flew out from underneath it. *Gone green, gone green, gone green.*

'You're not gonna stop me,' said Kenny irritably. 'I saw it in my dream, you showed it to me. There's a monster under the pier. What do you expect me to do, go back to sleep like it was all just a nightmare?'

Gone green, gone green, gone green.

'That's not what she would expect me to do.'

Gone green, gone green, gone green.

'Dora Lane. If she was in danger, do you think she'd expect me to run away? If that thing is under the pier then everyone is in danger. The cops don't believe me. My dad definitely won't. So I guess it's up to me.'

Gone green, gone green, gone green.

'It's just like my stories. Just like Gonagreen. The knight always has to slay the dragon before he can get to the princess. So that's what I'm gonna do, I'm gonna —'

But before he could finish, the cuckoo flew from its box and began darting from one side of the room to the other. Kenny ducked down, watching at it collided against the walls before spiralling down to the carpet and landing with a faint chirp.

'Jesus Christ! What the hell is your problem?'

The cuckoo stared at Kenny hopefully. *Pain, pain, pain.*

Kenny walked across the room and picked it up. 'Nice try...'

Scowling at the bird, he carried it toward the bed and nestled it onto the sheets. He was just about to give it a good telling off when another word echoed inside his head. This was a word he hadn't heard before. Not from the cuckoo, anyway. It was soft, and quiet, but it sank into his blood and seemed to get louder the longer it stayed there.

Afraid.

The word came over and over again, bobbing up and down from the depths of Kenny's mind, fighting for air and urging him to breathe it in.

'What, you don't think I'm afraid?' he asked once it had quietened. 'I am afraid. I'm terrified. But not of dying. I saw death a long time ago. I looked it in the face and was forced to make it a part of my life. I know death. But I don't know monsters. Not really.'

He began pulling more figurines and comics from the tub, burrowing all the way to the bottom. What he was looking for was squashed into the corner, crumpled and tattered, and scratched halfway to hell. He picked it up, then gave the cuckoo a stroke on the back.

'I'm not an idiot,' he said assuredly. 'I'm bringing the gun for protection, but I'm not gonna need it. You see, my dad told me about a farm he used to travel to for turkey hunting. The farmer there – Farmer Joe, I think his name was – had a bat problem that was driving him mad. They were screwing up everything. Contaminating the water, chewing the fruit, even spreading diseases. The only problem was, he couldn't find them. They weren't in the trees, the bushes, the barns. He looked everywhere.

'One day, he decided to light a bonfire in his backyard, burn up all the rotten hay and old fencing. And this wasn't a small bonfire, this was a big one. Half the size of his house. And hot. Like you could feel it all the way on the other side of town. Anyway, it turns out the bats could feel it too, because just by chance, he'd started the bonfire just a few inches above their hiding place. Pretty soon, it wasn't just smoke blocking out the sun. It was bats too. Hundreds of them, swarming around the farm before disappearing into the distance. The fire had driven them out of these tiny rabbit holes they'd been roosting in. To stop them coming back, every other Sunday, Farmer Joe would shove an oily rag into those holes and throw down a lit match.'

Kenny raised the box of matches in front of the cuckoo's face and it stared at them, its head tilting a little and its eyes, although black, glazed with the light of fear.

'You told me those people had made a home for the monster, all those years back. Well, I'm gonna get rid of it the same way Farmer Joe did.' Kenny pocketed the matches and shoved the tub back under his bed. 'I'm gonna burn its house down.'

4

It was approaching two in the morning, and Gaten was walking down the steps to the harbour. The storm hadn't let up one bit, and while that would almost certainly make things difficult, being on the water was something he was used to.

It was around fifteen years ago now that his uncle had left him the Iolanda, but he'd never been appreciative. Peter Dalbret had not been a very nice man. He'd smelled bad, for one thing. He'd smelled like rotten cigarettes and port wine – wine that had turned sour after being left in the sun too long. He'd also had two warts on both eyelids, so big they kept his eyes half-closed, which gave the impression he was constantly scowling at everyone. Ever since Gaten had swiped a pack of his cigarettes, his uncle had always treated him spitefully. Even at the age of fifteen, Gaten was just a no good, petty criminal, five or so years from his first stint in the county jail. Certainly a far cry from his brother, Theo, who was a shining example of propriety and prudence – before he decided on a certain lifestyle change, of course, though Uncle Pete didn't stick out life long enough to witness that.

As punishment for his thievery, it was decided that Gaten should accompany his uncle on some character building sailing trips. The Iolanda was a small sloop that he'd bought in a local auction, a rickety old thing that hardly ever got past ten knots. He took it out alone most mornings, but on Saturdays, Gaten would have to join him and quite literally learn the ropes – which was less of a character building exercise, and more of an excuse for his uncle to sit back, enjoy the oceanic breeze, and smoke around two dozen cigarettes.

This continued for around a year until Uncle Pete suffered a heart attack, but even death couldn't rid Gaten of the boat. Left to him in the will, the sloop had spent the last ten years bobbing in Cuckoo Cove harbour, slowly rotting away into a floating chunk of soggy wood. He didn't have the heart to throw it in the dump. Even though he hated him – and, man, did Gaten hate him – destroying his uncle's pride and joy seemed a little too far, even for a no good, petty criminal like Gaten. It was this point of weakness, however, that Gaten was now thankful for.

With his heart pumping, he walked over to the third slip, removed the cover, and climbed inside the rotting Iolanda. The wood beneath his feet felt spongey, and the ropes were covered with slime and seaweed, but Gaten didn't mind. All it needed to make was one trip and then, for all he cared, it could sink into the depths of the ocean where it belonged. Unwrapping the mooring line from the cleat, Gaten moved to the stern to find a jerry can. To his relief, the can in the storage locker sloshed with about two-thirds of its fuel remaining. He poured one-third into the tank and tried to spark the motor. It took several attempts before it was pulled out of its slumber – coughing a dozen times in an imitation of its owner – and then the boat was moving, surfing the water like a tired, bloated frog that had forgotten how to swim.

When it finally got into its groove, Gaten untangled the main halyard and let loose the sail. As if it was aware of its final hurrah, the boat picked up speed and cruised over the waves, travelling close to its maximum of ten knots. The pier awaited him just half a mile away. Despite the dark skies, Gaten could clearly make out its silhouette in the faded, flickering lights of Cuckoo Cove. According to the note, the call had been made at around nine-thirty that same evening, and while Gaten didn't know if that was true, he knew he was going to find out. If there was a way he could get actual proof that there was something out there, that maybe there *was* some kind of monster lurking in Cuckoo Cove, then perhaps everything could be changed. This road he had forged for himself was a dark one. Without his job, without his reputation, without his brother. But if he could see this thing for himself and pinpoint its location, there might be a way to light up the street lamps. All he had to do was hold his nerve, and hope that his uncle's boat could survive one last round.

It was doing a fine job so far. The sail remained fully set, willing the boat onwards, and it wasn't long before Gaten found himself closing in on the supporting structure of the pier. As he did so, the storm seemed to abate a bit, the rain pulling back as if holding its breath. The boat creaked and groaned on the waves, and Gaten eased the sail in response, slowing it down before returning to the motor. This time, it churned into life immediately, chugging the boat forward until it was underneath the framework.

Then the world around Gaten went quiet. Even in the darkness, he could make out clumps of cuckoos huddling in the crevices, sheltering from the tiny waterfalls that were hurtling down from the decking of the pier. While he felt calm, the racing of his heart told him otherwise. As soon as the sky was blocked, every inch of Gaten felt like it had been stung by adrenaline, draining away any remnant of whisky that had been lingering in his bloodstream. Nothing about this world felt blurred or distant. Everything was immediate. The water beneath the boat, the way the seaweed wrapped around the wood and metal, the steady, quiet call of the cuckoos. Gaten didn't have to go looking for any of it. He felt it. In his head, in his heart, in the way the hairs stood up on the back of his neck. He was completely sober to the world around him, to the point where he was a part of it, and knew almost everything that had happened, was happening, and was bound to happen in the next few seconds. But nowhere in that world did he see a monster. The waves rushed against the pier, the cuckoos chirped and shuffled, but as far as Gaten could tell, there was no other disturbance. The groan of the wood was not the low growl of a strange beast. The patter of water on his shoulder was not the falling drool of some hungry phantom. Though his heart told him to be afraid, his head told him there was nothing to be afraid of.

All the same, he pulled the throttle and cruised closer toward the end of the pier. Once he was up against the last piling, he cut it out and stood up, peering toward the woodwork and cupping his face with his hands. The wind was picking up again, the rain making it hard to see. Gaten thought back to the tape, and the shadow that had blocked out the light of Adrian's world. He remembered the toothless man and his ugly grin, and for a moment, he wondered if he really had gone crazy. Was a shadow really enough to go on? To tear up his beliefs and be convinced of a monster? *Yes*, he thought. *Yes it is.* It was like he had known right from the beginning, as soon as he saw that bloated, floating body bobbing up and down in the reservoir, there was something darker lurking within Cuckoo Cove. He'd known for a long time that this town was the home of monsters, and this was just another one he would have to deal with.

But now here he was, standing beneath the abandoned pier, and all he was looking at was a congealed mess of green slime and rotting wood. He didn't know what he had expected to see there, but he at least thought he'd see *something*. Anything that might confirm his fears and give him the answers that he needed. He sighed and held hard to the mast, steadying himself as the waves began to get louder.

As they did so, however, another sound came to join them. It fell like rainwater through the cracks of the pier, landing upon Gaten so softly that it wouldn't be noticed by anyone else – only Gaten, whose heart was still racing and whose blood was aflame with the roar of immediacy. Music. Strings. Drums. A voice. Faint and mellow, yet somehow still jubilant and raucous. Together they phased into a melodic hum, floating in the air like confetti in the wind, and Gaten tried to find the source of it. He was at the end of the pier, so he knew he was directly underneath the old ballroom, though he also knew no one had set foot in that hall for years. He shook his head and wondered whether all of the whisky had been pushed out of his system after all. But even after a rigorous shake down, the music remained. If anything, louder than before. More there. More real. And strangely more alluring. Like it was a golden ladder being lowered down from bright clouds, willing Gaten to climb it.

He didn't climb, but he did pull on the throttle and turn the boat into shore. Strange music which shouldn't exist wasn't a monster, of course. But it was something. And something was exactly what Gaten was looking for.

5

By the time he got onto the decking, the music had shifted to darker tones – tight, visceral. It rested on the wind like autumnal leaves, so quaint and colourful, and yet dead in its makeup. Gaten stood before the gates of the pier, breathing it in. Above his head hung the skull of the whale, large and smiling, with two great big dark holes staring him down from both orbits. The bone itself had been tarnished by years of rain and seawater now. The same thing which had kept it alive, now inciting its gradual, inevitable rot. Gaten grabbed the metal bars and climbed over to the other side. Beneath his shoes, the wooden decking was wet and slippery. He could see the waves moving through the cracks several feet below him. All traces of calm were gone from the world now, and instead, the waves seemed to crash against the pier with even more vigour, like they too had been seized by a surge of adrenaline. Holding on to the bannister, Gaten began walking to the end, his eyes darting from shadow to shadow, and his left hand hovering delicately above his gun holster.

From the outside, the ballroom looked just as dilapidated as the rest of the pier. Windows were boarded shut and graffiti was splattered across the paint. From the inside, however, Gaten could still hear the music. The trumpets, the strings, the sax. Loud voices echoed from within the walls, humming into the night like Gaten had stumbled across a nest of bees. Carefully, he approached the doors and tried to open them. They gave a little, but in the centre, just in front of Gaten's chest, he could see a lock holding both doors together.

Here was a slither of light that shone from within. A light that felt both warm and inviting, and yet cold and distant. Gaten leant into it. Through the gap, there were distant blurs. Gold, white, blue and black, swirling together in a haze. But after a few seconds, they began to right themselves. Features were coming through. Hair, faces, eyes, hands, holding firmly onto each others, and spinning. There were flowers too, Gaten could see. Roses, lilies and carnations pinned to dresses and suits, squeezed behind ears, and gripped between teeth. To the right side, there were groups in masks. Stringed, plastic dog masks, clipped beneath the nose to allow for the rotation of champagne flutes. To the left side, there were even more. Pigs, horses, and grasshoppers, if Gaten had to guess, though they could have been roaches or ants. They stood in batches of three, deep in conversation. Some were men, others were women, and some appeared to be both, judging by their muscular arms and beefy thighs that were shown off by scantily cut dresses.

'What the hell...' Gaten muttered, his heart beating hard against his chest.

After a few more seconds, he rubbed his eyes, blinked, and returned his gaze to the centre, where the dancers were beginning to part now. As the music swerved into something slower, hands let go and Gaten could stare deeper into the abyss, following the beam of light until it reached a face that he recognised. Gaten's brother was stood in the middle of the room, his back up against the stem of a giant champagne glass, and his hands softly caressing the hair of another man. Like Theo, this man was also dressed as a woman. He was wearing a curly, black wig, and he was clad in leather, with a long, black cape tied loosely around his neck. He was a tall, slim man, with olive-coloured skin and a radiance that enveloped even Gaten, standing outside in the chill of the night's storm.

He watched them for a while, jaw agape. Everything about what he was seeing seemed strangely impossible, like he was peeking into someone else's dream, or perhaps a nightmare that was on the turn. But it was real. Everything that was happening was happening right in front of him, and no matter how much he rubbed his eyes or shook his head, none of the picture changed. It only progressed and developed.

Like right now, this second. The man in front of Theo grabbed his hand and turned coolly toward the door, smiling happily and saying something that Gaten couldn't hear. He didn't see Gaten, but Gaten saw him. He saw his lean face, his bony cheeks, his dark eyes, full of life and death. Life, because they were glistening, and shining, and bright in the haze of spotlights. Death, because Gaten had seen those eyes before – empty, soulless, and trickling with goo once the body had been dragged onto the banks of the reservoir. Behind Gaten's shoulder, he felt that same body float down toward his ear, its cracked lips curling into a smile. It seemed to whisper,

Happy to see me?

And Gaten let out a silent scream. Because once again, somehow, terribly, he was staring into the eyes of Adrian Ramirez.

CHAPTER FIFTEEN

THE PUDDLE

1

The colours of aurora borealis still blazed in the night sky, streaked across the dome of the ballroom like an ancient painting. Sara had been watching them for at least ten minutes when Ava returned with a pair of drinks. She placed one delicately in Sara's hands, and she downed it like a baby downing a bottle of milk. When just the ice remained, she put the glass down at her feet and held both sides of Ava's head.

Around her, the party had achieved a delicate balance of wildness and serenity. The members of the secret Cuckoo Cabaret Club were smiling and cheering, some dancing under the glistening lights, others simply immersed in each other's company. Sara squeezed the curls of Ava's hair and stared into her eyes. They were sparkling and gazing into her soul with a strange intensity. She didn't have to knock, Sara let her in. They stood there in the music gazing into one another, like they were both as beautiful as the colours above them. Celestial events, basking in each other's suns and letting the warmth overtake them. Sara kissed her and started to shake. She felt like crying, but not in a bad way. She felt happy. Once again, her spirit was dancing, waltzing on tiptoes and twirling in Ava's shadow, exhausting itself until it fell into her arms. Ava leant back and read her mind.

'You're thinking of lying here with me, aren't you, little cuckoo? You're thinking of lying on this dance floor and holding me until the sun comes up and the colours fly away.'

Tears streamed down Sara's cheeks, her lips trembling. Ava wiped at Sara's face with her finger, lifting the teardrop to the lights before blowing it away with a *poof*.

'All in good time. I don't know about you, but I don't want to get trampled on. And those tears are ruining your makeup. Now, come on. Drinks, drinks, and more drinks.'

Ava took Sara's hand and began walking her toward the bar. Just as she did so, however, the doors to the ballroom opened so violently they nearly flew off their hinges. The band on stage stopped playing and the room went eerily silent. The darkness of the outside world spilled into the light, and standing in the centre of that darkness, drenched and shaking, was Gaten. His eyes weren't holes now. They were bright, alive, and burning with fear. As he stepped inside the Cuckoo Cabaret Club, Sara felt Ava's grip loosen. She looked shaken, as if Gaten's entrance had stripped away some of her mystery and revealed an actual, real person hiding underneath. Someone who could feel fear, and surprise, and all the things that an ordinary person could feel. Only Ava was not ordinary, and it didn't take long before she composed herself and that silky curtain was cast around her once again.

'Looks like we have a drowned cuckoo, everyone. Who kicked this one out of the nest?'

'No,' said Sara. 'He's not one of us.' She glared at her brother fiercely. He was the last person she wanted to see right now. He was a remnant of that other life Sara never wanted to think about again, a part of the storm she had managed to seal herself away from. 'What the hell are you doing here?' she hissed.

'Theo…' muttered Gaten. 'Theo, you're not safe.'

'No thanks to you. What is it, did you follow me or something? I came here to get away from you, Gaten. I came here to get away from all of you.'

'Theo, please listen to me. You're not safe.'

The rain continued to drop from Gaten's coat, creating a small puddle on the floor around his feet. Around him, the crowd was still deathly quiet, as if they were a machine waiting for another quarter to jolt them back to life.

'Theo, please —'

'Who's Theo?' asked Ava, her voice cool and probing.

Gaten looked at her and shuddered. He seemed as transfixed by Ava as Sara was, only this was a different kind of admiration. An admiration kicked up from some terrible pit of horror. He looked like he was a second away from fainting.

'My brother,' he said meekly.

'Oh,' Ava nudged Sara on the shoulder. 'Isn't that darling? He has a pet name for you, pickle.'

'Theo,' Gaten stared at Sara pleadingly. 'That man. I don't know what he's told you. But he's not who you think he is.'

'No,' Ava swivelled toward the band on the stage. 'Who is he, boys?'

And then the quarter was slipped back into the slot. On Ava's cue, the band catapulted into a melody. A burst of sax, trumpets, and horns bounced against the walls of the Cuckoo Cabaret Club.

'A GRAAAAAAND, SPANKIN' WOMAN!' Ava lifted her arms and sang, and the members of the Cuckoo Cabaret Club cheered in response. 'And you're just a man, in every sense of the word. Oh, my sweet, sweaty, chunk of testosterone. While I think it's wonderful you decided to enter our little club and explore your best self tonight, I can't help noticing you've used two wrong pronouns within the first minute of your introduction. It's rather killed the mood. So I'm sorry, but it seems you don't fit the Cuckoo code, and I'm going to have to ask you to leave.'

Gaten remained rooted to the spot, his face still pale and his eyes still glistening. The water had stopped trickling off him now. The puddle at his feet looked more like a thin sheet of ice.

'Adrian,' he whispered.

Ava's smile flickered. 'Is that my pet name? I don't much fancy it.'

'That's your real name. You're Adrian. Adrian Ramirez. I found you in the reservoir a week ago. You're dead.'

'Like I said, honey, the only thing dead in here is the mood.'

'Look,' said Sara, taking a step forward. 'I don't know what's gotten into you, Gaten, but you need to leave.'

'Theo, you need to trust me, I —'

'Trust you?' Sara interrupted him. 'Seriously? After everything you've done?'

'I know what I've done, and I'm sorry. But I'm here now, little brother, and I'm asking to protect you.'

'Protect me from what?'

'Him,' Gaten pointed at Ava. 'He's dangerous.'

Ava laughed, flicking her hair behind her shoulder. 'Oh, well you've got that right.'

'He's not who he says he is. He's Adrian Ramirez. The first body. The one we found at the reservoir. I don't know how he's here, I don't know how any of this is happening. But I do know you've got to step away from him right now.'

Ava twirled behind Sara and pulled her arms around her waist. She pouted at Gaten playfully. 'What a pity. We were just about to dance.'

Gaten glared at her, his fists clenching. Some of that fear had turned into anger now, Sara could tell. The moment Ava had touched her, a spark of fire had ignited behind Gaten's eyes, and now it was spreading rapidly.

'Tell me your name,' he said through gritted teeth.

'I'll tell you my name if you tell me hers.'

And just like that, the fire was dampened. Gaten went to speak, but nothing came out. Just a flush of warm air, the flame perhaps, extinguishing into nothing. Sara felt her heart sink. She felt like crying, but her tears had run dry now. All that was left of her was just a harsh despondency.

'Get out of here, big brother. Get out of here now and don't come back.'

Ava let go of Sara's waist, standing in front of her like a human shield. 'You heard the woman.'

'I'm not leaving,' said Gaten.

'Oh, I think you are.'

'You can't make me.'

'My sweet little pickle, we can do anything when we're caught up in the music. In fact...' Ava crossed her arms and began tapping on her leather sleeves. 'You've got me feeling a certain number. Something to kick the mood up a few notches.'

With a flick of her heel, Ava turned and galloped onto the stage, shooing the singer from the microphone. She glared down at Gaten with those great, shining eyes.

'Monsieur,' she said, her voice reverberating through the speakers. 'I think it's time we treated you to a favourite of ours. It's called the "Time Warp".'

Right on cue, the band started playing. The strum of an electronic guitar rebounded off the walls, accompanied by the steady, booming beat of a kick drum. Confetti rained down from nowhere, swaying from one end of the ballroom to the other, as if caught in the storm. As Ava started singing, the members of the Cuckoo Cabaret Club started dancing. Gaten was caught in a sea of people, all of them with their arms in the air and their bodies bouncing. He tried to squeeze through, pushing past as many revellers as he could, but it was all to no avail. The crowd was getting denser, and pretty soon Gaten was swallowed entirely. Sara watched on with her mouth open. Behind her, Ava pulled the microphone from the stand and sang,

'My cuckoos jump to the left!'

Sara watched as her brother was lifted into the air. What looked like a hundred glittery hands were holding him aloft, jumping toward the left side of the hall in obedience.

'And then they spin to the right!'

The crowd moved to the right, Gaten surfing from one end to the other.

'With their hands on his hips!'

Still held high into the air, Gaten was marched toward the open doors.

'They throw him into the night!'

Sara could hear him screaming, yelling over the music in one last desperate appeal.

'HE'S NOT REAL! THEO! YOU'VE GOT TO BELIEVE ME! HE'S —'

But before he could finish, the crowd threw him out into the storm, slammed the doors behind him, and let out a great, big cheer. More confetti rained down from the ceiling, and Sara turned to see Ava blowing a kiss.

'I'm no mystery, honey,' she said, placing the microphone back into its hilt. 'I'm just another cuckoo.'

2

Gaten watched in horror as the light of the Cuckoo Cabaret Club disappeared and the doors slammed to. A wave of applause erupted from within. The party continued as if nothing had happened, like Gaten had just been an irritating moth who'd flown too close to the light. But Gaten wasn't going to sit back and watch his brother get burned. With his teeth still gritted, he climbed to his feet and pulled his gun from its holster, reaching for the door. Before he could touch it, however, something made him stop. A strange silence befell the world around him. The applause inside the club cut out like it had been severed with a knife, and a sharp ringing began swirling between Gaten's ears. He stumbled backwards, holding his head in pain.

Walls. Clocks. Crying. Strawberries.

For a split second, Gaten was pulled back into a memory from twenty years back. He was ten years old, playing in the forest with his best friend, Rupert Common, splitting branches and using them for spears. A sharp, unbearable pain was eating into his pinky finger, and he was looking down to find a shard of wood slotted deep underneath his fingernail. He was feeling sick and vomiting, and his dad was attempting to slide out the splinter with a pair of rusty pliers.

Smoke. Coughing. Water. Ropes.

That shard of wood entered him again now, burying into his left eardrum and eating into the soft tissue around his skull. Disconnected words ran through his mind, and a maze of colours flashed before his eyes. Red, yellow, green, blue; a messy haze descended upon where he stood, and Gaten wished more than anything that he would find his dad in the midst of it, a wet tea towel in one hand and a pair of rusty pliers in the other.

Brother. Fighting. Puddle. Runner...

Just as the pain was getting impossible to bear, the colours disappeared and the pain stopped. The only sound remaining was the waves beneath the pier, such a relief that they sounded like a symphony. Gaten stood in the dark and tried to grab his bearings. He listened to them rushing in, then pulling back, then rushing in, then pulling back. But as the sound of the waves grew louder, he realised that they were changing, becoming instead deep breaths that were squirming through the cracks of the wood. A cold shiver ran through him and he felt the gun go loose in his hand. The pier vibrated and shook. Then, in the corner of his eye, Gaten watched as a huge talon curled around the bannister. It stayed there for several seconds, making the wood moan. Then there was another one, covered in what looked like gunk and seaweed, sliding over one of the lamp posts to pull a monster up from underneath.

The monster itself looked like a ginormous bat. Its torso was ragged and patched with fur, and its wings were black and rubbery. Its head resembled that of a werewolf, similar to the ones Gaten had seen in the movies, only this one had stark, bloody eyes, and so many teeth that they seemed to overlap each other, crammed into its mouth and fighting for space. Its gums were thick and dark, its ears high and pointed, and its body moved with such precision and grace that it didn't even appear to cast a shadow. In fact, it *was* the shadow. It skulked in the same way a vampire bat skulked, climbing carefully onto the roof of the ballroom until its belly was above the glass dome, and its wings drooped down on either side. It stared down at Gaten, unseeing, but at the same time seeing.

Why do you ruin my feast?

The words echoed inside Gaten's head, spoken but not spoken, high-pitched and yet strangely guttural. He opened his mouth and whimpered.

'You're it. You're the shadow. The monster.'

As if compelled by an unseen force, Gaten collapsed to his knees, the creature looming over him like a god demanding worship.

How could you see? How could you hear? My club wasn't meant for you. Nothing here is meant for you.

At that moment, Gaten slipped into another memory. He was staring at the monster, but looking into the eyes of Steven, Lucas, Billy and Derek. They were standing in a line, Derek with a Swiss army knife in his hand, and Steven with his fists clenched.

'I don't understand,' he murmured.

Ah, but the blood that runs through your veins runs through hers too. You are connected through stars and sky. Through blood and dreams. You are one.

Gaten watched as the rain fell from the monster's coat into the puddle that Theo was lying in. The monster appeared to smile.

Such a rotten memory. It moulds your soul, it does. You are not good enough. You would never be good enough.

'You're in my head...' Gaten said, trying desperately to shake the memory away.

The monster crept forward on the roof, making it creak. *And you are in my home. Ruining my feast. Making it doubt the world I'd created for it. Your rotten, moulding infection, tarnishing my soul just when I had got it so close to being perfect. Years and years I have waited. So many souls I have found that are not good enough. Souls like yours. But such a hunger needs to be appeased. Must be appeased. Why do you take away my fill?*

A long string of something gooey fell from the monster's mouth, sliding into the gutter of the ballroom. Gaten thought about his brother. He thought about him inside there somewhere, dancing obliviously with the body of Adrian Ramirez.

'Theo,' he whispered, a horrible realisation stinging his chest. 'You're talking about Theo.'

The monster continued to crawl closer. *Wasted time. Wasted hunger. Wasted days I have been nurturing this soul, nourishing it, so that it could nourish me. Now you have doomed it to die needlessly.*

Without thinking, Gaten jumped back onto his feet and raised the gun in front of his face, his finger tensing on the trigger. 'YOU'RE NOT GOING TO TOUCH HIM!' he cried.

And the ghost of what sounded like a laugh swirled inside Gaten's head. The monster's face remained as emotionless as ever. It climbed down from the ballroom and stood in front of Gaten with its spine arched. Now it was closer, Gaten saw its eyes were not really eyes at all. Both sockets were filled with strands of flesh, like veins, deep red and pulsing. He felt the gun go limp in his hand again.

Is it you who threatens me? The monster tilted its head toward him. *Yes, I am the shadow. And I have seen the light of your soul. Every part of it. Every story. I know what you did on the day of water. You ran and ran and ran. And you have kept running. She knows that. She remembers. She...*

The monster stopped. Gaten swore he saw it hesitate, like it was slowly realising something.

Oh, but the way she felt when she looked at you. That emotion. That story. Perhaps there is still hope. Perhaps that's the key. The last piece of the puzzle.

Gaten lifted the gun again. 'You're not... you're not going to...'

He tried to stay strong, stay firm, but he could feel his world going blurry. The memory of the splinter returned this time, and Gaten felt like he wanted to double over and vomit. The monster seemed to be able to tell.

Unless you can find the will to stop me.

It nudged him mockingly and, as if one of its talons had simply poked the weapon out of Gaten's hand, Gaten watched his gun fall from his fingers and land with a thud on the wet wood of the pier. The ghost of the monster's laugh returned, and it turned its back on him, climbing once more onto the roof of the ballroom. Gaten noticed a red light beginning to radiate from the glass dome.

You forsook this soul the day that you ran. Now it is mine. So do what you do best, runner...

The monster opened its mouth, revealing a glow of its own. A strange red sparkle was climbing its way up through its throat, and its terrible, fleshy sockets were starting to twist and bubble.

Run.

And Gaten listened to it. Without even picking up his gun, he turned on his heel and ran as fast as he could into the rain.

3

The red light bathed the club, casting every dancer in the shade of blood. The smoke machine was whirring now. Sara stood in the midst of a cloud, watching as the band switched instruments and dropped into a slow rendition of "As The World Falls Down" by David Bowie. The crowd swayed drunkenly, eyes closed, feeling the music. Not Sara, though. She kept her eyes on Ava, staring intensely as she approached and took her hand.

'Uh oh,' Ava giggled. 'That's a stern look, pickle. Should I be worried?'

'What did you say up there?' Sara asked quietly.

'I didn't say anything. I sang. It's a little song called "Time Warp", I thought you would've heard of it.'

'No, not that. Afterwards. You said something about being a mystery.'

Ava smiled. Despite the red light, her teeth shone whiter than ever before, polished and perfect, like you could lick them and they would squeak.

'Same thing I told you the other night. I'm no mystery, honey.'

Sara cast her mind back to that night in question. Ava had indeed said those exact words, and Sara had found it strange at the time, only she couldn't place why. But now she could.

'On the night we kissed, you said the same thing. Only those were my words. I said that to Tony at Salvador's, just before he ran away from me.'

Ava raised her eyebrows sarcastically. 'I think you may have had a little too much to drink, sweetheart.'

She giggled, but Sara didn't join in.

'Okay,' Ava relented. 'I suppose you didn't like my number. I know it might have seemed a little harsh, but us cuckoos have to stick together. People like your brother don't understand what we do. What we go through every day. When the sun shines on such tiny little worlds, they can't help but be blinded by it.'

Sara shook her head. 'I did like your number. You know I did.'

High pitched guitar notes echoed throughout the Cuckoo Cabaret Club. They were played beautifully, almost mournfully, and Sara thought about Luna. She thought about those moments she had been on stage at the Precious Star Bar, when she would be singing "Don't Dream It", and Luna would be standing there with a smile on her face, her eyes closed, and her hands on her heart. Those were happy memories, Sara realised now. Being up on that stage, singing that beautiful song. Looking at Luna and dreaming about a mirrorball. She pulled her attention back to Ava, and for the first time ever, she didn't feel that sense of lust, or love, or happiness. She just felt dizzy.

Distant. Like she was going to be sick. Ava squeezed her hand even more tightly.

'It's okay,' she said. 'You're shook up. I understand if you want to go after your brother. But can I ask you to do something for me first? Would you dance with me, my little cuckoo? Just dance with me a moment?'

Before she could answer, Ava held both her hands and pulled her calmly into the centre of the dance floor. Then Sara was really swaying. The red light poured down upon her and Ava rested her head on her shoulder. It was a warm hug, and despite how she was feeling – the confusion, the dizziness, the fever – Sara fell into it like it was a fluffy blanket on a rainy night. She listened as Ava whispered into her ear.

'Having someone like that in your head can be torture. It can bend you the wrong way, make you forget who you really are. But we know who you are, little cuckoo. We've always known. Your soul is such a bright one. Just broken a little. And suffocating. So we've tried to let it breathe. We want the best version of yourself. That's all we want. To appease our hunger.'

On the word "hunger", Ava wrapped her arms tightly around Sara's back, locking her into place. Everyone around them moved as if they were in slow motion. Some of them smiled at her, raised their glasses. An old man with thin, wiry wrinkles, a young woman with a tiara and plastic butterfly wings, a masked person dressed almost entirely in fishnet stockings. They parted to make way for her and Ava, allowing them to dance delicately as one.

'That's what we need, you see,' Ava whispered again. 'A soul that sings. Some of them out there seem so bright, but when you really look at them, when you gaze into the depths and surround yourself with their stories, you realise their fire was dampened a long time ago. Good. But not good enough.'

Ava's arms wrapped tighter around Sara, coiling around her body like a serpent. The smell of coconut and pomegranate started to disappear. When Ava leant up against her ear, all Sara could smell was sweat and dry ice.

'But yours was good, Sara. Salvageable. And that's what we've tried to do. We've tried to salvage you. Make you happier than ever. Make your soul shine, and sing, and be free. We've tried to complete you. We thought we knew how to do that. But perhaps we didn't know, because I'm holding onto you now, and I can still sense your unhappiness. A part of the puzzle is not complete. But that's okay. Shush, now. It's okay. Because we're dancing. We're dancing...'

As they swayed through the red fog, more members of the Cuckoo Cabaret Club started to appear. It was strange, but Sara could swear they were growing more familiar, like they were faces from a past life that had returned to dance with her. There, in the corner of the ballroom, drinking slowly from a champagne flute. Steven. Or was it Billy? The face looked so blurred in the bloody light, and every time Sara tried to make eye contact, he seemed to peer down and laugh into his chest. Here, now, another one. Definite this time. Sara saw one of the men pull his mask away from his face, and she gasped as she saw her father staring back at her. That same rough face. Those loose strands of hair, swept carefully along his liver-spotted head. She noticed his own glass, filled with a thick, black liquid, like shoe polish, which he sipped slowly and let dribble down his chin.

With a yell, Sara pushed Ava away and stumbled backwards, watching as she disappeared into the red haze. Then the lights cut out and the music stopped. For a few moments, all Sara could hear was her own breathing. Short breaths that sounded more like faulty machinery, whirring out of control and set to explode. She stood there in the darkness, staring frantically about herself. The gloom was too thick to see through now. It felt like she was floating in some great red ocean, somewhere faraway on a distant planet.

That's all we want... All we want...

This time, Ava's voice arrived in her head. It twirled from one side to the other, like she was still dancing somewhere inside there. In a desperate panic, Sara took a few steps forward, her arms outstretched. She tumbled into three members of the club. All of them had stopped dancing and were entirely still now. Above their heads, she noticed a bright orb begin to lower itself through the fog. A mirrorball casting thin shards of light in every direction.

I want your soul, the voice of Ava returned. Louder, fiercer, and wet, like it was lined with saliva. *I want to feel its brightness in the holy dark.*

Sara pushed the group aside and kept moving, her breaths growing shorter, tears running down her cheeks. She hit into another, taller figure, who turned and smiled down at her. She removed her mask, and Sara saw that it was Luna.

'No!' she yelled. 'No! Not you!'

I want to eat it. I want to taste it. I want to feel it inside me. I want to feast, and feast, and feast. I just need your soul to be perfect. Make it shine for me.

Sara spun around. In the red fog, she saw something that pulled her back into her childhood nightmares. The giant face of a monster was leering down at her, its eyes the colour of blood, and its mouth packed with what looked like a thousand teeth. A full-bodied scream tore through Sara, and she sprinted in the opposite direction. It felt like she was running for several minutes, like the ballroom had grown to ten times its size. She only stopped when her heel clipped against the edging strip of the dance floor, and she fell face first onto the carpet.

This soul runs like its brother, Ava laughed at her. *That's what he did years ago, and this is what he has done now. He has run away. Far away. And now it's just you and me. So shine for me, Sara. Shine, shine, shine.*

Sara saw the monster in the fog again. It was looming down from where the glass dome should have been, its mouth open wide and its throat glowing. She felt a hand grip her, and then another, and then another. Members of the Cuckoo Cabaret Club were pulling her onto her feet and holding her in place, her arms outstretched. Sara screamed and prepared for the worst. But then, out of nowhere, a gunshot rang out. Sara felt a sharp breeze whip past her right shoulder, and she watched as the monster reared back and roared, falling back into the smoke before disappearing into nothing. The club members let go of her one by one, running into the haze until just a single pair of hands remained. Their grip was firm, solid, and the skin was the warmest skin Sara had ever felt before. She turned around and found herself staring into the eyes of her brother.

'RUN!' Gaten shouted.

And then they were running. Sara felt Gaten pull her close to him. She squeezed his hand, feeling her heart leaping in her chest. Despite everything, her soul was suddenly ablaze with happiness. They weren't safe yet, but her brother being there had shot her with such an enormous relief that being safe didn't really matter anymore. She was with him, and he was with her, and a pantheon of monsters could rain down upon them and Sara knew that they would be alright. Because he had come back for her. He had put his life at risk to protect her. He loved her. And love was the most powerful thing a monster could face.

After a few seconds, Sara began to make out the shape of the doors. They were getting closer now, running fast through the fog, until they were right in front of the exit.

'YOU DID IT!' Sara cried.

Gaten yanked the doors open, but when the outside world was revealed, Sara knew that something was wrong. Because it wasn't the pier waiting for them on the other side. It was nothing. Just the storm, and a deep black hole that travelled all the way down to what looked like a giant, glistening puddle.

Sara shook her head and turned to her brother. 'Gaten, what do we —'

But her brother looked totally different now. His skin was white as paper, his face an empty, hollow mask, and his eyes were two glowing red orbs glaring deep into the pits of her soul. The voice of the monster echoed back into Sara's world.

Did you really believe your brother would come back to save you?

In the light of the mirrorball, Sara spotted a giant head peek back out of the fog, a thin smile full of teeth, dripping saliva onto the wood of the dance floor.

Thank you, Sara, it whispered happily. *You are good enough now.*

And then her brother clasped her shoulders and pushed, and Sara felt herself hurtling down, down, down, until she fell with a splash into the puddle, and everything went black.

CHAPTER SIXTEEN

THE SPIDER

1

The rain was easing when Kenny climbed over the gate of the pier. His sneakers were dripping wet from the journey, each puddle soaking right through to his socks. He wondered briefly whether frostbite was something that only happened in the North Pole, or if it could happen to kids in Cuckoo Cove. He felt like he was shaking uncontrollably – although whether he was shaking from the cold or the knowledge of what he was about to do, he wasn't entirely sure. Either way, he was resolute. It had taken him just thirty minutes to get from his house to the pier, and while the words "afraid, afraid, afraid" had been spinning in his head, he hadn't hesitated once. He'd inserted the cuckoo in the upper pocket of his jacket, shoving some toilet paper in there so it would feel at home. Indeed, it had been carrying on just as it had carried on back in Kenny's room, whispering the same words over and over again until Kenny felt dizzy. Perhaps that was the plan. But Kenny was a kid, and every kid in Cuckoo Cove knew the way to the beach, no matter how much a talking cuckoo tried to disorientate them.

And so Kenny had gotten there, and now he was standing with his back to the gate, the great expanse of the pier stretching out in front of him. He couldn't see any monsters. He couldn't see much at all, apart from the world directly lit by his flashlight. Thankfully for Kenny, however, he knew exactly where to point that flashlight. In the centre of the pier, there was a small, derelict pavilion surrounded by beaten-up deck furniture and smashed glass, with a sign that read:

UNCLE JOE'S FISH BAR

That was where Kenny was headed. With a deep breath, he bent toward his suitcase and removed two water bottles full of gasoline. His dad tended to keep several bottles in the garage to take with him on long hunting trips. Ever the good father that he was, they were stored right next to their supply of Dasani bottles – which *did* store water – and had been distinguished by a simple "G" written across the base in magic marker. Mandy had always argued with Kenny's dad about that, saying one of these days the bottles were bound to disintegrate and explode. And Kenny guessed she was right – for six of them, anyway.

He squeezed them under his armpits, picked up the box of matches, and slung the gun over his shoulder. Then he walked swiftly toward the pavilion, trying to ignore the cuckoo's more urgent repetitions of the word "afraid" as he got closer, and broken glass began to crack under his feet.

2

The pavilion wasn't hard to get into. All of the windows had been broken years ago, and while Kenny did manage to cut his thigh, he knew that was a small price to pay compared to what the monster could do to him. He kept quiet, and for some reason, he crouched down, scanning the inside. As expected, it was a broken wreck. Like a ship that had been lost at sea for decades, the woodwork was splintered and full of cobwebs, creaking in the wind and yet so deathly quiet you could hear a pin drop. The furniture was scattered about the place, broken into small pieces, and the kitchen equipment – the restaurant must have had an open plan – was so full of rust it looked like it had degraded into red coral.

That's where Kenny started. Approaching what he assumed were the ovens, he unscrewed the first bottle cap and started pouring gasoline onto every inch of the kitchen he could find, even going so far as to open the cupboards and splatter the piping.

'Reckon there's still gas in there?' he asked the cuckoo.

Afraid, came the cuckoo's response.

When he was done, Kenny moved on to the furniture, squirting gasoline over every chair, table, dresser, frame, even a great big wooden anchor that had fallen from its mount on the wall. Overall, a total of two bottles were used to soak the pavilion. Four more would be used to form the spider. Returning to his suitcase, Kenny removed the other bottles and headed back out of the window and into the rain. Unscrewing the third cap, he tilted the bottle upside down and walked around twenty yards diagonally, stopping only when he got to the bannister of the pier, where he let it pour through the cracks and onto the support beams. Turning the bottle upright again, he then walked to the left side of the pavilion and started anew – this time moving straight to the left. He repeated this act at every corner and every facade, walking diagonally, then straight, until eight arms of gasoline were stretching from the pavilion. On the last run, Kenny finished by making a circle back around and climbing back inside through the broken window, managing to scratch the inner side of his left thigh this time. He stopped in the centre of the pavilion, letting the last bottle run dry. Then he stood in silence for a few seconds, just listening to the rain. The cuckoo fidgeted uncomfortably in his pocket, and Kenny glanced down at it.

'I reckon we're in big trouble,' he said.

Afraid, came the cuckoo's response.

Kenny removed the box of matches from his waistband. The last line of gasoline should have been long enough to give him good distance when he lit the match, but this wasn't an exact science. Kenny had lit campfires before, he'd done that countless times, whenever his father had dragged him on hunting trips. But he'd never lit a pier on fire. He wasn't even sure if this would work, or whether the rain would make the flame the size of a candle. Either way, he was about to find out. With his fingers shaking, Kenny removed a match from the box and squeezed it into his palm.

'Okay,' he said to the cuckoo. 'Let's...'

But before he could say the word "go", something made Kenny stop. He realised now that the world around him wasn't so quiet anymore. The sound began as a gentle scratch behind his left ear, but then it grew into something deeper, a more rhythmic tapping. One two, one two, one two, with something strange and squelchy accompanying it, almost like the sound a boot made when you pulled it out of the mud. This sound lingered in the air for several moments, and when Kenny turned, he could see exactly where it was coming from. Whatever it was, it was hiding behind the broken anchor, right in the corner of the room, underneath another broken window. His cuckoo disappeared into his pocket. But Kenny had the rifle. Removing it from his shoulder, he clasped the gun in both hands and slowly walked toward it.

What was waiting for him behind the anchor was not a monster, however, but a bird. Another lone cuckoo that was standing above a dead rat, pecking frequently at its open torso, and ripping the flesh into tiny wet chunks. Although it wasn't a particularly pleasant sight, Kenny let out a nervous laugh, noticing as his cuckoo poked its head out of his pocket again.

'When you get back to your friends, remember to give this one a slap from me. Jesus, I nearly —'

CUCKOO!

Kenny leapt backwards with a yelp. The new cuckoo had stopped eating the rat now, and was instead stood on the anchor, staring Kenny straight in the eyes. Blood was dripping from its beak.

CUCKOO!

Another call, above Kenny's head. He pointed the flashlight up to the ceiling to find two more cuckoos staring down at him from the rafters.

CUCKOO!

Two more. Behind him. Emerging from holes in the woodwork. Kenny swallowed and took a step back, then he watched as the cuckoo with blood on its beak flew up to an open window, staring out of it almost tentatively. Kenny followed its gaze, staring along the pier, which was stretching into a darkness that wasn't quite dark anymore – more a murky haze, illuminated by a deep, red glow coming from the ballroom at the far end. Kenny tilted his head. The glow was throbbing, pulsing like a beating heart. And it was getting brighter, the redness spreading, until it lit the entire pier like a blood moon.

Afraid...

The cuckoo in Kenny's pocket curled up against his chest, but Kenny didn't pull his eyes away from the window. Out in the distance, he could see dozens of cuckoos darting from underneath the ballroom. They flew up into the night sky and disappeared into the clouds. Then there were more, about twenty yards from the ballroom, closer to the pavilion, fleeing from underneath the pier and flying into the darkness. Kenny watched them go, and then watched a dozen more, and a dozen more, and a dozen more. It was like a line of dominoes, one flock after the other, getting closer and closer to Kenny. Even the cuckoos in the pavilion left to join them. All except the one in Kenny's pocket, which was entirely hidden in the tissue now, whispering over and over again,

Afraid, afraid, afraid...

'Shh,' Kenny whispered back. 'It's okay. There's nothing to be afraid of.'

But it was hard for the cuckoo to believe that when Kenny didn't. Because both of them knew what might make the cuckoos flee like that. The monster under the pier was awake, and what was awake was moving. Kenny swallowed again. Then, like he knew what was about to happen, he crept into the corner and pointed his gun at the floor in front of him.

Terrified, he watched as a huge talon broke through the floorboards, scratching about the pavilion. It retracted, then both talons burst through, peeling back the wood like it was made of cellophane. And Kenny started to cry.

3

Carrots give you superpowers.

It never really felt like Sara came to. That is to say, the blackness didn't ever disappear. It just got harder, almost sharp. There were edges to it, corners. It felt almost like she was in a dark box, sealed away from the outside world, and she couldn't see anything but a vague outline of herself. Her hands, her torso, her dress. Parts of herself were starting to come to light, but the darkness was so strong, she wasn't really sure if she was seeing those parts or just imagining them.

You're not imagining it. I read this over the summer. They're rich in beta-cartons, which the body converts into vitamin A.

She felt like she was standing. In fact, she knew that for sure. She was standing on something, and it felt kind of wet and slushy. When she moved her feet, she could swear she saw some dirt being kicked up into the air, where it hovered momentarily before settling back down.

Vitamin A helps you see in the dark because it produces a pigment called rhodopsin. I know it sounds all science-y, but the bottom line is our parents aren't telling us lies. Carrots really do give you super powers.

Behind Sara's ear, she could hear the voice of Sebastian Borwell. This was the nerdy kid at school, the kid at the bottom of the social ladder, so she didn't want to be caught talking to him. Not while there were people around who were waiting to judge.

Who's around?

Everyone. The members of the secret Cuckoo Cabaret Club. They had all been surrounding her, and these were members of a cool and exclusive clique. If Sara's school days had taught her anything, it was that an association with nerdy people would kick you out of a cool club before you could even say "pickle juice".

There isn't anybody around that I can see.

But Sara knew that wasn't true. They had been there. All of them. They had been dancing together, swaying, drinking, happy, and she could still hear them now. She could hear their shoes on the dance floor. She could hear their chatter and their laughs. She could feel them looking at her, and Sara knew that must have been true, because years of being gay in Cuckoo Cove had taught her to know when people were looking at her.

So tell me where they are then. Look around. Have you been eating your carrots?

Sara looked at her hands and tried to make them out. She could see her nails, long and sharp. She could see her veins. Things were definitely starting to come to light, but she needed time, not carrots. She needed time to adjust to her surroundings and understand exactly what had happened and where she was, and sarcastic comments from a nerdy kid at the bottom of the social ladder wasn't going to help.

Hey, I'm the one putting my neck on the line talking to you, not the other way around. Don't you remember? I stopped talking to you after everyone discovered you were gay. You thought you were cooler than me, but you slid all the way down the social ladder. Now you're the one at the bottom.

Sara went to lash out, but she couldn't see Sebastian Borwell anywhere. Just the blackness. So she shouted into it.

'I'm never gonna be as low down as you, Seb! You and your books, and your zits, and your never ending *Discovery* channel facts that nobody wants to hear.'

No, I mean it, Theo. You're at the bottom. All the way at the bottom. Look up.

There was a moment. Then, hesitantly, Sara peered up at the ceiling. Above her, the blackness dissolved into a funny sort of sparkling blue. It glistened and shifted, rippling like the colours of aurora borealis, and just above that, Sara could see dozens of pairs of shoes and high heels. The members of the Cuckoo Cabaret Club were dancing, and drinking, and smiling down at her. A new voice whispered into Sara's dark world.

Kinda makes you feel suffocated, doesn't it?

This voice sent shivers up Sara's spine. It was the voice of the bully, Steven Harris, pressed right up against her ear.

I guess I didn't want you to fall this deep into the puddle, Theo. But I had to teach you a lesson. There are no gay towns in America, and if we had let you carry on, you'd only go and spread the sickness. It's like a cancer, you know? You gotta deal with that shit early.

Sara tried to shove him away, but again, she just lashed out into nothing. 'Leave me alone, Steven! You're not in my life anymore! It's just me and the club now! I'm out of the puddle!'

But as soon as she said it, everything started flooding back to her in a tidal wave. She had been in the club, but everything had gone wrong. There had been red smoke, and monsters, and running, and her brother, but not really her brother. She had been pushed into the puddle and she had fallen all the way down. Now that was what she was looking at. She was standing right at the bottom of the puddle, kicking up the muck and dirt, and above her, the members of the Cuckoo Cabaret Club were dancing on the surface.

The puddle, Steven confirmed. *That's it. The puddle. You're in there again, and this time, it doesn't look like you're getting out. You know how I know that? Because Sebastian Borwell is full of shit.*

Sara held her head in her hands. A great, throbbing pain was pulsating through her brain now, making it feel squeezed. She felt like being sick, but when she tried to hurl, another voice replaced Steven's and she jolted straight upright.

It's not the carrots, said her father. *I thought I'd raised you better than to believe a thing like that. Then again, I thought I'd raised you better than to become the person that you are. Parading around in dresses. Wearing wigs, makeup, and doing god only knows what. I haven't had many disappointments in my life, Theodore, but you're certainly one of them.*

Sara crumbled down to her knees. She didn't even try to lash out this time. She had been living and lashing out at this voice for years and years, and she knew by now that it didn't do any good.

It's not the carrots, her father repeated. *It's you. That thing out there pushed you into this puddle, and now it's feeding off your soul, your life, your very being. And honestly, I'm glad. Your soul has been rotting ever since you plastered that shoe polish across your face. If this thing wants to feed off that, then it can be my guest.*

Sara let go of her head and looked down. Her father was right, she realised. Right in the centre of her chest, she could see a small, red light, faded and faint, but growing a little brighter every second. Her entire body was starting to glow.

'I don't understand,' Sara muttered.

But really, she understood just fine. Because she wasn't just looking at this light, she was feeling it. The light was eating away at her, soaking into her veins and emptying them. She was getting lighter, and lighter, and lighter, but rather than float to the surface of the puddle, she could only feel herself sinking down, crumpling like old paper and drowning. The red light was draining her of all substance, turning her into a shell of a human being, until it was just her memories left. And soon, perhaps, not even them.

Not even me? her father asked.

But Sara didn't want to hear him. If she was going to be left down here, she wanted to be left with only the good people in her life. The people who had cared for her, and loved her, and treated her well. So Sara curled into a ball and made herself think hard. Hard about Luna. Hard about the Precious Star Bar. Even hard about Gaten, despite the fact he had run away from her for a second time, and left her in a nightmare she'd never get out of. She thought hard about all of them before the red light swallowed her completely and they were gone. And she was gone. And it was only this puddle left. And those people up there on the surface. Dancing on what was – and Sara understood this quite clearly now, perhaps always had done – her deep and shallow grave.

4

The pavilion shook. Kenny watched as the monster peered out of the dark hole, its face large and hungry, and its teeth drooling with wet gunk. It glared at him with red eyes, its gums peeled back, seething.

Another one comes to ruin my feast...

The cuckoo buried itself deeper in his pocket, but the voice that echoed inside Kenny's head wasn't the bird's anymore. It was a harsh voice, low and gurgling, and it lingered between Kenny's ears like a throbbing migraine. He moaned and shook, the gun slipping from his grasp to point down at the floor.

A young soul, this one. Quiet. Small. But long since bled. Already, you would not be good enough.

Quite slowly, the monster lifted its talons and pierced them into the floorboards, using its wings to lift itself out of the hole and slide across the floor. The gasoline smothered its belly, matting the fur.

Why are you here? it asked. *The feast has already begun. You can't spoil it now.*

'I didn't... I wasn't...' Kenny stuttered, and for some reason he felt himself dribble. 'I wasn't going to do anything...'

The monster's head tilted, and for a moment, Kenny thought it was squinting at him. But as he looked closer, he noticed that its red eyes were masked with crimson flesh and veins. The monster was blind.

I suspect this soul does not tell the truth. How it shivers and quakes and cries when it talks. Out of all the souls I have seen, this is the most weak and pathetic. Wet and tiny. And unloved.

Kenny held the gun tighter. The monster was blind, but it was looking at him. Well, not at him. *Inside* him. The monster was staring into his soul, but that didn't mean it could tell what he was doing. If it didn't have eyes, then Kenny had a way out. Slowly but surely, he began lifting the nozzle of the gun up from the floor.

No love from its father, who craves to cut the cord on its previous life. No love from the woman called Mandy, who wants the father all for herself. No love from the girl who it has tried to cling onto, again and again and again, only has never succeeded.

The gasoline squeaked and sludged as the monster moved closer, and a wide, mocking smile began to stretch the corners of its mouth.

The girl he calls Dora...

Letting out a cry of anguish, Kenny aimed the gun straight at the monster's face, but the monster was too fast. In a flash, its left talon rose into the air and hurtled across the room like the shadow of a lightning bolt, striking Kenny in the face and sending him catapulting into the wall. The gun flew out of his grasp, and the cuckoo fell from his pocket, flying chaotically around the room before disappearing through the hole in the floor. Kenny moaned, but he didn't feel any pain. All he felt was something warm and wet travel down his cheek and his neck, and a funny sensation in his stomach that reminded him of being on a rollercoaster.

The monster leered over him, drool oozing from its gums, and its dark and fleshy sockets bubbling. *It thinks I cannot see, but I can see everything. I can see your soul, little child. I can see the lonely story in front of me.*

Kenny watched as tiny droplets of blood trickled from the monster's left talon, like water dripping from a tap that hadn't quite been turned off all the way. He realised after a few seconds that it must have been his blood. He touched at his wound hesitantly, but his face was so numb, it felt like dipping his fingers into a strangely warm puddle.

A soul that chooses to imagine other worlds rather than live in its own. I can set you free, if you'd like. If this is not the world you'd like to live in, perhaps it is I who can send you to another.

Knowing his time was done, Kenny closed his eyes and prepared to be sent into a deeper kind of darkness. Like the talon that had swept across his face, this too felt strange and unexpected. He had played out this moment many times in Gonagreen, and every time his character died, it always felt like a big and momentous occasion. This felt small in comparison. There was no grand music, no emotional last speeches. Death had been inflicted upon him by a giant, shadowy monster, but that didn't make what was happening any grander. The whole thing was like falling into a sleep full of magic and mystery, yet was proceeded by a twitch and a fart. Any moment now, he would be gone. And the only thing remaining would be an echo of his last whimper.

But the whimper never actually came. Instead, there was just a roar and a moan, and Kenny opened his eyes to see the monster lurch backwards, its wings twisting around its body to cover its face. Perhaps because of the ringing in his ears, or perhaps because he'd been thinking so hard about death, Kenny hadn't heard the gunshot. But he knew there must have been one, because smoke was pouring from the nozzle of his rifle, which was now gripped firmly by a tall and pale looking man in the corner of the room.

The man watched as the monster writhed in pain, sliding back over the gasoline-soaked floor before crawling into the hole like a wounded spider. Then he pulled Kenny to his feet.

'What the hell are you doing here?!' he shouted.

Kenny shook his head. 'I... I don't...'

'Get out of here and run. Just run and don't look back.'

'Who are you?'

'I'm the police.'

The officer pushed him, but the world around Kenny felt like a see-saw. It tilted him from one end of the room to the other, and in a daze, he found himself falling back into the arms of the officer. He reached toward his pocket, trying desperately to find the matches.

'I said go, kid!'

'You need to come too,' said Kenny in a jumbled slur.

'I'm not running! Go now! Before it comes back!'

This time, the officer marched Kenny to the open window and practically threw him out of it. He landed in a heap on the wood of the pier, and as soon as he did so, he felt a huge, stinging throb in his cheek. The pain had finally caught up with him. Blood was pattering down his chin and through the gaps of the wooden decking and, as if the strike of the talon had happened just two seconds ago, he felt like his face was on fire. Climbing to his feet, he ran almost drunkenly across the pier, and didn't stop until he reached the gates. Breathing hard, he clambered over them, landing miraculously on his feet. As if trying to put as much distance between him and the monster as possible, he then staggered onto the beach and collapsed.

When he fell, the box of matches fell with him, sliding out of his back pocket and landing with a light thud on the rocks. He turned to look back. The ballroom was still glowing red, and the sky behind it was still dark, but thin rays of light were beginning to peak over the ocean now. They cast the foundations of the pier in a gentle, pink haze. And just there, where the wood met water, Kenny could see a small, broken boat tied loosely around the first column. He stared at it for a few seconds. Then he felt his hand curl around the matchbox, squeezing so hard that a match broke free and landed almost magnetically into his bloody palm.

5

Gaten walked slowly around the pavilion, gripping the rifle. At first, he'd thought the creaks and scratches coming from underneath the pier were cuckoos, but the pain in his head told him otherwise. The gunshot should have been enough to kill any living thing, and yet the pier was still bathed in red, sparkling in the first rays of rising sunlight, but laden with the heavier, darker red, which continued to pour out of the glass dome of the ballroom. Gaten would bet anything that, if the monster were to die, then the red light would die with it. And so he walked and he listened. The groans beneath him were growing louder, stretching from one side of the decking to the other. Perhaps he imagined it, but the decking seemed to be moving, like some great heat was bending it out of shape. He stood still and tried to spot a shadow.

'If you're in my head,' he whispered, 'then listen to this. I'm going back for her. I'm going to save her.'

There was a second. And then the monster responded to him, its voice so clear it could well have been hanging directly below his feet.

This soul is foolish as well as cowardly. You cannot save the one called Sara. I'm feasting on her as we speak.

The pain in Gaten's head swelled, and he looked once again at the ballroom. The dome seemed to be swelling too. Swelling with a bloody light that seemed to be getting brighter, pulsing every few seconds. Every part of him wanted to race inside and get his brother out, but he knew he would be racing into a trap. If his brother was going to be saved, then the monster needed to die, and he had to be the one to do it. He gripped the gun tighter.

'What do you mean, feasting?' he asked, though what he wanted to say was: *show yourself, you fucker. Be a good shadow and get closer to me.*

As if it knew what he was thinking, the monster took a few seconds to reply, and when it did, its voice sounded more distant.

So many souls I have searched for. It seems you've been searching too. I can see now, you've been following in my footsteps.

Gaten frowned. 'You eat souls…?'

The voice grew closer again, like it couldn't help it. *Not souls. Just one soul. Hers.*

Gaten lowered the gun to the decking and began treading softly around the pavilion once more. 'But three people are dead. You killed them.'

They ended themselves. I just pushed them to their conclusion. What else am I to do? I see only souls. I find the brightest, the purest, for the big feast. But they were not good enough. Their flames were dampened, so I extinguished them completely to spare myself from returning to them.

'You killed them to save time?'

A fire was beginning to sizzle inside Gaten's chest now. Impatience, fear and fury were pulling at the strings of his own soul.

Weep for them all you wish. They did not die for nothing. I eventually found my feast, and you cannot stop it now. I am devouring her. Swallowing her soul. And it is delicious.

Gaten gave in to the fire and shot randomly into the decking. The wood seemed to move once more as the bullet pierced it, curling like a wave until it broke and erupted five feet in front of him, throwing Gaten backwards. The monster landed on the pier with a heavy thud, its teeth bared and its red, sightless eyes somehow piercing. Gaten saw the side of the monster's face where the bullet had struck. It looked creased and sunken, the fur burned away and the flesh revealed. But it wasn't bleeding. It wasn't incapacitated at all. A heavy stone sank into his gut. The monster was un-killable, he realised. It was going to be stood between Gaten and his brother no matter what he did, and shooting it would be as useless as closing his eyes and wishing it away. He let go of the rifle.

In the distance, a voice called out to him, high-pitched and shrieking.

'OFFICER! OFFICER! RUN!'

With tears blurring his vision, Gaten turned to see the small figure of the kid on the beach, his arms waving madly.

'I'm not running anymore,' he whispered.

The monster laughed sharply. *You think me a monster, but I am not a monster. I have not killed. And when I have finished my feast, I will rest. Until the next one. But if you do not run now, you will make me a monster. And I will be happy for it.*

Despite the pavilion blocking his view, Gaten could see the red light of the dome beam brighter, rising above the monster's head to form a crown. He thought about his brother in the midst of it, standing alone and afraid, praying to be let into his bed. To curl up by his feet and pull the sheets tight. To melt away his nightmares and share his dreams. And that was enough. With gritted teeth, Gaten climbed to his feet and stood before the monster, fists clenched.

'I'm not running,' he said again.

So step toward me. Step toward me and bleed.

Gaten went to take a step forward, but as he did so, something else caught his attention. The smell of something burning filled his nostrils, and he looked down through the gaps of the pier to spot something bright and fiery travelling slowly across the water. It was hard to say for sure, but it looked like his uncle's boat, making its final voyage. Onwards to where, Gaten didn't know. But the puddles surrounding him gave him a good clue. He could see them in the sun now. Strings of shining liquid merged with the rainwater and travelled around the pavilion, shimmering rainbow colours in the morning sunrise. Gaten stumbled backwards, and the monster leered at him furiously.

The runner cannot help himself! But you have stepped into death already, and I have a feast to finish!

As if to suck him in, the wings of the monster opened and flapped. But only twice. The second time, they were licked with flame. Gaten wasn't quite sure, but it felt like the monster caught first. It became enveloped in a thick, blue fire that seemed to light it all in one go, and then the air around him exploded. First underneath – that must have been the Iolanda – and then right in front of him, the pavilion erupted in a flash of blue light, disintegrating into chunks and pieces.

Gaten was thrown backwards again, further this time, and when he landed, he felt a strange surge of something wet and hot travel up his back. It lingered there for several moments, then appeared to wrap itself around his body like a snake, curling under his armpits until it began to hurt. His ears were ringing, but he could still hear the monster. It was screaming and roaring, twirling in front of Gaten like it was performing a dance. Its fur coat was totally ablaze and its face was stretched in agony.

THE FEAST! THE FEAST!

For the first time, the monster was nearly incoherent. Gone was the calm, premeditated voice that had sunken so poisonously into Gaten's head, and in its place was a voice full of fear, of chaos, and a fury so powerful it seemed almost incomprehensible. It was like the emotion had been ripped from the depths of another hell, deeper than the one on earth, and entirely alien. Gaten watched as it jumped from the pier and flew into the sky.

THE FEAST! THE FEAST!

Chunks of burning fur dropped from its belly. Thick fireballs rained down upon the pier, stopping only when the monster crashed onto the ballroom, and its wings wrapped around the glass dome.

PROTECT THE FEAST! PROTECT THE FEAST!

The monster screamed in pain again. Then its yells twisted into a language Gaten couldn't understand. It flapped even more wildly and cast itself off the glass, flying straight up into the sky and twirling like a spinning top. After just a few seconds, it disappeared completely into the clouds, and Gaten was left to stare at the ruin it had left behind.

His own body was screaming now. He had a sense that the hot, wet feeling was a flame of his own, steadily melting away his clothes and eating into his skin. But despite the pain, he remained dead still. The only thing he cared about was being smothered in a different red light. The ballroom was breaking apart and burning, and inside was a soul that was entirely unaware. Gaten blinked against the smoke that was beginning to seep from his own body, and he yelled at the top of his lungs,

'SARA!'

6

Sara...

Sara's father stared at her, his sweaty forehead reflected in the surface of the puddle.

A name that you plucked out of the sky and stitched onto your chest. It doesn't mean anything. Not like the name I gave you. That name meant something. The name I gave you matters.

His words arrived with such a barrage of heat and flame that Sara felt like they burned through her body, sizzling into her skin and making her grimace in pain. She closed her eyes and rocked back on her feet, just as she did when she was a kid and was preparing for another onslaught of insults that were bound to come. Only this time, they didn't come. What came instead was something Sara couldn't understand. A slur of words spoken from dozens of different voices. She could hear Steven in there, and she could hear her mother. She could hear Gaten, and Luna, and Justin, and Sebastian too. Everyone and anyone Sara had ever known was there in front of her, and sure enough, when her eyes opened, her father was gone, and a line of bodies were standing in his place.

Homo non est homo. Homo iocus est.

They stood with their backs to her, motionless silhouettes of all shapes and sizes, repeating the words all at the same time.

Homo non est homo. Homo iocus est.

'What?' Sara whispered.

Homo non est homo. Homo iocus est.

'I don't understand.'

One of the shadows with spikes on its head shuddered, convulsing violently, and the other bodies started doing the same.

Homo non est homo. Homo iocus est.

After a few moments, Sara realised they weren't convulsing at all. They were laughing, shaking uncontrollably and patting each other on the back, like one of them had just told a joke that had brought the house down. As they laughed, the line of bodies started spinning, twisting around Sara and getting faster, and faster, and faster. All the while repeating,

Homo non est homo. Homo iocus est.

The bodies turned into a jumbled mess of laughing darkness, and in the gust of the whirlwind, Sara felt herself being lifted off her feet. She floated in the midst of them, gazing up at the surface of the puddle and watching as it began to warp into something a little brighter.

Homo non est homo. Homo iocus est.

No. Not brighter. Whiter. The blue, rippling surface turned into a white sheet with lines and creases. It was thicker too, and Sara could see what looked like a corner of a duvet poking out on the left, dangling by a few inches. The whole thing looked like a giant bed.

Homo non est homo. Homo iocus est.

Sara reached out her hand and cried, but her cry was just hot air in a world that was steadily getting hotter. It felt like arms of fire were wrapping around her legs, pulling her down, and when she craned her neck, she realised that was exactly what was happening. Through the tunnel of bodies, another red light was being churned into her reality. It looked like the light that was radiating from her chest, only darker. It grabbed at her feet and coiled tightly around her skin, pulling her toward it.

Homo non est homo. Homo iocus est.

Sara screamed and kept reaching for the bed. She could feel her whole body vibrating. Something both soft and hard was seeping from her chest, her clothes, her pores. It felt like the last remaining essence of her spirit was finally being ripped away. Or not ripped away. Eaten. The grip of the light was eating into her and getting stronger – not just wrapped around her legs, but *inside* her legs, travelling up through her groin, her stomach, into her veins and pouring around her heart.

Homo non est homo. Homo iocus est.

The tunnel of bodies continued to spin faster and Sara felt herself shrinking, becoming insignificant in the red mist. Like a speck of dust in a gush of water. The puddle was being emptied, and she was spiralling down the drain.

Homo non est homo. Homo iocus est.

Sara closed her eyes and realised she really didn't want to die. She knew she had never been able to fight her nightmares, but she never suspected they would actually get her – that they would morph themselves into something real and suck her into such a deep, dark hole that would be impossible to pull herself out of. But that's what was happening. Sara was falling into her final nightmare, and all she could do was take one last look at the bed and reach out her hand. Without meaning, without reward, she knew that. But still. Reach. Because if there was one last thing she was going to do, before being swallowed completely by the red light, it was to reach for something better, and hope there might be something up there reaching for her too.

With that last thought, the red light engulfed her. But just before it swallowed her completely, Sara saw the duvet move, the sheets shift, and a giant hand reach down from the bed. It travelled through the tunnel and curled around her, wrapping her into its palm.

Then everything happened so quickly. A great, terrible scream echoed inside her ears, and she felt the strands of red light unravel inside of her. In the dark throat of the tunnel, the red light fell away, tumbling into the blackness as Sara was pulled up, up, up, through what had just a few seconds ago been the surface of the puddle. And sure enough, when she was on the other side, she found herself gasping for breath with a barrage of water cascading from her skin.

7

Then the ballroom again. Sara's brother stood in front of her, his eyes wide with fear and his skin red and scarred.

Surrounding him was fire. Great pillars of flame had erupted around the hall, which was now no longer the secret Cuckoo Cabaret Club, but was just a vast, dilapidated space of dark, broken wood. When Sara breathed, a barrage of smoke was pulled into her lungs and she choked, falling into Gaten's arms. Sparks of light blew up around her and she felt the fire lash her face. She wanted to pass out, but she fought off the blackness and held her brother tightly.

'If you're real,' she whispered to him, 'hold onto me and don't let me go.'

Although her voice was quiet, Sara felt her brother hold her more tightly than she had ever been held in her life. He pulled her across what had once been the bright, glistening dance floor and over toward the exit. Waves of fire swooped over Sara's head, and so she dipped down, keeping her face tight to her brother's smouldering coat. After a few moments, she saw the doors of the ballroom, burning too. They opened onto the pier, which was billowing smoke into a cool, red sunrise, and Gaten dragged Sara across the decking.

'WE'VE GOT TO JUMP TOGETHER!' he yelled over the roaring flames.

They stopped at the banister, and Sara looked down into the ocean, stark blue and foaming around the columns of the pier. Yet another puddle that she was being told to jump into. As if he knew what she was thinking, Gaten grabbed her hand and looked her straight in the eyes.

'Together...' he repeated.

Another explosion of fire roared behind them, and Sara felt herself squeeze his hand back. Then, together, they climbed onto the banister, took one last breath, and leapt into the air.

They didn't let go of each other all the way down, and even when they crashed into the waves and everything went cold, their hands were still wrapped as one.

CHAPTER SEVENTEEN

SOMETHING FLIES

1

Something here lets go of its feast and gives in to a sharp, thunderous rage. It swerves through the clouds and feels the light of the sun on its back. It feels raindrops caress its burning skin. It feels the wind biting against its face. Something here feels all the elements extinguishing the fire that had been hugging its body, making it scream, and roar, and snarl. But the fire inside its soul remains, hotter than ever before. It drives something here to oblivion and makes it fly and soar with purpose. Such a purpose. Something here has a million thoughts and wishes that race around its head in a hurricane, and all of them lead it to one solitary mission: to kill, to kill, to kill. To avenge its ruined feast and put out the souls responsible. Three souls in total. But first the small one, the one that had burned its home and left it to sink. Something here swoops through the clouds and flies directly toward the soul called Kenny.

2

Kenny saw the shadow before it had even broken the cloud layer. Like flashes of black lightning, something had been flying in and out of sight above him, blurred and indistinguishable, but now very real. The monster was hurtling through the sky with its wings stretched, and even from the beach, Kenny could make out its terrible, blood-filled eyes glowing red in the morning sunrise. He knew this had been coming. As soon as he set the boat alight and burned the monster's home, he knew it would bay for blood. For his blood. And that there would be no use in running. So he stood there without moving, staring at the shadow as it got closer, and closer, and closer, and out of nowhere, lunged to the left and started to spin.

3

Something here is going to kill the soul called Kenny, but the soul called Kenny doesn't deserve to die. What deserves to die is the voice in our heads, the shadow in our dreams. The one who whispers things. Evil things. The one who has been with us for so many years, and has made itself a part of us. The one who has stolen our life, and made us hungry. So hungry and so afraid and so lost, for so long and for so far.

Something here wants to kill, but we do not want it to kill. Not the soul called Kenny, who has shown such light, such understanding, such freedom. Not the soul that has immersed itself in the promise of a distant land and has made us do the same. To dream of another world, where we are not shackled by something's hunger, and darkness, and desires, and death. We will not let that happen. We will soar to protect the soul called Kenny. And if the cold waters of the world below lead to another called Gonagreen, then we will be happy in our flight.

4

As far as Kenny could tell, the thing that had made the monster swerve to the left was just a dot. A simple black dot that seemed harmless, and yet was fast and lethal, swooping down over the monster and digging itself into its back. Then more arrived, flying down from the clouds and charging toward the monster, and it was then that Kenny realised they were cuckoos. Hundreds and hundreds of cuckoos, wrapping themselves around the monster and burrowing their beaks into its flesh, making it spin and spiral.

He could hear the monster screaming, but for the first time, the voice didn't seem to be in his head. It was out there. A scream of fear and fury that echoed from inside the cloud of cuckoos and begged hopelessly for its salvation. Only it didn't look like there was anything to salvage. The monster was completely covered now. All Kenny was watching was a flock of cuckoos performing one last dance in the morning sky, pirouetting in the sunrise before hurtling down toward the ocean.

The scream continued until the waves cracked and the black cloud disappeared into them, cutting off the voice and causing a great explosion of seawater. The monster didn't come back up. The cuckoos didn't either. The water bubbled and frothed. It gushed, rippled, and choked. But it didn't break. It didn't change. It calmed and grew still, quietly reflecting the fire on the pier and the fire on the horizon, out there, where the sun was now turning from a deep, fierce red to a light shade of pink. Beaming gently.

5

A sharp ringing remained in Gaten's ears when he clambered onto the shore, his hand still wrapped tightly around Sara's. The world around him was blurred and hazy, like he was still standing amidst the smoke on the pier, and he felt strangely heavy. If Sara hadn't been with him when they jumped into the water, he was sure he would have sunk all the way to the bottom. Like it was his will – and only his will – to keep her safe that had kept him afloat. But now he had got to the beach, and there was still the monster left to deal with.

'Where is it?' he choked, staring into the bleeding face of the young boy. 'What happened to it?'

'It's alright,' he heard the boy reply. 'It's dead. My friend killed it. You look hurt, sir. You look really hurt.'

'What friend?'

'My cuckoo.'

On the word "cuckoo", the boy fell to his knees and began to cry, and Gaten felt the last of his will easing, falling away into something soft and quiet, and leaving nothing but the blurry haze. He turned to his left, squeezing Sara's hand again.

'Sara, I'm...'

But Gaten couldn't hear his voice anymore. The ringing was too loud. The haze was too strong. Things were getting bright and dark at the same time, and he felt like he was disappearing. Like perhaps he was back in the ocean, and he was taking one last look at the surface of things before he was swallowed into the sand. He could see Sara look at him and her eyes widen. She mouthed something, but Gaten lifted a hand to stop her. He didn't want her to talk, because he wanted to say something to her. Something he should have said a long time ago, and should have been saying for the rest of his life – though his life appeared to have only a few short moments left now.

'I'm sorry, Sara. I'm so sorry.'

The look on Sara's face told him the words had been said, and they could now rest on the cool, morning breeze, just as Gaten could rest. He felt the blackness really approaching then. There were flashing blue and red lights racing toward the beach, and he saw Sara push the crying kid toward them. Then she was crouching over Gaten, holding his head. Just a single point of whiteness in the dark. She was saying something and crying, only Gaten couldn't make it out. He just lay there and held onto her, feeling strangely comfortable. The pain of the fire had gone now, the pain of his regrets gone with it. He lay there knowing that he had run the right way this time, and he had done all he could. All he could. Even in the face of the darkest nightmare. All he could. And now for dreams. Now for sinking into his bed, with Sara there beside him, where she should have always been.

He closed his eyes and then, silently, he wished her good night.

And out of the black, whispering fire,

CHAPTER EIGHTEEN

THE DANCING

1

The school corridor was humming in contempt. Students with sagging backpacks stood with their backs to the walls, taking him in, judging. Some wore smirks and others wore smiles, mocking smiles that were taut at the edges. Some even revealed teeth, glaring at him with eyes that appeared to glow red under firelights. And they whispered things. Mean things that, while unintelligible, squirmed into his mind and made his thoughts unbearable.

Kenny's imagination was ablaze. Keeping his head down, he pulled his books out of his locker, held them tight to his chest and marched toward the exit. The light outside cleansed him somewhat, but there were still children around. Big children and small children who were standing in clusters in the schoolyard and staring bullets into his soul. He saw a boy put a finger to his eye and droop it down, mimicking what the scar had done to Kenny's face. He saw a girl make the "crazy" sign, sticking her tongue out as she twirled an invisible strand of hair around her head. But Kenny marched on, keeping his head down and praying he could make it to the gates without running into an incident. Unfortunately, he only made it about ten yards before an incident ran into him.

'Going somewhere, Crazy Kenny?'

Harland Thomas barged into Kenny, sending him flat onto his back with a breathy 'OH!' Before he knew it, Harland, Edward, and Aidan were standing over him, their smiles stretched.

'Yeah,' he breathed painfully. 'Home.'

'So soon?' asked Harland.

Kenny shuffled, collecting his books from the wet grass. 'You know, not all of the bells are for lunch. Some of them mean school's out.'

'Reckon he's dragging on your weight, man,' said Edward.

Harland's smile flickered. 'You play football, don't you Kenny?'

'Uh-huh.'

'So you know you gotta weigh at least forty pounds to make an impact at right tackle, right?' Harland grabbed at his belly, which was protruding a little from his *Jets* shirt. 'This ain't peanut buttercups, this is teamwork.'

'Yeah,' said Kenny. 'I get it. I was kidding.'

Only Kenny wasn't kidding. Harland Thomas had gotten fat, and the whole school knew it. Kenny wasn't sure what had made it happen. Perhaps the school's Christmas menu had improved, or perhaps he'd become too cocky for his metabolism. Whatever it was, anything that gave Kenny an edge in the race to Dora's heart was something to be celebrated. Holding in a smirk, he squeezed his books under his armpits and went to stand, but Harland's outrageously heavy boot slammed down hard on his chest.

'You think you're funny, huh? Like shit you were kidding, you weedy asshole.'

'I'm not weedy,' wheezed Kenny.

'Another lie. I don't think I can trust a word that comes out of your mouth. None of us can. Unless, of course, you put the record straight about how you got that scar. And the truth, this time.'

'I've told people the truth.'

Aidan laughed. 'What? That a monster was hiding under the pier and you killed it?'

'I never said I killed it.'

'Yeah, of course. That's the part we were having trouble with.'

'That's the part I would have trouble with.' Edward grinned, his yellowed front teeth on full display. 'Hell, if there was a monster, I couldn't imagine this kid doing anything other than hiding under his mom's bed and making a puddle on the carpet.'

'My mom's dead,' said Kenny.

'Dad's bed, then.'

At that, Kenny shoved away Harland's boot and clambered to his feet. The three boys snickered and feigned a worried 'oooh' in response.

'You know what I think happened?' said Harland. 'I think Crazy Kenny realised he's never gonna be able to throw a ball further than ten yards. I think he realised he's so weedy, the coach would rather pick a twig with legs at quarterback. I think he realised his biggest achievement in life is climbing to the top of the Indian post, which is getting smaller every year.'

Kenny glanced toward the Indian post at the edge of the schoolyard. It did indeed look smaller than it did a year ago. But then, ever since the cuckoo had flown into his life and said the word "pain" over and over again, everything had looked smaller to Kenny. Everything but Harland Thomas, of course.

'I think Crazy Kenny wanted to come up with something better,' he continued. 'So he took a knife from the kitchen cupboard and came up with a story.'

'Then how do you explain the pier burning down?' argued Kenny.

'Shit if I know. But what I do know is that there wasn't no monster. You're just coming up with this story to impress my girl.'

'Dora's not your girl.'

'Look at that, boys.' Harland patted his friends on the back. 'As close as we'll get to a confession. Well, she's not your girl either, is she, Crazy Kenny? But I guess you'll find that out at the Christmas Cuckoo tonight. Unless you're too busy fighting some more monsters.'

Officially reaching his limit, Kenny threw caution to the wind and pushed past them, making for the gates of the schoolyard and leaving his books wet and crumpled in the mud behind him. He didn't look back until he reached the Indian post, where he was relieved to see that, rather than follow him, Harland and his friends had decided to place their attention on his books, charging around the playground and throwing them between each other like they were frisbees.

'Rather them than me,' Kenny muttered.

And out of nowhere, another voice muttered back.

'I wouldn't care what they have to say, Crazy Kenny.'

This voice was quiet and gentle, and just about as sweet as the sweetest of honey, dipped in sherbet and melted strawberries. Dora Lane emerged from behind the Indian post with a small, cherry lollipop resting seductively on her bottom lip. She looked just as beautiful as the day Kenny had met her. Her blonde hair was dangling in two delightful ponytails, her pert cheeks were dimpled and rosy, and her bright eyes were glistening with an irresistible shade of chocolate. Kenny could almost hear his heart flutter in wonderment.

'Crazy Kenny,' she repeated, sizing him up. 'That's an unfortunate nickname, don't you think?'

Kenny stared dumbly for a few seconds. 'Uh, yeah. It's not fortunate.'

'It doesn't even rhyme. And besides, I've always thought it should be up to the person to choose their own name.' Dora rested her shoulder against the post and gave her lollipop a long, hard suck. 'What do you want to be called?'

'My name...?' replied Kenny unsurely.

'Which is?'

'I'm Kenny. You know me. I'm in your math class. We talked that one time in the school corridor. You know, after I climbed the Indian post.' He pointed to it, as if Dora might assume he had climbed some mountain in India.

She squinted, then tapped her beautiful, long fingers on one of the engraved faces in the wood. 'Oh yes, that was you. Right to the tippy-top-top.'

Kenny nodded enthusiastically. 'Uh-huh.'

'I reckon you'd look even better climbing this with that scar on your face.'

'You like my scar?'

'Oh yeah, I think it's cute. Gives you a kind of devil may care vibe.'

Once again, Kenny felt his heart fluttering. He realised he was slouching a little, so he puffed out his chest, like he had seen Harland do, and he pouted his lips into a smoulder. He stopped almost immediately when Dora laughed at him.

'You know, it's funny I haven't seen you around more. I would've thought I'd remember someone like you.'

'I...' Kenny was about to reiterate that they saw each other every day in math class, but he thought better of it. If there was one thing he knew about girls, it was that you had to act cool. Almost uninterested. Like she was nothing more than a cuckoo digging in the stones at Cuckoo Cove beach. He slouched again, because perhaps that looked better.

'Tell me, Kenny,' mused Dora. 'Are you any good at dancing?'

Kenny hesitated. 'I'm not sure. I've never really danced before. Not *with* someone, anyhow.'

'Do you reckon you could dance with me tonight and look good while doing it?'

At that moment, Dora's eyes flashed a brighter shade of chocolate, and her face turned a little more hazy. The world around Kenny went into a funny sort of spin, and he had to stop himself from falling back onto his buttocks. He mumbled something incoherent.

'I've seen the way the school looks at you' continued Dora. 'You're a real mysterious type now. They'll all be looking at you tonight, but if you're dancing with me, then they'll all be looking at me too.'

Kenny attempted to shove some words back into his

mouth. 'I thought you might wanna dance with Harland Thomas.'

The lollipop made a wet popping sound as Dora pulled it from her cheek.

'I was thinking about it,' she said. 'But he's gotten fat.'

'He said that's for football.'

'He's fat.' Dora took a step forward, sizing Kenny up again. 'And while you're not perfect, I reckon you'd look good on the dance floor. If you're with me, of course.'

'You want me to dance with you...?'

'I never said that.'

'I feel like you just said that.'

Dora smiled and bit the lollipop between her teeth. It made a delightful clicking sound this time, and Kenny swallowed giddily. Even with a lollipop, this girl was a masterful temptress.

'You're talking crazy, Crazy Kenny.' She crunched down on the lollipop and it turned into tiny scarlet shards on her tongue. 'See ya tonight.'

And then she was gone, flicking the stick into the dirt and waltzing across the schoolyard, her ponytails bouncing. Kenny watched her go, his heart still flapping inside his chest like a butterfly. She had said, 'see ya tonight', but Kenny had heard, 'see ya under the mirrorball.' And every part of him wanted to jump for joy. But he didn't. He was cool, detached, and uninterested. He gave the Indian post a friendly tap and strutted over to the gates, smiling giddily.

2

It had taken Kenny a whole month to look in the mirror. After the skin graft was complete and his wound had been patched back together, Kenny knew he had been left with something that would change his life forever. The scar travelled from his left temple to his eyebrow, and the way the skin had rested had caused his eyelid to constantly droop halfway shut. He had cried when he finally saw himself, even more so than when he dreamt of his cuckoo. But these tears were selfish ones. They were borne entirely out of self pity and lost dreams, and that only made them sting harder.

Although it appeared those dreams hadn't been lost after all. Kenny jumped down onto Adamson Avenue with the same smile still wide across his face. He'd always known telling the truth about the monster would be a long shot, especially with Dora, who was so down to earth, but he hadn't thought his scar could be his salvation. If he'd only known that a few months ago, he would have taken up lion taming rather than football, but he supposed that didn't really matter now. What had happened had happened, and the monster's scar was the one Kenny was left with.

He watched himself walking in the passing shop windows. It was strange, but even when he had been unable to look in the mirror, and had only acknowledged the scar by poking at it tentatively, he had always been sort of glad that he had it. In many ways, it was a rope that kept him tethered to that night two months ago. Sara had told him countless times that there would be no point in trying to explain what had really happened. They had to come up with their own story about how the pier burnt down, and for the most part, Kenny had gone along with it. But if the school yard was a place for tall tales and truths alike, then Kenny was going to tell his. He had recounted the story with every detail: finding the cuckoo, having the dream, going to the pier, facing the monster, and he had done it all in the knowledge that no one would believe him. Over the years, he knew the story would be forgotten, and even Kenny himself would learn to live on without it. But that wasn't what he wanted. What he wanted was to remember. To live with every detail and hold the weight of that night tight in his chest. He wanted to remember the monster, the people it had taken, the nightmares it had created, and he wanted to remember his cuckoo. His lost, broken cuckoo that had been so small, and yet had made a sacrifice so big. All of it was a weight he wanted to carry, and so, while the tales might go cold, he knew that the scar would always bring him back. Even when the red eyes grew faint and the voice of his cuckoo echoed into nothing. His scar would tie him into the memory and burn what happened deep onto his soul.

Plus, it looked cool. And Dora liked it. And so he was happy. Still smiling, he turned a corner and knocked on the door of the Precious Star Bar.

3

Sara was sitting atop a stool with her head buried inside her notebook. Her knees were glossed in white paint, and her dress was torn at the hem, but that was nothing compared to Carl.

'Goddamn half-assers,' he gurgled through running tap water, his face dunked in the sink. 'Fancy priming the walls but refusing to paint them. Bullshit you have to wait seven hours. It's the goddamn night of the goddamn relaunch.'

Sara hummed absently. 'Goddamn.'

'Yeah, you said it, Sara. Goddamn.'

There was a knock on the door, and Carl bumped his head on the tap as he jerked upright.

'Goddamn it! If that's Hawbury Hardwares, tell them it's already painted, and most of it on my face. Then invite them in so I can claw em'.'

He curled his fingers and hissed like a cat. Sara closed the notebook and tread softly across the bar, careful to avoid the near-emptied pots of paint. She opened the door to find the small, scarred face of Kenny Townsend staring up at her.

'Well?' said Carl. 'Is it my new scratching pole?'

'I think this one's been scratched enough, Carl.'

'Very funny,' said Kenny.

Sara smiled at him. 'Go ahead, kid.'

'Cuckoo. Scar. Dancing.'

'Dancing. Huh, that's a new one.'

Ever since the night on the pier two months ago, Kenny had been a constant presence in Sara's life. At first they would simply meet and talk about what had happened, trying to make sense of things. But no one could ever make sense out of something like that. The nightmare had been too big, the consequences too monstrous. And so Sara had decided on something smaller. Every day. Three words. Just three words to summarise what Kenny had been thinking, and feeling, and crying about. And hopefully, after a little while, everything would become a little smaller, the emotions more manageable, until he could understand the kind of person he had become in the aftermath.

Sara felt like he needed something like that. It would have been easy to let Kenny go back to his ordinary life, where he would keep the events of that night buried in his chest. But if Sara had learned anything from the puddle, it was that burying things alive never seemed to work out well. Pretty soon they would find a way to claw back through the dirt and grab the first thing closest to them. That had happened to her, and if she'd put distance on Kenny, she knew it would've happened to him too. Every kid was the same, after all. No matter their race, their religion, or their sexuality. Every kid needed three words. To throw the spade behind their shoulder, and learn to live with the things they'd rather hide.

Sara walked over to the stool and sat herself back down, and Kenny went to follow her.

'UH-UH!' Carl pointed at him threateningly. 'Take one more step, kid, and I can wave goodbye to my licence. The powers that be hate us affiliating with kids.'

'Who's the powers that be?'

'Everyone.'

Sara chuckled. 'Go easy, Carl, no one's watching.'

'Everyone's watching.' Carl looked at her seriously, then returned to the sink and renewed his scrubbing session.

Kenny stuffed his hands in his pockets, lingering on the spot. 'I was just gonna say, I talked to Dora today.'

'Oh yeah?' said Sara, although her attention was back on her notebook.

'I think she wants to dance with me. You know, at the Christmas Cuckoo tonight.'

'That would explain the third word. Well done, kid. I'm proud of you.'

A moment passed. Kenny wrinkled his nose as he sniffed in the paint, scanning the room with a false sense of interest.

'Looks good,' he said unenthusiastically.

'Like shit,' gurgled Carl.

The Precious Star Bar had taken four weeks to get to this point. Carl had been intent on boarding the place up, but Sara had convinced him not to. It was strange, but in the darkness of the last two months, the Precious Star Bar had become a sort of refuge in Sara's mind. A place where she could close her eyes, and sing her songs, and feel something other than the deepest of despairs. Only she didn't know why. This place had never been perfect. Far from it. But it had been the stage for good things and good people, and perhaps there was something important in that. Things were different, of course. The *ELECTRIC SLUT!* chair was gone, and the smoke machines along with it. More importantly, one of the two hearts that had pulled it all together was missing, and the beating of the bass would always sound a little emptier as a result. But every stage needed different lighting eventually. And perhaps, if they waited long enough, the curtains might open onto act two.

'Hey, Sara,' said Kenny. 'Now that you're gonna be here more often, do you reckon we could do the three word thing over the phone? It's just that Adamson Avenue is kind of a trek.'

Sara raised an eyebrow suspiciously. 'And?'

'My legs get tired.'

'Aww. You hear that, Carl? Kenny's legs get tired.'

Carl kept his head in the sink. 'Try living in my sixty year old body, kid. Every part of you will get tired. And I mean every part.'

'Powers that be,' Sara murmured.

Carl kept quiet.

'It's just a bit more of an effort, you know?' Kenny argued.

'Face to face. That's how this works. I don't make the rules.'

'You kind of do.'

'Oh,' Sara flicked her wig over her shoulder. 'That's right.'

'So what's wrong with a phone call?'

'Sorry, Kenny. So long as this is working, we're gonna keep doing it.'

Kenny huffed. He knew by now that Sara was stubborn. Once she had her mind set on something, more often than not, that something was going to bend to her will. He scratched at his head and took one last shot.

'You don't know it's working...'

Sara flashed a smile at him. 'Do you remember your last word yesterday? It was "monsters". Today, it's "dancing".'

The last word. And a powerful one at that. Kenny let out a big sigh and gave up.

'The dance is tonight,' he murmured. 'You don't have to come, you know.'

'You in a room with those dickwads? I'm gonna be there.'

'So what is it? Are you my bodyguard as well as my therapist?'

'I'm not your bodyguard, I'm theirs. Kenny, most people wet the bed when they have nightmares. You went after yours with a gun and some gasoline. Those kids don't know what they're up against.'

'You wanna make sure they don't beat me up.'

Sara shrugged. 'Some monsters are worse than others, yes.'

'Great. Well, I'll see you at four then. See ya later, Carl.'

The sink made a splutter in goodbye, and Kenny turned onto his heel, closing the door of the Precious Star Bar behind him.

'It's clever,' Carl gurgled as he turned off the tap, grabbing one of the nearby bar cloths to wipe his face.

'What's clever?' asked Sara.

'The three word thing. You should do it too. What happened that night affected you more than it affected him.'

Sara hesitated slightly. She hadn't been planning on telling Carl what had really happened that night on the pier. She never thought he'd believed it. But one month ago, during a rainy evening full of whisky and fizz, she had decided to do it. Even if Carl didn't believe her, she reckoned he deserved to know what had happened. But the funny thing was, he *did* believe her. Without question, he had believed every word she said. About the secret Cuckoo Cabaret Club. About the monster and what it had wanted. He had taken it all in, and when Sara had asked him why he was so sure she wasn't crazy, he had simply said, 'Luna's stories were never fiction to me. We both believed in monsters'. And that had been that.

'Who's to say I'm not doing it?' Sara replied finally.

Carl threw the cloth in the sink. 'Proceed.'

A few seconds passed. Then Sara cleared her throat.

'Precious. Stars. Luna.'

In an instant, Carl's wall crumbled a little. His jaw shuddered, and the ghosts of a thousand yesterdays swam in his eyes. He flickered a broken smile. Then, quite slowly, he took Sara's hand and squeezed. Such a squeeze. Hard, yet gentle. He said something about changing the pipes and paced downstairs into the basement, but Sara knew he was going there to cry. He did that sometimes. And then he would come back, his wall rebuilt. And things would carry on, the memory of Luna still with him, but comfortably so. Just as it was with Sara. So she let him cry and returned her focus to her notebook. So far, she had listed twenty songs for the Precious Star Bar's big reopening. Just as Luna would have wanted, they were all sung by Cher.

4

The Christmas Cuckoo was an annual school dance that took place in the community centre on Redwood Street. It was originally a small affair, but over the last few years, the party had grown to be a town-wide celebration, with local shop owners hosting pop-ups and raffles, police officers putting on demonstrations in the parking lot, and even the local carnie loaning a few rides for the nearby park.

This year more than any other, it seemed that no one could resist the fun. The street leading up to the centre was full of people, and as Sara walked through the crowd, she took note of how happy they all looked. To them, the last few months had been nothing but a bump in a perfectly straight road, with nothing effectively extraordinary enough to write home about. They even looked at her the same. Small glances, slight smirks. Kids pointed, of course, but that was only natural. She was more alarmed when the adults pointed. To them, she still didn't belong, but Sara knew she shouldn't expect anything less. It was her life that had changed forever, not theirs. And so she would have to deal with them in the way she always did: with a kiss and a wink, and a dream that one day, they wouldn't see her as the alien.

Once she was through the crowd, Sara made her way into the community centre, passing her ticket to the doorman as she did so. The centre itself was decorated with tinsel and Christmas lights, and at the far end, a sparsely decorated Christmas tree was displayed beside the adults-only punch table. In the centre of the room, there was a large dance floor full of children, some of whom were throwing baubles – that had clearly come from the once well-decorated Christmas tree – and being chased by the school janitor. "Fairytale of New York" by The Pogues was reverberating out of the speakers, and two sets of parents were arguing with the DJ to switch it off. In the corner of the room, Sara could see Kenny talking with a bunch of people she hoped were his friends. He caught her eye and smiled, and Sara smiled back, grabbing a cup of punch before reclining on the bleachers. She remained watching for a few minutes, drinking her punch and taking in the atmosphere, but when the song changed and the lighting went red, she had to close her eyes.

Even two months later, Sara was still being caught out by the red light. It gnawed into her chest and threw her right back into the secret Cuckoo Cabaret Club. To Ava and the dancers, and the monster leering at her through the smoke. Once upon a time, that place had been a shining light in a world of darkness. But really, it had just been another lie. Something to suck her in and turn her inside out. To swell her soul until it was good enough for the feast. Gaten had saved her from that, but once the club was gone, her soul hadn't miraculously got better. The monster's talon had inflicted that scar on Kenny's face, but Sara had been scarred in a different way. She had been scarred on the inside, the part of her that really mattered. And it still wasn't right. Not really.

In that first month, she had thought about giving up completely. She remembered standing knee-deep in the ocean, wishing she could let the tide wash her away and leave her soul to rot in the water. Because what else was left? That same world she thought the secret Cuckoo Cabaret Club could save her from, it had only made her weaker to it. Left her with the knowledge that there was no easy answer. That some thorns stuck in the side and bled forever. It wasn't the monster that nearly killed her, it was the lie. The secret. And the road ahead after that secret had been uncovered.

At the time, the cold embrace of the sea seemed like one she could readily dissolve into. Only she didn't give into it. And over the days and weeks, things did start to get easier. But there would always be work to do. Like now, this red light. It reminded her that things still didn't make sense. Life and how to live it. And while she acted strong, just a single light pull could place her back in the water. But she was trying to be okay, at least. And the good thing was, she had people who could help with that.

As if on cue, a hard, blistered hand rested upon hers.

'Red light's off.'

Sara opened her eyes to find her brother sitting next to her. He wore dark shades, and his neck was covered by a long, black compression collar. He was sporting a loose shirt, but Sara could make out wet patches from the gel that lathered his torso. His body had been ripe with bandages ever since that morning on Cuckoo Cove beach. The burns he had suffered were all second degree, and he'd spent most of the last two months receiving mesh grafts, dressings, physiotherapy, and a collection of painkillers and nerve blocks. He complained often, but Sara didn't feel sympathy. At one point, she had thought she'd lost him completely. She'd thought his first true embrace since she'd called herself "Sara" would be his last, and that he would burn and burn forever in the pink light of that sunrise. But he had survived. Wounded, different, but survived. And as far as Sara was concerned, everything he complained about was actually something to be thankful for. Even if he didn't quite see it that way yet.

She held his hand tightly. 'How did it go, big brother?'

'Well,' said Gaten, 'it's looking like five months in the slammer, followed by a mandatory mental health programme. With all the stuff that's come out about me in the press, Justin wants to come down pretty hard to clear his name. But he's not unreasonable. In light of my service, he's offered to speak for me in favour of a suspended sentence. So long as I admit I was wrong about everything.'

Sara took that in. 'You should do it,' she said after a few seconds.

Gaten looked at her. 'I wasn't going to.'

'It doesn't matter now, does it? We've lied about you burning the pier down, we might as well wrap it all up in a neat bow. Either way, Hadero stays where he is.'

She stared down at the floor, hating even the taste of Justin Hadero's name in her mouth. Gaten shuffled on the bench and scratched irritably at the back of his silicone-covered neck.

'No ending is perfect,' he said.

'And this one is far from it. I mean, this town will never know what you did for them.'

'Just so long as one person knows.'

Sara felt her brother's hand squeeze tighter, and she looked at him, her momentary swell of anger replaced with something that mattered. Something, once again, to be thankful for.

'How are you?' she asked softly.

'Truth or a lie?'

'Always truth.'

Her brother thought for a few moments. 'Better. But not good. You?'

Sara smiled sadly. 'Snap.'

At that moment, the music around them changed and the lights grew sharper on the dance floor. Sara looked up to see Kenny being led into the middle of it. His hand was being held by a girl, taller than him, with blonde hair and shiny skin. Her bright blue dress looked like it was made of ice under the mirrorball, and the small, plastic tiara, which sat perfectly atop her head, was sparkling like a diamond. She pulled Kenny close and they began dancing, swaying slowly through the crowd. Sara watched them with a smile, but her smile dropped when she noticed the girl's eyes fixed on a boy in the corner. He was larger than Kenny, better looking, and he was staring at the pair of them with a fierce scowl plastered across his face.

Gaten chuckled. 'Poor kid.'

'Do you think he knows?' asked Sara.

But before her brother could answer, a group of four men, perhaps fathers, walked past, and one of them slapped the cup of punch out of Sara's hand.

'Queer,' he said simply. And the others laughed.

Sara watched them congregate at the punch table and stare at her, their eyebrows raised, as if they were waiting for her to rush the dance floor, touch one of the kids, and turn them gay with a *zap* and a *bang*.

Gaten nudged her on the arm. 'Don't let them bother you.'

'Bother me? They do a lot more than that. They smother me. Everything does. You know what I've realised? Out of the four people we know the monster targeted, three of them were gay. It was looking for the brightest souls, the happiest, the shiniest. And it picked us. What does that say about you lot?'

One of the four men flicked some invisible hair over his shoulder mockingly. It was strange, but in this light, he looked a little like Ava. His olive skin, his large dark eyes. Only it wasn't Ava that Sara was remembering, it was the monster. A lure in the form of Adrian Ramirez, the boy who had hidden his wig in a water tank in an effort to save himself, because that was the only thing he knew to do when monsters were chasing him. To reject his true form and hide it in dark water.

'Except all of our souls were smothered,' Sara continued. 'Adrian's, Luna's, mine too. But mine had the most potential, I guess. All I needed was the secret Cuckoo Cabaret Club. A road toward happiness. Something I could never achieve out here.'

Gaten repositioned his glasses. 'I don't know about that.'

'About what?'

'Happiness isn't something that's given to us on a platter. It's something we have to create ourselves. A candle in all this blackness.'

'Very poetic.'

'Look at Kenny.' Gaten nodded toward the dance floor. 'You think he doesn't know?

The music picked up in tempo, and Sara watched as Kenny twirled the pretty girl around his arm. His smile was wider than Sara had ever seen it, but there was something else there on his face. Not the scar, which was almost impossible to see in the glare of the Christmas lights, but something else. Something that cut through the smile and made it almost sad. It was then that Sara realised that her brother was right. The kid was not stupid. Something deep inside of him knew that his dreams weren't coming true. That Dora was not in love with him. And yet he had still decided to hold her and be happy, knowing that tomorrow might not bring good things. For now. For this moment. He had chosen to dance.

Sara wavered. Then she sniffed, stood, and offered Gaten her hand. 'Come on, then.'

'What are you doing?'

'Dance with me, big brother.'

Gaten hesitated. 'Sara, I'm covered in gel sheets.'

'So some of them might fall off, and you might hurt in the morning. But you won't now.'

Gaten looked around the room, as if searching for an excuse. But then he looked into Sara's eyes and saw something. Sara didn't know what, but it must have been something convincing, because it was enough to make him stand and take her hand.

The next thing she knew, they were on the dance floor, with the mirrorball spinning above their heads. Songs changed from fast to slow, and Gaten and Sara were there for all of them. Spinning and waltzing and swaying. Laughing and joking and smiling. After a while, it felt like they were the only two people in the room. Just them and the darkness, holding onto each other and dancing. At one point – though she wouldn't have been able to put her finger on it – Sara even felt a spark of something happy ignite in her soul. It wasn't big and it wasn't brilliant. It wasn't some great realisation, or even something she would remember the next morning. But it was meaningful. The world went quiet, and every bad thing was replaced with something good.

And life became a beautiful wonder.

THE END